GEMMA WEIR

THE MONTANA MOUNTAIN MAN SERIES

BELONGING TO THE MOUNTAIN MAN

Belonging to the Mountain Man
Montana Mountain Men #6
Copyright © Gemma Weir
Published by Hudson Indie Ink
www.hudsonindieink.com

This book is licensed for your personal enjoyment only.
This book may not be re-sold or given away to other people. If you would like to share this book with another person, please purchase an additional copy for each recipient. If you're reading this book and did not purchase it, or it wasn't purchased for your use only, then please return to your favourite book retailer and purchase your own copy.

Thank you for respecting the hard work of this author.

All rights reserved.

This is a work of fiction. Names, characters, places, brands, media, and incidents are either the product of the authors imagination or are used fictitiously. The author acknowledges the trademark status and trademark owners of various products referred to in this work of fiction, which have been used without permission. The publication/use of these trademarks is not authorised, associated with or sponsored by the trademark owners.

Cover Design by Kirsty-Ann Still, Pretty Little Design Co.
Formatting by LJDesigns

Also by Gemma Weir

Montana Mountain Men Series
Property of the Mountain Man (Montana Mountain Men #1)
Owned by the Mountain Man (Montana Mountain Men #2)
Kept by the Mountain Man (Montana Mountain Men #3)
Claimed by the Mountain Man (Montana Mountain Men #4)
Saved by the Mountain Man (Montana Mountain Men #5)
Belonging to the Mountain Man (Montana Mountain Men #6)
Loving the Mountain Man (Montana Mountain Men #7)

Montana Mountain Protectors Series
Blaze (Montana Mountain Protectors #1)

Alphaholes Series
Obsession (Alphaholes #1)
Obligation (Alphaholes #2)

The Archer's Creek Series
Echo (Archer's Creek #1)
Daisy (Archer's Creek #2)
Blade (Archer's Creek #3)
Echo & Liv (Archer's Creek #3.5)
Park (Archer's Creek #4)
Smoke (Archer's Creek #5)

Archer's Creek: The Next Generation Series
Hidden (Archer's Creek: The Next Generation #1)
Found (Archer's Creek: The Next Generation #2)
Wings (Archer's Creek: The Next Generation #3)

The Kings & Queens of St Augustus Series
The Spare - Part One (The Kings & Queens of St Augustus #1)
The Spare – Part Two (The Kings & Queens of St Augustus #2)
The Heir – Part One (The Kings & Queens of St Augustus #3)
The Heir – Part Two (The Kings & Queens of St Augustus #4)

*For everyone who reads this book –
Buy batteries.
I'm not sorry if my characters offend you.
I take no responsibility for any babies
made as a result of reading my stories.
Yes, you'll need to leave your feminism at
the door.
Oh... and you're welcome LOL.*

* * * WARNING * * *

After the hate I've gotten over my last two releases, I think it's time to extend the warning again.

My heroes are assholes. They are not PC. They are at times morally ambiguous, behave like cavemen and sometimes they'll do whatever it takes to get their heroines pregnant.

Please, please, please don't read this book thinking I'm exaggerating about how OTT and alpha these characters are, because you'll hate the book and then write a scathing review saying both me and my characters are psychopaths.

This book contains an over-the-top, jealous, unreasonable, possessive asshole.

If you consider unapologetic alphaholes unacceptable, or feel their behavior is in some way abusive, then this isn't the book or series for you.

If you're a naysayer who thinks what I write is romanticizing domestic violence and abuse then please, please stop reading now.

This book isn't a guide to dysfunctional relationships, it's fiction. My books are fantasy, this isn't real life, it's a romance novel and should be read as such.

We all know in the real world throwing a woman over your shoulder, messing with her birth control or stalking her and letting yourself into her home is a one-way ticket to either a restraining order or the mental hospital. But I'd like to think that in fiction it's okay to agree that these things are incredibly sexy. Please do not kink shame me or my enthusiastic readers for finding these extreme alphahole behaviors hot, maybe if you read this book with the pinch of romantic salt it was intended to come with, you might like it too.

Please heed this warning, my books will make you question your feminism so I suggest you leave it at the door while you live in the world of my creation for a little bit, then pick it back up on your way back out. It's okay to like this kind of story, because that's all it is, a story, a few hundred pages of fantasy intended to titillate and excite, not to change your life.

If you're easily offended this isn't the book for you. But if, like me, you love a guy who is so obsessively in love with his girl that he will snarl, demand, punish and fuck her until she gives herself to him completely, then read on and welcome to the world of my Montana Mountain Men.

For a full list of trigger warnings for each book please check out my website www.gemmaweirauthor.com.

Chapter One

Bay

Yet another woman I've known my entire life sidles up beside me, smiling coquettishly as if they're waiting for me to blink and suddenly fall in love with them. This isn't the first time this has happened to me, it's not even the first time this week. For the last few years, ever since Beau fell for Bonnie, and news of Barnett men succumbing to love at first sight filled the small town we live in, women have been lining up like cattle wanting to be my *one*. The girl I'll instantly fall for and turn into a caveman nutjob for, just like my brothers have.

It's pathetic how these women have lined up hoping I'll choose them or what-the-fuck-ever, and as much as I've tried to be polite, my patience has worn thin of grown-ass women I've known my whole life throwing themselves in my path. You'd think by now they'd have given up, but they haven't. If anything, as my brothers have been taken off the market one by one and the pool of available Barnett brothers has dwindled, they've gotten worse. There isn't a single woman left in town who hasn't brought their car into our garage for an unnecessary service, or dropped by with cookies or a casserole they just so happened to have made too much of. I've been propositioned more times in the last three years than I have the rest of my forty-two years on earth and honestly, I'm sick of it.

Flashing her a bored, dismissive tip of my lips, I walk away from her and into our tiny office sanctuary, that's so oily and grimy I've yet to find even the most desperate of female prepared to step inside.

Unlike my brothers, I'm not interested in finding my woman. I enjoy being single, I like meaningless one-night stands, and I have zero intention of becoming a mindless caveman just because I fall in love.

That's not to say I'm not happy for my brothers, because I am. I adore all my sisters and I'm genuinely excited that our home is full of my adorable nieces and nephews. I love kids, I just don't ever see myself having any of my own.

"Jesus, if I have to change another oil filter, I'm going to lose my damn mind," Penn scowls, flopping down in the chair in front of my desk. Despite the perpetual smell of gasoline and the dirty, grease-stained walls and furniture, my office is actually cleaner than it appears at first glance. The reception space at the front of the garage is where we greet customers and it's immaculately clean, but this is our private space, and a bit of grease and oil doesn't bother us in the least.

"You'd think now that Lulu and I are married and have three fucking kids together, the women would stop thinking I'm available. I get why they stalk you, but why me?" my brother whines.

"Maybe you need to start wearing a sign around your neck," I suggest sarcastically.

He flashes me the bird, with the hand with his wedding ring on it, and scowls at me. "You and Cody need to hurry up and find your women. Once we're all taken, the rumors will die down until the kids are old enough to get hit with the family legacy."

"Do you think it'll happen the same way for the girls? What about Poppy?" I ask. "She's a Barnett too."

"My baby girls aren't allowed near a boy they're not related to until they're in their thirties," Penn snarls.

"Bro, you're fucking screwed. Lulu, Alice, Cora and Bonnie are all only in their twenties and married with kids, and if Teddy has anything to do with it, Juni will be pregnant before she turns twenty-one. There's no way you're going to stop Poppy, Bluebell or Hyacinth dating, at least Mav, Fox and Wilder will be able to scare off any little assholes that come calling for their cousins," I laugh.

"I'm going to take my babies to school every day and eyeball any little fuckers who think they're good enough for my girls," Penn says, his expression completely serious.

Unable to help myself, I laugh. "Bro, chill out. Poppy is one and Bluebell and Hyacinth are only four months old, you don't need to worry about getting your shotgun out for a few years yet."

"I can't fucking wait for you to find your woman, the moment you lay eyes on her you'll be as crazy as I am."

"Never going to happen. I know you all expect me to jump on the love train, but I'm good just the way I am. I'm too old to be thinking about settling down and having kids, I'm happy to stay single and keep my life calm and uncomplicated."

"You don't mean that, just look at me. I was fine with a different fuck for every day of the week until I found Lulu. She's perfect for me and now I can't imagine anything worse than touching another woman other than her. I had no idea I had a thing for pregnant women until she was swelling with my babies, now I'm counting down until I can breed her again."

"And how does Lulu feel about you wanting to get her pregnant again?" I ask with a smirk.

"I think she suggested scheduling me a vasectomy or a castration, but she'll come around. Another fucking amazing thing about finding your woman... no condoms. My swimmers have the GPS coordinates locked down and once the twins are sleeping through the night, I'm going to keep my wife pumped full of my cum until she's bred again."

"She's going to kill you. It's going to be almost as bad as when Cora found out Huck knocked her up again."

Penn hisses between his teeth and grimaces as we both remember the way Cora kicked Huck in the balls two weeks ago when she found out she was expecting again. "Huck's lucky she didn't cut his dick off in his sleep. The funny thing is that he says he really didn't mess with her birth control this time, although after last time I don't blame her for not believing him."

"We need to get back out there," I sigh, nodding my head in the direction of the door. "We have another four oil changes booked in this afternoon. But from now on, I'm going to start scheduling Callum to deal with all the fuckbait jobs, then we can focus on the actual repairs and avoid all the legacy bunnies that won't take no for an answer."

"Sounds like a plan to me. The upturn in business the last couple of years has been great, but I'm servicing Lindsey Hollis's Honda again for the sixth time this year today, and if she tries to grab my dick like she did last time she was here, I'm banning her."

"Agreed," I nod. "I'll let Callum know about the change in scheduling going forward."

Pushing up from my chair, I grab a bottle of water from the small refrigerator I keep stocked in the corner of the room and head back out into the garage, forcing a smile to my lips as Laura Becksworth pushes her tits out and struts toward me.

"Nice to see you again, Miss Becksworth, what can I help you with today?"

***

Loading the last of the dirty dishes into the dishwasher in our family's shared kitchen I add a detergent tablet, close the door, and set it to run. We all have our own apartments, but we still end up eating together most mornings and evenings. Our family of seven is now bigger than ever before since Alice and Granger's son, Fox, Beau and Bonnie's son, Wilder, and Lulu and Penn's twin girls, Bluebell and

Hyacinth, were all born. That now makes seven brothers, five sisters, three nieces and three nephews, as well as more extended family than I can list without me needing to draw a diagram.

I love it, almost as much as I don't. Most of the time I enjoy the commune feel to our home, but on occasion I miss the times when it was just me and my brothers shooting the shit and chatting about the women we were fucking. I don't even remember the last time the seven of us were together without all of the women and kids.

Bidding good night to my family, I push open the door to my apartment and step inside, closing it behind me and exhaling a weary sigh. The space that was once my bedroom is now the entrance into my apartment. I have a living, dining, kitchen space, two bedrooms and two bathrooms, and even though I've been living in the space for nearly two years now, it still feels a little odd not to be going to sleep in my old bedroom. The others have all changed and personalized their space, Penn has even built an add-on to his to increase the size of the living space and incorporate two more bedrooms and a playroom. But my apartment is still pretty empty and anonymous. I'm not sure why I'm reticent to decorate and personalize it, but every time I sit down and try to think about how I want my home to look, I hit a brick wall.

Kicking off my shoes by the door, I glance down at the empty wall that I really should fill with a shoe rack, promising myself that this weekend I'll look at paint chips and furniture and make a real effort to make this place home, rather than just a space to sleep and store my clothes.

It's too early to go to bed, but the thought of sitting alone on my couch is too depressing. With a houseful of babies, the days of action movie binge nights on the seventy-inch flat-screen TV in the main house with my brothers for company are long gone.

Padding into my bedroom, I wince at how lifeless and boring it is in here too. The walls are white, the comforter and sheets on the bed are black, and the only other furniture in here is a dresser Granger made me from a tree I chopped down from the yard behind our home when I was a teenager. It's rustic and worn, but my dad and I felled the tree together and then he taught Granger how to build the dresser. It was one of the last things we did together before he died.

Turning on the light in my bathroom, I strip out of my clothes and climb into the shower. Twisting the dial and waiting for the water to heat, I step beneath the spray and wash, mechanically cleaning my skin and hair, making sure all of the oil is gone from my arms and beneath my fingernails.

Once I'm finished, I turn off the water, grab a towel and dry myself, putting my dirty clothes and towel in the hamper, before walking naked into my bedroom and climbing onto the bed.

My cell beeps and I reach for it, opening it to find a text from a woman I've been casually seeing for a few months. Rochelle is a lovely divorcée with two kids and zero interest in anything beyond complication-free sex on the nights her kids spend at their father's.

ROCHELLE
Hey Bay, Pete has the boys fri-sun this week, do you fancy coming over?

Sighing, I consider her offer. The sex is fun, and I enjoy knowing she has as little interest in making this anything more than sex as I do, but I can't find enough enthusiasm to say yes. I met her in a bar when she was out celebrating her divorce with her girlfriends. We were both a little drunk and when she asked me if I wanted to go home with her and help her celebrate, I'd agreed. My cell beeps again.

ROCHELLE
Picture

It's a picture of her naked body from the neck down. She's tall, her skin a deep-rich-ebony color. She's a real gym bunny, regularly going to the gym every day after work, so her body is tight and she could easily pass for being in her twenties, even though I know she turned forty not long after we first hooked up. Her nipples are a deep-pink color and hard in the picture as if she pinched them a moment before she took it. There's a glimpse of her pussy visible through the neat line of hair that covers her folds. She's gorgeous and I should be eager, imagining all the things I could be doing to her if I were to go, but I can't seem to find any enthusiasm. I don't know if it's that things have run their course with her, or if I've just lost interest in everything right now.

My life is good. I have a great job, and a fantastic family. I'm mortgage-free, I make good money and I'm still young enough that my dick works and enjoys being inside a woman. But just lately, a veil of disinterest has settled over me and I don't know how to get rid of it.

I'm not unhappy and there's nothing in my life that I'd change, but something keeps niggling at the back of my mind that says I need more, I just don't know what that more is.

Lifting my arms up behind my head, I exhale slowly and consider what to reply to Rochelle. She won't be too disappointed if I tell her that I'm busy, but it's a lie and as a general rule, I consider myself a pretty honest person.

> **ME**
> Stunning, honey, but I think it might be time for you to get back out there and find someone to treat you like the queen you are.

The moment I hit send, I know it's the right thing to do. I could go to her place and fuck her this weekend, but it feels like an asshole move to arrange to fuck someone when you've lost all interest in them. Putting an end to this thing now is the best thing to do.

My cell beeps and I open the text.

> **ROCHELLE**
> So that's it?

> **ME**
> It's been fun though, right?

> **ROCHELLE**
> A lot of fun. Thanks for all the orgasms. Take care, Bay.

> **ME**
> No, thank you! 😊 Take care, Rochelle.

Dropping my cell to the comforter beside me I wait for the regret to kick in, but it doesn't come and I exhale a slow, relieved breath. If I was going to fall for anyone, Rochelle would have been perfect. The sex is great, she's happily independent, she doesn't need me in any way, and we could have rubbed along quite comfortably together, living separate lives, while still enjoying each other's company.

The fact that I feel nothing, not even any mild discomfort about ending things with her over text, confirms just how shallow of a connection it was. Given that she wasn't even slightly bothered by me telling her we were done, means she obviously wasn't feeling anything deeper than me either.

Connecting my cell to the charger cable, I place it on my bedside cabinet and crawl under the covers. I don't have a TV in my room, so it's dark and quiet as I close my eyes and try to clear my mind. Instead of the calm silence I'd hoped for, more disquiet fills me.

Opening my eyes again, I stare up at the ceiling. Why is it, in the dark of night, your mind starts to ask you the questions you refuse to think of in the light of the day? I don't want to consider that I'm unhappy with my lot in life, but as I lie here alone, lonely and bored with my existence, I'm forced to wonder if it's time for a change?

Chapter Two

Missy

I shouldn't be here.

I know I shouldn't be here, but it's literally the only option I have.

I can't; won't spend another night in the house with *that* man and if my only other alternative is a little breaking and entering, then so be it.

When I spotted the old, rusty-looking RV last week, I stored the memory of it and the realization that it could be a safe haven for me as a last resort in the back of my mind, but I never thought I'd be using it so soon.

When my uncle showed up at mine and my nana's house in New Mexico four years ago, I thought he was sent from heaven. Nana's health was poor and we'd just had a letter informing us that she didn't qualify for disability anymore, because she hadn't filed the right form. Honestly, if he hadn't shown up, I'm not sure how she was planning to find the money to pay the rent that month. At sixteen, I was too young to get a proper job and so Uncle Ernie seemed like the knight in shining armor we'd both been praying for.

Not wanting to rock the boat, I never complained once when he insisted we pack up our apartment and move away from the only home I'd ever known. I changed schools, accepted sleeping in a windowless basement, and made sure he knew how grateful both me and Nana were that he'd taken us in.

When she died a year later, I wasn't sure what would happen to me, but once again, good old Uncle Ernie saved the day. He told me he'd signed all the paperwork to become my legal guardian, so that I wouldn't have to go into the system. He told me he loved me, that we were family, that we could take care of each other.

Stupidly, I believed it all. I accepted the home he offered me, I basked in the familial support and I loved him like the uncle he was. Except, the day I turned eighteen, he woke me up with a surprise.

Turns out, good old Uncle Ernie isn't actually my uncle at all, he's my second cousin. When he found out my paternal grandparents set up a trust for me, he tracked me and Nana down, knowing I'd gain access to it when I turned eighteen. Then he played the long con for two years, pretending to care about me, while the whole time it was a lie just to get an inheritance I hadn't even known existed.

He broke the news of what a fucked-up asshole he was by pinning me to my bed on the morning of my birthday. His pervy eyes had raked all over my body, while he rubbed his disgusting dick in his sweat-stained pants with one hand, forcing the other between my legs as he threatened to use my body as repayment for his hospitality... unless I signed over my inheritance to him without even knowing how much it was.

Terrified, and without another option, I signed the paperwork and he got my money. But the Joke was on him, because apparently the grandparents I never met—and never even knew existed—didn't want me to blow all my money at once, and only gave me access to a percentage of my trust when I turned eighteen.

When he found out it wasn't going to be the payday he was expecting, Ernie was furious. He'd showed his hand too early and even though he'd gotten access to the ten thousand dollars in my trust, he was determined that every penny my grandparents had left me was going to be his. I considered running away, or even going to the police, but with nowhere to go, no proof of his threats and no money, I had no choice but to stay put.

He couldn't get the rest of my trust until I turned twenty-one and I had nowhere else to go, so we made a deal. My perverted, disgusting non-uncle promised to keep his hands to himself, and I agreed to sign over the rest of my inheritance the moment I turned twenty-one.

To keep me to my word, as soon as I graduated high school he got me a job and arranged to have my salary paid directly into his checking account. He says the money he takes covers the rent for my room and the cost of food and utilities. But we both know it's a way of making sure I never have enough money to run.

I've never stopped striving for freedom from him, but every time I've managed to squirrel away enough dollars for a bus ticket out of town, he's found the money and taken it, leaving me right back at square one. Without a penny to my name, he's kept me stuck here and completely dependent on him, while we both count down the days until he can steal the rest of my inheritance from me and I can finally be free.

What Ernie doesn't know is that for the last six months, I've been working overtime, covering other people's shifts under the table for cash and stashing the money at work. I don't quite have enough for a deposit on a room somewhere in a shared apartment yet, but I'm hoping that in the next few weeks I'll have enough to quit, then I can take my final paycheck and leave.

Everything was going okay, until two days ago when Ernie The Asshole got drunk and broke through the lock on my door while I was sleeping. His dick was hard and he had enough beer in his system not to care if I'm young enough to be his daughter, or that I'm his meal ticket—but only if he keeps his hands and every other part of his body to himself.

Luckily for me, I sleep pretty much fully dressed in sweats and a T-shirt. I've also been taking a free self-defense class at the old folks' home I work in, so I took the bastard to the ground and attempted to send his balls back up inside him before I got my ass out of his house.

Rather than go home, last night I volunteered to do the night shift at work, and then slept in the on-call room today. I'd hoped to pick up an extra shift tonight as well, but no one needed me to cover. Which is how I find myself behind a garage trying to figure out how to break into an RV. With my cell in my hand, playing a YouTube tutorial on how to break into a car door, I try to push the wire I'm holding into the gap between the frame and the glass, only there isn't a gap, or at least not an obvious one and instead of sliding, the wire is bending.

Rolling my shoulders back I turn the wire around, holding the bent end and using the still flat end to try to mimic what the guy on the video is doing, only his wire looks different from mine, because I'm using an old wire hanger I found near the dumpsters, behind the garage.

Frustrated, I throw the wire to the ground, grabbing the RV's door handle with both my hands and yank at it. The door opens so suddenly that I lose my balance and fall onto my butt.

"The door was open," I laugh, cursing my stupidity for not even checking, as I push up from the ground and brush the dirt from the back of my jeans. Glancing around me, I check to make sure no one can see me, but the RV is hidden from the street between the garage and the self-storage warehouse that's next door.

Climbing into the small space, I pull the door closed behind me and immediately feel awful. Someone owns this and I'm trespassing. I've broken the law; this is a felony. The urge to leave is strong, but the need to not go to Ernie's house is stronger. I've been a victim of circumstance for too long, but I refuse to be around him when there's a very real chance he could get drunk and decide his need to play out his perverted fantasies is greater than his desire to steal my inheritance.

I still have no idea how much money is waiting in my

trust for me. Ernie has all the paperwork, but he refuses to let me see it, which suggests that it must be a pretty substantial amount. Enough at least to make it worth keeping me around for the three years he's had to wait until he can take it from me.

If Ernie was a more intelligent guy, he'd have read the small print in whatever paperwork he had and known that only a percentage of the money was going to be accessible to me at eighteen. That said, if he was less of a money-grabbing douche, he'd have also realized if he'd have just asked me for it, I'd have given him every cent I had because until my eighteenth birthday, I'd genuinely thought he'd loved me like a daughter, or at least a beloved niece—which is exactly what I thought I was to him.

Looking back, I can see some things I should maybe have questioned, like the hugs that went on just a little too long. Or the clothes he bought me that were too grown up and revealing for a teenager. Now that I know he's an asshole of the first order, there are lots of things that should have been red flags, but for two years, he had me completely fooled. I thought he was just the cool uncle that swooped in and saved the day.

I shudder at the memory of the salacious look on his face as he woke me up on my birthday, his hand cupping his junk, his thinning hair greasy, his two-day-old stubble patchy and ugly. He's only in his late forties but he looks closer to sixty, and not in a silver fox way, but in a *one more piece of fried chicken away from a heart attack* way.

Suddenly, being arrested for trespassing seems like a much more appealing option than being within a mile of his house and him.

Shuffling into the small interior of the RV, I sit down on the worn blue seat cushion and take stock of the space. It's old, but surprisingly clean and warm. Luckily, it's springtime, on the cusp of warmer days and lighter nights. I'm not sure how I would have fared if it had been winter, because the temperatures can plummet at night this close to the mountain and freezing to death is definitely not the way I want to go.

Lowering my purse from my shoulder, I pull out the foil blanket I stole from the supply cabinet at work and start to open the packet. The material is rustly and loud as I unfurl it, but if the temperature drops, it'll keep me warm. Next, I take out the inflatable pillow I bought at the dollar store. It's one of the ones that people use when they travel on a plane. It's not ideal, but it's not like I can carry around a real pillow, so this is better than nothing.

Blowing it up, I hook it around my neck and sigh to myself. Unclasping my belt from my jeans, I twist it around the door handle a few times. It won't stop someone from getting in if they really want to, but hopefully it'll slow them down long enough for me to wake up and be ready to run or fight or whatever.

I eye the cushions and then the sneakers on my feet. It feels rude to put my shoes on the cushions, but I don't want to be unprepared to make a run for it if I need to, so I silently apologize to whoever owns this RV, then twist to the side and lie down along the seat, pulling the foil sheet over me and moving the neck pillow until it's as comfortable as I think it's going to get.

It says a lot about my life that I feel more relaxed and safe sleeping rough in an RV at the back of a garage than I do in my own home, but as I drift to sleep, it's without any of the terror I've felt every night since my eighteenth birthday.

***

Waking up, I'm dimly aware of the sound of someone knocking on the door. It can't be my door, because Ernie stopped knocking six months ago. Now he just walks straight in unless it's locked, then he yells and kicks at the door, always eager to remind me of the threat he could be if I decide to step out of line.

"Hey." An angry voice joins the knocking. "Hey, get the hell out of there or I'm calling the police."

Jolting upright, the foil blanket falls away from me and I blink through the film of sleep as the silhouette of a man—a big man—glares at me through the window. As I watch, wondering how I'm going to get out of this situation without being arrested, the angry snarl on his face dissolves and instead, a worried expression replaces it.

"What the fuck? You're just a kid."

I want to snap at him, tell him I'm not a kid, that my childhood truly ended the day I turned eighteen. But instead, I feel tears fill my eyes, because he's going to call the cops and I'm going to get hauled to jail. I was so close to freedom, and now the risk that avoiding Ernie has forced me to take, has ruined it all. "Please don't call the cops," I whimper, wishing I could be stronger, but this moment has stolen all the strength and resilience I've had to find to get through the last couple of years since my life imploded.

"Come on out of there, honey, I'm not going to hurt you, or call the cops."

"You're not?" I ask, dubiously.

Shaking his head, he takes a step back and offers me a wry grin. "Nah, I figure if you're using this old heap of junk as a bed, there must be a pretty good reason. Come on into the garage, the coffee machine is on."

"You don't even know me and you could just be saying that to get me to trust you," I say, struggling to understand why this man is being nice to me, instead of reporting me to the police.

"No, I don't, but we can change that. I'm Penn Barnett, this is my garage and this"—he taps on the roof of the RV—"is my sister's RV. Why don't you tell me your name?"

I shake my head, refusing to tell him who I am.

"Well, it's nice to meet you, whatever your name is. Come on in, you look like you could use a hot cup of joe."

I know I probably shouldn't trust him, blind trust in people is what's gotten me into the mess I'm currently in. But for some reason, this man doesn't evoke even a twinge of fear in me. It's not that he isn't intimidating looking, he is. He's huge and broad and his muscles are the type that look like he could crush watermelons in his biceps. But despite that, I don't think he has any bad intentions toward me. That's why instead of running away the moment I can, I find myself following him across the small yard and into the garage.

The smell of oil and gasoline hits my nose as soon as I step into the building and it's oddly familiar, although I'm not sure why. I don't drive and I've never had any reason to be inside a car workshop before.

"How do you take your coffee?" Penn asks, leading me to the back of the space where a metal bench holds a tabletop refrigerator, a coffee machine and a microwave.

"Missy, my name is Missy McCormick, and cream, two sugars please."

Grabbing two mugs, he fills them both with coffee, then adds cream and sugar to one mug and pushes it along the bench to me.

"Thank you," I say quietly. "I'm sorry about sleeping in the RV, the door was open and I swear I didn't touch anything, or do any damage, I just needed somewhere to stay for the night, I promise I won't come here again."

Penn's brow furrows and his lips part as if he's going to speak, but a different male voice calls out.

"Penn, you in here? Bryan just called; he wants us to start the refurb on that Mustang he sent us pictures of the other day."

"Back here," Penn calls, frowning at me slightly, before he looks to the other side of the workshop.

A moment later, the most attractive man I've ever seen in real life steps into view. If I wasn't already leaning against the bench, I'd have to grab hold of it for support, because I swear my legs buckle a little just from the effect seeing him has on me. I've had a couple of boyfriends in the past, Uncle Ernie actively forbade me from dating, but I was a teenager and so I've kissed and fooled around a little, but I have never, never had a visceral reaction to a man the way I am to this one.

Perhaps it's because he is one-hundred-percent man,

without even a hint of boy in sight. I have no idea how old he is, thirties, maybe older, but he's gorgeous. Tall, super tall, well over six feet, with muscles I can see from here are tight and firm. His hair is a brown color so dark it could even be black; his skin is tan and even dressed in scuffed jeans and a Henley, he's sexier than most men could ever wish to be. "Holy shit," I whisper beneath my breath, but I must speak louder than I thought, because Penn chuckles beside me.

"Who are you?" tall, dark and sexy asks, his eyes taking me in and then grimacing.

"Bro, this is Missy McCormick, I found her sleeping in Alice's RV this morning," Penn tells him.

"What?" he questions, glancing from Penn to me and back again. When his gaze settles on me, I fight the urge to preen a little. "How old are you?"

"Twenty," I tell him, hating the way he seems to physically flinch in reaction.

"Jesus," he mutters.

Placing my mug of coffee back down on the counter, I pull my purse a little higher onto my shoulder. "Thank you for the coffee, and I'm so sorry about breaking into your RV, I promise not to do it again. I'd really appreciate it if you didn't call the cops, although if you feel like you need to, I'll understand."

"I already told you I wasn't going to get the cops involved," Penn says.

"Thanks," I say, dipping my gaze to my feet, embarrassed. "I should get going." Turning, I take a step toward the exit, not wanting to run, but needing to get away while I have the chance.

"Stop," the new guy orders.

My feet freeze to the spot.

"Come back here."

I don't know why I do it, but I spin around and retrace my steps until I'm back leaning against the metal counter.

"Explain why you were sleeping in the RV."

"I'd rather not."

"Why?"

"Because it's not really any of your business. I'm sorry I slept in there, I already apologized to Penn. I didn't have a choice, but I promise it won't happen again."

"I'm going to need more than that. You're a kid, where are your parents? Do they know you're not at home in bed where you should be? Why aren't you in school?"

Crossing my arms stubbornly over my chest I glare up at the new guy, my lips pressed firmly together.

"Maybe you should try introducing yourself to Missy before you start demanding answers from her," Penn says, his tone gruff and unexpected.

"Bay," the guy growls.

"Excuse me?" I ask confused.

"I'm Bay Barnett."

"Oh," I say, suddenly incapable of forming full sentences.

"Missy, this is my brother," Penn says, his gaze moving from me to Bay and back again, an odd expression on his face.

"I should really get going," I mutter, feeling off-kilter and uncomfortable beneath Bay's penetrating gaze.

"Not until you answer my questions," Bay demands, matching my body language and crossing his own arms over his chest. As well as making him appear intimidating, the position also makes his arms look more delicious and ripped than before, and I have to swallow down an audible sigh of appreciation.

Masking my blatant attraction to him, I huff out an annoyed breath and drop my arms to my sides. "My parents are dead, so no, they don't know I'm not in bed and I graduated high school a while back and not everyone gets to go to college."

"Where are your family then?"

"Gone too."

"Are you homeless?" Penn asks, his voice significantly kinder than Bay's.

"No, not technically," I tell them illusively, not willing to admit that sleeping rough might actually be safer than going home.

"So, you have a place to stay, you're just choosing not to stay there?" Penn asks slowly.

Not really wanting to answer the question, I twist my head from one side to the other and then reluctantly nod.

"What's your address? I'll take you home, someone will be worried about you," Bay growls.

"Dude, didn't you just hear her, she doesn't want to go home," Penn snaps, glaring at his brother.

"I really should get out of your hair." Smiling gratefully at Penn, I take a step forward, but Bay steps into my path, stopping me.

"I don't think I've ever seen you around town, be

difficult to miss that hair," Penn smiles, nodding to my flame-bright-ginger hair.

Grabbing a strand, I twist it uncomfortably and wait for the redhead jokes to start. I've been compared to a carrot, a match, a battery, you name it, I've heard it all before and now the insults thinly disguised as jokes slide right off my back.

"You're not from Rockhead Point?" Bay asks after an awkward silence when the teasing I was anticipating never comes.

"No," I admit.

"But you work here?" he asks.

I'm nodding before I can think better of it.

"Where?"

"I should go," I say again, not wanting to walk away from the angry, beautiful Bay, but knowing that I need to.

"That isn't happening," Bay snaps, fury lacing his tone.

I glance to Penn, trying to figure out what's going on, but he's not looking at me, he's staring at Bay with wide, shocked eyes.

"Her?" he asks him.

"Shut up," Bay snarls.

"Bay?" Penn questions.

"I know, I said shut up." Glaring at his brother, Bay turns his steely gaze back on me. "I'm giving you a ride to work. Don't bother trying to lie to me and tell me somewhere fake, I'll be walking you in and chatting to the staff to make sure you actually work there."

"Why do you care? If you're going to call the cops, just do it, I already told you I'll understand."

"Are you planning on going home tonight?" he asks, staring at me with intense eyes.

I look away, unable to hold his gaze and lie to his face.

"That's what I thought. Where are you planning on going? You obviously don't have friends you can stay with, or any family who can look after you. I'm not going to let you sleep somewhere dangerous again. I have an apartment above the garage."

"No," I hiss.

"I'll collect you after you finish work and bring you here and help you get settled upstairs."

"No," I argue a little more emphatically.

"Yes, little Imp, that's what'll be happening. And before you get any ideas about running, if I have to, I'll sit at your work all day to ensure you don't try to slip away before I collect you."

"It's not worth trying to argue with him," Penn laughs, obviously amused.

"I don't know you, I'm not staying with you," I tell him.

"You're not staying with me. I don't live there, I live about twenty minutes up the mountain, both Penn and I keep apartments here for when we need some space from the rest of our family. It's safe, it's empty and it's a hell of a lot better than sleeping in a cold RV without a lock or wherever else you were thinking of sleeping tonight."

"I don't—" I start to halfheartedly argue.

"Don't bother arguing, this is how it's going to be. Now let's go, we can grab you something to eat on the way."

Before I can even formulate another protest, his palm is around the back of my neck and his huge, perfect body is behind me, making me feel a hell of a lot more than just fear as he crowds me, steering me out of the garage and toward a big black truck parked outside.

Walking me to the passenger door, he opens it, then grips my hips with his huge hands and lifts me into the cab, placing me in the seat and leaning over to strap me into the seat belt.

The gesture is as weird as it is adorable and if I wasn't a little pissed at his over-the-top take-charge attitude, I'd probably be swooning at the gentlemanlike behavior. I'm not sure why I'm going along with this. I know I should run, there's no way for him to track me down—not that he'd have bothered. So why am I here in this big brute's truck?

"It's because he's beautiful," a little voice inside my head whispers to me. If he didn't look the way he does, I'd definitely have run, him being so goddamn attractive is undeniably part of the reason I'm here. But more than that, there's something about him, something that's drawing me to him, instead of urging me to flee.

Since the moment I laid eyes on him, it's like peace settled over me. Which is weird because since his gaze landed on me it's felt like a swarm of bees are buzzing beneath my skin. He's far too old for me, probably even old enough to be my dad if he'd had kids young. Not that it matters, a guy this hot won't be single, he'll have an equally hot wife and two-point-four beautiful mini-me kids.

When he climbs into the truck and closes the door, I'm pretty sure I absorb all of the oxygen inhaling his delicious scent. It's man, soap, mint and leather, he smells like what I imagine a new car smells like, and it's intoxicating.

"Where am I taking you?"

"Mountain View Pines," I admit reluctantly, inhaling slowly to try and get my head in gear and calm down the ridiculous, childish reaction I'm having to this beautiful, scary man.

"The old folks' home?"

"It's a retirement facility," I say without thought, parroting back the description that's drilled into everyone who works there. Apparently calling it a retirement facility instead of an old folks' home allows them to charge significantly more to all the old folks they con into moving in.

"So, it's an old folks' home," he mocks playfully.

I shrug. "Yeah, it's an old folks' home."

"What do you do there?"

"Mainly a lot of cleaning. I've been working there since I graduated, and jobs that involve a mop and bucket is about all they trust a twenty-year-old to do."

"Do you like it?"

I shrug again. "I like the residents."

"But not the other people you work with?"

Babette, the manager, is a friend of Ernie's, that's how I got the job in the first place and the reason he's been able to take all my wages every month. Her open dislike of me is also the reason the other staff think it's okay to be mean to me. They know she won't do anything to stop them from giving me the worst of the jobs. "Not particularly."

"What about friends?"

"What about them?" I ask.

"Do they know you're sleeping in shithole RVs?"

"They went to school out of state, I only get to see them on the holidays when they come home," I confess, feeling a wave of sadness wash over me when I think about how much fun Mallory and Heather are having away at school. I was too ashamed to tell them about Ernie's betrayal when it happened. I always make an effort to say hi when they come home to visit, but the differences between our lives have changed our friendship and it wouldn't feel right to burden them with my problems now.

"So, you're all alone?" His voice is gruff, but the tone is softer and I hate the pity I hear.

"Don't make me out to be a pathetic loser, last night was the exception, not the rule. Plus, I have plans, big plans that don't include me sleeping in abandoned campers."

"I don't think you're a loser or pathetic, I just feel bad that you're alone. I live in a house with seventeen other people, I can barely hear myself think for people."

Wow, he has a wife and more than a dozen kids, that's crazy, although I bet he's a good dad. Now that I think about it, the way he's swooping in and trying to take over my life right now is a typical dad thing to do, or at least what I imagine good dads do. "You and Penn are brothers?" I ask, even though I already know the answer.

"Yep, I'm one of seven."

"Wow, seven, that's a lot of siblings. You must have liked being from a big family if you had fifteen kids."

His brow furrows and he turns to look at me. "I don't have any kids."

"You just said you live with seventeen other people."

"I do. My six brothers, five of them are married and

between them they have six kids so far."

"And you all live together?" I gasp. It's both sweet and a little appalling that he lives with his whole family. I can't imagine wanting to live with so many married couples and kids, it kind of feels a little hippieish.

"Not in the way you're thinking, we're not in a cult or anything, although I suppose it does sound like a commune when I say it out loud. We converted our family home so we each have our own apartments, connected to the main house."

"Oh, and your wife is okay with that?" I'm fishing, but I don't really know why. He's too old for me, and it's clear he thinks I'm a kid who can't take care of herself judging by the way he's bossing me around.

"No wife, or girlfriend or significant other," he growls angrily.

I've pissed him off, so I nod, clasp my hands together in my lap and keep my eyes forward. I can feel his gaze repeatedly landing on me, but I don't react. I don't know this man, or why he's driving me to work or offering me a place to stay. I wish I didn't need his help, but I do, and although sleeping in the RV was a hell of a lot better than going to Ernie's last night, I know it's not even a short-term solution to my problem.

It's another six months until I turn twenty-one. Ernie might want my inheritance, but apparently, it's no longer enough of an incentive for him to keep his hands to himself, and I refuse to become any more of a victim to him than I already am.

If Bay wants to be my savior, then I'd be stupid not to

let him, and a bed in an apartment with a lock is definitely better than my other option, which is to take the money I have stashed at work and run. I should have enough for a bus ticket out of state, and then maybe enough for a shitty motel for a few days until I can find a job. The main problem with that is, if I don't find a job as soon as I get to wherever I'm going, I have nothing to fall back on and then homelessness really might be a reality.

Bay pulls the truck to a stop outside the small bakery I've passed, but never had the money to try out before.

"Come on, let's get some breakfast," Bay says, killing the engine and unfastening his seat belt.

"I'm fine thanks, I'm not really a breakfast person," I tell him, not wanting to admit that I don't have even a dollar to my name. The only cash I have is hidden in Mr. Prentiss's mini safe in his suite. He spotted me trying to squeeze some balled-up cash into my sock one day and I ended up confessing everything to him. He's a very sweet old man, who offered to give me enough money to get away. I refused of course, but I accepted his offer to keep my stash safe in his suite just in case Ernie ever found out about the cash I have and got my boss to check my work locker.

"Let's go, breakfast is the most important meal of the day."

"Honestly, I'm fine, I promise not to run away while you go get yourself something." My stomach picks that exact moment to growl loudly and I blush, my cheeks turning hot and pink.

Without saying another word, Bay climbs out of the truck, circles the hood and opens my door. Leaning over me, he unfastens my seat belt then lifts me out of the seat like I weigh nothing.

I expect him to step away, but instead of giving me any space, he leans in, curls his huge hand around the back of my neck and squeezes. "Don't lie to me, little Imp. Now let's go get you something to eat."

Chapter Three

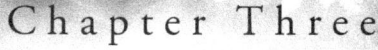

What the hell am I doing? Goose bumps pebble along the skin on her arm and I don't know if she feels this thing between us or if I'm scaring the crap out of her, but either way, I just can't force myself to step away.

When her eyes finally lift to meet mine, it's like clarity smacks me upside the head and I know fighting this will be futile. My woman, my one, my fated person is a girl less than half my age.

I should be arrested for all the things I've fantasized about doing to her in the last five minutes in the truck together. I've envisaged all the depraved ways I could use her body until her throat is hoarse from screaming my name, her pussy is swollen and dripping with my cum and her ass cheeks are bright red from the spanking I've given her.

How could this have happened?

I was happy; well maybe not happy, but I was content on my own. I didn't want a woman, and I certainly didn't want a barely out of her teens, runaway enchanted forest imp who's a walking problem waiting to happen.

If I'm doomed to be tied to one person, why couldn't they be my age, sensible, mature and self-sufficient? Instead, everything about Missy is messy. Her hair is sleep rumpled, her clothes are creased, there are dark circles under her eyes and she's just a little too skinny, which I think is probably from lack of food and not a style choice.

She's everything I don't want in a woman, so why is it that I'm reluctant to release her from my possessive hold? I like the way it feels to have my palm wrapped around the nape of her neck. I'm not the type of guy that feels the need to lay claim on a woman in public, but I want people to look at the way I'm handling her and know she's mine. Lacing my fingers with hers, I lead her into the small bakery that's been here since I was a child and force her to pick something to eat. The urge to care for her is strong, and I have to fight my need to carry her back to my truck and feed her to make sure she's eaten.

What the fuck am I doing?

I'm not a complete asshole, I'd still help her even if she wasn't mine, I'd never let a scared kid go hungry if I could do something to help. But this isn't just civic-mindedness, this is an intrinsic need to take care of what's mine. Only I can't keep her.

If she was ten years older, I'd say fuck it and claim her,

but she's not. She's twenty—god, I hope she's twenty and not lying about her age. She's a kid, even if her eyes are filled with a maturity much past her young age.

It feels wrong for me to want her the way I do, but even after a night spent sleeping rough in an abandoned RV, she's still beautiful. Her hair is bright coppery red, orange and fiery the moment the light hits it. Each strand is a corkscrew curl that bounces when she moves, falling past her shoulders and down to the middle of her back.

Her body is all woman, big tits, a tiny waist and an ass that has my palm tingling with the urge to slap it and watch as it wobbles. Her skin is pale and there's a smattering of freckles across her nose and cheeks, stopping just above her rosebud mouth.

I'm going to hell.

She's so young and so innocent and so mine, but I can't touch her. I won't be the old dude with the woman young enough to be his daughter. I won't tie her to a man twice her age when she should be enjoying being young and free and stupid.

After she picks a muffin, I order a slice of peach pie, two sandwiches and two bottles of water, never letting go of her hand as I pay. Then I lead her back to the truck and lift her into her seat, relishing the feel of her skin beneath mine, even from the innocent touch.

"I…" she starts. "I don't have any money, but I promise I'll pay you back. Once I've left town, I'll post you the money back, I promise." Her cheeks are flushed red again, her embarrassment painful to watch.

"You don't owe me anything, I wouldn't take your

money, Imp."

"Why do you keep calling me Imp?" she asks.

"Guess you just remind me of one, a tiny little mischievous forest creature, more fun than a fairy, but not quite as naughty as a pixie."

I'm not sure how it's possible, but her cheeks go even redder. We both fall silent for a minute as I slowly drive across town to the old folks' home she works in while she eats her muffin, and I rein in my need to insist she eat more. When I park my truck in the lot of the huge modern-looking building, her eyes go sad.

"You okay?" I ask, wanting to know what's causing her to look that way and how I can stop it.

"Oh," she startles, snapping her head around to look at me. "I'm fine. I should get to work though."

"Stay there, I'll come help you down."

"I can—"

"You'll stay there until I come get you," I interrupt, trying not to snarl at her and only partially managing. Jumping out, I open her door, annoyed that her seat belt is already undone and I won't have the chance to lean over her to unclip it. Wrapping my hands around her waist, I lift her out, letting her breasts brush against my chest as I lower her to the ground. "What time does your shift finish?" I ask, not capable of letting her go just yet.

"Eight," she whispers, almost as if she realizes I'm struggling with control right now and doesn't want to set me off.

I nod, then force myself to let go with one hand and then the other, hating every inch of distance I put between us. "I'll walk you in."

"There's no—"

"I'll walk you in," I insist. Remembering the sandwich and water I bought, I grab it from the truck and hand it to her. "Here, put your lunch in your purse."

"Thank you," she says, looking up at me with wide green eyes that I could fall into and never escape from.

"You're welcome, Imp." I take her hand again and she lets me, walking beside me like it's the most natural thing in the world. Even though we probably look ridiculous together I want to pull her to me and take a picture, just so I have a memory of the one time I allowed myself to be like this with her. For the rest of the day, she's mine, but once she's safe in my apartment I need to leave her alone. I need to allow her to be twenty and meet a nice guy her age and not be lumbered with a middle-aged asshole who still lives in his childhood home.

Pushing open the door, I hold it for her to walk through. I expect her to try to free her hand from my hold, but she doesn't, stepping into the foyer and waiting for me to move in behind her.

"My locker's just through there, I'd show you, but only staff are allowed back there," she says, her smile sweet and warm.

"I'll be here at eight. Be here."

She nods, but I pinch her chin between my thumb and forefinger and tilt her head back slightly. "I mean it, Imp, be here at eight, I'll be seriously pissed if I have to track your ass down."

"Why do you care, Bay?" she asks me, her eyes earnest.

"Because I just don't seem to be able to help myself," I confess, leaning down and pressing my lips against her cheek.

"Missy, where the hell have you been?" an angry male voice shouts from behind us.

Instinctually I spin us, putting Missy behind me.

"Who the fuck are you?" the guy sneers, eyeing me up and down, then looking away the moment he meets my eye.

"I could ask you the same question," I say, taking an instant dislike to this slob of a man who's trying to step around me to get to my girl. He's short, maybe five feet six, or seven, with a paunch that's rolling over the top of his stained jeans. His hair is dark and greasy, thinning on top but styled in a way that he's trying and failing to hide it. His face is flabby with some acne scars and two days' worth of patchy stubble. He looks like a douchebag and judging by his attitude and demeanor so far, he acts like one too.

"I'm the uncle of the girl you're manhandling."

He's her uncle? If that's true, why is she still hiding behind me and not rushing to explain why she didn't come home last night?

"You're not my uncle," Missy snaps, moving to step to my side.

Reaching around, I keep her protected, ensuring that my body is between her and her uncle, or whoever he is.

"I don't know what the fuck you're playing at, but you need to explain where the hell you were last night." the guy snarls, his lips turning into an ugly sneer.

"I'm not explaining anything to you, asshole," Missy snarls angrily.

"You owe me an explanation, I'm the only family you've got. Who the hell do you think you are speaking to me like this?"

"We both know you couldn't give a crap and we're not family."

My eyes widen as I wonder where my sweet little imp has gone, because the hellcat who's trying her best to get around me and at this guy, is nothing like the girl I met this morning.

"We have a deal, you little bitch, you don't get to run out on me."

"Yeah, we had a deal, but then your disgusting drunken ass broke my door and let yourself into my room in the middle of the night."

A snarl falls from my lips and I glare menacingly at the fat, ugly asswipe in front of me. He broke into her room? This is the reason she's sleeping rough, because of this asshole. Hell no. I don't give a fuck who this guy is to her, nobody gets to be in her room at night, not even me. I might not be able to touch her, I might not be able to claim her as mine, but I can sure as fuck make sure she's safe.

"You need to watch what you're saying. You live in my house, you eat my food, I pay for everything. I got you this job and I can take it the fuck away. Remember that, you little bitch, everything you have in life, it's because of my generosity. Now get your shit, I'm taking you home."

"I don't know who the fuck you think you are, but if you ever come near Missy again—"

"Who the fuck are you?" the asshole demands, looking at me like he doesn't think I'm going to beat the shit out of him in a minute.

"I'm the motherfucker who's going to kick your ass into the middle of next week if you ever speak to this girl like that again."

"Is this where you were, fucking this Neanderthal? Jesus, I didn't raise you to be a whore."

"Not unless I'm your whore, isn't that right, *Uncle* Ernie," my imp says, poison dripping from every word.

Spinning around, I look down at my woman, *my woman,* and try not to react to what she just said. But she's not looking at me, all her vitriol and anger is aimed at the man standing in front of us. The man who says he's her family, but who breaks into her room drunk in the middle of the night.

"You're as crazy as your mom was, she infected my brother—"

"He wasn't your brother, he was a distant cousin, did you even really know him? Or was it just all about money?" Missy snaps. Her eyes wide, as if she can't believe she just said that. Then gasping, she covers her mouth with her hand and takes a wary step back.

Turning, I look at Ernie The Asshole, whose eyes are narrowed with a hatred I've only ever witnessed in movies and never in real life. "I'll see you at home, Missy," he says slowly, menace lacing each word.

No, nope, no, there is no way I'm letting her go near this guy ever again. I might be trying to tamp down the caveman alpha male who wants to haul his woman over his shoulder and take her back to his cave and ravage her, but there's no way I can allow him to threaten her. He hasn't said he's going to harm her in explicit words, but the intention is there and so blatant I just can't let that stand.

Snapping my hand out, I grab the front of his shirt and haul him the two feet between us, lifting him onto his tiptoes so I can look him in the eye. "You will not talk, look, touch or even breathe in her direction ever again. I don't give a fuck if you are dying on the floor and she's the only one who can save you, you'll make your peace with an extended stay in hell rather than even acknowledge she exists."

"She's my niece," he wheezes out.

Turning, I look at Missy, arching my brow. "Are you his niece?"

Shaking her head, she glares at him. "He told me he was my uncle, but he's not, he's my second cousin."

For a second, I try to figure out if that actually makes them related, then realize it really doesn't matter either way. "I'm guessing after your choice of sleeping arrangements last night, you don't want to go back to live with him?"

Quickly shaking her head again, she glances around us, noticing for the first time that we've attracted a bit of a crowd.

"She's not your niece and she doesn't want to live with you anymore."

"She owes me," he hisses, his eyes bugging out a little as he turns and glares at Missy.

"How much?"

"What?"

"How much does she owe you?"

"Everything, she owes me fucking everything and she stays until I get it."

"Gentlemen," someone calls from beside us.

Turning, I glare at the balding guy in a uniform, with security embroidered across his chest, who is standing with a woman wearing a severe black business suit. The moment my anger is focused on him, the security guard takes a step back and holds his hands up in a conciliatory gesture. "What?" I growl.

"Sir, we have a strict, no-violence policy here at Mountain View Pines, so I'm going to ask you to please release Mr. Harrison and take a step back before we have to call the sheriff," the woman says, her tone no nonsense and cold to the point of glacial.

Glaring once more down at Ernie, I reluctantly loosen my hold on him and take a step away, herding Missy back, keeping her behind me and almost hidden from view.

"Miss McCormick, this…" suit lady pauses, sneering at me, "Gentleman is with you?"

"Yes, ma'am," Missy replies. "He was kind enough to give me a ride to work, he didn't know who Ernie was and when he approached me aggressively, he stepped between us to make sure I was safe."

My Imp's voice is quiet and a little kowtowed and I hate it, I'll take her anger over this meekness toward the woman that I'm guessing is her boss.

"Hmm," the suit sniffs, glaring at me again, before she looks to Ernie, her expression softening a little. "Mountain View Pines is an elite retirement facility. We pride ourselves on the quality environment and service we offer to our clients."

"I understand that, Ms. Lockley," Missy nods solemnly.

"Due to this," she sneers again, looking at me, "scene you have created here this morning, I have no other alternative but to terminate your employment effective immediately due to gross misconduct."

"What?" I shout. "You can't fire her because of something I did."

"This has nothing to do with you, Mr...." she trails off, waiting for me to tell her my name, but Missy speaks.

"Of course, I'll just collect my belongings from my locker. Stuart can accompany me and then I'll get out of your way. I'll stop by HR and they can issue my final paycheck," Missy tells them calmly, too calmly almost.

Everyone freezes for a second as if they were all waiting for Missy to make a scene, but instead she just lifts her chin almost regally and looks to me. "Thank you for the ride, Bay."

I open my mouth to tell her this is bullshit, but before I have a chance, she turns and walks away with Stuart, who I'm assuming is the security guard trailing after her.

Suit lady and Ernie have a heated, whispered conversation, before they remember I'm here and both turn to glare at me.

"I suggest you leave, before I call the authorities," suit lady sneers.

Ignoring her, I look to Ernie. "I meant what I said, you stay the fuck away from her. I don't give a shit what you think she owes you, you stay the fuck away, or I'll make you."

"Is that a threat?" suit lady gasps.

"Nope, it's a warning." I know I sound like a shitty

mobster in a film right now, but there's so many unknowns here I don't know what else to do. Missy is a stranger to me, I don't know her, or her family situation. I have no idea what's happened that has led this asshole to believe that she owes him something, or if that's a physical something like money or a metaphorical something. I'm out of my depth here and even though a part of me wants to just beat the shit out of this asshole, until I have more information, this vague threat will have to do.

"I'm calling the police," suit lady snaps.

"Don't bother, I'm leaving," I growl at them, eyeing them both before I turn and head to the exit. Standing beside my truck, my hands clenched into tight fists, I wait for my Imp to come back out. After ten minutes, I wish I'd gotten her cell number, but I'm not even sure if she has one. I didn't get the chance to tell her that I'd be waiting for her. Would she know? Or would she assume that I'd just leave?

After another five minutes I march back into the main entrance and find Missy huddled into the wall while Ernie crowds her, his beady eyes hooded and angry. I can't hear what he's saying, but he's gesticulating threateningly and then he grabs the purse she has pressed tightly against her chest.

I'm barely aware of moving, but in the next second, I'm between them. Reaching behind me, I curl an arm around her, urging her to lean into my back, to use me as shelter from anything that threatens her.

Like she was always meant to, she curls against my spine, her fingers twisting the fabric of my shirt. The moment I feel her safe and protected, I turn my attention to the asshole trying to intimidate a twenty-year-old woman who he claims is his niece.

"I warned you, I told you to look the other way, to never speak or touch or even acknowledge her again."

"Look," he hisses, his voice high and feminine. "I don't know who the hell you are, or why you think you can get involved. I'm sure she's a good fuck, but this is a family matter so you need to mind your own goddamn business." Shards of spittle bust from his mouth as he speaks and I cringe at how disgusting it is.

"Imp, did you get everything you needed?" I ask her, ignoring the douchebag.

"I need to say goodbye to one of the residents, but he's not here right now, other than that, yes I have everything," she says quietly.

"Missy, we're going home, we have a lot to discuss. As a family," Ernie says through gritted teeth, trying to sound caring and not like the fucking asshole he really is.

As much as I want to pick her up and carry her away, I can't just take over her life. "Do you want to go home with Ernie, or come with me?" I ask. If she says she wants to go with him, I might well lose my mind, but I don't tell her that, giving her the illusion of a choice.

"Can I come with you?" she asks.

"That's exactly what I want," I tell her, turning around so instead of her being pressed to my back, she's now sheltered against my chest.

"Missy," Ernie says her name like it's a warning, but I don't give her a minute to respond, guiding her straight out of the front door and to my truck.

"Missy," Ernie yells, following behind us.

When he yells again, she flinches and her steps falter.

"Ignore him, I've got you, babe," I whisper as I unlock the truck, open the door and lift her inside, refusing to acknowledge the grown-ass man who's chasing us across the parking lot, screaming at us. Closing her door, I climb into the driver's seat, start the truck's engine and drive away, keeping an eye on Ernie as he screams obscenities and watches us leave.

Once we're about half a mile away from the old folks' home, I pull to the curb, put the truck in park and turn to look at her. Her ratty black purse is on her lap, her arms wrapped protectively around it. Her eyes are unfocussed, staring ahead, but she's obviously not even aware of the fact that I've stopped.

"Are you okay?"

Inhaling sharply, she turns slowly to look at me and shakes her head. "That was a lot."

I nod, agreeing with her.

"I can't go back."

"To your job or to Ernie's place?"

"Both," she whispers, lifting her hand to her mouth and biting at the nail on her thumb. "I got fired and left home." A slightly manic laugh falls from her lips. "I can't go home. I couldn't anyway, but now I really can't." She laughs again. "Mr. Prentiss has all my money in his safe, I literally don't have a penny to my name."

"I thought you went to go pick up your final paycheck?"

"They said they would pay it into my account." She giggles manically, but there are tears sliding down her cheeks.

"That's okay then, right?"

"Not really," she mutters. "Because he has my wages paid into his account."

The hairs on the back of my neck prickle and my shoulders tense. "Why would he do that?"

"Because he's an asshole."

"So, you don't think he'll give you the money?"

Her laugh is so unexpected that I think I actually flinch. "Well, I haven't seen a penny of the money I've earned there in the last year and a half, so I doubt he's going to suddenly become altruistic now."

"He takes your salary? The money you earn at your job?" I ask slowly.

"He takes everything, I literally don't have a single dime right now. He allows me to eat the food in the house and he got me a bus pass so I can get to work, but other than that he makes sure I don't have any money at all."

"Why? Why does he think you owe him?"

Dragging in a sharp breath, she sits up a little straighter in her seat. "I'm sorry, none of this is your problem and I can't apologize enough for dragging you into my drama. I've managed to get a little cash working extra shifts at Mountain View without Ms. Lockley knowing, and one of the residents offered to let me keep it in his safe in his room. I'll grab it from him later and then I'm going to get on a bus and get the hell away from here before Ernie realizes that I'm really not planning on going back."

"Missy, if you think I'm just going to let you get on a bus with no money, nowhere to stay and no job, you must be fucking delusional," I snarl, my entire body tense with how wrong everything she just said feels.

"Bay, we don't know each other, we met less than an hour ago when your brother found me sleeping in his RV. Honestly, I appreciate you not calling the cops and getting me arrested and I'm grateful for the food, the ride and the way you stepped between Ernie and me, but you've done enough. I can fight my own battles and look after myself."

Forcing my teeth together to stop myself from telling her she's mine, that she belongs to me now, I nod slowly, letting her know that I heard her. Then I pull away from the curb and back onto the street. "Can you drive, Missy?" I ask her lightly.

"No, Ernie said he didn't want me to do drivers ed because he felt it was dangerous and not properly supervised. He doesn't drive either, or at least I don't think he does. He's told me an awful lot of bullshit over the years, so I'm not really sure what's true and what isn't at this point."

Nodding again, I drive, taking a right turn, then a left. "Where did you and he live? I know it's not in Rockhead Point, or else we would have bumped into each other before, it's a small town."

"Our house is in Wilderwood, it's a couple of towns over, about thirty minutes by bus."

I nod, making small talk as I drive.

After about ten minutes, she stills, looking out the window. "Where are we going? The garage is in town, I guess I assumed we'd go back there."

"We're not going to the garage," I answer simply.

"Oh, I thought..." she trails off. "It doesn't matter, as

soon as I can get my money from Mr. Prentiss, I need to leave anyway."

Grinding my teeth so hard I'm a little worried I might break one, I stay silent, not demanding she stay, or warning her that even though I'm fighting it, I'm not sure I'll ever be able to let her leave. I won't turn into my brothers; I won't lose my shit and claim this girl. But if that's the truth, why the fuck am I halfway up the mountain instead of back at the garage, showing her the apartment?

"Bay," she asks. "Where are we going?"

"My place."

Chapter Four

He's taking me to his place? What the hell does that mean? Since the moment I met both him and his brother, I've felt an almost endless amount of trust in them, but has that been misplaced? I'm a twenty-year-old girl in a car with a virtual stranger. What the hell am I doing allowing myself to be this vulnerable?

"What do you mean you're taking me to your place?" I shout. "Stop the car. I don't want to go to your place, I don't know you." I can hear the sound of my own panic but I can't stop it. The realization that if Bay turns out to be a total psycho and no one would ever know where to look for my body hits me, and I claw at the door, trying to open it and bail out.

"Stop," he snaps, his voice taking on a dominant tone

that I haven't really heard before.

My fingers stop pulling at the handle and I still, but I don't know why because my mind is spinning in circles, telling me to run, to flee from this man who has driven me to work, bought me food and protected me from Ernie.

"Look at me," he demands.

Slowly, I turn to face him and the moment our eyes meet, I feel something settle inside of me and the tension in my shoulders relax.

"I'm not going to hurt you. I'm taking you to my home, my whole family lives there with me, remember? One of my sister-in-law's brothers is a deputy in the sheriff's office. I'm going to give you my cell phone and you're going to call him and ask him if you're safe with me, okay?"

He holds out a cell phone to me and I snatch it off him, Googling for the number and then dialing it.

"His name is Cameron Cunningham," Bay tells me, his tone quiet and nonthreatening.

"Rockhead Point Sheriff's department," someone greets when the call connects.

"Can I speak to Deputy Cunningham, please?" I ask, not taking my eyes off Bay.

"I'm afraid Deputy Cunningham isn't working today, I'm Deputy Moseley, can I help?" a female voice asks.

I pause, think for a second and then speak. "Do you know Bay Barnett?"

"Sure, Bay and his brother own the garage. Is there some kind of issue?"

"I'm not sure, I'm with Bay right now, we don't know each other and he said that Deputy Cunningham could vouch for him."

The deputy laughs, her voice sweet and high. "Oh wow, another one bites the dust, huh? I can vouch for him, Bay and his brothers are good people, I don't know him really well, but this is a small town and, well it's impossible to not know of everyone. His brother Huck is married to Deputy Cunningham's sister and Cam likes the whole family, has dinner with them all at least once a week. If you have any issues, feel free to call me back though, you can ask for Deputy Moseley or Miranda, I'm on shift for the next three days. Okay?"

"Okay, thank you, Deputy, my name is Missy McCormick, if I turn up dead or am reported missing, the last person I was with is Bay Barnett."

"Okay," she laughs again. "I'm sure I'll be seeing you around town, Missy, you take care now."

"Thank you," I tell her, then end the call, but instead of returning the cell to Bay, I hold it in my hands and look up at the man beside me.

"Cam wasn't there?" Bay asks.

"No, I spoke to a different deputy."

"I heard," Bay nods. "We're here."

We pull off the road and onto a gravel driveway that meanders for a while before revealing a massive log home. Despite the size of the it, the house seems to nestle into the countryside, almost blending with the trees behind it and the miles and miles of mountain wilderness in the distance.

"Home sweet home," Bay says, pulling to a stop behind several other cars and killing the engine. "Stay there, I'll get your door," he warns, quickly climbing out and circling the truck. Just like he's done every other time, he opens my door, leans over me to unfasten my seat belt and then lifts me out like I weigh nothing and it's perfectly normal to be carrying around someone you just met.

He doesn't ask me for his cell back and somehow, I find that reassuring. Like if he was really kidnapping me—which is basically what he's done—he'd want to take away all my ways of calling for help and by letting me keep the cell, he's reminding me that I'm not really a prisoner.

Capturing my hand in his, he closes my door and then leads me toward the house. We pass several SUV's, all with baby seats in the back and those blinds they put on the windows to stop the sun from shining on the kids.

When he pushes open the front door I pause, wondering for a second if I should run. I have no idea why I'm being so compliant; if it was any other man bringing me halfway up a mountain to his home, less than two hours after meeting him, I'd be running so fast in the opposite direction there would be burn marks beneath my feet. But there's just something about Bay that just makes me feel safe.

I'm not sure if it's that he put himself between me and Ernie, or that he waited for me at Mountain View. Maybe it's that he cared enough about a stranger to make sure I'd eaten, or maybe it's all of it. Whatever it is, it doesn't feel like we only met this morning, it feels like I've known him and trusted him my whole life.

The fact that he's tall, dark and handsome is probably helping too. If he was short, fat and ugly, I doubt I'd be being as trusting and as stupid as I'm being now, no matter how shallow that is.

The sound of people hits me the moment I step inside and instead of the house being quiet and empty like I'd expected, it looks like we just stepped into a day care center. Four women are all sitting in a huge open-concept living room surrounded by baby paraphernalia.

"Bay, is everything okay?" a beautiful brunette asks, standing up with a toddler balanced on her hip.

"Hey Lulu, yeah everything is fine. I'd like you all to meet Missy." Squeezing my hand slightly, Bay pulls me from where I was hiding behind him, guiding me around him until I'm at his side and being stared at by four of the most gorgeous women I've ever laid eyes on.

The woman he just called Lulu looks at me, then to Bay and then behind her to the other women, before a huge grin spreads across her face. Rushing forward, she thrusts the toddler at Bay before she throws her arms around me and hugs me like we're best friends reunited.

"Oh my god, it's so nice to meet you," she gushes. She's shoved out of the way and a redheaded woman takes her place, squeezing me tightly. When she releases me, another brunette smiles warmly and hugs me, whispering, "It's so wonderful to meet you," into my ear before she steps back, revealing a stunning blonde woman behind her.

I expect the blonde to dive on me next, but instead she waves shyly. "Hi Missy, I'm Alice."

"Hi Alice," I say, waving back.

"Oh fuck, we just hug bombed her without even introducing ourselves," the redhead laughs. "I'm Cora, this is Bonnie," she points to the other brunette. "And this is Lulu."

"Hi," I say awkwardly. I have literally never been greeted so warmly in my life. Did Bay call ahead and tell them we were coming?

"Sorry, Imp, I should have warned you that my sisters are crazy," Bay laughs. "It's going to take you a while to get everyone set in your head, but Lulu is married to Penn, who you met earlier. "This…" He leans down and blows a raspberry on the cheek of the toddler in his arms. "Is their daughter Poppy, and their twins Bluebell and Hyacinth are just over there." He points to a pink bassinet where I can just see two babies wearing matching pink hats with bows on them. "Cora"—he gestures to the enthusiastic redhead—"is married to my brother Huck, he's at work right now, but you'll meet him later, their son Maverick is the one trying to climb out of the playpen."

"Mav." Cora gasps, darting across the room and scooping the little boy out of the pen. "I swear you get more like your father every day," she scolds, booping her son on the nose with her fingertip while he grins unabashedly, his hair a mop of strawberry-blond curls.

"Alice, the only one yet to dive on you is married to my brother Granger and their son Fox is no doubt sleeping peacefully, he's the most laid-back baby I've ever met. And then Bonnie is married to my eldest brother Beau, their son Wilder is…" His eyes scan the baby chaos in front of us and then land on a chunky baby swaddled in a blanket in a second bassinet. As if he heard his name being spoken, Wilder opens his eyes and lets out a baby scream, his face screwing up and getting red as he loudly ensures he has everyone's attention.

"You had to say his name, didn't you?" Bonnie scowls at Bay. "It's taken me an hour to get him to go down."

"Sorry," Bay winces, then looks to me. "Wilder has colic, he's been screaming the place down all day and night."

I nod, like I have any idea what baby colic is. I really wasn't expecting to be introduced to his family, or that his sisters, or sisters-in-law would be this excited to meet a stranger. It doesn't make any sense, and that makes me uncomfortable. As a general rule, people's behavior is simple and understandable. Some people are generally nice and that's cool, but the way I was just greeted like I was a soldier returning from war is weird.

"Do you want a drink?" Bay asks, seeming almost awkward as he takes my hand again and steers me toward the open kitchen area.

"Why am I here, Bay?" I ask, pulling my hand free of his hold and taking a fortifying step back.

"Honestly, I don't really know," he confesses weakly.

"Maybe you should just take me back to town. I can get my money from Mr. Prentiss and then get on a bus."

"And go where?" he snaps, a savage expression morphing his face.

"Away," I sigh, wistfully.

"You're so fucking clueless, Imp. How are you going to take care of yourself once you get there?"

"I'll get a job, like every other person in the world," I snark.

"And where will you sleep while you wait to save enough money for an apartment? On the streets? In the bus station? Or were you hoping to stumble across another unlocked RV wherever you went, too?"

"Don't make me sound like a moron, I'm not stupid, but it's not like I have loads of options here either. I can't go back to Ernie's. I got fired from my job. I don't have any friends or family in Wilderwood. If I'm starting over with nothing, why can't I do it somewhere new, somewhere without any bad memories?"

"So stay here," Bay says.

"What?"

"Stay here. We have a spare room that no one's using, you'll be safe and you can work at the garage, we need someone to work reception."

"I don't need your pity, I'm not some kid that needs to be parented."

"Oh, trust me, Imp, I have no interest in being your fucking parent," he growls.

"So why? You don't know me, we only met this morning, why do you care? If I'd woke up a little earlier, Penn would never have found me and we'd have never have met, so why does it matter? Why bring me here?" I ask, needing to know the answers. People aren't altruistic, nobody does something just to be a decent human, not without there being something in it for them.

Bay lifts his hands and rubs at his temples. "Because…" he trails off. "Because I want to, okay? You need help and I can offer it, just leave it at that."

"What do you want in return?"

His head snaps up and his eyes flare with anger. "I don't want anything, Missy."

"No one helps someone the way you're offering to help

me without an ulterior motive."

"That's not true, but if it is, then maybe I'll be the first. Come on, let me show you your room."

"I don't know, I appreciate the offer but—"

His hand lands on the base of my spine, and I shiver as the heat of his palm makes tingles prickle along my skin.

"I'm not taking you to the bus station, I'm not taking you anywhere, so move your ass and I'll show you your room," he growls, urging me to move with the pressure of his hand on my back.

"Bay."

"You can either walk, or you can go over my shoulder, result will still be the same."

A shocked gasp falls from my lips and I twist around and stare at the beautiful man behind me. "Did you just threaten me?"

"You can call it a threat if you want," he says, still propelling me forward until we reach a door on the back wall. Lifting his hand from my back he leans around me and opens it, then curls his fingers around the nape of my neck and he guides me into the beautiful space that looks more like a hotel suite than someone's guest room.

"This is your guest room?"

"This used to be my parents' room, after Mama died it stood empty for years, but the girls did a full refurb on it a couple of years ago. To be honest, other than Alice when she first met Granger, no one has ever used it. It's yours for as long as you need it."

"Don't you need to ask the rest of your family before you offer me a place to stay?"

He shakes his head. "Nope, they'll be fine with it."

"I don't—"

"It's done, so drop your purse and your jacket and I'll get us some drinks," Bay tells me, ignoring my attempt to argue.

I expect him to leave, but instead he waits impatiently for me to do as he says, then he takes my hand and leads me over to the huge couch where his sisters and all the babies are sitting. Cora pats the spot beside her and I sit down, watching Bay walk over to the kitchen and start to make a fresh pot of coffee.

"Soo," Cora singsongs, "tell us everything. How did you and Bay meet? Why aren't you freaking out about the whole 'mine' thing?" she giggles.

Furrowing my brow, I look at her in question. "We met this morning, well actually I met Penn first. I…" I swallow, hating that I have to confess how I really met the Barnetts. "Until a couple of days ago, I lived with my second cousin Ernie. Some stuff happened and I had to leave and well, I saw an RV behind the garage and so I…" My cheeks blush bright red. "I needed somewhere to sleep. Penn found me there this morning. I was expecting him to call the cops, but instead he was just making me a coffee when Bay came in and well, there was an altercation at the place I worked and I got fired and then Bay brought me here."

"So, when did he tell you that you were his?" Bonnie asks excitedly.

"I don't know what you mean."

"Did he go all growly? I mean they always go growly, but did he like, try to kidnap you or anything?" Cora giggles.

"Kidnap me?" I gasp. "Why would he kidnap me?"

"Not like kidnap, kidnap. Although Huck kind of did it to me, but I mean more like sweep you off your feet and steal you away," Cora says with an exaggerated wink.

I must look as confused as I feel, because all four women are staring at me.

"He didn't tell you that you're his?" Lulu asks.

I shake my head. "No. Why would he? We met about two hours ago."

"You're not from Rockhead Point, are you?" Bonnie asks.

"No, I've lived in Wilderwood for the last four years."

"Okay, well if you were from here, you'd know all about the Barnett legacy," Cora starts.

"No," a deep voice snaps from beside us, causing all of us to turn our attention to where Bay is standing with a tray of mugs and a plate of cookies.

"I don't understand," Bonnie says, her brow furrowed.

"Mind your business," Bay snarls at her.

She flinches like he's slapped her and then narrows her eyes on him. "Bay."

"Bonnie, this is nothing to do with you."

"So, she's not?" she trails off, looking pointedly at me.

"This is nothing to do with you," he says through gritted teeth.

"She's here," Cora argues.

"Look," I interrupt. "I'm happy to go if someone can take me down to the bus station."

"No," all five of them say at once.

"I've obviously caused some kind of issue and I'm only

here because Bay didn't tell me where he was taking me until we were already halfway here."

"You haven't caused any issues, Imp, my sisters are just being nosy pains in the ass, ignore them. Now how do you take your coffee?"

A strained silence swirls around us as Bay doctors everyone's coffees and hands them out. There's a slight reprieve when the babies start to wake up and the women all rush around making bottles and finding pacifiers and diapers.

I've never felt more uncomfortable in my entire life. Obviously, there's something else going on here that I don't understand. Maybe this isn't the first time Bay's brought home a stray, or maybe they thought I was someone else? Regardless, it's clear that I need to leave. The problem with that is I don't really know where I am and Bay was pretty adamant that he won't be dropping me off at the bus station, at least not today anyway.

A yawn slips from my lips and I nestle back into the squashy couch, watching as the women all bustle around, ordering Bay to help as they manage the six kids. I'm exhausted just watching. Kids freak me out, tiny humans with constant demands. My earliest memories aren't great and according to my nana before she died, I was a bit of an asshole until I started at middle school. I'm not sure if I was or not, but I think maybe Nana was just done with child rearing. Then I got dumped in her lap and she was too good a person to not take me in.

A second yawn stretches my jaw and I allow my eyes to fall closed for a moment. Considering I slept in an RV last night, I got more sleep than I usually would, but even being here in a stranger's home I feel safer than I have at Ernie's since the day I turned eighteen.

My body has finally decided to slip out of high alert. A normal person would be more wary here, but somehow, I instinctively know that Bay won't hurt me, and he won't allow anyone else to hurt me either. I don't know how I know it, but I do. I'm safe here and I want to cry, because I'm safer with someone I met this morning, than the man who sought me and my nana out, told us he wanted to help and then raised me for years.

The pretense has always been what's bothered me the most about what happened. It's not the money, you can't miss what you've never had and as I never even knew the inheritance existed, signing it over to Ernie wasn't the end of the world to me. But knowing that he pretended to care about me every day for two years, before he revealed his true motives, that hurt.

Since my eighteenth birthday—when I woke expecting to celebrate coming of age with the uncle I adored, and instead found a sexual predator who coerced me into giving him money by threatening me and using his physicality to pin me to my bed and tell me all the things I could trade for what I owed him—I'm not sure I've ever felt safe enough to relax.

Knowing Ernie arranged my job at Mountain View Pines, I could never fully let my guard down there either. He kept me so dependent on him for every little thing I needed, even asking someone for help felt out of reach.

I can't explain why Bay is the person who's changed

everything, and maybe he isn't. Maybe I made the change when I decided to sleep anywhere rather than at Ernie's where he held the threat of rape and sexual abuse over my head. Maybe I'm the catalyst for me finally being able to free myself from his hold over me.

Yes, I like that better. I don't want to be saved, I want to save myself and being here, with this sexy, good, beautiful, caring man was my choice. He might have whisked me to his castle on a mountain—or log home, but you get the gist. Either way, he brought me here, but trusting him is my choice and even though I have absolutely no evidence to back up my gut feeling, I know this is a place I can be free, even if it's only for an afternoon.

Tomorrow I'll take charge again, I'll pull on my girl boss panties—metaphorically, of course, my panties are the cheapest available at Target—and set my life on the path I want it to be on. But for today, I'm going to let Bay Barnett stand between me and the big, bad world.

I know letting go should make me feel lighter, but instead I go heavy, letting this couch carry my burden, just for a little while.

My eyes flutter shut and, this time, I don't fight it. I've been scared, tired and broken for almost two years and as I fall asleep, I rejoice in the warmth of the Barnetts, their home and family.

Chapter Five

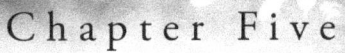

From the corner of my eye, I watch as her muscles relax and she slumps back into the couch. I know I shouldn't have brought her here, into my home, my life, my family, but I wanted her here; I wanted to know what it felt like. Unfortunately, it feels so right I know I'll torture myself with the feeling for the rest of my life.

I can't keep her. She's too young, she has too much life to live, too many plans for me to tie her to me. If she was even ten years older I might do it. I might take her and claim her and fill her with my babies so she'll always be mine. But my Imp is twenty, a baby in comparison to me.

She hasn't told me what's really going on with Ernie, the uncle who apparently isn't her uncle, but I'm smart enough to know whatever it is, it's not good. The moral, decent part of me knows I should take her to the bus station, give her enough money to get her set up in a decent apartment and then let her go. But the inherently male part of me is burning with the need to possess my woman. And she is mine.

She's everything I don't want, young, broke, needy. I should be running in the opposite direction, but instead I'm pissed that she doesn't know she's mine, that she can't tell she belongs to me now. For a moment, as I listened to my sisters asking her about how we met, I thought she might tell them she felt this instant jolt of lust and passion, that I was hers, but of course she didn't. She hasn't got a clue about my family's curse or how it might affect her.

A part of me wanted them to tell her, to explain that me bringing her here could only mean one thing. That she's mine, that she belongs to me now, but in the end I couldn't. I can't, won't do that to her. I won't tie her to me when she's not even old enough to have had a chance to decide what she wants out of life.

My sisters are fussing with the babies, who all seem to recognize that one is awake and then wake up to join in the fun. Lulu plops a wailing Hyacinth in my arms and hands me a bottle. For a second, I turn all my attention to the tiny baby girl, the twins are four months old now, but they were super tiny when they were born, so even though they're older than Wilder and Fox, they still seem small in comparison. Pushing the teat into her mouth, I smile down at my niece when she goes silent and immediately starts to suck.

When I look up again at Missy, her eyelids are fighting to stay open and there's a soft smile on her lips that makes me want to lean over and press my mouth to hers, just to see if she tastes as soft and sweet as she looks.

I hate that she can't ever be mine. I don't want the life I'll force on her to be her future, but I still want to possess her and own her in every way humanly possible. Everything about her calls to me, from the coppery flame color of her hair, to the Cupid bow of her lips. I can see myself corrupting all of the youthful innocence she carries with her like an aura of purity. I can imagine pushing her to her knees, knotting her hair around my fist and then using her mouth as my own personal play toy.

I'm not the kind of guy you allow anywhere near pure, innocent, inexperienced girls. I need a woman who knows what she wants and can keep up with what I need. My dick is not in control and I can go months without sex, but when I'm getting it, I'm a machine, and I'm yet to meet a woman who can keep up with my libido.

Rochelle was the closest I've ever come to finding my match in the bedroom. On the occasions when I'd visit for the weekend, we'd fuck over and over until her body was too exhausted to keep up, then she'd crash for a few hours and then we'd start all over again. We never spent enough time together to see if she'd be able to keep up long term, but she did better than any of my other hookups.

Missy might be mine, but there's no way I could treat her the way I have my conquests in the past. There's no way I could pin her to the bed with a dildo stretching out her ass while I fucked her pussy. There's no way I could face fuck her until tears and spit coated her cheeks, and there's no way I could spank her ass until the skin was hot and pink then come all over her, rubbing my release into the punished skin and both her holes.

I'm an asshole, but I'm not that much of an asshole, and that's why tomorrow I'll do what I need to do. In the meantime, I'll torture myself with her presence, and fuck my hand knowing she's asleep in the room next door.

Glancing back down to Hyacinth, I smile at her again, watching as her lips spread into a smile in return. For a moment I imagine holding a different baby girl with a shock of copper red hair and her mother's smile. My heart starts to beat uncontrollably and I close my eyes, forcing away the vision that will never come true. When I open my eyes again, I glance over at Missy and find her asleep, her head lolled slightly to the side.

Somehow, in sleep she's even more beautiful than when she's looking at me with all that quizzical wonder in her eyes. She's a puzzle, sweet and coy, but she has a backbone that I can't help but admire. I don't claim to understand even a little of what's going on in her life, but she's not cowering under the weight of it, her back is straight and her chin is high. She's a fighter and it's yet another thing that's drawing me to her.

Lulu follows my gaze and smiles a little at the sleeping Imp on the couch. "You need to tell her," she whispers.

"No, I don't."

"Bay, is she yours?"

I stare at her for a long moment then nod once.

"Then how can you possibly think you'll be able to let her walk away? You're a Barnett, it's only a matter of time until you lose your mind and go all crazy alpha caveman on her, the girl needs to at least understand what's going on and be given time to process it."

"I'm not going to claim her, so she doesn't need to worry about me losing my shit."

"What?" Cora gasps, joining in the conversation.

"She's twenty, I'm more than twice her age. It's not fair of me to take away her chance to be young and free and tie her to an old man."

"You're hardly an old man." Bonnie scoffs. "There's a bigger age gap between me and Beau and you weren't telling him to leave me alone."

"That's different," I snap, then immediately lower my voice. "You're from here, this is your home and you had no plans to leave. If you'd had your feet out the door, sneakers tied tight so you could run away, I might have told him to leave you be."

Bonnie scoffs. "He wouldn't have taken any notice anyway. But age is only a number, just because she's young doesn't mean you should get to make this life-changing decision for her. It's not just your choice to take away."

"It is my choice. I'm not going to lumber a girl like her with a guy like me."

"A guy like you?" Lulu questions. "Bay, you're hardly a bad guy, any woman would be lucky to have someone as great as you."

"I know I'm not a bad guy, but I'm not looking for a woman and if I was, it wouldn't be someone like her."

"Someone like her? I've known her for thirty minutes and she seems adorable. What's wrong with her exactly?" Cora hisses, ever the feisty protector. She was a firecracker when Huck first met her, but since she had Maverick, she's become a real mama bear and all the wives are her cubs.

"I don't mean it like that. I like her, of course I fucking like her, she's mine and I'm fighting the urge to throw her over my shoulder and lock her in my apartment until she can't breathe without thinking of me, but I won't. Maybe she'd go along with it now, but when she figures out I stole her life from her, she'd hate me."

"Do you think any of us will end up hating your brothers? They all did pretty much exactly what you just described to us, have they stolen our futures from us? Huck deliberately got Cora pregnant, Granger lied and tried to trick Alice into marrying him, Penn refused to leave Lulu alone and Both Beau and Teddy became full-blown stalkers to get me and Juni. Do you really feel like your brothers have done something wrong?"

Swallowing thickly, I try to figure out what to say so I don't sound like an asshole or piss off almost all the important women in my life. "A part of me does think they all did you wrong, yeah."

All four women stare at me like they have no idea what to say, because I essentially just took a shit on all of their marriages and now the words are out there, I can't take them back. "I'm not saying that what y'all have isn't the real deal. I know it is and I know my brothers' worlds start and end in this room with all of you. But a part of me has always thought that maybe no should have been no and when you fought against them, they maybe should have let you go."

The silence is so deafening I can hear the sounds of my heart pounding in my chest. Even the kids are quiet, and tiny Hyacinth is lying in my arms, betrayal etched in her beautiful eyes.

"I'm not sure if I should slap you or hug you," Cora says quietly.

"If I'm honest, I'm not sure which you should do either," I reply.

"You're wrong," Alice says quietly. "If Granger had accepted my no and walked away, I'd be across the country somewhere, alone, hating myself and convinced that I was so toxic and awful a person that I shouldn't even allow myself to have a proper conversation with anyone. If he'd have walked away when I told him he shouldn't be around me, I wouldn't be here, with all of you."

She's so quiet that sometimes I think we all forget about my most reserved sister, she's the sweetest, kindest most gentle woman I've ever met and to hear her say that she once thought she was toxic and awful makes a lump of emotion catch in my throat. "Alice."

"I don't need you to tell me that I'm nice or whatever. I know I'm not what I thought I was, or most of the time I do. But Granger saved me, he saw more than I ever allowed myself to see in the mirror. He patched up all my broken pieces and sewed them back together with a part of him. He's everything I never thought I deserved to pray for, and I'd be lost without him. He gives me more than I could ever give back, but he loves me and I love him and that's all because he refused to let me fight him, when he knew we were meant to be together. How do you know that's not what you are to Missy?"

Cora, Bonnie and Lulu all look at me expectantly, but

I don't have an answer, because I honestly have no idea. I don't know Missy, I know she has some shit going on in her life and that whatever it is, she didn't feel safe to go home and she'd rather camp out in a cold, empty RV. But she's asleep now, does that mean she's just exhausted or that she feels safe and secure enough here with me and my family that she could relax?

I try to force myself to look away, but my eyes just won't stray from her beautiful face, or flame-bright hair. Sighing, I try to imagine telling her she's mine, that some fucked-up version of fate decided that she's the perfect woman for me, but I just can't. There's not a version of that scene that doesn't end with her calling me a psycho, perverted asshole and running from me, and I wouldn't blame her.

I'm twice her age. For all I know she might not even be attracted to me. I don't know if my brothers ever considered that, or if they just knew they were good-looking bastards and assumed the women they knew were theirs felt the same. Objectively, I'm aware that I'm attractive to women. Rochelle was only my latest fuck buddy in a pretty lengthy back catalog of willing bed partners, but I've never touched anyone more than ten years younger than me, let alone twenty years. For all I know she could be repulsed by the idea of a man old enough to be her dad trying to lay claim to her.

No. I won't do it, I can't be the type of guy who ruins her future to secure my own. Now, I just need to figure out how the hell I let her go.

Missy's lip's part and a soft snore falls from her lips. I can't help but smile. A part of me wishes I could just leave her here on the couch where I can watch over her, taking in every moment I have with her, before I have to say goodbye, but she's obviously exhausted. Once Hyacinth finishes her bottle, I burp her, then lay her down on the couch beside her mama. Carefully, I slide one arm around Missy's back and another beneath her legs, being cautious not to touch her inappropriately, no matter how much my body wants to explore hers. Lifting her from the couch, I cradle her against my chest as I carry her into the guest room and gently lay her down on the bed.

Exhaling, I crouch down at the side of the bed, lift my hand and brush away a strand of hair that's fallen across her face. She's so beautiful and my heart stutters as I imagine stripping her naked and learning the dips and curves of her body while she sleeps so peacefully. If I could make her mine, I'd start every morning by priming her cunt with my fingers, before filling her with my dick and waking her up by fucking her and giving her my cum.

My cock twitches, but I refuse to adjust it, in case she wakes up and finds me with my hand down my fucking pants. Being this close to her is testing my resolve. I could crawl onto the bed beside her, slide my fingers beneath the waist of her leggings and tease her pussy until she's wet for me. Then when she woke up, I could roll her onto her stomach and hold her legs apart while I feasted on her, licking and sucking at her pink folds until she gushed for me, coming all over my face.

A desperate groan forces its way between my lips. No, this can't happen. Pushing myself upward, I turn my back on my perfect little Imp and leave the room, closing the door silently behind me. That was it, that was my moment of weakness, I can't let it happen again, no matter how much it feels like I've left my heart and soul in the room with her.

I'll do what I can to help her get back on her feet, and then I'll let her go and I'll return to my life of shallow sex and empty, lifeless walls. Now I know she exists I'll hate every minute, but better I be the one who suffers rather than her. Tying her to me would ultimately cause her pain and I never want that for her, ever.

Ignoring the pained looks on my sisters' faces when I step back into the family room, I slump down onto the couch, scooping Poppy up when she waddles over to me, her arms in the air. She's almost two now, but she's still the adorable little monkey who stole all our hearts the first time her mama brought her here to meet us. "Hey, Princess."

"Unka Bay, boo-boo." She holds her arm up to me, showing me the Minnie Mouse Band-Aid she has on her elbow.

"Oh no," I coo, lifting her arm higher and pressing a kiss against her skin, snuggling her close, her soft brunette curls tickling my cheek when I lean my chin against the top of her head.

"Betwa now," she nods, lifting her pudgy hand to pat at my cheek.

I chuckle, loving how one toddler can make my whole soul feel a little lighter, just by being here. Poppy might not share DNA with Penn, but that's never made an ounce of difference to him or any of us. She's my first niece and she owns a piece of my jaded and disinterested heart.

Jumping off my lap, she rushes over to her toys, all

of her attention on the twin baby dolls she's fussing over, poking plastic bottles at their faces while she imitates what her mama is doing with her baby sisters.

"You're making a mistake," Bonnie says quietly, as she changes Wilder's diaper while he stares on with wide-eyed wonder for his mama.

I shake my head, not willing to argue with her when I know she won't change my mind.

***

Missy sleeps for three hours and for the entire time, I fight the urge to go and watch over her, to stand guard and absorb every moment that she's here. I thought allowing her to leave would be hard, I never expected it to be impossible, but every second that passes by with her here whittles away at my resolve to keep my hands to myself.

A part of me thought that I could convince her to stay here for a month or two. That I could keep her safe, give her a job at the garage and pay her ridiculously well. Then when she finally climbed aboard that bus that will take her to a future that doesn't involve me, she'd have enough of a buffer to keep her safe until she gets a job wherever she's going. But I know that won't be an option. If she stays here longer than a night, I'll lose my mind.

I'm starting to see that the caveman I never planned to be, might be a little closer to the surface than I'd like. She's mine, and with every second she's here with me, I convince myself that I might just be selfish enough to ruin her life to keep her.

"You should go and check on her," Alice suggests.

Pursing my lips, I shake my head.

"Would you like me to?" she asks, her sweet voice a balm for my increasingly ravaged psyche.

Smiling, she strokes Fox's cheek, then walks to the bedroom door and knocks softly. After a second, Missy speaks and Alice opens the door and disappears inside. If it were any of my other sisters, I'd worry about them telling Missy the story about my family, explaining who she is to me, but Alice won't. She's still the quietest and most steady of all the girls. Bonnie, Cora, Lulu and Juniper all adore my brothers, but if shit went down, they'd leave and be fine. Alice looks at Granger like he's the only reason she can breathe and I'll never admit it, but sometimes the utter devotion in her eyes when she smiles at him makes me a little jealous.

I've never pried into their relationship, but from the way she defers to him, looks to him for guidance and seeks his eyes whenever she's in doubt, there's something a little deeper than just love between them. All of my brothers, except Cody, have admitted that they enjoy an element of control in their relationship with their wives, but for Granger and Alice I wonder if it's more than that. Given what she told me today, that he sewed her broken pieces back together with some of himself, it makes sense.

I'm not aware that my eyes have been firmly fixed on the bedroom door, until it opens and my heart jumps to my throat as I wait for Missy to emerge. I only met her this morning, but going three hours without seeing her is making the blood running through my veins burn and itch with the desire to ensure she's okay.

Alice steps out and then pulls the door closed behind

her and I frown, looking from my sister to the door and back again. "Is she okay?" I ask.

"She's fine. Tired and confused, anxious and overwhelmed."

"I should…" I jump up from my seat, ready to go to her, to check she's okay, but Alice's hand on my arm stops me.

"Bay, if you're serious that you're not planning to claim her, then you need to leave her be. If you go barging in there right now and become her savior; like I can see you're desperate to do, you'll hurt her when you set her on her journey to where ever she ends up. Don't do that. It's not fair. If you want to do what's right, you'll march your butt in there and tell her she's yours and that you'll do anything to make her happy, but if not, then sit down and don't play games."

It's possibly the most strength I've ever heard in Alice's voice and it's enough to keep me rooted to the spot. "I don't want to hurt her."

"I know," she sighs sadly. "I'm going to get her some clean clothes and then she's going to take a soak in the tub. She hasn't told me much, but I know what fear, sadness and worry look like, and that girl in there has all those things etched into her soul. You need to tread carefully. If you can't step lightly with her and you still insist on being an idiot and letting her go, then walk away and let Granger and I help her."

I'm shaking my head before I've even really processed her words. "She's mine," I growl.

"I know," she smiles.

"I can't…" I trail off, unsure what I can't do.

"I texted Beau, they're all on their way home, apparently your idiocy calls for guys' night," Bonnie says with a lethal smirk.

Well fuck.

Chapter Six

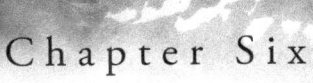

Waking up on a huge, cloudlike bed is awesome! My bed at Ernie's is small, hard and tainted with awful memories, and no matter how many times I wash the sheets or how many years pass, the bed still smells like Nana. This bed is enormous, at least a king size, maybe bigger, and the comforter has that crispy feel that you get with new sheets. The room smells floral, but not in an overpowering way, more like the way meadow flowers do in the middle of summer.

Instead of feeling worried or anxious, I wake up from my nap relaxed and rejuvenated. For a moment I wonder how I got from the couch to this bed, but a part of me knows that Bay more than likely carried me here—he seems the type to scoop the damsel in distress into his arms to save the day.

This house feels like a home. Not like my previous living situation, and now I think back on the two years I spent with Ernie before he revealed his true intentions, I realize his place never felt like a real home.

Sighing contentedly, I close my eyes and rub my hands against the cotton comforter. I love this bed, the only thing that could make it any better is if Bay were in it with me.

Holy fuck, where the hell did that thought come from? Obviously Bay Barnet is a beautiful man, but it's not like he brought me here to have sex with me—I'm still not entirely sure why he brought me here, but I know it wasn't for that and I need to get my head out of the gutter and be glad that I have somewhere safe to stay tonight.

All of my giddy daydreams about Bay fade away and the startling realization that I can't ever go back to Ernie's settles in their place. When I ran the other day, I never really considered that I wouldn't be going back there, I didn't even pack a bag, I just grabbed my purse and left.

I'm still in the clothes I hurriedly threw on, then sneakily washed at work. I don't have any ID, the photos of my nana or even a change of underwear. If I was desperate, I might have been able to sneak in and just avoid Ernie, but after the altercation with him and Bay, that's no longer an option. He got me fired deliberately and I know if I try to go home, he'll do something awful and then keep me locked down for the next six months until I turn twenty-one.

A soft knock on the door pulls me from my spiraling melancholy thoughts. Standing, I pad quickly to the door and open it. One of Bay's sisters is standing on the other side, her long blonde hair, shiny and poker straight.

"Hi Missy."

"Hi," I trail off, unsure of her name.

"Alice," she smiles. If she's offended that I forgot her name, she doesn't show it. "Would you mind if I came in for a moment?"

"Of course not, this is your home," I gasp, taking a step back and allowing Alice to enter.

"I stayed in this room, the day I met Granger," she says wistfully, stroking her fingers over the bed. "I always forget how pretty it is in here, you're only the second person to ever use it. My sister prefers to stay in a hotel when she comes to visit. I think she's worried we'll try and induct her into the cult she's convinced this place is," she giggles, her voice high and sweet.

"She's not from around here?"

"No, she's in the Army, she just got transferred to a barracks just outside of Houston. We have a weird relationship. Anyway, I just wanted to come and check on you. Are you okay? Is there anything you need?"

I quickly shake my head, not wanting to seem even slightly ungrateful for these strangers showing me so much kindness.

"How are you feeling? You crashed out on the couch; you must have been exhausted."

"It's been a stressful few days," I say, trying to sound elusive and just feeling like an asshole for not being honest. "Ernie, my second cousin who I've been living with, got drunk and decided to break down my door in the middle of the night. He's…" I pause, deciding how to word it. "He's an asshole sober, he's significantly worse with a gut full of whiskey. Anyway, I grabbed my purse and left, then I swapped with a colleague and worked a night shift at the old folks' home I worked at so I didn't have to go back home, and obviously you know that last night I slept in the RV out the back of Bay and Penn's garage. I have a plan, it's just that I didn't think I'd need it this soon."

Alice nods and I'm surprised to see there's zero judgment or pity in her gaze. "The RV is actually mine. I lived in it for five years. I've been spoiled since I moved in here, but I remember how uncomfortable those seats were, no wonder you were so tired. I imagine you're aching from head to toe too. You should take a bath; the tub is huge in this room and I know I have some muscle relaxing bath salts if you'd like?"

"No, I couldn't," I start to say.

"It sounds like it's been a rough few days for you, Missy. I won't pry, it's not my place, but know that you're safe here, there's a lock on this door and no matter how much whiskey is drunk, there's not a soul in this house who would try to open it. I can't pretend to understand how you're feeling, but I've been alone and scared, and I know I would have taken any opportunity I had to snatch a moment of peace and quiet if it was offered to me. My clothes will probably be too big, but Bonnie is a similar height to you so some of her stuff should fit."

"Oh no," I start.

"Missy," Alice holds her hand up to silence my protest. "It's okay to accept a little help sometimes, and none of it comes with any strings or expectations. Not everyone is an asshole who wants something in exchange for kindness. Now I'll go grab you something to change into and you run the tub."

Swallowing thickly, I nod, blinking to stop the tears that are threatening to fall from escaping. "Thank you."

"You're welcome."

Once she's gone, I shake out my hands that I hadn't realized were trembling so badly. Is this who I am now, someone who questions any act of kindness? I don't want to be that jaded, and the only person who has ever made me feel that way is hopefully no longer in my life.

Today was the turning point, the catalyst for change. Maybe fate or whatever else in the universe guides you to end up in the exact place you were meant to be, decided to do its thing and steer me toward that RV and the family who own it.

If a nap, an offer of a soak in the tub, and a clean change of clothes with the assurance that they expect nothing in return, can nearly bring me to tears, then it's clear how much this moment was needed. Today is the start of the rest of my life, away from Ernie and his twisted web of lies and onto something new, something better.

Stepping into the bathroom, I take a second to marvel at the soft-gray stone tiles and enormous egg-shaped bathtub that stands in the center of the room. If this is what their guest bathroom looks like, the rest of the house must be stunning. Twisting the faucet open, water gushes out and steam immediately starts to plume upward. Pushing in the plug, I watch, mesmerized by the water, the sound calming my racing thoughts. There's another knock on the door and

Alice peers around it, lifting up a pile of clothes for me to see.

"Bonnie wasn't sure what you'd want to wear so she grabbed you some yoga pants and a hoodie, I hope that's okay," Alice says.

"That's great, thank you."

"Here's the bath salts too, they smell delicious and you'll feel like you had a massage after you've had a soak with them. I have no idea what's in them, but Cora's mom bought us all some at Christmas and they're amazing." Placing the pile of clothes and the jar of salts on the counter, she flashes me a smile before opening the door and goes to leave. "Enjoy your soak, Bay's making lunch, but we'll keep yours warm until you're ready, so don't rush."

"Thank you, Alice."

Her smile grows, but she doesn't say anything, she just leaves, closing the door behind her. Crossing the room, I turn the lock, even though I don't feel unsafe here. Living with my pervy, threatening non-uncle has made locking doors feel more normal than it should. I lock the bathroom door too, before I strip out of my clothes and take a moment to rinse out my panties in the sink and then lay them over the heater to dry. They'll probably still be wet when I have to put them back on, but there's no way I can wear someone else's clothes without underwear.

Lifting the jar of bath salts up, I open the lid and inhale the fragrant scent of lily of the valley flowers. Nana's perfume that she only wore on special occasions had the same smell, and I find myself smiling as memories of the woman who raised me almost my entire life fill my mind.

Nana was ornery, cantankerous, formidable and the best person I've ever known. Losing her broke my heart. She was the only parent I've ever really known and remembering her now, feels bittersweet. Using the tiny wooden scoop inside the jar, I pour some of the salts into the tub and listen as they hiss and spit when they make contact with the water. Then I close the lid, placing the jar on the counter and slide into the bathtub, turning the tap off with my toe.

Exhaling wearily, I slide beneath the hot liquid and let it cover me, soaking my hair and face before pushing back to the surface. I wipe my eyes and rest my head on the side of the tub, and for the first time in too long to remember, I allow myself to relax.

I'm not sure if it's the peace, the heat of the water or the soothing scent of Nana, but I feel all the fear that's kept me going the last couple of days seep out of me and melt beneath the heat of the cleansing water.

There're tiny bottles of body wash, shampoo and conditioner and I use them, scrubbing myself until I feel refreshed and clean for the first time in years. Showering at Ernie's always felt like a dangerous temptation and whenever possible, I tried to use the facilities at work rather than give him the opportunity to find me naked and exposed.

Until right now, I hadn't realized how draining being constantly alert and on guard could be, and now that I'm free of him, my body doesn't know how to cope without all of the adrenaline.

Drying myself with one of the huge pale-pink towels that are stacked on a floating shelf, I debate putting on my dirty bra. My breasts aren't big, I can go without a bra, but as I lift up the yoga pants, I find a soft cotton bralette and matching panties with the tags still attached beneath the hoodie Alice bought for me.

There are no prices on the tags, but I make a mental note to ask Alice how much they were so I can pay her back. Wearing fresh underwear makes me feel like a new person and it's so much better than putting on the bra I've been wearing for three days, or the panties that are still wet.

I dress in the yoga pants and hoodie before searching for a brush to untangle my long hair. I eventually find a comb in the medicine cabinet and start the task of getting all of the knots out. Pulling my hair over my shoulder, I twist it into a braid and fasten a band around the bottom.

My feet are bare, but I don't want to put back on dirty socks and the worn wooden floors are smooth and warm. Padding barefoot to the bedroom door, I pull in a slow, calming breath, and unlock it, twisting the handle and opening it. I take a step out of the room that I've started to consider a sanctuary and back into the open living space.

Before I fell asleep, only Bay, Alice, Bonnie and two more of the sisters whose names I've forgotten were in the house with all the children. Now it's like the cast of *Magic Mike* all decided to visit and the family room is packed with beautiful men, who all stop what they're doing and turn to face me the moment I take a step away from the door.

"Err, hi," I say shyly, feeling heat bloom in my cheeks.

"Hi Missy," Penn, the only familiar face among all the newcomers, calls.

"Hi Penn."

"Imp," Bay says, striding forward to me. "Let me

introduce you to the rest of my family." He takes my hand the way he's been doing since we met this morning and pulls me forward, and I let him, like it's the most normal thing in the world.

Five other men are all standing with Penn, and even if I didn't already know they were Bay's brothers, it would be obvious when they're all standing together like this. They're all tall, built, and too good-looking for there to be so many of them all together in one room.

"This is Beau, Granger, Huck, Cody, Teddy and this beauty is Juniper, Teddy's wife. You already met Penn."

"Hi," I say with a slightly intimidated smile. All of the guys are tall like Bay and they tower over me like the most attractive wall in the world.

"Everyone, this is Missy."

"Hi Missy," Beau, the first guy Bay introduced me to, says.

I smile, my cheeks burning with embarrassment. I don't seem to be able to speak. Bay on his own is gorgeous, but all the brothers together is almost too much.

"We're all excited to meet you."

My brows pull together in confusion, why would they be excited to meet me? Beau's gaze moves to the right and he frowns. I turn to Bay and find him mouthing silently at his brother, but when he realizes I'm looking he immediately stops and smiles instead.

"Are you hungry?" Bay asks, his grip on my hand not loosening even though there's no reason for him to be holding me.

"Err sure." I look between the brothers and notice them

all communicating silently. There's something else going on that I have no idea about and it's starting to make me wonder what the hell it is.

Bay leads me away from his brothers and toward the kitchen where there's a huge Crock-Pot full of gooey, cheesy macaroni and cheese. Scooping some onto a plate, Bay adds some salad to it and then carries it to the enormous dining table, pulling out a stool and placing the plate in front of me. "I'll be right back," he says, then heads off to a door on the far side of the room.

As I dig in, the newcomers all help themselves to the food, and suddenly the chairs around me scrape along the floor and I'm surrounded by Barnetts.

"How old are you, Missy?" one of the guys asks.

"Twenty," I say, smiling up at someone as they place an ice-cold bottle of water in front of me.

"Same as me," a beautiful woman says from across the table. "I'm Juni by the way, this one's wife," she says, pointing at the brother with the lightest hair color. "He's Teddy, but no one will be offended if you forget names, there are so many of them," she laughs.

"You're married at twenty?"

Juni rolls her eyes and giggles. "Once these cavemen have you in their sights, everything tends to happen at warp speed, but as you met Bay this morning and you're living here already, I guess you've figured that out."

"I'm not living here," I scoff lightly. "I just need to go and get my money from a friend and then I'm planning to move out of state."

Her brow furrows and her fork pauses halfway to her

mouth. "I don't understand. How are you and Bay going to be together if you're moving out of state?"

"What do you mean? Bay and I aren't together."

"But he told you about the whole legacy thing. I mean I thought it was bullshit too, but it's worked for five out of seven brothers, so as ridiculous as it sounds, I've been converted to believe it too," she giggles, as the men beside me become painfully quiet.

"Treasure," Teddy says.

"What?" Juni smiles. "None of us believed that you guys find your women through love at first sight until it happened to us. I'm sure Bonnie, Cora, Alice and Lulu have told her their stories, I might as well give her mine too. It's obvious Bay hasn't done a Huck and actually kidnapped her, else she'd be begging one of us to help her escape, so she's clearly taking it better than the rest of us did."

My fork falls from my fingers and hits the plate with a clatter. "What are you talking about?"

Beau exhales. "He hasn't told you, has he?"

"Told me what?" Suddenly all that safe calmness I was feeling evaporates and the familiar edge of panic replaces it.

"Imp."

Bay appears at my shoulder and I snap my head around to glare at him. "What the hell is going on?"

"Finish your lunch and then we can talk," he says, his tone resigned, his eyes... sad?

I'm not sure what he plans to tell me, but I have a horrible feeling it's going to ruin this slice of solace I'd found in the Barnetts' guest room. Pushing away from the table, I stand up.

"No, eat," Bay snarls, glaring at the rest of his family that are all still at the table and trying not to look at us or make it obvious that they can hear everything we're saying.

"I appreciate everything you've done for me so far, but honestly I think it might be best if you just take me back down to town."

"No," Bay snaps. "Just..." he pauses. "Let's go outside and I'll explain, it's not bad, I promise."

When he reaches for my hand, I pull it back and his lips fall into a frown that makes my heart thud painfully behind my ribs. It feels like I hurt him, but that makes no sense because we're strangers. He's just a nice guy and I'm just the girl whose life is falling apart.

He eyes my hand for a second longer, then sighs, turns and leads the way to a side door that opens onto a patio area with huge outdoor couches. There's a gas patio heater set to the side of the seating area and he lights it and turns back to me. The stone beneath my bare feet is freezing and when he notices I'm not wearing shoes or a coat, he scowls, then marches toward me. His hands wrap around my waist as he lifts me off the ground, spins and deposits me down onto the couch.

I've barely had time to open my mouth to protest when he disappears back into the house, returning with a huge jacket and a blanket.

"Put this on," he growls, manhandling me into the coat before he covers my legs with a blanket.

"Bay, it's not that cold out here."

Resting his hands on his hips, Bay exhales, tipping his head back and staring at the sky for a moment before sitting down on the other end of the couch, as far away from me as he can get without sitting on another seat.

"What's going on? Is this some kind of fucked-up cult or something? Because honestly, I have no interest in being saved by your messiah or whatever," I snark, trying to hide my unease with attitude.

"Don't curse, Imp, I don't like the way it sounds on your lips," Bay says.

"Bay."

"I know, I just don't know how to tell you any of this without sounding like I'm losing my mind."

"Maybe just spit it out," I suggest with a shrug, fidgeting as I wait for him to confess to whatever everyone else in the house already seems to know.

Pulling in a long, low inhale, he drops his chin and looks down at me. "My daddy used to tell us that he knew my mama was going to be his wife the moment he set eyes on her. He said that it was like being hit by a train and being struck by lightning all at once, and that once it happened, he knew there would never be anyone else but her for him for the rest of his life."

I nod slowly, like I understand what he's saying, but other than thinking it's a cute story, I'm not sure what he's hoping to explain by telling me.

"It took Beau a full year to realize that Bonnie was his. He said he felt this insane pull toward her from the moment he saw her at the coffee shop she worked in, and from that moment on he never looked twice at another woman because he knew Bonnie was his, that she was the only one for him. Huck saw Cora and he said it was just like how our daddy described it, that she was his and he'd do anything to keep her. Granger married Alice less than a week after he met her, because she was his and he didn't see the point in wasting time when fate had dropped the woman of his dreams into his lap. Penn almost got arrested the day he found Lulu because he stalked her to work and then followed her home. And well, Teddy, he made a few mistakes but he knew Juni was his one from the very first second. We call it our family legacy, but maybe saying it's a curse might be a better description. However you label it, it doesn't change things. Barnett men find their women and that's it. Instant love, lust and possession. We have no control over it, we can't help it and from what my brothers have told me, it's impossible to fight it."

"So are you telling me…" I pause, not sure if I'm actually getting the gist of what he's saying. "Are you doing a really bad job of telling me that you think I'm—"

"You're mine, Missy, and I'm so fucking sorry."

Chapter Seven

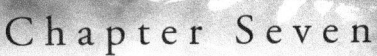
Bay

From the moment I laid her down on the bed and closed the door with me on the wrong side of it, I felt like there were ants crawling beneath my skin.

I hate it. I hate this pull to her that is already starting to make me feel like a madman, and I know is only going to get worse the longer I deny who she is to me. Alice took Missy some clean clothes to wear and ever since she came back, my sister has been staring at me with a mixture of pity and disgust—something else I hate.

I don't want or need anyone's pity. I'm not doing this to become a martyr, I'm just saving both me and her from a lifetime of crazy-possessive bars. She's too young to end up caged by me and I know that's what I'd end up doing. Hell, she's here, halfway up the mountain, stranded and unable to leave because I decided it was safer to bring her here than take her to the perfectly safe apartment over the garage.

In the first couple of hours, I've already taken over and made decisions for her. But that shit's not cool and I did it without even thinking about it. I just took charge and it felt natural and normal, and nothing at all like spending time with a woman like Rochelle. If I'd have brought her up here without her permission, she'd have had my balls squashed between her fingers and I'd have expected her to.

With Missy, I made a choice for her, because deep down inside, I know I'd need that. For the first time in my entire life, with her, I want a woman to be submissive and reliant. I'm a fucking monster.

The time between Bonnie calling Beau and my brothers all getting home en masse felt like an endless eternity. Knowing that my Imp was naked and wet in the room next door taunted me until my dick was so hard, I had to excuse myself to go and jerk off in my bathroom. I've never come so fast or so hard in my life.

By the time I got back out, Beau, Huck, Teddy and Juni were walking through the doors. I love my family, I really do, but I don't need to know what they think or feel about my decisions, because at the end of the day they're my decisions, not theirs. But one look at my big brother's face, and I knew I was getting his opinion whether I wanted it or not.

Before he had a chance to open his mouth and spout the 'she's destined to be yours' bullshit, Penn, Granger and Cody turned up and suddenly it was a party. When the bedroom door opened and Missy stepped out, I knew it was only a matter of time until someone told her the truth, but I never expected it to be Juni.

How I thought I could keep this from her when she was in my house, surrounded by people who all truly believe in the Barnett legacy, I don't know. Maybe subconsciously I wanted her to know.

Once she's covered in a blanket and wearing my jacket, I tell her the basics about the curse and how it's affected my brothers.

Her brow furrows and she looks up at me from beneath pale lashes. "So are you telling me…" She pauses, obviously confused. "Are you doing a really bad job of telling me that you think I'm—"

"You're mine, Missy, and I'm so fucking sorry," I confess, both hating and loving how right the words sound as I say them aloud.

Her pink rosebud lips part, and she makes an *O* shape that I have to fight really hard to not imagine sliding my dick inside. "You're sorry?" she asks slowly.

Nodding, I force my gaze to drop from hers, not wanting to look at her and see the horror and revulsion in her eyes.

"Why?"

"Why what?" I ask.

"Why are you sorry?"

"Because you shouldn't have to deal with my fucked-up family bullshit."

"Oh," she says quietly. "But this is how all your brothers met their wives?"

"All except Cody and well, me," I say with a nod.

"I'm confused," she says with a hint of huff to her tone.

Unable to resist, I lift my gaze and look at her. My heart skips, it fucking skips just from the way she looks, wearing my jacket, all bundled up and cared for, by me. A vision of taking care of her, of pulling her onto my lap as I feed her, of carrying her to bed, stripping her naked and spreading her legs until her wet cunt is revealed to me hits me like a sledgehammer. I've always preferred my women to be bare, but the idea of her having a neat line of red hair on her cunt drives me a little insane. I imagine holding her thighs wide and watching as my fat dick stretches her cunt until she squirming because even after fucking her every day, I'm still just slightly too big for her petite body to fully accept. My mind gives me an image of her clawing at my arms as I fuck her hard and deep, filling her with my cum and then holding her legs high to keep all of my seed inside her, willing a baby to take root in her womb.

"Fuck," I hiss to myself, blinking out of the vivid daydream, hoping that my hard dick isn't as obvious to her as it feels to me.

"That's not really an explanation," she says calmly.

"I shouldn't have brought you here."

Her brows lift and a pinch of hurt crosses her expression, although it evaporates almost immediately. "Why did you then?"

"Because this fucking curse turns us into asshole cavemen," I confess, wincing when I hear how bad that sounds.

"So, you don't want me to be here? Because I asked you to take me to the bus station and you said no," she tells me, sounding so fucking young and innocent.

"That's not... I didn't..." I stutter. I sound like a fucking teen trying to talk to his first crush and failing miserably. "I just want you to be safe, tomorrow we can figure out what your plan is."

"So, this family legacy?" she pauses, waiting for me to speak.

"Curse," I snap, "It's a fucking curse and it's not something you have to worry about, I won't let it affect your life. Now, you should go back inside and finish your lunch, it's too cold to sit out here today." Not waiting for her to respond, I stand up and turn off the patio heater that's keeping the air around us more than warm enough for us to be outside and comfortable. I don't want to keep talking about this with her. It's bad enough that I've had to confess who she is to me, there's no way I'll ever confess that I'm already starting to feel proprietary about her and like I have a right to be a part of any decision she makes.

Reluctantly, she moves the blanket off her lap and stands up, her dainty toes pale against the dark stone of the patio. Moving without thought, I scoop her off the floor, carry her into the house and place her back down on her seat at the table. None of my brothers say a thing about me carrying her around like she's a fucking princess, but then why would they? When I risk a glance at Missy, her brow is furrowed in confusion and... is that a hint of hurt in her expression?

She blinks, and whatever I thought I could see is gone, and all that's left is the same sad, lonely defiance she had when I first saw her this morning. My lips part and I start to tell her again why I won't be derailing her life, but Beau appears at my side, his hand landing on my shoulder.

"Missy, will you be okay here with the girls tonight? It's guys' night." Beau asks her, pinching my shoulder tightly when I move to speak.

"Oh," she blinks. "If one of you wouldn't mind running me back down into town, I was actually planning on visiting a friend and then playing bus roulette anyways. I don't want you to think you need to worry about me."

"Nonsense, we're happy to have you here for as long as you want to stay, consider the guest room yours. Plus, Bonnie has been craving some new company and the rest of us haven't had a chance to get to know you yet. Do you have Bay's number? If you have any issues, just text and we'll come right on home."

"Oh, no, I…" she stutters. "That's really not necessary."

"Actually, why don't you give me your cell and I'll program all of our numbers in, that way you've always got someone to call," Beau says, railroading Missy the way he does Bonnie when he's not getting his way. Of course, his firecracker of a wife always fights back tooth and nail, but my Imp is completely defenseless against him.

"Cell, honey," he says again.

"I don't have a cell."

Every muscle in my body tenses and an unexplainable rage starts to bubble from my toes, shooting upward in a wave so strong it threatens to explode out of me. "You don't have a cell?" I ask quietly.

"No," she shrugs.

"Why the fuck not?" I growl angrily. How is it possible in this day and age that she doesn't have a cell? Hal is nearly eighty and he has a fucking cell phone. Missy is twenty, she should be glued to social media or whatever the fuck normal twenty-year-old women do.

Her eyes narrow a little and her lips part and I know, I just know that I'm going to fucking hate whatever comes out of her mouth, but Beau speaks, silencing her. "Okay, well we can swing by the store and grab one for you, it's not safe not to have a cell, even if it's only for emergencies."

"Oh no, I don't need a cell and I don't have any—"

"You're taking the fucking cell," I snarl, interrupting her.

"Bay."

"You're taking the fucking cell. I'll add you to my plan."

"No," she gasps.

"Behave, Imp, see you later," I say, then walk away before she can argue and make me crazier than I already am.

Grabbing the keys to the big SUV we have, I stride out the door, clenching my neck muscles so stiffly I'm in pain, as I forbid myself from looking back at her. I knew fighting this would be hard, but with every new thing that comes out of her mouth, the harder it's getting.

The door opens and one by one my brothers emerge, striding over to me. I throw the keys to the SUV to Beau and he catches them in one hand and opens the driver's door. He slides behind the wheel as the rest of us fill the back seats, and Cody takes the passenger seat. No one speaks as the engine starts and we pull away from the house.

"So…" Huck starts.

"I don't want to talk about it until I've got a beer in my hand," I say.

Twenty minutes later, we push through the doors into Barney's bar and head over to the table we normally sit at when we come here to spy on the girls on their girls' nights out. It's not a secret, they know we do it, but they tolerate it, because they know how jealous and overprotective my brothers are. *"Missy would learn to tolerate it too,"* my inner voice whispers to me, but I punch it in the face until it shuts up.

"What can I get y'all?" an unfamiliar waitress asks as she sidles up to the table.

"Two pitchers of beer and wings and nachos for the table please," Teddy says, smiling at the girl, making her blush as she nods, then stumbles and backs away.

"Juni will kick your ass if she sees you flirting with another girl," Penn says.

"I wasn't flirting," Teddy growls, "I was being nice, I have no interest in anyone except my wife."

"Stop stirring shit," Beau says, slapping Penn around the back of the head. "We're here to find out what the fuck's going on with Bay."

Six sets of eyes all turn and look at me and I scowl, crossing my arms over my chest defensively. "There's nothing going on with me."

"Bullshit," Huck hisses. "You found your woman, yet you're here with us, instead of balls deep, working on making us another niece or nephew. Something must be going on."

"Look, just because she's mine, doesn't make her *mine*," I argue.

"That's the most stupid shit that ever came out of your

mouth. She's yours, so she's yours. She might not fall onto your dick, but that doesn't mean she belongs to you any less just because you have to work at it," Penn says.

"I don't plan to work at it. She's not mine in any of the ways that matter and I intend for things to stay that way." At my declaration, all of my brothers fall silent. The waitress appears at that moment with two large pitchers full of beer, seven glasses and the food we ordered. She doesn't mention the blatant tension that's bouncing between us, and no one says anything until she leaves.

"I don't understand," Granger says quietly. "Are you seeing someone? Does Missy have a husband or a serious boyfriend she's committed to?"

"You know I'm not seeing anyone, or at least not beyond sex and no, she's single as far as I'm aware, but to be honest I haven't asked."

"Then I don't understand what the issue is?" Teddy says.

"She's twenty," I tell them, like those two words should be all the explanation they need.

All of them stare at me like they're waiting for me to say more, but what else is there to say.

"Her age? That's the problem?" Granger asks slowly, like he's waiting for me to contradict him.

"She's twenty. She can't even come in here, she's not old enough to legally drink. She's barely out of fucking high school and I'm forty-two. I'm literally old enough to be her fucking father. It's wrong on so many fucking levels."

"That's it? You've got your panties in a bunch over a fucking age gap?" Huck laughs. "Jesus, bro, age is just a number."

"Bullshit. Age is just a number when it's five years, maybe even ten, but when it's over twenty years and the girl is practically a child it's basically a felony, it's fucking wrong."

"There's twenty-two years between me and Bonnie, I didn't see you telling me I was doing something wrong when I was dragging her into the house over my shoulder and fucking her six ways till Sunday? Were you thinking it then? Have you been sitting there calling me a sick motherfucker since I brought her home?" Beau asks, his voice dangerously low.

I love my big brother, I really do. When we lost our dad, he stepped up and became the surrogate parent to all of us, even me, when I was only a few years younger than he was. He's pissed at me right now, but he's hurt too, and it sickens me to think I've made him feel that way. Because I honestly never considered the age gap between him and Bonnie was an issue.

Sighing, I lift my head and look at my brother like a man. "I've never thought you and Bonnie were anything but perfect for each other, you know that."

"So what makes it okay for me, but not for you?" he demands.

"I don't know," I confess, "but I know I can't do this to her."

"Do what?" Penn asks. "Do you have some nonnegotiable shit you think is going to be an issue for her? You swing both ways? Like to be pegged? Or are you a sadist or something? Do you want to brand your name into her ass and collar her? Whatever the fuck your kink is, you should talk to her about it, you'd be surprised how fucking perfect she'll end up being for you. Fate has this shit down, I can almost guarantee she'll find whatever you think she'll run from hot as hell and in the end, she'll be your dream woman."

"No, I'm not into pegging!" I snark at my brother. "It's nothing like that. It's just she's young, she's still a kid and I'm a stuck-in-my-ways man in my forties. I have less than nothing in common with a girl who hasn't had a chance to live yet, and we all know that if I claim her, she never will."

"And that's what she wants?" Cody asks.

"All I know about her is that she's planning to get on a bus and move out of state. She doesn't know where, just not here," I tell them.

"Do you know why she wants to leave? She was sleeping rough yesterday; she's obviously got stuff going on in her life right now. Maybe she just needs you to give her a reason to want to stay," Penn offers.

"And what? Tell her she's mine, tell her that just being in the same house as her is driving me crazy, how I want to own her and fuck her and put my baby in her belly. How I want to tie her to me so tight she'll never get free and that if by some miracle she did, I'd hunt her down and drag her back kicking and screaming? Yeah, that's going to make her want to stay in a place she doesn't want to be with a stranger old enough to be her parent. No, I'm not going to ruin her life just because I'm an asshole."

My brothers are all looking at me with a mixture of concern and annoyance, except for Cody who just looks kind of horrified.

"So, you're what? Just going to put her on a bus and never see her again? You think you're going to be okay with that?" Teddy asks incredulously. "Because there's no way I could let Juniper go, even if I knew it was the best thing for her. Maybe that makes me a selfish bastard, but I know ultimately, I can make her happier stuck here with me than she could make herself alone somewhere else."

"She's too young. This fucking curse messed up, I didn't want a woman and if I ended up with one, I wanted her to be mature and settled and independent. Not a girl half my age who doesn't have a job, hasn't experienced life, fuck, she might even be a fucking virgin. She's got some shit going on with an uncle who isn't an uncle and, fuck. No, just no, I can't do it, I won't do it. Not to me and not to her either."

"All those things you just gave as reasons not to claim her, are the reasons she needs you to. She was sleeping in Alice's old RV, running from some kind of family situation, she's young, obviously fairly innocent and from how it appears, in desperate need of love, family and support. You can give her all those things, so why wouldn't you?" Cody asks passionately.

"She's not what I want," I tell them, hearing how wrong the words sound as they pass through my lips.

"I think that's bullshit. But if that's honestly the way you feel, if you're one-hundred-percent confident that you'll be ruining her life by claiming her, then I'll claim her. She's beautiful, closer in age to me and although I know she's not mine, I'm drawn to her," Cody says straight-facedly.

Rolling my eyes, I shake my head. "That mindfuckery

might have worked on Teddy, but it won't on me. I'm not going to hulk out, because I know you're just trying to provoke a reaction from me."

As I wait for him to smile, to tell me he's just messing with me, my heart starts to beat a little quicker, heat rising through me in a tide that makes each of my muscles clench and tighten as it works its way through my body.

"I'm not trying to force a reaction; I'm being completely serious. The moment I turned and saw her earlier, something about her called to me. I thought it was just me recognizing my new sister, but given time and a chance, I'm sure it could turn into something more. If it'd happened in a bar before all this family legacy stuff, I'd have taken it as a sign of interest and gone to buy her a drink. I won't be an asshole about it, but she obviously needs help and I'm happy to be the person to do that for her."

Beau, Granger, Huck, Penn and Teddy are all staring at Cody like they have no idea what the fuck is happening, and at me like they're waiting for me to lose my fucking shit. Is my brother seriously sitting here and telling me he feels a pull to *my* woman? I might not be planning to claim her, but that doesn't mean she's any less mine, and there's no way I'll ever let him have her.

"No," I growl, the sound more animalistic than human.

"I'm not asking permission," Cody tells me boldly. "If you're planning to let her walk away, what does it matter if I go with her? You might be okay with putting her on a bus, but I'm not. I can run my business from anywhere, my foremen can handle the jobs in Montana and I'll start a new crew of guys in whatever state we end up in. I've got plenty of money, I can take care of her and I already planned to expand Barnett Construction out of state anyway."

"You'd leave?" Granger asks, shocked.

Cody nods. "Not forever, but for a few years, sure."

"You are not having my woman," I shout.

"She's not a toy you can write your name on, then throw to the bottom of the toy box. She's a human, a person. If you're prepared to let her walk away then it shouldn't matter to you if I follow. We might be good friends, or we might end up as more, I have no idea, but I know I can't just let her leave and never see her again," Cody tells me, his eyes alight and filled with righteous indignation.

"She's mine," I growl, sounding just like the caveman I promised myself I'd never allow this curse to make me.

"Not if you don't claim her, she isn't," he says defiantly.

"I can't." My voice sounds ragged and defeated, despite the anger still pumping in my veins.

"Bullshit," Cody says, slamming his fist down onto the table and shocking the shit out of me. Cody is the calm brother, the quiet, reasonable, normal one of us, but right now he's angrier than I've ever seen him and it's because of Missy. My Missy.

"Maybe we should all just calm down," Beau says. "Bay, is the age gap really that much of an issue?"

"Are you telling me you've never sat back and thought fuck, my wife is twenty-two years younger than me?" I snap.

"Of course I fucking have," he says back.

"And?" I prompt.

"And every time I think it, I remind myself that I'm the

luckiest motherfucker in the world. My wife is hot as fuck and twenty-two years younger than me. She's beautiful, feisty, loyal, and she drives me to distraction in a way a woman in her forties probably wouldn't. But she's *my* woman. I own her body, heart and soul and she owns me in all the same ways. When you have what we have, our ages seem irrelevant, because they are. Bonnie is perfect for me, because she was always meant to be mine and I was always meant to be hers. Fate made me wait until she was old enough to show me who she was to me. From the moment that I saw her and knew I couldn't live without her, there was no way I was going to make something as unimportant as age stop me from claiming the missing piece of my soul," Beau says, leaning forward in his seat, his eyes imploring me to actually hear what he's saying.

"But—" I start to argue.

"If you ask me if Bonnie is what I envisaged the woman I'd marry to be like, you know I'm going to say no. But the truth is, my baby girl is so much more. She lets herself need me even though she's more than capable of looking after her own life. She gives me her trust, her body, her love and lets me be exactly what we both need. I could have found a woman, hell, none of us have ever struggled to find willing pussy, but there's no one else on the planet who could give me everything I need and all the things I had no idea I even wanted, other than her."

Chapter Eight

Missy

Once all the men leave, I'm left with the wives and kids. It feels kind of archaic and a little sexist, until Lulu pulls out a blender and starts whipping up a batch of margaritas, then suddenly instead of being left behind while the menfolk go out to the bar, I'm in the middle of the Barnett women's impromptu girls' night in.

I'm not much of a drinker, but when Lulu hands me a salt-rimmed glass, I take it and try not to feel too awkward in a roomful of virtual strangers.

"I'm so sorry about earlier, I had no idea Bay hadn't explained the whole 'mine' stuff. I would never have just blurted it out like that if I'd known," Juni tells me guiltily.

I smile, grateful that I seem to have the names of this huge family almost memorized now. "It's not your fault,

Bay should never have brought me here."

"Nonsense, this is exactly where you should be, as soon as he pulls his head out of his ass, he'll be claiming you and putting a ring on your finger," Cora giggles. She's the only one without a cocktail.

"Don't you like margaritas?" I ask.

"Oh, I love them, but Huck the asshole knocked me up again."

"You're not happy about it?" I cautiously ask.

Sighing, she rolls her eyes, then places her hand over her flat stomach. "No, I'm happy about it, I'm just convinced that he had something to do with me being pregnant, even though we agreed we were going to wait another couple of years before we had another one."

"I don't understand, did he forget to use a condom or something?" I ask, cringing a little about talking about birth control methods with someone I only met today.

"Fuck it, you're going to hear the story anyway," Cora laughs. "The Barnett family legacy, this thing they're convinced makes them know a woman is theirs, well it also makes them go batshit crazy. When Huck first started chasing after me, I was more than happy to fall onto his dick. You've seen him, he's a seriously hot man. But I would have been happy with some low-key easy sex and he was not okay with that. He was all in from the get-go and when I wouldn't fall in line with his insta-marriage full-blown relationship, he messed with my birth control pills, then spent weeks fucking me until he planted a lifelong commitment in my womb."

I know my eyes are wide with shock, but instead of

being angry, Cora is smiling and giggling. "When I found out what he'd been doing I left him and well, lots of stuff happened, he kidnapped me and kind of held me hostage for a little while, but it all worked out obviously. I forgave him, on the understanding that he wasn't allowed anywhere near my birth control ever again. I even started getting the jab instead of the pill after Mav was born, just in case he got any ideas. He loves getting me pregnant and ever since I gave birth, he's been trying to get me to say yes to having another baby. I said I wanted to wait and then conveniently, bam, baby in my belly." She points at her stomach.

"So did he do something?"

"Not according to my doctor, she gave me the usual bullshit, that the shot isn't one-hundred-percent effective and blah, blah, blah."

"Is that how the rest of you got pregnant too? Did they all mess with your birth control?" I ask a little shakily.

"No," Lulu says, placing her hand on my arm and squeezing lightly. "Huck is the only one who has a death wish. Although Penn wants us to get pregnant again already and the twins are still tiny. But Cora wasn't lying when she said they go a little crazy when they find their person. Penn lost his mind, the day we met he sat in the reception at the law office I work at all day, then followed me home. He refused to leave me alone for even a second."

"Granger brought me here the day we met and convinced me to marry him five days later," Alice tells me shyly.

"Beau followed me around for a year before he realized I was his, then he literally threw me over his shoulder and carried me into his bedroom." Bonnie laughs.

"Teddy propositioned me first, but once he realized I was his fated one, he stalked me relentlessly," Juni adds.

"Bay apologized," I tell them, a little dismayed to admit it after hearing how they'd been pursued. "He said it was a curse and that he was sorry, but he'd make sure not to let it affect me or my life," I tell them, watching as their faces all morph into almost identical pity-filled gazes. "He told you already," I surmise.

"He thinks he's too old for you," Alice confesses.

"But if he was feeling what the others all felt, if he really thought I was his, he wouldn't be able to resist, right?"

No one speaks and I smile sadly. "It's okay. Maybe he's wrong, maybe he's just feeling mixed up and I'm not his one, or whatever. That would make more sense, I mean he's him and I'm me."

"What do you mean?" Juni asks.

"Just that he's gorgeous and so self-assured and big and manly, and I'm a mess. We're so different, I could understand him not wanting to hitch himself to my wagon, my life is a disaster."

"He'll see sense," Lulu assures me.

"I don't think so, but I appreciate you all being nice to me. I mean it's a nice idea, right? That your perfect man falls instantly in love with you. But that kind of fairy-tale stuff doesn't happen to me. Tomorrow I'll go and collect my money, pick a bus, and I can get on with starting the rest of my life. Bay will just become a distant memory."

"Missy…" Alice starts.

"I'm not just going to sit around and wait for him to decide he wants me, especially when I don't even know if

I want him."

"Are you attracted to him?" Cora asks, a mischievous gleam in her eyes.

"He's very good-looking."

"There are lots of attractive men out there, you didn't really answer the question," she says, arching her brow.

"Yes, I'm attracted to him. I mean, obviously he's a lot older than me, but he's fit and he's definitely not rocking a dad bod. But I'm not into men that aren't into me and if he's fighting fate herself not to be with me, he obviously feels pretty strongly about this."

"You could test his resolve," Cora suggests.

"Cora," Alice says in a chiding tone.

"What?" Cora asks with fake innocence. "He hasn't said he doesn't want Missy, just that he won't allow the Barnett legacy to affect her life. I say we test his mettle. If he really is determined to let her walk away, then so be it, she can pick her bus and get out of town. If he's talking out of his butt and really he's as obsessed with her as the others are with us, then he'll haul her ass back here and into his bed faster than you can say 'I'm a fucking idiot.' It's a win-win."

A giggle slips from my lips. "You're a little bit evil, aren't you?" I ask Cora.

"I just enjoy provoking Barnett men, especially when they're being idiots. Bay knows he wants you; he knows you're his, but he's being stubborn for no reason and that makes him a moron. And I have zero tolerance for stupid people. If he was actually planning on letting you go, he wouldn't ever have brought you here."

"What do you mean?"

"The guys all agreed long before any of us came into the picture that this house was their home and not their hookup pad. They decided that the only time they'd bring a woman here is if she was their woman—the one they want endgame with. I was the first woman to ever stay the night here," Bonnie says.

"But surely…" I trail off.

"Bay has an apartment over the garage he could have taken you to. You'd have been safe there; you could have stayed there until you were ready to leave town and that would have been it. But he didn't take you there, he brought you here, halfway up the mountain with no way for you to leave unless one of us takes you. He might think he isn't going to claim you, but he's halfway there already and as soon as he gets over himself, he'll be on you like white on rice," Cora chuckles.

"And that's it then? If he decides I'm his, I have no other choice in the matter?" I ask, not liking the sound of that. I've had all my choices taken away for a really long time, I don't want to have to give them up again now for a man I barely know.

"Of course you have a choice," Alice says in her quiet, reserved tone.

"Bay's been kind to me, but I only reclaimed my life today. I don't want to give it back up again tomorrow."

Suddenly instead of the anticipatory, excited matching gleams in the women's eyes, they all soften and look at me with concern and worry.

"It'll be okay, Bay isn't like that," Juni tries to assure

me.

"But you've all just told me that's exactly what he'll be like. Between these brothers, they've stalked, kidnapped, forced you into pregnancies… If he suddenly gets it into his head that I'm his, he'll take away my choices without thinking twice about it. Maybe if I loved him, eventually I'd be okay with him doing that, because my choice would be him. But not now, not when the only things I know about him are that he owns a garage and apparently comes from a long line of crazy."

"Missy, it's—" Bonnie starts, but I interrupt her.

"It's not like that? You five just spelled it out for me and it's just like that. If *he* decides I'm his, I have no say in it. And if I argue, he'll do whatever it takes to win. Jesus, I've jumped out of the frying pan with my psycho not-uncle and into the fire with a man who may or may not force me to marry him. God, my life would be so much simpler if I was a lesbian."

There are sounds of agreement before the ladies all look between themselves like they're silently trying to formulate an argument to counteract all the stuff they've just told me. But it's out there now and nothing they say to backtrack will make a difference. "I think I should leave, nothing good will come of me being here. Either he'll decide I'm his or he won't, but I refuse to be an obligation or to allow him to become another noose around my neck."

"Or you could flip things around and force him to play on your terms," Cora suggests, a hint of a smile tipping up the corners of her lips.

"Oh, I like that," Bonnie laughs.

"I'm not so sure—" I start.

"Why not? You've already said you're attracted to him. If you pursue *him,* you can see fast if this is something you might want and then if it isn't, one of us will drive you to the bus station and it'll be his own fault for not treating you like the gift you are. He's being an idiot and if it takes losing you for him to recognize it, then so be it," Lulu says passionately.

"I've never pursued a guy, especially not a guy like Bay. I haven't really even had a proper boyfriend. My not-uncle told me I wasn't allowed to date while I was in high school and then well, after…" I trail off, not really wanting to admit how much of a fool I was. "Anyway, I've never even been on a date, I'm a virgin for goodness' sake, how on earth would I even start trying to seduce a man like Bay?"

"I was a virgin when I met Beau," Bonnie confesses, "He loved the idea that he'd be the only man I'd ever been with. Knowing Bay, he'd probably lose his mind and have a ring on your finger ten seconds later if you told him, so it might be best to keep that to yourself for a while."

Groaning, I let my head fall back onto the couch cushion behind me. "I can't do this. I'm not sure I even want to."

"Don't you think you'll always wonder if Bay was the guy you were meant to be with if you don't even give it a chance? Now you know what's happening, just flirt a little, talk to him and see what he has to say. Before I met Granger, I assumed I was meant to be alone forever, if he hadn't forced the issue, I'd have gotten in my RV and left, never knowing that my other half was here just waiting to find me," Alice says in her quiet impactful way.

After dropping so much information in my lap I need a year to sort through it, the girls tend to the kids, chatting amiably about this and that, always making sure I'm a part of the conversation even though I have no idea who most of the people they're discussing are.

Juni tells me it's her turn to cook and I offer to help, needing something to do to keep my mind off the mess my life is. Between us, we make meatloaf, mashed potatoes, corn and buttery rolls, and my mouth waters even as I'm reminding myself not to get too comfortable here. Tomorrow I fully intend on taking myself and my meager belongings back down to the bus station.

For a minute, when I'd heard all their tales about being claimed and belonging, I'd felt a surge of hope. It's been so long since I've belonged to anyone that being Bay's and a part of this strange but close-knit family felt like a bigger dream than I could ever hope for.

Now. Well, now I'm not sure if belonging to Bay Barnett would be a dream come true or a nightmare brought to life. Either way, it won't be happening. I saw his face when he told me his feelings for me are a curse, he meant it and I won't be the obligation he stupidly brought home and couldn't get rid of.

The guys turn up just as Juni and I are dishing up the thirteen plates of delicious-smelling food. Poppy and Maverick ate earlier and the babies are all either in bed or in the mobile bassinets that have been placed beside the table.

I manage to avoid looking at Bay, although I became instantly aware of him the moment he stepped into the house. Being away from him for a few hours seems to have helped firm my resolve and by the time the food is gone and the guys have cleaned up, I'm ready to escape into my bedroom for the night and hide until I can escape in the morning.

Like they're drawn to each other, the men gravitate to their women. Beau lifts Bonnie onto his lap, Huck cradles Cora's stomach, whispering in her ear as she alternates between scowling at him to smiling. Granger takes Alice's hand and she seems to sag into him like he's instantly relaxed her, just from being near, and Teddy steals a giggling Juni away the moment he can, disappearing behind a door that I'm assuming leads to their rooms.

Even though I know I should leave; I pause, watching them interact with each other.

"It's beautiful, isn't it?" a voice asks from behind me.

Startled that I've been caught, I jolt and turn, expecting to find Bay, or Penn, but instead it's Cody, the only other single Barnett left. "What?"

"How much they love each other," he says, glancing over to where Penn, Lulu, Poppy and the twins are sitting together chatting, as Poppy carefully helps her mama feed one of her sisters.

Sighing, I smile wistfully. "Yes, it is."

"I'm sorry my brother is being an ass."

"You don't need to apologize, and he isn't being an ass, he's being honest. I don't know if this legacy or curse or whatever is really real, but either way, he doesn't want it and I can respect that."

"He'll change his mind, I know he will, but if he doesn't; I want to help you, you're family now. Will you sit with me a minute, tell me a little about yourself? Bay is so caught up in himself he hasn't bothered to ask I'm guessing."

"I was actually just going to..." I point in the direction of the guest room.

"I'll make you a cup of coffee, it's early and I'm guessing you just want to hide from him and this whole mess."

"Okay," I agree, nodding.

"Perfect," Cody smiles, and I'm shocked by how beautiful he is. To be honest, of all the brothers, he's probably the least instantly impressive. That's not to say he's not attractive, he is, but it's more understated than the rest of his family. He's tall, still towering over me, but his build is broader, more thick than defined muscle, although I'd guess that if I were to wrap my hand around his bicep, he'd be firm and strong. His hair's thick and a rich-chocolate color and his skin is tan, like he works out in the sun. He has tiny lines at the sides of his eyes when he smiles and for some reason that I simply can't explain, I want to throw my arms around his neck and ask him to hug me.

He leads me over to the kitchen and holds out one of the stools at the breakfast bar for me. Quickly making me a mug of coffee, he adds milk and sugar how I like, before taking the stool beside me and turning to face me.

Resting his elbow on the counter, he holds his own coffee with the other hand and focuses all his attention on me. It's disconcerting to be looked at like I'm the most interesting thing in the world, but instead of wilting beneath his gaze, I relax, biting my tongue to stop myself from spilling every secret I have.

"So, tell me something about you. How old are you?"

I giggle. "I'm twenty."

"Bay already mentioned that you've been living in Wilderwood, but is that where you were born?"

"No, I was born in New Mexico, I lived there until I was sixteen, then I moved to Montana and I've been here ever since."

"And you've been living with…" he trails off, waiting for me to fill in the gaps.

"My second cousin."

"What about the rest of your family? Are you close with them?"

"I don't have any other family," I tell him simply. I don't miss the flash of sympathy in his eyes, but I don't need him to feel sorry for me, you can't miss what you've never had.

"Your parents?" he asks cautiously.

"They died when I was a week old. They'd taken me to visit with my nana and my dad forgot formula, they went to the store to buy some more and were both killed in a car accident."

His gasp reminds me how shocking it must be to hear my tale of woe, but to me it's just something that happened. I don't remember my parents; I don't even have any photos of them. Nana wasn't someone who hoarded memories so there just aren't any, or at least none I've ever seen. I know I look a lot like my dad, that he had red hair like I do, or at least that's what Ernie told me when we first moved in with him. At the time, I assumed the comparison brought him comfort. Now, I'm sure he probably meant it as an insult.

"I'm sorry."

"That's okay, I never knew them so I've never missed

them, at least not in a visceral sense," I shrug.

"Are you close to your nana?"

"I was, she died six months after we moved to Montana. She raised me, because there was no one else to and she wasn't prepared to let me fall into the system. She used to tell me she'd done her child-rearing years with my mom, but she tried her best."

"What about your dad's family?" Cody asks, pain and sadness flashing across his expression.

"Until Ernie turned up, I didn't know I had any," I confess, swallowing down the pang of longing that always hits me when I think about my dad's family. I never knew them and as far as I'm aware, they never made any effort to see me, or get in touch after my dad died. But they must have known about me to leave me money. I'm angry that they never wanted to know me, but there's a part of me that still wishes I'd at least gotten the chance to meet them before they died.

"This place must seem like a madhouse to you," he laughs lightly.

"It's definitely different," I say diplomatically.

"We've all moved out at one point or another, but we always end up right back here eventually. I'm the only one who didn't come straight back to Rockhead Point after school."

"Oh, where did you go?"

"I own a construction company, so I spent a few years once I'd graduated learning my trade, cutting my teeth and working every aspect from a basic laborer to more skilled jobs, right up to project management and liaison. I wanted to make sure that when I started my own thing, I could do everyone's job and know if things were being done well. It also gave me a chance to travel a little and build up a reputation for being good at what I do. By the time I came back to town, I had a small team of great guys and my work's only grown from there," he says, pride spilling from every word.

"That's great. Do you still enjoy it?"

"I love it. I have a home base here, but I have jobsites all over the state and I'm looking at pursuing some contracts out of Montana too. Some days, I pitch in and build houses or factories or offices, others, I'm in a suit meeting with property developers or senators or mayors. There're never two days the same."

I smile, because his joy is so contagious.

"Do you work? Or are you in school?" he asks.

"Until today I worked at Mountain View Pines."

"The old folks' home?"

I giggle. "Yes. I've been working there pretty much since I graduated from high school."

"Did you like it?"

"I liked the residents, but the manager, she wasn't the nicest boss. When she wasn't around it was good."

"What the fuck, Cody?" Bay snarls, storming across the room and looming beside us.

"What?" Cody asks calmly.

"You're serious?" Bay demands, glaring at me then back to his brother.

"I don't see what the problem is, I'm drinking coffee and getting to know Missy a little better. What's the issue?"

Cody asks, but there's something in his tone that tells me there's more going on here that I don't know about. Either way, this isn't my home, my family or my argument, so I slide down from the stool I'm sitting on. "I might go and get some sleep. Thank you again for letting me use the guest room. Night, Cody." Without waiting for either of them to speak, I dart across the living room and into the bedroom, closing and locking the door behind me.

Chapter Nine

Bay

"Fuck," I mutter to myself as I watch Missy practically sprint across the room and into the guest room.

"What the hell is your problem?" Cody demands, anger lacing his familiar features.

"My problem is you trying to move in on *my* woman."

"I'm not moving in on *your* woman. I was having a pleasant conversation with the girl you plan to drive to the bus station tomorrow. Do you know she doesn't have anyone? No one. Not a single other living relative other than some second cousin that she doesn't seem particularly close to."

"I met the cousin, or uncle or whoever he is, he's an asshole. What happened to her parents?" I ask before I can stop myself, she mentioned they were dead this morning, but she didn't tell me anything else, and I didn't try to find out because I don't want to know more about her. The only way I'm stopping myself from laying claim to her is by keeping my distance, reminding myself over and over that she's not what I want and that I'm not going to ruin her life by tying her to me.

"Both her mom and dad died in a car accident when she was a week old. She lived with her grandmother until she died when Missy was sixteen. She's alone, Bay, completely alone and she's sweet. What the fuck is wrong with you? I only just met her a couple of hours ago and I want to wrap her in a blanket and tell her everything is going to be okay. She needs to be taken care of, to be loved and cared for. Why are you fighting this so hard?" Cody growls angrily.

"Because I don't want to care for someone. I want a woman who doesn't need me, who can look after herself and just wants to exist by my side."

"Bullshit. You don't want that, you're not hardwired that way, none of us are," Cody scoffs, jumping down from the stool and pushing past me. "Beau, what was your gut reaction when you first saw Missy?"

"That she needs a hug, a good meal and a real man to take care of her," Beau answers immediately.

"Huck?" Cody calls.

"That someone needs to feed her and make sure she's looking after herself," Huck answers.

"Penn?"

"I was pissed when I saw someone curled up asleep under one of those shiny emergency blankets they give to victims at the side of the road, but then when I saw it was her, with all that red hair and sad eyes, I just wanted to make sure she was alright," Penn admits.

"Do you need me to go ask Granger or Teddy too?" Cody snarks. "Missy is perfect for you and your inherent need to care for someone. You'd hate being with someone who was independent and didn't need you, that's not who you are. I know it's what you've become used to with your fuck buddies, but you're attracted to those women because you know it'll never be anything serious. Missy is endgame, she's sweet and kind and a little bit broken and she needs you. I don't understand why you don't see that."

"She's too young."

"Yep, she's too young, too innocent, too vulnerable, too nice, too inexperienced. Anything else you want to use as an excuse to let your perfect woman walk away?" Cody snarls angrily. "I'm serious, big brother, if you let her go, I'll follow. I won't let her end up alone and forgotten just because you're an asshole who can't see the best thing that will ever happen to him is right here in front of him."

"You'll stay the fuck away from her," I hiss, standing straighter as I take a menacing step toward my brother.

"No. You've got until tomorrow morning to stop being a martyr and man the fuck up, else I'm stepping in," Cody warns, glaring at me as he spins on his heel and stomps over to his door, stepping through and slamming it behind him.

"I can't be what she wants," I tell the rest of the room, but I'm speaking more to myself than any of the rest of them.

"You don't know what she wants," Alice says pointedly.

I don't really understand why it is that my quietest

brother- and sister-in-law are advocating so hard for Missy. Do they know something I don't? Perhaps Alice sees another lost soul in Missy? The circumstances behind Alice being alone might be different than why Missy is, but the end result is still the same. She admitted earlier that she feels like Granger essentially saved her, and I can see why she'd want that for Missy, if she does in fact need saving. But I can't be that for her, and I only made things harder for myself and her by bringing her here.

Regret makes my stomach ache and my chest bang painfully. My heart physically hurts at the realization that I'm going to let her go. Since I saw her this morning, I've known it had to happen but until now, right this second, I wasn't sure I could do it. That I could allow her to walk out of my life and move on without me.

Tomorrow morning I'll drive her to get her money, then I'll buy her a bus ticket to wherever she wants to go. She told me she doesn't have a bank account, but I have a few thousand cash in my apartment that I have put aside for emergencies. It'll be enough for her to use as a deposit on an apartment and to get her through until she can find a job.

This is the best thing for her, for both of us. She's not what I want and I'm not what she needs.

Ignoring the concerned eyes of my family, I turn my back on them and make my way into my apartment, forcing myself not to look at the door to the bedroom she's sleeping in. I've done little more than torture myself by bringing her here, giving myself a permanent reminder of her in my space, my home.

Closing the door behind me, I cover my face with my

hands and breathe in and out slowly. I can do this. I can let her go, even though it feels wrong on every single level. She might be mine, but this way, she has the chance to do bigger and better things. She can be whoever she wants, wherever she wants. The only future she has here with me is with a ring on her finger and as many babies as I can put in her belly.

Resigned, I head for my bedroom, strip down to my boxers and flop back onto the comforter. My mind swirls with every reason why I should march my ass over to the guest suite, throw her over my shoulder and carry her back in here with me. I can imagine the way she'll smell, the way she'll taste, the sounds she'll make that will drive me insane until I can barely survive without being inside of her. A part of me wonders if I should just do it, if I should claim her, just once, just so I know what it's like. I'm pretty sure she's not a virgin, but she's definitely inexperienced and I won't do that to her, I won't use her like that just to slake my own lust.

Instead, I close my eyes, slide my hand down to my dick and imagine all the way's I'd touch her, all the things I'd do and say to her if she were here. It's a pale comparison, but it's enough for my dick to harden and my balls to pull up as I groan her name and spill my seed onto my stomach.

With my rapidly softening dick still gripped in my hand, I open my eyes and stare up at my bland ceiling. All of the lust my fantasy had evoked is gone and what's left behind feels hollow and dirty. Grabbing the shirt I just took off, I clean up as best I can and crawl into bed. There's no way I'll sleep, but just for tonight I'll enjoy knowing she's here, she's safe and for this moment in time, she's still mine, even if when the sun rises… she won't be any longer.

***

At some point I must fall asleep, because the next time I open my eyes, pale early morning light is bleeding through the sides of my blinds, sending streaks of light across the dark sheets on my bed.

Nausea and dread accompany wakefulness and thoughts of Missy fill my mind. I don't have any idea how I'm going to broach the subject of taking her to the bus station without feeling like the world's biggest asshole or convincing myself that it'll all be okay if she stays.

Yesterday I suggested she could work at the garage and stay until she has enough money to leave, but after a day of being in close proximity to her, I know that's not an option. It took all of my self-control and a healthy dose of self-loathing to keep my hands to myself, another day with her and I'll have my dick inside of her, coating her slick core with my cum before dinner.

As soon as she's eaten breakfast, I'll drive her down to the old folks' home to get whatever cash she said she stored in her friend's room, and then put her on a bus. It's the only thing that makes sense.

Dragging my ass out of bed, I turn my shower to cold and punish myself with a freezing blast of water that makes me suck in sharp hisses of breath. By the time I'm clean, my teeth are chattering, but my resolve is firm and I dress and slip out into the main house where Beau is preparing breakfast for everyone.

"Morning," he says quietly.

"Hey."

"You're up early."

"Got plenty to do, might as well get an early start."

"Oh yeah?" Beau questions gently.

"Missy needs to go collect some cash she has stored in a friend's room at the old folks' home, and then I'm going to drop her at the bus station."

The spatula Beau's holding falls from his hand and lands on the counter with a thud. "Are you fucking serious?"

"This is the best thing for everyone. I'm going to give her some cash to help her get settled and then leave her alone to live her life."

"You're a fucking idiot," Beau scoffs, turning his back on me and dismissing me in a way my brother has never done before.

Pouring myself a cup of coffee, I sit on the couch and watch the door to the guest suite. When it hasn't opened an hour later, I stand up and walk over to it, lifting my hand and knocking gently.

It feels like forever before I hear the door lock disengage and the door opens. Then she's there right in front of me, and my heart is banging against my ribs like it's trying to get free of my chest.

"Hi," I force out past arid lips.

"Hey."

"There's breakfast out here."

She nods, then glances behind her back into the room. "I should really get going, I need to go and get my money from Mr. Prentiss. I'm not sure where I'm going to end up, but I'd like to get there in the light rather than at night if I can."

"You're not going anywhere," my voice screams inside my head, but I don't say it aloud, instead I nod. "Come and eat, then I'll drive you back down to Mountain View Pines."

"I can call a cab—"

"They won't come this far up the mountain," I interrupt.

"Oh. Well, if you're sure, I don't want to be any trouble."

She's so fucking young and sweet and for the first time, I truly realize that it's going to kill me to let her leave. I step to the side to let her pass me and manage to keep my hands to myself as she walks over to where everyone is quietly sitting. Even the kids seem to feel the somberness filling the air and they stay quiet, the little ones remaining asleep and the older ones eating without making a fuss.

I fill a plate with pancakes and pass it to Missy, not bothering to take any food for myself. My stomach's tied up in so many knots, there's no way I could eat now if I wanted to. Trying not to stare at her, I drink my coffee and discreetly take in every detail of her face. Her skin is pale and so smooth, it looks like she could be made of porcelain. Freckles are sprinkled across her nose and cheeks down to her rosebud pink lips that are plump and perfect for feasting on. Now that I'm taking the time to memorize her, I can see her eyes are a deep-green color that shines and they seem to change color when she moves. Her hair is red and alive with curls that make her look like the princess on a film Poppy made me watch with her.

She's perfect and mine and I don't want to give her up. With every second that passes, it's one less I'll get to spend with her, and I have no idea if I'm being selfless or just incredibly stupid, but either way I'm going to do it, I'm going to drive her away. What's that cliché saying? If you love it, let it go. Well, I don't love her, but I could, I could let myself fall in love with her so easily.

Breakfast seems to be over in the blink of an eye and as the plates are cleared away, my entire family all seems to be watching me, waiting for me to do something, anything.

"I'll just grab my stuff. Bonnie, thank you for loaning me the clothes, I'd have washed them, but I have no idea where your machine is," Missy says, her cheeks going pink.

"Oh, there's no need to worry about that," Bonnie says with a wry smile.

"I just want to thank you all for your hospitality, I'm a stranger and you welcomed me into your home, I'm really grateful."

"Where will you go?" Cody asks, glaring at me even as he speaks to Missy.

She laughs nervously. "I don't really know. The world's my oyster, right? I figured I'd get to the bus station and see where the next bus is heading, then I'd go there."

"We never got a chance to get you a cell phone yesterday, but you should take all of our numbers, that way if you need anything you can call one of us," Beau tells my girl, his brow furrowed in concern.

"Oh, you don't need to worry about me, I'll be just fine." Missy smiles, then walks away from the table, me, and my family before disappearing into the guest suite. No one says a word, but I can feel all of their eyes are on me. I wish I could make them understand, but right now I don't think it matters what I say. All they can see is me letting my woman leave, something none of them would ever do.

Granger goes to speak, but before he has a chance, Missy is back, her small used-looking purse hung over her shoulder. One by one, my family all hug her and say goodbye. The girls do their best to convince her to stay. Bonnie suggests she could move in with her dad, Lulu suggests she could stay with Chloe, Penn offers her his apartment over the garage and Juni tells her there's a spare house on Smokejumper Alley, but Missy waves them all off.

"Thank you all, I appreciate the offers, I really do, but…" She turns and glances at me for a second before looking away. "But I think it's time for a fresh start." She looks at me again. "Are you ready? I don't want to take up too much of your day."

I nod, swallowing past what feels like razor blades in my throat. Missy smiles, gives my family another wave, then calmly heads toward the front door. Following on autopilot, I move to lift her into my truck like I did yesterday, but she scrambles in, closing the door before I get close.

It shouldn't be a shock that she doesn't want me to touch her, I all but told her yesterday that she's destined to be mine, but I'm not interested. Honestly, I'm amazed she hasn't punched me in the face—or the balls. Sighing, I climb into the driver's seat and start the engine. It doesn't take as long as I wish it would to get down into town and to Mountain View Pines Retirement facility.

Pulling into the parking lot, I kill the engine and move to climb out when she stops me. "I'll only be a minute; you don't need to get out. If you'd prefer, I can just walk to the bus station, it's not far."

"I'll wait," I growl.

"Oh okay, I'll be quick."

Throwing open the car door, she's out of her seat and halfway across the lot before my clenched jaw finally relaxes enough for me to argue about accompanying her. I decide I'll give her ten minutes, any longer and I'll go in, just in case she needs help. *"She doesn't want your help, you rejected her,"* my inner voice reminds me, and I fucking hate that even my own psyche is giving me shit over the way I'm treating her.

She's exiting the building and rushing toward me a moment later, opening the passenger door and clambering in. "I really don't mind walking; I know you need to get to the garage."

It suddenly dawns on me that she doesn't have any luggage, nothing but the ratty purse she's hugging to her chest. "Where's the rest of your stuff? Do we need to go pack up your things?"

"Oh." She shakes her head. "No, I don't have anything else I need to take with me."

"You only have the clothes you're wearing, you need your things," I growl.

"I don't want any of it. None of it is mine, Ernie paid for it and I don't want anything he bought for me. Plus, it'll just be something else he'll accuse me of owing him," she says with more anger in her tone than I've heard since he tried to accost her yesterday.

"You can't leave town with nothing."

"Why? Look, I appreciate your concern, Bay, but what I do or do not have isn't really any of your business. I'm not worried about having no clothes, I can buy stuff whenever I get where I'm going. Right now, I'm more concerned with getting to the bus station and getting on with my life away from here."

"I'll take you to Cora's store, you can pick some things—"

"No," she shouts. "Just stop. You don't owe me anything, I'm not your girlfriend or your responsibility. I know this whole legacy/curse thing has you feeling a bit crazy, but you don't need to be nice to me to make up for the fact that you don't want me. We don't know anything about each other, the age difference is, well…" she pauses, inhaling slowly. "It's an issue, but the truth of the matter is you don't have any kind of obligation to me. If I'd picked somewhere else to sleep two nights ago, we would never have met. Thank you for all your help the last couple of days. I hope you find whatever it is you're looking for. Now I'm going to walk—"

"You're not walking," I say, my words terse as I start the engine and pull out of the parking lot before she can jump out of the truck. As I pull to a stop at the bus station, everything feels wrong. I shouldn't be doing this, I shouldn't be letting her go, it's wrong, so fucking wrong. But as she leans across the center console and presses a soft kiss to my cheek I can't move. My throat is choked with emotion and I don't say anything, I don't say a fucking word.

"Goodbye, Bay," she whispers, smiling at me with a smile that I've never seen on her lips before and hate with every cell in my body.

Then she climbs out of my truck and walks away.

She's walking away and I can't move even though I know I should be chasing her, that I should be stopping her from leaving because she's mine.

She's mine, my heart, my soul, my woman and I just let her go.

Chapter Ten

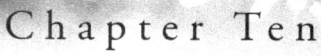

Tears fill my eyes as I press a kiss to Bay's cheek before climbing down from his ridiculously high truck. I shouldn't care, I've only known him for a day, but I still feel like I'm leaving a little part of myself with him, even as I'm walking away. I don't look back, I can't because I'm not entirely sure I'll be able to keep going if he's still there and I know I'll be a little heartbroken if he's already left.

The bus station in Rockhead Point is tiny, there're some local buses that run from the other small towns like Wilderwood where Ernie lives, but to get anywhere else I'm going to have to catch a bus to Bozeman and then onto somewhere else from there.

My envelope of cash is in my purse that I'm clutching to my chest, but the few hundred dollars I have in there aren't going to get me far. At the counter I buy a ticket to Bozeman, and the attendant tells me that it's boarding so I need to hurry. Darting across the asphalt, I jump onto the bus a moment before the bored-looking driver pulls the lever and closes the doors.

I think a tiny part of me thought that maybe Bay might change his mind, that he might race after me, stop the bus with some grand gesture where he tells me he can't live without me. But of course he doesn't, and as the bus pulls out of the station, I keep my gaze down on my hands in my lap, knowing I won't be able to bear seeing the empty curb where his truck was parked.

It takes about forty-five minutes to get to Bozeman and by the time I'm following the line of passengers down the steps and off the bus, I'm almost excited—almost. Unlike the station at Rockhead Point, this bus station has a computerized wall that displays all the buses that are departing, what stand they're at, and where they're going to. My eye follows the display up to find the next bus leaving is heading for the city of Madison in the state of Wisconsin.

I've never been, but then I've never really been anywhere other than New Mexico where I was born and Montana. Wisconsin could be exciting. I don't know much about the cost of living there, but surely it can't be as expensive as, say, New York City. Full of resolve, I grip my purse tightly and stride over to the ticket office.

"Hi there, how much is a ticket to Madison?" I ask the attendant.

"Bozeman to Madison is one hundred and twenty dollars," the bored-looking woman says, not looking up from her computer screen as she speaks.

A hundred and twenty dollars for a bus ticket is way more than I'd expected to pay, although I'm not sure why I thought it would be cheap, it's got to be close to a two-day drive from here, and even though it's more than I anticipated, it's still got to be much cheaper than flying.

"Wisconsin, huh?" a voice says from behind me.

Turning, I feel my jaw go slack as Cody Barnett smiles back at me.

"Cody?"

"Hi Missy."

"What are you doing here?" I ask, my brow furrowing with confusion.

"Do you want the ticket or not?" the attendant asks.

"I'm sorry, ma'am, we just need a minute, we'll step over here so we're not in the way," Cody says, placing a hand under my elbow and carefully pulling me to the side, allowing the next person in line to step up to the window.

"I need to buy my ticket," I protest, pointing toward the counter where the disinterested attendant is now serving someone else.

"We need to talk before you do," Cody says, smiling softly down at me.

"I don't understand."

"I know," he nods. "I don't really know why I'm here. Well, no, that's a lie, I know exactly why I'm here, but it doesn't even really make any sense to me, so I'm not sure how I can explain it to you."

"Maybe just spit it out, because I have a bus to catch," I laugh.

He laughs too and suddenly I relax, because he's just one of those people who instantly makes you feel better. "Okay, here goes. You know we have this legacy thing?"

I nod cautiously.

"Don't worry, I'm not going to tell you that you're mine or anything. But I am drawn to you. I don't know why and I don't know the reason, but I do know I'm not prepared to let you disappear, so I have a proposition for you."

"A proposition?" I ask, taking a step back.

"Oh god no, not that kind of proposition," Cody says quickly. "I run a construction company, I've been looking to expand out of state, so my proposition is that you come and work for me."

"Why? I've never worked on construction, I was a janitor," I cry.

"I'm not suggesting you grab a hammer and start installing drywall," he laughs. "I was thinking you could help out in the office, maybe answer the phone, or well, I don't really know, we can figure that out later."

"Why are you doing this? If this is because your brother rejected me—"

"It's not," he assures me quickly. "I don't know what for and I don't really understand why, but I know, right here in my chest," he slaps at his heart. "That you're supposed to be in my life."

"I think you just feel bad for me," I tell him, shaking my head.

"If I just felt bad, I'd be handing you an envelope full of cash and a plane ticket, I wouldn't be here, with my bags packed in my car, ready to move across the country with you.

"You what?" I shriek.

"Crazy, right? But I'm serious, I have a suitcase full of my clothes, my laptop and everything else I need to carry on running my business. Come with me. We can go to Wisconsin if that's where you think you're meant to be, or you can throw a dart at a map and we can go there. I don't care, I just know that this is where I'm meant to be, helping you."

Shaking my head, I look up at his face, at his earnest, excited eyes. "You're insane."

"Distinctly possible," he chuckles.

"I'm not sleeping with you."

"Agreed," he says, holding out his hand to me. "What do you say?"

"This is crazy."

"Completely crazy. But kind of exciting, right?" Cody smiles.

"Okay," I nod. "Yes, why not?"

"Yes," Cody fist-pumps, dropping his arm across my shoulders and leading me away from the ticket desk and toward the exit and the street. "So, Wisconsin or dart? How are we picking?"

***

Three Months Later

In the end, instead of using a dart and a map, we used a random state generator Cody found on Google to pick where we went, which is how we ended up in Burlington, Vermont. It took us three days to drive here and about two minutes once we got here to realize we were in a town very similar to Rockhead Point, only on the other side of the country.

Those hours and hours of driving gave Cody and me a chance to really get to know each other in a super intense way, and by the time we hit the Vermont border, I had a new best friend.

It turns out that driving for three days and being forced into close proximity is a seriously bonding experience. We talked about everything from school to relationships to pizza toppings and the weird thing is, we figured out that we had loads in common.

On the third day and a couple of thousand miles away from my not-uncle, I told Cody about Ernie. It took me over an hour to convince him not to drive all the way back to Montana so he could beat the shit out of him.

Cody booked us into a tiny inn the first night we got here, they only had one room left and he insisted on paying. As I lay in my bed, staring over at Cody in his, I realized that maybe I was never intended to meet Bay that day, I was meant to meet Cody. I'm not attracted to him and he's not attracted to me, but he's the brother I never knew I needed. I had no idea how much I needed rescuing that day and even though Bay and the rest of the Barnetts were wonderful, it was Cody who saved me when he turned up at the bus station.

Once we got the lay of the land in Burlington, Cody rented us a two-bedroom apartment and put me to work helping him open a new branch of Barnett Construction. Within days, he'd set up meetings with the local officials in all the biggest cities in Vermont, secured us an office to work out of and started interviewing for a new local construction crew. Thankfully, Cody was super patient with me, teaching me the ropes and helping me earn the salary he insisted on paying me.

To say the Barnett clan was shocked to hear Cody had upped and moved out of state was an understatement. I tried not to eavesdrop whenever he called and spoke to them, but it's hard not to hear an eleven-way video chat in a small apartment. We haven't spoken about his family's reaction, in fact we don't talk about them at all, although I know he speaks to them all almost daily.

In the last three months, we've lived in a weird kind of bubble. We work together, live together and spend all of our time together. In such a short span of time he's become my family and I honestly have no idea where I'd be, or what I'd be doing if he hadn't turned up at the bus station that day.

"Hey," he calls as he strolls back into the office.

"Hey, how did the meeting go?" I ask, hitting send on the email I've just finished typing, then looking up from my screen at him.

"It went great, he gave me the rundown on that tender you found for the renovations on the city library, and I'm confident we can be competitive with our offering," Cody tells me, smiling happily.

"That's awesome, winning that contract would be a massive boon for us. Barry called to let you know that the job out in Missoula got the final sign-off from the certification board, so they'll be packing up and moving all the crew and equipment straight over to the school jobsite in Helena."

"Great, could you let Fran know that we can send final payment invoices for that one?"

"Of course."

"Have you eaten?" Cody asks.

"What time is it?" I say, glancing at the clock in the corner of my screen. "Oh shoot, it's after two. No, I planned to go and grab something for us both, but I forgot."

"You need to eat," he chides, his brow furrowed in concern.

"Cody, you've been force-feeding me hamburgers since we met, if you don't stop I'm going to be the size of a truck."

"You're still too thin, I'm just taking care of you."

"I know," I sigh. "But you know I can take care of myself, right?"

"Family," he reminds me, like he does every time I hint that I can look after myself and don't expect him to fuss over me.

"I know." I roll my eyes playfully.

"Let's go and grab a late lunch, I have some stuff I need to talk to you about."

"Are you leaving?" I blurt, my heart rushing to my throat and making nausea swell in my stomach.

"No," he says quickly. "Of course I'm not leaving." Pulling me from my chair, he wraps me in his strong arms and holds me to his chest. "I'm not going anywhere, Mis, you know that, and if I did, you'd come with me, that's what family does."

"You left all your family to come here with me," I utter quietly.

"That was different, they have each other, you didn't

have anyone."

"I know you miss them."

"I do miss them, but I've lived apart from them before, and I speak to them every damn day. It's not like Bay's..." He stops speaking suddenly and I push away from his chest and look up at him.

"It's not like Bay's what?"

Cody inhales slowly, then sighs. "It's not like Bay's talking to me."

"What do you mean? Why wouldn't Bay be talking to you?"

Lifting his hand, he cups my cheek and then presses a brotherly kiss to my forehead. "You know why, Mis."

I feel my brow furrow in confusion. "He's not talking to you because you're here with me? I don't understand why that would make any difference to him."

"I kind of..." Cody starts then trails off. "Let's go get lunch and I'll explain while we wait for food, I'm starving."

I nod, but a part of me wants to demand that he explain what he means right this second. Why would Bay care that Cody was here with me? He drove me to the bus station, he didn't ask to keep in touch, or even show any real care about what happened to me after I left Rockhead Point. So, what does it matter that I'm in Vermont with Cody? Maybe it's because he thinks I'm the reason Cody left. I suppose I was. Their family is so close and then I came along and one of them upped and left and moved across the country without even saying goodbye.

They probably all hate me. I don't know why, but the thought makes my chest tighten. I don't want the Barnetts to hate me. They were all so kind to me and in return I stole one of them and spirited him away. God, they must think I'm an asshole.

My mind swirls with thoughts and recriminations the whole time it takes us to walk to the small Chinese restaurant that does a working lunch menu just down the street from our office. Cody holds the door open for me and I step past him and into the small, dimly lit restaurant.

From the outside, the place looks a little run down, with chipped paint and dated decor, but the food is unbelievable and at lunch they do a taster menu where they deliver a dozen small portions of food on a platter.

Cody orders our usual and drinks, then settles back into the worn booth seat.

"So...?" I prompt.

Rubbing his hand over his face, he sighs. "Remember the day we met, when you stayed at the house while us guys went out for drinks?"

"Yes, of course I remember."

"Well, Bay was being an idiot. He was so determined that he wasn't going to claim you, that he was too old and you were too young and that the legacy was a curse and all that bullshit."

"Okay," I say, trying not to wince. Even three months later, it makes a pang of hurt spark in my chest if I think about the way Bay rejected me. I understand his reasoning, in part I almost agree with him, but I'm not going to pretend it wasn't a blow to my pride that he was happy to walk away from his fated person, just because that person was me.

"Yeah well," Cody pauses again, grimacing slightly. "I

might have told him that if he wasn't going to claim you, I would."

"What?" I whisper-shout.

"I know, I know. But I thought a bit of healthy competition might be the boot up the ass he needed to see you were perfect for him and he'd stop being such a fucking douche canoe."

"You never? You don't feel that way about me, right?" I ask cautiously.

"No," he blurts. "No, you feel like my sister. I told you I was drawn to you, but it's never like a sexual thing. I just said that to try and provoke him. And now…" he trails off.

"He thinks we're together like that?" I gasp, my eyes wide.

"I'm not sure. I've told the others we're just friends, but Bay won't speak to me at all," he confesses on a tired sigh.

"You need to go and see him. I won't be the reason you fall out with your family. Do they all hate me? Do they think I'm a terrible person who stole their brother?"

"No, of course not," he laughs, reaching over and squeezing my hand. "They'd rather me be there, but they get why I'm here, well, kind of anyway. They think we should both just go back to Rockhead Point."

"You can, if that's what you need to do. I'll miss you, but I'll be okay, I can find a smaller place and—"

"I'm not leaving. Starting up a second branch of Barnett Construction was always my plan, it being here almost on the East Coast is perfect and I'm not going anywhere. But we will have to go back to Rockhead Point soon."

"What, why?"

"Okay, so don't kill me, but after you told me about Ernie and your inheritance, I had my lawyer do a bit of digging into your family."

"Why?" I ask. On the journey down here, I'd confided in Cody and told him all about Ernie. I'd told him about the way he'd gotten me to sign my inheritance over to him and then his threats and control when he'd realized there was a second trust that I couldn't access until I turned twenty-one. I'd also told him that I didn't care about money that was coming from family who couldn't make the effort to even look me up to see if I was okay. As far as I'm concerned, Ernie's welcome to it.

"Because that money is yours. Your grandparents went to the effort to put it into trust for you."

"I don't care about the money. I don't even know how much it is. All I know is that inheritance has been a part of a really ugly period in my life and I'm happy to never think about it again. Hopefully when I don't claim it when I turn twenty-one, it goes to look after pigmy goats or something instead of to him."

"Well, let me tell you what my lawyers found out."

"Fine," I sigh, thanking the waitress for my drink as she places the glasses on the table.

"Did you know your dad's family was Irish?"

I shake my head as I sip at the cold soda in my glass.

"Apparently, he was born in Kilkenny in Ireland. Before he came to America and met your mom, he was married to a woman named Moira and they had a daughter called Elizabeth."

Sucking in a sharp gasp of air, I grab the edge of the

table tightly. "I have a half sister?"

He nods. "She was two when your dad came over to America. I don't know why he came here, or if his marriage to Moira was over before he left, but judging by the time line, he met your mom as soon as he got over here and they got pregnant with you. Obviously, you know they died when you were only a few days old. They never got married and when he passed, he was still legally married. All of his estate went to his wife, but from what my lawyer found out, it was five or six years after he passed before his family found out he was dead. The trust was started in your name just before your sixteenth birthday. I don't know for definite, but I don't think your paternal grandparents knew about you before then."

I can hear everything he's saying to me, but my ears are ringing and his words don't make any sense. "They didn't know about me?"

"I don't think so. My lawyer can reach out to the lawyers who handled their estate if you'd like, but with them both passed, you'll never really know for sure. Anyway. The value of the trust isn't public knowledge, but it was set up so you'd get access to a lump sum when you turned eighteen, some at twenty-one, then more at twenty-five. I'm assuming Ernie didn't know that, but it certainly looks like he tracked you down with the sole intention of stealing that money from you."

"When did they die?"

"Your grandfather passed a month after they started your trust and your grandmother just a few weeks after that. I'm not sure what caused their passing, but I'm sure we could find out if you wanted."

I shake my head. "They, they didn't know about me."

Taking my hand again, he squeezes tightly. "They didn't know about you, and once they found out, they put the trust in place to provide for you after they'd gone."

In and out, my chest moves, pulling in oxygen, but I still feel light-headed, like my heart is beating too fast and I can't quite find enough air.

"Hey," Cody calls, jumping up from his seat and scooting in beside me. "It's okay, just breathe, it's okay."

"I thought they didn't care," I say through gulps of air.

"I know, but they did. They just didn't know about you."

"Do I have any other family?"

"You had an aunt, but she was a lot older than your dad and she passed before your grandparents did. She had a son, who had a son, that's Ernie. He's your second cousin, but from what my lawyer could find, he's always lived in the US and only ever met your grandparents a handful of times when he was a kid. I don't know how he found out about you, or why he decided to track you down to steal your inheritance, but judging by his dad's criminal record, being a thieving asshole runs in the family."

"He told me he was my uncle," I say absently.

"I know."

"I thought he cared about me. He looked after me and my nana for years before he showed his true colors." I'm rambling. Tears fill my eyes, but instead of blinking them away I let them fall, too shell-shocked to care that I'm crying in a restaurant.

"He's an asshole, Mis, you can't allow him to take

anything else from you and the only way you can do that is by going home to claim what's yours."

For a second, when his words register in my mind, I think he's talking about Bay, that he thinks I should be claiming Bay. But then I realize he means the money, my inheritance, the trust my grandparents set up for me. The grandparents that maybe didn't abandon me like I'd thought, the ones that maybe didn't even know I existed.

It's all too much. I thought I was alone, but I have family, a half sister. When I got in Cody's car with him all those months ago, I thought I was starting over, a new beginning in a new place. A new me, not encumbered with shitty non-uncles and money I've never cared about from a family who didn't want to know me. But now, after everything Cody just told me, this fresh start doesn't feel so fresh anymore.

I'm not sure if I'm grateful for what he's found out, or angry that he's brought my ragged history into the present, when I was starting to feel like someone new, someone worthwhile.

I've never told Cody, but I heard the argument Bay had with his family after they thought I'd gone to bed that night.

"I don't want to care for someone. I want a woman who doesn't need me, who can look after herself and just wants to exist by my side."

On days when my mind fills with what-ifs, when I wonder how my life would look now if Bay had done what all the other Barnetts had done and claimed me, doing whatever it takes to make me his, I remember the way he sounded when he told his entire family that he saw me as someone who'd always need him, who couldn't take care of herself.

His voice is the one I taunt myself with when I feel out of my depth trying to do a job I have zero experience with. It's the voice I envisage when I feel sorry for myself and wonder if I should have just stayed as Ernie's pathetic little ward. I never want to be that stupid, needy, pathetic girl who needs to be helped through life because she's not capable of doing it on her own.

Cody's never treated me that way. From the day he picked me up, he never gave me stuff, he offered me a job and then when he tried to give me my first paycheck, he accepted it when I gave it back to him to cover everything he'd bought me those first few days. He never once questioned it, he just took it back and told me he'd cover groceries that month and I could do it the next.

My life now is mine. I pay my way. I own my shit. Cody might fudge a little on exactly how much my half of the rent is, and I'm sure it's not normal for a boss to buy lunch every day, but I work hard, well beyond normal office hours. The stuff we do for each other now balances, we're equal and I love it.

A part of me wishes that it'd been Cody who'd seen me and decided I was his fated woman instead of Bay. I'm not attracted to him, but I could see myself being incredibly happy spending the rest of my life with my best friend.

"Mis?" Cody calls, dragging me back to the present as he wipes the tears from my cheeks and gives me another squeeze.

"Sorry."

"It's my fault, I shouldn't have just piled it all on you

like that. I wasn't sure how else to explain without just telling you everything."

"No, it's okay. I'm glad you told me, it's just a lot, you know."

"You turn twenty-one in three months, we can fly in, see the lawyer, sign whatever paperwork you need to sign, then fly right back if that's what you want."

"You can't fly in and not spend time with your family, I know how much they miss you and how much you miss them. Plus, you need to sort things out with Bay, explain that you were just provoking him."

"How about we both fly in and stay at my place for a while, everyone would love to see you, they ask after you all the time."

"I can stay in a hotel; you stay and spend time with your family and I'll do the lawyer stuff and then come home."

Cody leans back a little so he can look down at me. "Is this because you don't want to see Bay?"

"No, of course not," I lie.

His smile is blinding and full of mischief. "Well, if you're not trying to avoid my asshole brother, there's no reason to pay for a hotel. We can stay at mine."

Chapter Eleven

Bay

Three months and three days earlier

"**G**oodbye, Bay."

I'm frozen, listening to her say goodbye even though it's not what I want. It's wrong, so fucking wrong and I should be stopping her, but I can't move and I don't know why.

"Because you're no good for her," a voice whispers inside my head, but that can't be true, can it? She's mine, I know that right down to my core, she's mine and she should be here, with me, in my life, in my truck, in my bed.

My limbs still refuse to cooperate and my ass feels glued to the seat as my heart argues with my conscience. A part of me knows I should let her go, but the rest is demanding I hunt her ass down and keep her.

It could be a moment, or an hour that I silently debate with myself, but the moment I decide I'm selfish enough to ruin her life just to keep her in mine, I'm off my seat and running across the bus station.

Only she's not here.

There's only one bus waiting to depart and I ignore the protests of the driver as I rush on board, searching the seats for her, for my Imp, but she's not on the bus. She's not in the waiting room, or the bathroom I enter. She's gone and I have no idea what to do.

"I'm looking for my…" I falter, wondering what to call her. Woman? Girlfriend? Fiancé? Life? None of them seem enough, but too vague all at the same time. "She's young, bright-red hair, beautiful."

"Not seen any redheads," the attendant at the ticket counter says, not even glancing in my direction.

"Are you sure? I dropped her off at the curb."

"Nope," the attendant says again, her gaze still firmly fixed on the screen of her monitor.

Growling, I turn away from the counter and stalk toward the stands where the bus I invaded has now left from. "Fuck," I hiss beneath my breath. How the fuck am I going to find her? I let her go. I fucking let her go. I'm an idiot, an asshole of the first order and I probably deserve to be alone for the rest of my life just for allowing my Imp to leave without making her mine.

Stomping back to the counter again, I bang my fist against the plexiglass screen between the attendant and me. She jumps, lifting her gaze to me for the first time and scowls.

"Violence is not tolerated here at the Rockhead Point Transport Terminal," she says icily.

"I just wanted to get your full attention," I say, flashing her a cold smile. "What buses have left in the last fifteen minutes?"

Sighing, she purses her lips together and after flashing me a glare, looks down at her screen again. "The circular to Bozeman left seven minutes ago, the twice daily to Billings left four minutes ago."

"That's it?"

"That's it." She looks at me again and sneers. "Next." Blatantly dismissing me, she pointedly lifts her gaze and looks over my shoulder to the person behind me.

Hissing angrily, I step aside, grasping my hair in my hands and tugging tightly. She must have gotten on the bus to Bozeman, but that left nearly ten minutes ago. Turning, I race through the people lining up to buy tickets, making my way back to my truck a few minutes later.

Jumping into the driver's seat, I start the engine and gun the accelerator, pulling away from the curb with a screech of my tires. The moment I start driving, my mind blanks and I suddenly have no idea how to get to fucking Bozeman. I've driven to the bigger city to the west of Rockhead Point, hundreds of times, probably more, so why is it now, when I'm chasing after the woman I should never have let go, that my mind empties and my internal map is off fucking line.

My foot lifts off the gas, and I shake my head as my brain refocuses and I turn my truck back in the direction of the city and Missy. It takes me nearly twenty minutes to catch the bus, and I follow it all the way to the station where an angry man in a Bozeman City Bus company uniform lowers a barrier, blocking my path and forcing me to park in the lot.

I can hear the sound of my heart beating as I jump out of my truck and take off at a sprint, pushing my way past the people walking down the sidewalk until I'm beside the bus. The empty fucking bus.

Wading through the busy bus station I search for a glimpse of her, convinced that I'll be able to spot her hair no matter how big the station is, or how many people there are here, but I can't find her.

If I'd have asked more questions, done something other than think about why I couldn't keep her, then maybe I'd have some clue which bus she's planning to get on next. But I didn't. I didn't want to question her about where she'd want to land next, because I was too busy thinking I knew what was best for us both and because of my arrogance, I've lost her for real this time.

When my brothers have been idiots with their women, the farthest they've run has been the next town over or a couple of hours away. But she could be on her way to anywhere by now and I have no idea how I'd go about tracking her down. I don't even know her date of birth.

I search for over an hour, checking every seat on every bus just in case she's on there, but it's like she's vanished. The attendant at the ticket counter didn't remember seeing her, and without any more leads, I've hit a dead end.

She's gone.

I'm not proud of how I spend the next couple of days.

I barely remember getting home and falling into several bottles of whiskey. I know my family is worried about me, but what the fuck can I even say to them? That I fucked up everything, that I'm an idiot.

Three days later and with the worst hangover I've ever had, I stumble out of my rooms and into the main shared living space. It's lunchtime on a Wednesday but my entire family is here, staring at me, pity in their eyes.

"You look like shit," Cora says, eyeing me with disgust.

"Look better than I feel."

"Are you expecting sympathy, because I doubt you're going to get it," she says, too loudly and a little shrill.

Groaning, I slump down onto the couch, letting my head fall back onto the cushions and covering my eyes with my hand. "Why are you all here? Shouldn't you be at work?"

"We're not all here."

Dropping my hand, I scan the people around me. "Cody's the only one with anything to do today?" I ask, closing my eyes as pain explodes in my skull.

"Cody's not at work," Beau says.

"I'm sure you can have your intervention without him," I scoff. "I know what a fuck up I am. I let her go. I watched her walk away from me and by the time I figured out what an idiot I was it was too late. I chased her bus to Bozeman and then she disappeared. She's gone and it's my own fucking fault. I deserve to be miserable for the rest of my life, because I let her go and I have no idea how to even start trying to find her."

"We know where she is," Cora says coldly.

Snapping my eyes open I bolt upright. "What?"

"We know exactly where she is," she says, her lips pursed.

"Peaches," Huck says, his tone warning.

"What? This is all his fault, I'm not going to sugarcoat it for him," she snaps back at him.

"Maybe we should—" Alice starts.

"Missy's with Cody," Bonnie says with an angry glare.

"She's here?" Jumping out of my seat, I move toward Cody's door.

"No. They're not here," Beau says, sighing tiredly.

Swinging around, I scan the faces of my family. They're a mix of pity, anger and sadness. "Then where the fuck are they?"

"Vermont," Granger says.

"Ver... What?" I yell.

"Cody and Missy are in Vermont," Juni says, her voice soft and full of sympathy.

"Why. Are. They. In. Vermont. Together?" I seethe.

"Because you're a fucking moron," Cora snaps.

"Peaches, I swear," Huck growls, but Cora spins around to glare at him.

"Don't even start with me, he needs to hear this, he fucked up and there's no point sugarcoating things, or pandering to his fragile male ego." Turning, her glacial stare lands on me. "What did you think was going to happen, Bay? Did you expect her to spend the rest of her life pouting and miserable that she missed her chance at *you?* Sorry to burst your bubble, but that was never going to happen. You told that girl to her face that you weren't interested. Worse, you told her that she was yours, made just for you, destined to be your mate, your partner, your love, and then you told her you didn't want her."

I flinch, but Cora continues unperturbed. "You fucked up and she left. The way I see it, you don't deserve her, because clearly that girl has been through some stuff and she still had enough self-worth to hold her head high and leave with as much dignity as you allowed her. If Cody is smart enough to see her for the diamond she is, then good on him. But know this, Bay, your woman and your brother are gone and the only person to blame for that is you." Her voice breaks and Huck curls his arm around her, turning her to face him just as tears fill her eyes.

I watch as her shoulders silently shake. "Peaches, you're fucking killing me, baby, I fucking hate it when you cry," Huck coos, stroking her hair as he holds her tight to his chest.

At the start of her angry tirade I'd been ready to argue, to call my brother a traitor, to rant and rave about how fucked up things are, but Cora's words have sucked all of the wind from my sails. How can I blame anyone but myself? Cora's right, I told Missy I didn't want her. Why would she care that I'm sorry now?

"The next flight to Vermont is tomorrow morning," Penn says, laying a hand on my shoulder and squeezing tightly.

"Is she okay?" I ask, not making eye contact with anyone.

"Cody called a couple of days ago to let us know that he and Missy were together and that they were headed to Vermont. Other than a couple of texts, we haven't heard anything else from them. Depending on where they end up, they should be there by now, or at least they will be by the end of the day," Beau says, his voice low and free of emotion.

I nod, but I'm not sure why. A part of me knows that I should be feeling something. Anger or heartbreak or just something, but all I feel is numb. Cody told me that he was drawn to her, he told me that If I let her go, he'd follow her. He warned me that this was his exact plan, but now that he's done it, now that he's claimed my woman. *My woman.* All I feel is empty.

"Where do you want to sit, flight's pretty empty so…" Penn trails off, waiting for me to answer.

"I'm not going to Vermont."

"Why the fuck not?" he asks.

"I can't," I admit. "What could I even say to her at this point?"

"Sorry might be a good start," Lulu snaps.

"Would you forgive this? I knew her for a day and I spent the entire time rejecting her over and over again. Would you accept an apology and then follow me back to the place you were desperate to get away from?"

"No, I wouldn't," Lulu agrees, her voice clear and unwavering.

"I told her she wasn't what I wanted, that this thing between us was a curse. Cody followed her when I let her go. He swooped in and saved her, and now he's taken her to the other side of the country, leaving his family and his home behind. If you were her, would you leave that for a guy who dismissed you?"

"No, I wouldn't," she agrees again.

"So, you're just going to do nothing?" Teddy asks, incredulity lacing each word.

"I don't fucking know," I shout. "I have no fucking clue. All I know is that my chest feels like it's been ripped open and my heart is gone. It's in fucking Vermont, falling in love with my brother." The words pour out of me in a rush and once I'm finished, melancholy and anger and betrayal replace them. "Fuck this, I need a drink." Standing, I brush off my family's concerns and head back to my room. Grabbing the last remaining bottle of whiskey, I twist off the top and lift the bottle to my lips, pouring the liquor into my mouth and waiting for the bliss of oblivion to hit.

***

"What the fuck?" I shout, jolting awake as freezing cold water hits my face, shocking me upright as liquid fills my mouth and nose.

"Get up," Beau demands, placing the now empty water jug down on my coffee table.

"Fuck off," I growl, wiping the water from my face with my hands, then stripping my soaking wet shirt off and dropping it to the floor.

"Enough fucking moping, either go get your woman, or man up and get your ass to work. Penn's been holding the fort while you've drunk yourself into a stupor for the last five days, your time to mope and feel sorry for yourself is over."

"Fuck you. Like you'd be any different if you'd lost Bonnie."

"Firstly, I could never lose Bonnie, because I'd never

let her leave, I'd tie her ass to the bed before I'd let her go and secondly, if my woman was in another state, you can be damn sure I'd be on a plane tracking her ass down and doing what the fuck ever it took to bring her back to me. I sure as fuck wouldn't be drinking whiskey like it's water and moping like a little bitch."

"I'm not fucking moping."

"Sure as hell looks like moping to me. Now what's it going to be? Vermont, or work."

"Tell Penn I'll be in once I've had a shower."

Beau scoffs and shakes his head. "You're a fucking idiot."

***

It's been a week since I drove Missy to the bus station and stupidly let her go. Four days since I found out she was with my brother. Three days since Beau dumped water on my head and told me to either go get my girl or suck it the fuck up. Since then I've got up, gone to work and functioned, but all of my thoughts are with Missy.

It doesn't seem to matter what I do, if I sleep or don't sleep, if I drown myself in whiskey or stay sober, all I can think about is her. Regret is my permanent companion and I'm not sure how to live with that. Is this my life now? Am I going to spend the rest of forever feeling like half my soul is missing?

Cody calls most nights, but even though I know it's my own fault that I'm here alone and he's with her, I can't seem to stop hating him. I haven't spoken to him, because I'm worried that if I do, I'll say something that I'll never be able to take back and If I do that, what the fuck will happen if he and Missy get married and have kids? If I destroy my relationship with him, I'll not only lose him, I'll lose all access to her too... Even if all I'll ever have is seeing her from a distance on the arm of my baby brother.

***

One Month Later

The familiar chirp of the video call on the laptop has all of my family rushing over to crowd around the small screen, eager to see Cody. Everyone misses him, his absence has left a gaping hole in all of our lives.

I miss him too, but my feelings are overshadowed by my anger and jealousy. Every day that Missy isn't here with me is an extra day she's with him, and even though I love him, I fucking hate him at the same time.

He calls most days at the same time, but I still haven't spoken to him. I don't want to see them together, although if she's part of the calls I never hear her. A part of me knows I'm being a pathetic asshole and feeling sorry for myself, but the thought of her with *him* is more than I can bear.

I've bought and canceled five plane tickets but I'm honestly not sure what the fuck I'll do if I allow myself to go after her. She's mine; I believe that right down to my marrow. She belongs to me, and the way I feel right now is my punishment for not claiming her the moment I saw her.

If I get on a plane and end up in the same state as her, I'm honestly not sure there's anything or anyone, including her, that could stop me from taking what's mine. When Huck lost his shit and kidnapped Cora, I thought he'd lost his fucking mind. Right now, that seems like a pretty mellow reaction to his woman trying to run away from him.

With each day that passes, I feel my control slipping away and I'm pretty sure I'm on countdown to losing my motherfucking mind. The only question that remains is if anything can be salvaged with my relationship with my brother if I break into his apartment and steal back my woman.

***

Two Months After That

The moment my plane lands in Vermont, I swear every hair on my body stands on end because I'm so close to her. It doesn't matter that I couldn't get a seat on the flight to the closest airport to where she is, or that I still have nearly a thirty-minute drive to get to the town of Burlington, where Cody and Missy are sharing an apartment overlooking Lake Champlain. I'm here in the same state as her for the first time in three months and my dick is rock hard just in anticipation of seeing her.

I don't have the right to be sexually aroused, but my dick hasn't gotten the memo, because as far as he's concerned, we'll be claiming Missy as soon as we get to her. The brain in my head—the one on top of my shoulders—knows that, more than likely, my dick isn't going to be getting wet any time in the foreseeable future, but if three months without her has taught me anything, it's that I have to fucking try.

It's been twelve weeks, three days and about twelve hours since I let my stupid fucking hang-ups ruin my life. I'd like to say that the way I treated Missy was an aberration, but that would be a lie. In the last three months I've gone backward and forward more times than I can mention trying to decide if by cementing *my* future with her, I'd be ruining *hers*. A part of me still believes she's as completely wrong for me as I am for her, but apparently, I'm selfish enough not to care. Because here I am, in Vermont, chasing after my happily ever after while planning to steal my brother's.

I still haven't spoken to him since he left. I'm pissed at him for leaving, for being with her and for being right too. He told me I was being an idiot, he warned me I was wrong and I ignored him. Hell, he even told me exactly what he planned to do and it still came as a shock when he did it.

This is the longest I've ever gone without speaking to one of my brothers and I fucking hate it. Even if I were to swallow my pride, how the hell am I supposed to tell him that he doesn't get to keep the woman he was prepared to move halfway across the country to be with?

I don't want to lose Cody, but Missy is mine and I can't fucking live without her. Before I knew who she was, it was easy to say I didn't want the legacy to hit me. Once I found her, I used that as a way to hide from what she made me feel. I'm a fucking coward. I never knew that about myself until I laid eyes on her, but from then, right up till the moment I ran after her at the bus station, I've been fucking terrified.

Maybe if I'd told one of my brothers that, things would have turned out differently, but when I saw her for the first time, my gut reaction was fear. A girl like Missy is so much more than a fuck. So much more than a casual arrangement with no expectations or hurt feelings. But I knew the moment she looked at me that there could never be anything casual about my Imp.

Now it's three months later and I've fucked things up so badly, she might never forgive me, but I can't walk away. Every thought, dream, nightmare, everything is her. She's who I fall asleep dreaming of and wake up thinking about. She's bewitched me and it turns out I don't ever want to be freed.

Somehow, I need to make her forgive me, convince her we belong together and make her see that I'm a better choice than my brother, all without losing my shit, embracing my inner caveman, knocking her out and taking her back to Montana.

Anticipation hums in my veins as I pull into the lot for Missy and Cody's apartment block and park in the space next to Cody's car. Inhaling slowly, I stretch out my tense muscles and take in the serene view of the water in front of me. Cody's always loved the water, so it doesn't surprise me that he'd choose to live on the lake. He told me the only thing he missed about where he went to school in Cali was being close to the water.

I luck out when I reach the door to the building, catching it as someone exits. The entire flight, I tried to decide what I was going to say to them both when I got here, but even after four and a half hours in the air, I'm still no closer to figuring out how I'm going to handle this.

My brother is in a relationship with my soul mate. Yep, that's some Jerry Springer shit right there. I know it's an asshole move to be here right now, they've been together for months, but I couldn't sit at home knowing she was moving on without me, if there was even a hope that she might give me a chance to throw my hat in the ring.

My hands shake as I lift my fist up and rap it against the door. Thud, thud, thud. My heart bangs against my chest as I wait for a glimpse of her, but when the door opens it's not Missy, it's Cody in the doorframe.

His fist snaps out so quickly I don't see it coming before it smashes into my face, making me stagger back. Righting myself, I lift a hand to my cheek, bracing myself for another punch, but when I glance up at my brother, he's not angry, he's smirking.

"Jesus, bro, it took you fucking long enough," Cody laughs, throwing his arms out and pulling me in for a hug that has me stiffening in his hold.

"I..." I start, then stop, unsure what the fuck to even say.

"It's been three fucking months, you fucking asshole, I gave you ten days at the most."

"I..." I pause again. "What?"

Cody laughs, releases me, then steps back. "Come in, I'll get you some ice for your face, Missy just went to the store."

I don't understand why he's smiling. If I'm here, he must know it's not to wish him and my woman well, so why isn't he pissed? He punched me—which I totally deserve—but then hugged me and now he seems pleased to see me.

"Coffee, soda or beer? I'd offer you something stronger, but Beau told me you were hitting the sympathy juice pretty hard for a while, so I won't encourage you."

"Err, beer," I mumble, shell-shocked. I follow Cody as he leads me into the living space where two dark fabric couches overlook a fucking amazing view of the lake. The kitchen is at the back of the apartment and then two doors lead off into rooms to the right.

"You want anything to eat?" he asks happily as he hands me a bottle of beer and takes one for himself, grabbing a packet of pretzels from a cabinet and tipping them into a bowl.

"No, thanks."

Placing the bowl of snacks down on the coffee table, Cody flops back onto the couch and I slowly sit opposite him.

"I got to say, bro, I was starting to lose hope, I thought I was going to have to get Mis back to Montana before you pulled your head out of your ass."

"What the fuck is going on?" I ask, so confused I'm starting to wonder if this is actually just a dream and I'm going to wake up back in my bed at home.

"What do you mean?" Cody asks, his brow furrowed.

"I mean, why are you pleased to see me? You know why I'm here."

"Why the fuck wouldn't I be pleased to see you? And I'm assuming you're here to sort things with Mis."

"And you're okay with that?"

Sitting up straighter, Cody leans forward and stares at me. "What exactly do you think is going on here?"

"You're living with Missy, you moved across the damn fucking country to be with her," I explain slowly, having to spit the words out.

His lips tip up into a slow grin, then his shoulders start to move as a soft chuckle breaks free. Narrowing my eyes, I try to figure out what the fuck is so funny, but before I get a chance to ask, he's laughing loudly, his eyes watering as his whole body shakes with the intensity of his mirth.

Does he think it's funny that I'm here? Or that I think I have a chance of taking her away from him?

Jumping up, he claps me on the shoulder and then shoves me a little. "Come here, I want to show you something."

"What?"

"Come on," he urges, stepping around the couch and heading across the apartment.

Reluctantly, I stand and follow him. He pauses beside the two doors that lead to their bedroom. I don't fucking want to see where they sleep, but my protest dies on my lips as he opens the first door, not stepping inside as the scent of rose hits my nose. The room is obviously feminine, the sheets on the bed a pretty floral pattern that is both girly and modern. There are bottles of products on a dressing table and a bathrobe hanging over a door that I'm assuming is a closet.

I'm surprised that Cody is happy living in such a feminine space, but my brothers are whipped enough to let their women decorate however they want as long as they're happy. I glance up at my brother, expecting to see his triumph, but instead it's amusement that's etched into his smile. Crooking a finger at me, he takes a step to the side and opens the second door, revealing another bedroom. This one has black sheets on the bed, a massive flat-screen TV mounted on the wall and is impeccably neat and tidy, just like my brother's apartment back home.

My lips part on a silent breath as I glance at the two rooms, then back to Cody. "My room," he says, pointing to the room in front of us. "Missy's room," he says, gesturing to the other.

"You don't…" I trail off, incapable of asking him about them sharing a room.

He shakes his head slowly side to side. "No, it's not like that. I figured since you were here, the others had told you."

"You said—"

"If you hadn't refused to speak to me for three fucking months, you'd know it's never been like that," he snaps angrily.

"You said—"

"You think I'm fucking your girl?"

"You said—"

His scoff is low and full of bitterness. "I was trying to goad you into realizing what a fucking idiot you were being. Do you really think I'd ever touch a woman that belonged to you? What the fuck is wrong with you?"

All of the air leaves me in a shame-filled exhale. "I…" My mouth goes dry, because I have nothing to say, no excuse to give, because I did believe he was capable of that. I thought he'd followed her and seduced her into his arms, his bed. "I…"

"Nothing, you've got nothing, have you?" Cody asks with a disgusted huff. "I'm not sure what's worse, that you were prepared to let your fucking soul mate leave or that you'd think so poorly of me. Is that why it's taken you so long to get your head out of your ass and come claim her? Because you thought we were shacked up here together? Or are you just so fucking self-absorbed that you were too busy trying to decide if you wanted her before you came and fixed your fuckup?"

"I thought I lost my chance," I admit quietly. "I realized I'd made a huge fucking mistake about five minutes after she got out of the truck at the bus station in Rockhead Point, but by the time I chased after her, the bus to Bozeman had already left. I chased after it, and followed it all the way into the city, but they wouldn't let me follow when it pulled into the station and by the time I found somewhere to dump the truck she'd gone. I drank myself stupid for three days and then when I sobered up enough to tell everyone what had happened, they told me that you and she were together here."

"So, you assumed I was fucking her?"

"You told me you were drawn to her, that if I fucked up, you'd claim her," I growl.

"I am drawn to her and I have claimed her. But not as my fucking woman, as my sister and best fucking friend. What the hell do you think would have happened to her if I hadn't found her that day in Bozeman? She had two hundred dollars to her name and the ticket she was about to buy to Madison would have taken almost every fucking penny she had. She'd have been on the streets within a couple of days on her own. She had nothing, just her ID, the clothes she was wearing and those couple of hundred dollars, that's it."

"I had money to give her, but I froze, I…"

"You shouldn't have ever let it get that far," he yells at me. "You should have seen the angel she is and you should have had a ring on her finger that same day. I used to look up to you, Bay, you were so put together, the most capable of all of us. Beau's temper has always kept him wound tight, but you, you were cool, calm and in control. But this, the way you handled this wonderful, special, beautiful soul. You don't fucking deserve her."

"I know." I nod. "I know I don't deserve her and I tried to stay away, I thought you two were together and I tried to leave you be. I tried to leave you both alone, but I can't because she's mine, Cody, she's mine and I can't fucking live without her."

"What?" a soft feminine voice says from behind me.

Spinning around, I see her, standing by the front door, her hair hanging in loose curls over her shoulders. She looks different than the last time I saw her, healthier, less afraid. I should have been the one to help make that change in her, but instead it was my brother, the one I've thought badly of and refused to speak to for months.

"Hi Mis, Bay came to visit," Cody says, glaring at me as he steps around me and strides over to her, taking the grocery bags from her hands and pressing a kiss to her forehead before taking them into the kitchen and slowly emptying them.

"Hi Bay," her voice breaks a little. "Cody never mentioned you were coming to visit. Can I get you a drink or something to eat?" she asks, overly politely.

"He didn't know."

"Oh, well surprises are nice, I know he's been missing his family, so it'll be good for you guys to catch up," she says, fake brightness lacing each word as she follows my brother into the kitchen, standing close beside him, grabbing the groceries and turning her back on me as she slides them into the cabinets.

"I didn't come here to see Cody." I wait for her to ask why I'm here, but she still has her back to me, her arms frozen in the air in the middle of sliding a box onto a shelf. "I came to see you."

The box falls from her hands, hitting the floor with a thud.

"Maybe I should—" Cody starts to say.

"No," Missy shouts quickly, spinning and grabbing onto Cody's arm with a tight grip.

"Okay," Cody says, looking up at me for a second and then shrugging. I get why he's picking her over me in this moment. I don't deserve his loyalty. I could have asked any of my brothers or sisters what was going on between Cody and Missy at any time in the last three months, but I've point-blank refused to hear or speak about them and now that childish behavior has come back to bite me on the ass.

Would I have come sooner if I'd known they weren't together romantically? Possibly. But there's no way of knowing that either way. I'm here now and it turns out I need to make things right with my brother as well as trying to prove I'm not the self-centered asshole I showed myself to be the last time I saw Missy.

"Missy, do you think we could talk?" I ask cautiously.

"Why?" she asks caustically.

"Because I need to apologize, I—"

"Apologize for what? You haven't done anything wrong, at least not to me. We met once, one time, Bay. You helped me, you gave me a ride, I'm not sure what you think you have to be sorry for?"

"Missy."

Forcing a fake smile to her beautiful, full pink lips, she lifts one hand into the air. "Shoot, I forgot my laptop at the office. I'll go and fetch it, it'll give you guys some time to catch up," she says, snatching her purse from the counter and her keys from a bowl beside the door before she leaves.

Staring after her, I exhale wearily, rubbing my palm over my two-day-old stubble.

"It's going to take more than an apology," Cody says, shaking his head at me.

"I've fucked up so badly."

"Yep," he agrees, not bothering to sugarcoat it. "I still can't believe you thought I moved in on your woman."

"I haven't exactly been myself recently," I confess, stepping forward and leaning against the counter. "Losing her was a lot harder than I thought it would be."

"That why you're here? Because it sucks being alone?"

"No."

"Then why?"

"Because without her, nothing works, nothing makes sense, the light feels dim, the dark endless. I'm broken and she's the only thing that can fix me."

Cody nods, some of the anger fading from his face.

"What do I do?"

"Honestly, bro, I'm not sure you deserve her, or my help."

My chin hits my chest as I let my head fall forward and exhale. "I know. I'm sorry. I've got excuses, but they're all bullshit. I should have listened to you, you were right, but I thought I knew better, I thought I was doing the right thing."

"Just because she's younger than you?"

"I'm old enough to be her dad," I cringe. "I'm in my forties, compared with her, I'm practically an old man. She's young, she's so damn innocent I feel like a fucking felon just thinking about the things I want to do to her, and more than that, I want to tie her to me. I want to take her home and keep her there, I want to put a baby in her belly, then another, then another until I'm shooting blanks and too fucking old to breed her anymore. I'm going to steal her future and I know I shouldn't, it's why I was willing to let her go, why I've stayed away until now. But apparently, I'm selfish enough to do it, to take her and keep her and own her. Because the moment I convince her to let me touch her she's going to belong to me and I'll never fucking let her go."

Cody's eyes go wide and he stares at me for a long, shocked second. "Well fuck."

"Yep," I laugh.

"You went caveman."

"I passed caveman two months ago. I'm nothing but hers now, her man, her Neanderthal, her fucked-up, too-old stalker. I'm a fucking train going at full speed toward the end of the track and complete annihilation and I don't care, it's her or oblivion."

"Jesus, Bay, maybe I will break out that whiskey. Is this what I have to look forward to? Losing my damn mind."

"I haven't exactly been comparing notes with the others, but if I had to guess, I'd say yes. When you find your woman, don't let her go. Don't ever fucking let her go, because this, it's fucking torture. So please, fucking help me, please."

Cody's brow furrows into a deep ridge and he steps over to me, throwing his arms around me and pulling me into a tight hug. "Of course I'll help."

I hug him back just as tight. I hadn't realized how much I'd missed him until now, but although I'm here for Missy, I need him to come home almost as much. Our family won't be complete again until we're all back in Montana where we're supposed to be.

"So, what do I do?" I ask as I release him and follow him back over to the couches again.

"Look, there's some stuff you need to know about her, but I'm not going to tell you. She's legit become my best friend and I won't betray her trust to give you insider knowledge. what I will tell you is that I've never met anyone who needs to be looked after more, but is so used to taking care of herself that she wears her strive for independence like a bulletproof vest."

"What the fuck do I do with that?" I ask him, exasperated.

"No fucking clue," he laughs. "When we got here, I rented this place and an office space. I helped her get set up with a bank account and I employed her. She's smart and worth every penny of the salary I pay her, but when she got her first paycheck, she insisted I take it back to cover the costs of everything I bought her when we got here. I've been secretly paying it back into her account in small amounts that I'm telling her are expenses, but she was adamant that we be equal, that she contribute and pay her own way."

"But you pay for the apartment, right?"

"Of course, but she thinks she's paying half the rent. She isn't, I pay four times what I told her it costs, but she pays me what she thinks is half each month and we take it in turns buying groceries. I would love for you to just scoop her up, put her on a plane and take her home so you can take care of her, but she isn't going to go for that."

"Do you think she'll come home with me eventually? You've got a nice view and all, but home is Montana."

"Eventually, yeah, maybe. Soon, hell no."

"Fuck," I growl, reaching up to tug at my hair. "Looks like I'm sleeping on the couch."

"There's a hotel—"

"Hell no," I snarl. "I'm not leaving, I'm going to be right here, all the fucking time. I'm going to be here when she wakes up, eat every meal with her, be the last person she sees before she goes to sleep. I'm going to do whatever the fuck it takes to make up for the damage I did when I let her get out of my truck that day, and then once she doesn't hate me, or whatever the fuck she feels for me now, I'm going to claim her as mine and fill her with a baby."

"Jesus, bro," Cody laughs, lifting his beer bottle up like a toast.

Tapping my bottle against his, I lean back against the cushions, watching the door for Missy to come back. It's time to start making my woman see that I might be an asshole, but I belong to her now, just like she belongs to me.

Chapter Twelve

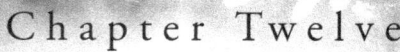

Glancing down at the laptop inside my purse, I close the door to my apartment behind me and rush toward the elevator, desperate to get away from my new home for the first time since we moved here.

Bay is here.

Bay is here!

In the three months that've passed since I climbed out of his truck, planning to get on a bus to my new future uncertain and alone, I thought I'd built up how beautiful he was in my head.

Cody is attractive and he definitely shares characteristics with his brother, but Bay is gorgeous. Since the moment I saw him, sprawled across the couch that's usually mine, my heart has been beating a staccato rhythm in my chest, and my vagina has been drooling in appreciation of the hot man in my seat.

His hair is slightly longer, a little rumpled and the stubble on his face and the bags beneath his eyes all suggest that he either had a rough trip to get here, or maybe there's something else going on that no one told Cody about.

Despite his slightly disheveled appearance, he's still hot as hell like he was the day I met him and he unceremoniously rejected me. I thought he was the most attractive man I'd ever seen then, but now, when his image has been plaguing my dreams for three months, he seems even more perfect. When he followed me into the kitchen, I was reminded just how big he is. His tall frame is built with broad shoulders and tightly muscled arms that make the memory of him picking me up and carrying me across his patio like I was weightless replay in my mind.

I only heard a moment of what he was saying when I walked back in.

"She's mine and I can't fucking live without her," he'd said, but surely that's not why he's here. He can't be talking about me, because that doesn't make any sense. He said I wasn't what he wanted; he was adamant that his feelings for me were a curse. So, it's ridiculous to think he's here for me.

I hope he's visiting to fix things with Cody. Since he told me why he and Bay weren't speaking I've been racked with guilt at being the cause—albeit unknowingly—of them falling out. Cody shouldn't have ever suggested that he wanted me in that way just to wind Bay up, but Bay rejected me, so what does it matter if I'm here with Cody?

Once I'm in the hallway outside our apartment, I pause,

unsure where I'm going to go. I don't have a car, or actually know how to drive, so wherever I'm going it's got to be somewhere I can walk to. Moving on autopilot, I get down onto the street and walk across the lot and toward the shops and bars that are still bustling with life. There's a coffee shop Cody and I sometimes use and I head toward it, flinching slightly at the shrill buzz the door makes when I step inside.

The comforting scent of rich, freshly brewed coffee surrounds me as I step inside and quickly order myself a cup, then retreat to a table pushed up against a wall in the corner, cradling the mug in my hands as my mind drifts back to Bay.

"Could he be here for me?" my inner voice asks.

A surge of hope barrels through me so fast I don't have time to shore myself against the onslaught of feelings just a hint of the thought provokes. It shouldn't matter to me. He rejected me, fought against his instincts—the same instincts that were strong enough to evoke kidnapping, forced pregnancy, stalking and so many more messed up scary, romantic things in his brothers.

I shouldn't give a fuck if he finally came for me, but the blood-filled traitor in my chest doesn't care and neither does the greedy, thirsty bitch between my legs. I'm wet and jittery and just too damn excited, and I have no idea what the hell I'm even supposed to do with that.

No one has wanted me since my parents died. My nana looked after me out of duty and familial obligation, but if there had been someone else offering to care for me, she'd have handed me over in a heartbeat. Ernie was only ever interested in my money. The boys at school just wanted to fuck me, mainly because I was still a virgin and became a challenge. My friends cared about me, but once their lives took them away to college, they moved on.

The only person who's cared about me, just for me, is Cody. He isn't hoping for romance or love, he didn't come after me to piss his brother off or use me. He just knew we were going to be important to each other and so he forced his way into my life.

"*She's mine and I can't fucking live without her.*" His voice rings through my ears and I mentally flinch.

He told me I was his back in Rockhead Point, but I never felt claimed or like it was anything more than words. Because while he was declaring his ownership in one breath, he was telling me he didn't want me with the other.

Am I okay with him changing his mind?

Honestly, I don't know. My brain isn't okay, not at all. The sensible part of me wants to kick him in the balls and tell him to fuck off. The rest of me wants to throw myself into his arms and belong to him, because I want to be his, to be owned, be claimed, be wanted more than I want my next breath.

I'm a virgin—practically a nun. Because my non-uncle refused to let me date in high school and then soured me on a physical relationship when he used the threat of rape and abuse as a way of keeping me in line.

But I want Bay. If I'm honest with myself, I have since he walked into the garage that morning and I first laid eyes on him. He's beautiful and he made my body heat up in a way I've never experienced before him. In a purely physical way, he's perfect, but if he's here for me, he's not going to accept me using him to experience sex with.

Panic makes my chest hitch up and down too fast. I'm out of my depth, Bay is an adult man in his forties, he could be into anything and I'm clueless. No wonder he didn't lay claim to me, who wants to end up with a frigid, inexperienced girl when they could have a mature woman capable of being everything he could want and need.

"But he's here," my pesky inner voice chimes in again.

My anger at his dismissal and rejection three months ago is almost overshadowed by my desire to be his. His sisters, the other women who have found themselves caught up in the Barnett legacy, or curse, seemed so sure, so confident in the love of their husbands. Until I met them, I'd never known people that secure, that proved that love like that can actually exist. The only marriages I've seen in real life have been those of my high school friends' parents, and all but one had been unhappy and ended in adultery, misery and ultimately divorce.

In the single day I spent with the Barnetts, it gave me hope, then shattered all of my dreams, and even though I'm battling with my excitement that he's here, I've been broken too many times before and I can't allow him to do it again.

My life is different now, I'm different than the girl he met and that's in no small part due to Cody and the new life he's been helping me build. I want Bay, there's no point denying it. He was right that back then, I'd have been needy and clingy, because I was such a mess. But not anymore. Now I have a job, I have my own money, I have a sense of self-worth that standing on my own two feet has allowed to build inside of me.

I might want to be Bay's, I might let him claim me—if he wants to because there's no point denying how he makes me feel—but I refuse to be that pathetic, clingy little girl. If I'm going to belong to him, it won't be because I need to be saved.

After an hour and two cups of coffee, I pull my jacket on, grab my purse and stand. Smiling at the barista behind the counter, I step through the door and out onto the sidewalk, hitch back my shoulders and head toward my home.

Since I left the apartment, the sun has drifted down beyond the horizon and stars have replaced it, filling the sky and twinkling majestically over the expanse of lake our apartment overlooks.

The neighborhood we live in is fairly safe, but I still feel that prickle of fear all women feel walking alone at night and I blow out a sigh of relief once I close the door to the building's lobby behind me.

I was woefully unprepared to see Bay earlier, but now I'm calmer, more composed and prepared to be around him and hear him out, if he wants to speak to me. Turning my key in the lock on our door, I push it open and step inside. Garlic, rich sweet potato and herbs scent the air and I breathe in and smile appreciatively. "Something smells good."

"I made pasta," Cody says from the couch where he and Bay are sitting, their postures relaxed.

"Awesome. Do you need me to make garlic bread?"

"Nope, already in the oven."

Nodding, I kick off my shoes, place my purse on the floor beneath the side table, drop my keys in the bowl, then grab three bottles of beer from the refrigerator. "How's your visit going? You guys all caught up?" I ask, trying to force nonchalance into my voice as I slide onto the couch beside Cody.

"Yeah, we're good," Cody says, glancing at Bay with a smirk.

"Missy, I was..." Bay swallows and inhales sharply, looking surprisingly nervous. "Could we maybe talk?"

"Sure," I shrug.

"Really?" He sounds so surprised I have to swallow back a smirk.

"I'll go check on dinner," Cody says, jumping up and darting into the kitchen like it's a mile away from us, not a few feet.

"How is everyone? Is Cora starting to show?" I ask, nervous and unsure if he's actually here for me, or if I'm way off the mark.

"They're fine, but I'm not here to talk about my family," Bay snaps.

"Okay." Lifting my beer to my lips, I take a drink.

"Cody lets you drink? You're not even fucking legal yet."

Arching my brow in horror, I lower my bottle down and stare at him. "I'm not a child Bay, I'm twenty. Cody doesn't let me do anything because he's my friend, not my keeper."

"I know," Bay sighs, scrubbing at his face with his palm. "Fuck, I'm fucking this up already."

"Why are you here, Bay?" I ask, unable to keep quiet and force him to lead the conversation like I'd planned.

"For you."

I wait for more, but he doesn't say anything else, just

stares at me with those expressive eyes and that perfect face. His hands are clenched tightly in his lap. Actually, his entire body is taut and tense.

"Why?"

"Because you're mine," he says simply.

"I was yours three months ago. You said it was a curse, you said you didn't want me, you rejected me." There's no point in sugarcoating it. I might want to throw myself into his lap and beg him to hold me, but I won't, and I need to understand why things have changed for him.

"I'm an asshole, babe, a fucking asshole and I'm so fucking sorry," he says, leaning forward, his body filling the space across the coffee table and making me feel penned in by his sheer size.

"I already told you, you have nothing to apologize for—"

"I have so much to apologize for it'll take me a lifetime to make it up to you." He interrupts me. "I was wrong, so fucking wrong."

"Why now? It's been months, so why now all of a sudden have you flown halfway across the country to apologize to me. It's not like we were in a relationship, it was a day." I'm being a bitch, but I can't stop because I'm hurt and even though I want him, it doesn't make his blatant rejection sting any less.

"I froze."

"What do you mean?"

"When I took you to the bus station. I knew it was wrong, I knew I wanted you to stay, but I froze and my arms and legs wouldn't move. It wasn't until you'd gotten out of the truck and gone, that I finally got my senses back and chased after you, but it was too late. You'd gotten on the bus and gone. I chased after you, followed the bus all the way to Bozeman, but then I lost you again. I thought you'd gone forever. Not going to lie, I was a mess. It took me a few days to come out of it, and by then you were with Cody, almost on the opposite coast."

"You came after me?" I ask on a shocked gasp.

He nods.

"Why?"

"Because you're mine, you belong to me, Missy, and I knew it then, but I freaked out and then it was too late and you were gone. I tried to stay away, for all the reasons I tried to let you go in the first place, but when it comes down to it, I can't just let you live your life without me, I can't pretend that you don't have me and that I don't want you."

A silent puff of air escapes my mouth and I stare in shock and awe-filled confusion. "I…" I swallow, clearing my throat. "What do you want from me, Bay? What are you hoping is going to come from you being here?"

"I want you to pack your stuff and come home with me. I want you to marry me and I want to spend the rest of our lives making up for missing out on these three months together."

"You want to marry me?" I splutter.

"Yes."

"We've never even kissed."

Like I've waved a red rag at a bull, Bay stands up, steps over the coffee table, curls his arms around my waist and lifts me from the couch like I weigh nothing at all. His arm slides under my butt, encouraging me to wrap my legs around him, while he curls his finger under my chin and lifts my mouth onto his waiting lips.

The kiss is like nothing I've ever experienced before. His tongue immediately takes control, sliding between my lips and forcing me to kiss him just the way he wants. The hand that had gently lifted my chin, slides down to wrap around my throat, his thumb softly caressing the pulse point that's thrumming erratically beneath his touch.

The arm supporting my weight is somehow squeezing my butt and I moan. I legit moan as my pussy heats and drools excitedly. Sexual desire stronger than any I've ever felt before consumes me and I grind my pelvis, begging for something, anything to take this to the next level.

The action must be instinctive, because this is as far as I've ever gotten with a guy and I'm clueless as to how things go from here. Obviously I've watched porn, I understand the logistics of sex and foreplay and all that stuff. But there's a hell of a difference between watching actors on a screen and experiencing it for yourself.

Before my eighteenth birthday, I'd begun to explore my body and even managed to get myself off a few times. But after Ernie pinned me to my bed, his hard cock pressing excitedly into my stomach as he threatened to hold me down and force his way into my body, my room and bed felt too tainted by him to be a space safe enough to explore what made me tick.

But right now, there's nothing but unexplored want and need and desire crashing through me. Bay lowers me down enough until his rock-hard cock is pressed against the needy place between my thighs and I let out another embarrassingly desperate groan.

"Put her down, Bay, dinner's ready and I don't want to watch a live sex show while I eat," Cody yells.

A masculine, annoyed grunt slips from Bay and I expect him to put me down, but instead he rolls his hips, holding me in place as his dick presses against me. "When I get you home, I'm going to keep you in our bed for a month. I'm going to have my dick inside you from the moment we wake up to the moment we go to sleep. I'm going to mold that tight pussy of yours to the shape of my cock and keep you so full of my cum that I'll have to plug you with my fingers to stop it from dripping out of you. I'm going to fuck your cunt, your mouth, your ass and your tits, and you're going to scream yourself hoarse when I make you come so hard over and over that you'll forgive me for being a stupid motherfucker who was willing to let the best thing that will ever happen to him walk away. I'm going to apologize with my mouth, fucking you with my tongue and fingers until you're so wet your thighs and the sheets will be soaked with your cream. Then I'll slide my dick into you again and make you come as many times as you want before I fill you up. I'll own your body, Missy, but you'll own my soul."

I'm struck dumb, my lips open on a gasp that might be shock or desire.

"Let's eat and then we can go to bed and I can start apologizing to you." His smile is all sin and any response I can think of dies on my lips, because really, what the hell do you even say to that?

Laughing, he releases my throat and pushes his hand

between my thighs, cupping my sopping core over my pants. "This is mine now. Nobody but me touches it. Not you, not a vibrator, nothing but me. You get me?"

I know my eyes must be painfully wide, but he doesn't back down at my shock, he just smiles. "This is what it is to be owned by a Barnett, my little Imp. I tried to let you run, I tried to stay away, but it didn't work and now you belong to me, heart, soul and cunt. Time to get used to it."

Not waiting for me to reply, he gives my sex a squeeze then reluctantly pulls his hand away and carries me over to the dining table. I wriggle to get free, but he just turns me and sits down with me in his lap, leaning down and whispering into my ear. "Better get used to this, babe, once we're home, you'll be eating with my dick inside one of your holes. Imagine how fucking hot it'd be to have dinner while my dick is buried in your ass, your tightness just keeping my cock warm while we eat. Then the moment we're done, I'll bend you over the table and fuck you until you scream."

A shudder rushes through me and I feel his soft, low chuckle vibrate beneath me.

"For fuck's sake, I'd forgotten what it was like to live surrounded by sex-crazed couples. Is that it? Are you together now?" Cody asks. "Got to say, I wasn't expecting it to happen so quickly, but I suppose Bay's got three months of caveman crazy stored up, so maybe I shouldn't be surprised."

"Yes," Bay says at the same time I say,

"No."

"Yes," Bay says again, the single word so gravelly and stern that he's practically warning me not to argue.

"Okay," Cody laughs, elongating the word. "I'm going to eat, then I think I'll head down to the bar and make myself scarce for a few hours while you figure that out."

"Thanks, bro," Bay says, lifting his fist up and pushing it across the table for Cody to bump.

Bay refuses to let me off his lap, and honestly, I only make a halfhearted effort to get free, before just settling back against him and eating. When he feels me relax, the arm that was banded around my waist loosens and after a while, his hand lowers until it slides between my legs, cupping my sex possessively. He doesn't try to touch me more, or arouse me, he just holds me, like he's laying claim and his touch is just to remind me.

A part of me knew I wasn't going to be able to fight him if he tried to claim me, but I'd expected my anger to last longer than the five minutes it had taken him to kiss me. As much as running and making him chase is appealing, letting myself indulge in him sounds better.

No one has ever spoken to me the way he did. I doubt the boys at my high school could even imagine all the things Bay just told me he wants to do to me and if they did, I imagine I'd have been appalled. But when Bay spoke about touching me, licking me, fucking me and owning *all* of me I wasn't horrified, I was excited.

The disgusting sexual things Ernie threatened me with, only repulsed and terrified me, they tainted all thoughts of me and sex. But the way Bay spoke and described all the things he wants to do, had me on the verge of an orgasm just from his words.

"Eat," Bay prompts, but I'm not hungry so I push my

plate away.

"Eat," he says again.

"I'm done."

Clearing his throat, Cody pushes his chair back from the table. "I think that's my cue to go get my bar on. You good with me leaving, Mis?"

I nod. "I'm fine," I assure him, and it's the truth, I feel perfectly safe with Bay, I always have, and that's another reason why his rejection was so hard to take, because for a very brief moment he became my safe harbor and then just as quick as I found him, I lost him again.

"Cool, call me if you need me," Cody says, ignoring Bay's angry glare and feral growl as he leans down and presses a kiss to my cheek. "Love you, Mis."

"Love you too," I tell him, watching my best friend grab his jacket and keys before he disappears out the door, leaving me and Bay all alone.

"I'm never not going to fucking hate that," Bay snarls.

"Get used to it," I snap, pushing up and trying to stand from his lap.

"Did you just tell me to get used to it?" he laughs, banding his arm around me tighter, refusing to let me leave.

"I'm not going to stop loving your brother just because you decided to pull your head out of your ass," I tell him matter of factly.

"I don't want to talk about my brother. I want to taste your sweet, wet pussy."

Inhaling a sharp gasp, I wiggle in his lap, my eyes widening when I feel the long, hard proof of his arousal beneath me.

"Bay," I whine, hating how needy I sound, but too far gone from his closeness and dirty words to fight it.

"You eat first, then after, I'll eat you," he orders, and it is an order, his tone not allowing any argument. Stabbing some pasta with his fork, he brings it to my mouth, holding it there until I part my lips and allow him to feed me. It's weird and not at all what I'd expect from this huge alpha male, but I chew and when I swallow, he brings the next piece to my lips, then the next until I put my hand on his arm, stopping him.

"Enough?"

I nod.

Holding me gently, he eats his own food, offering me a glass of wine I hadn't even noticed was on the table. Once we've both eaten and our glasses are empty, he shocks me, standing quickly, then flipping me around and up and over his shoulder, smacking my ass playfully as he starts to walk. "Time for dessert, babe."

"Bay," I gasp, then giggle as I bounce around, my head hanging down, my hair falling over my face. "Put me down, I'm going to be sick."

"Pick a number."

"What?"

"Pick a number."

"Three hundred," I gasp as he opens the door to my bedroom and carries me inside.

"Three hundred it is." Lowering me to the floor, he doesn't give me a moment to reacquaint myself with being the right way up before he grasps hold of the bottom of my shirt and lifts it up and over my head in one smooth pull. In quick, efficient movements, he removes my bra, then peels my jeans and panties down together, throwing them over his shoulder as his eyes ravage my nakedness.

"Fucking hell, Imp, you're perfect."

"Sex doesn't change things; I don't forgive you," I say, fighting the urge to cover myself with my hands.

"I don't forgive me either, but this isn't just sex and it will change things for us. Are you a virgin little Imp?"

Biting my lip, I nod.

"Good. Once your virgin blood is coating my dick, that's it, babe, I don't expect you to forgive me yet, but once I take you, there's no out, there's no changing your mind or wanting to be free, you'll be mine completely. But first, I'm going to taste you. You're going to come on my tongue, then on my fingers, then again while I lick your clit and finger your ass, then when you're so wet, I know I'll fit, I'm going to slide my big cock into your tiny, virgin cunt and fuck you like I own you, because I do."

"Bay." Shaking my head I make a sound of protest, but he ignores me, dropping to his knees and using his hands to spread my thighs wide enough for him to push his face into my sex. "Oh my god," I shriek as his hot tongue touches my core for the first time.

I'm naked and he's fully clothed on the floor with his face level with my vagina, licking and sucking on me like my sex is his favorite thing in the world. "Fuck, you taste delicious," he growls, turning his face and nipping at the skin on the top of my thigh.

Making a sound that I've never heard myself make before, my fingers find his hair as he continues to eat me.

His teeth scrape against my clit and I mewl as an orgasm so strong that my legs give way barrels through me, threatening to bring me to the floor. Except I never hit the ground, Bay catches me, lifting me up as he stands.

"That's one, babe, two more to go before I give you my dick. I'm going to need to stretch you out with my fingers so you can take me, my cock's big and you're small, but I can't fucking wait to watch your cunt swallow it until you're gaped wide, split in two and helpless to take whatever I give you."

My stomach clenches in anticipation at his words. "I want to see you," I gasp as he lays me down on the bed so my legs are hanging off the end, my butt perched on the edge of the mattress.

Lifting his eyes, his gaze locks with mine before he parts my legs, holding me open with his hands. "After I watch you come on my hand." Running a finger through my folds, he teases my sensitive clit before dipping lower and holding my pussy lips open so he can look at me. "I'm going to shave you so I can see this pink hole. I'm going to ruin you, babe, make it so your body craves me and your mind wants me and your heart needs me just to survive. You and your pussy are mine and I'm a possessive bastard."

My back arches off the bed as he pushes one finger into me, filling me and making me moan.

"So fucking tight. Do you have a vibrator? Have you fucked yourself with it?

"No," I shake my head.

"I'm going to get you one, then I'll make you fuck yourself with the toy while I watch. You'll slam it into your cunt over and over, but it'll never make you come because your pussy will only come for me. From now on, the only way you'll come will be when I make you." As he speaks, he slowly pumps his fingers in and out of me, adding a second, then a third until the sound of my arousal fills the air as he fucks me, doing something that makes a shard of bliss zoom up my spine every time he fills me.

"Oh god," I whine, lifting my butt up, searching for something, but I'm not sure what.

"I've got you, babe, let it go, come for me," he coaxes, and at the sound of his voice something unravels and tightens all at once. I come with a cry, but he doesn't stop, thrusting his fingers until I collapse down onto the bed, my breath ragged.

"No more," I rasp.

"Just one more, then I'll give you my dick," he purrs, dropping his head to lick at my clit.

At the first touch, I mewl, my clit sensitive, but he doesn't stop. His tongue flicks and licks and his teeth nip as he pulls his fingers from inside of me, leaving me feeling empty until something probes at my asshole, making my entire body tense.

"Relax, Imp, I'm just playing," Bay coaxes, using a gentle but constant pressure against my ass until I unclench enough for his finger to slide into me. "That's it, babe, I'm going to stretch this impossibly tight ass out until my dick can slide right in, but for now it's just my finger. I'm going to make it feel so good, you'll crave it."

His tongue doubles its efforts on my clit as he slowly fucks my ass. I should hate it, but I don't. The forbidden sensations only seem to heighten the bliss when his tongue flicks over my clit, teasing me until I'm panting and writhing beneath him, pushing my ass back onto his finger, urging him to fuck me harder, deeper, more. I come on a cry, squeezing my eyes tightly shut as my toes tingle and pulse, joy radiating upward until my whole body is jerking.

When the shudders and tremors subside, I blink my eyes open and find a shirtless Bay above me. One of his hands is stroking circles on my thigh, while the other is gripping his dick. His massive, *massive* dick.

Oh my god, his dick is huge. Too big. Porn big. There's no way that's going to fit and I'm not sure I want it to. Bay told me that after we had sex, my vagina would be molded to his shape, he hadn't mentioned that would mean it'd be stretched possibly beyond repair.

"No," I gasp, snapping my knees together.

"What's the matter?" Bay asks, pushing his huge hand between my thighs and forcing them open.

Jesus, his hands. I should have known how terrifying his dick was just from the size of his palms. This is why I need girlfriends, because they could have prepared me for a guy with a big dick, they could have warned me what to look out for—and avoid.

"That's not going in me. You'll split me in two, no, not happening."

Bay's laugh is low and rough, and my pussy that was terrified two seconds ago starts to drool in anticipation. "It'll fit, babe; I promise."

"No, you'll ruin my vagina," I gasp.

He climbs onto the bed, holding my thighs open as he

moves between them, his fingers sliding into my sex and pumping in and out. "Ruining you is exactly what I plan to do," he rasps, pulling his fingers free and immediately replacing them with the head of his dick, spearing me before I have a chance to protest again.

"Oww, fuck," I cry as a burning stretch scorches between my legs and he slowly fills me, backing off, only to push in a little deeper once more.

"This is going to hurt, babe, nothing I can do to stop it, but I'm going to do what I can to make you feel good. Next time, it'll blow your fucking mind. You ready?"

"Condom," I pant.

"Not happening," he smirks, pressing his lips to mine as he pushes forward and impales me fully on his enormous cock.

I scream into his mouth as pain, sudden and awful, rushes through me. It subsides quickly into a raw burn and an uncomfortable fullness. "Condom," I pant again, my voice ragged as he releases my lips.

"Never, I'm never putting anything between me and this cunt."

"Bay, I'm not on any birth control." Apparently, he doesn't see this as a big problem like I do, because instead of being worried, he smirks.

"Bay," I cry, wiggling beneath him and pushing at his chest in an attempt to get him to move and put on a condom. Smirking, he gathers my wrists together with frightening ease, pinning them to the bed above my head and holding them there with just one of his hands.

"I could get pregnant."

"I fucking hope so." He laughs, holding me still as he starts to move, slowly retreating, then sliding into me again, stretching me wider each time, making the burn change into a painful heat that hurts but in a nice way. My legs move on their own, curling around him and holding on, as he claims me in the most primeval way.

"Fuck, your cunt is strangling me, this is going to be quick, Imp, but it's going to be a rough night, because I'm already desperate to be in you again and I'm still balls fucking deep. I'm going to fuck you again and then again. Then I'll do my best to give you some time to recover."

His hand pushes between us and starts to rub at my clit as his thrusts become firmer, harder and faster. The pleasure his finger is creating is at odds with the burning in my core, but when I come, it's like the pain morphs with the bliss, pushing me into an odd orgasm that makes my head swim and a foggy haze fill my sight.

"Shit, fuck," Bay chants, slamming into me, groaning as he finds my lips and kisses me while his hips twitch and his shoulders tense beneath my hands. Ending our kiss, he moves his lips to my jaw, then my neck, peppering reverent kisses on my skin while his hand cups my cheek. "You're mine now, little Imp," he whispers against my ear. "Ruined and owned all in a single night. You should have run farther when you had the chance, because I'll never let you go again."

I don't speak, I'm not even sure I can. A part of me expects him to roll off me and go to sleep, but even in the brief time I've known Bay, I should have realized that wasn't what was going to happen.

Instead, he slowly slides his dick out, then stares down at where we were connected. "Fuck, Missy, your pussy's all swollen and pink. Your blood and my cum are all creamed together in your slit."

His words make me feel squirmy and wrong and I start to press my knees together, but his hands stop me.

"You're such a good girl for taking my dick, keep your legs open, I love seeing you like this, freshly fucked and full of what I've given you." His fingers stroke over my clit and then push inside of me, making me flinch. "I'll clean you up in a minute, but be my good girl and let me push all my cum back inside of you."

His praise makes the uncomfortable feeling from mere seconds ago dissolve and replaces it with a warm sensation that makes happy tears prickle at my eyes. I'm sure there's an expensive shrink somewhere who could analyze the shit out of how I'm feeling, but something about hearing him say good girl makes me want to throw myself into his chest and hug him.

He fingers me for a few more minutes, then shuffles down the bed and presses a kiss to my mound. "Stay here, I'll get a cloth."

"I can just have a shower."

"No," he says forcefully. "Let me take care of you."

He wants to take care of me. God, why does that sound so good? As I watch, he stands from the bed and pads over to the bathroom, returning a minute later with a washcloth in his hand.

"Spread your legs."

"Bay."

Climbing onto the bed, he ignores my attempt at a protest and pushes the washcloth between my thighs, forcing my legs open as he carefully wipes away the blood and arousal. The warmth of the water soothes my sore, pulsing vagina and once I'm clean, he wipes his dick, removing all the blood from his skin.

Standing, he drops the cloth in my hamper and scoops me off the bed, carrying me bridal style into the bathroom, where he deposits me beside the toilet. "Pee," he orders, then turns and walks back into the bedroom, not closing the door behind me.

A part of me thinks I should protest his order, but I remember reading that using the bathroom after sex prevents UTI's, so I sit and wince as the stream of pee starts. After I'm finished, I search the bathroom for my robe, or something to cover up with. Being naked felt okay when he was intent on making me come, but now it just feels awkward.

Anxiety and fear hit me all at once. I had sex with a guy I don't know. I gave my virginity to a man more than twice my age, who made all kinds of fucked-up promises that he obviously won't keep, and now I feel weird and self-conscious.

"What's the matter?" Bay asks.

Snapping my head up, I turn, realizing he's standing in the doorway, still unapologetically naked, his dick still kind of hard and pointed directly at me.

"I was just looking for my robe. Did you book into a hotel?"

"I'm not staying in a hotel, unless you don't want to stay here with my brother. There's a flight home tomorrow morning we could get, we could be home and in bed before dinner."

"Home?"

"Home. Montana, Rockhead Point."

I finally resolve that no matter how hard I look, there's nothing to wear in here, so I wrap my arms around my breasts and glare at Bay. "I live here, this is my home."

"Now, yeah. But we can't live in Vermont."

"You can't," I say. "But I can."

"What the fuck is happening right now?" Bay snaps, closing the distance between us and lifting me off the floor, supporting my weight with his hands under my butt. "We can't live in fucking Vermont, Missy. I have a business to run."

"Can you put me down, I can't have a conversation while you're holding me like this."

"No," he snarls. "Now what the fuck do you think happened tonight?"

"We had sex," I say, managing to swallow down the "duh" that's on the tip of my tongue.

"We didn't just have sex, Imp. I took your virginity. I told you the moment my dick was inside of you, you were mine. I told you that you'd belong to me, that I'm going to keep you full of my dick and my cum. A few minutes ago, I was wearing your virgin blood like a badge of fucking honor. You belong to me, Missy, we're going to go home, we're going to get married and we're going to live happily ever fucking after," he says angrily.

"Bay," I start.

"No. I know I fucked up. I know you don't forgive

me. I don't fucking forgive myself either, but you can hate me, you can be angry at me, you can scream and shout and punish me for as long as you need to. But you'll do all that with me, in our fucking home in Montana."

Shaking my head, I try to argue. Because I don't hate him, not really anyway. I'm angry at him, I'm hurt, but I don't need to punish him, that's not the type of person I am. But this is my new life, my fresh start, going back to Montana would be taking a step back and I've come too far to do that, even for the man who's holding me and looking at me like I'm his everything.

"I don't want to go back to Montana, Bay. I like it here. I like this apartment, I like my job, I like living with Cody."

"Cody can't stay here forever. For fuck's sake, this game is over, Missy. You ran, I chased. I caught you and now you're mine, let's go home." Bay sounds exasperated, a little confused and patronizing as hell.

He's still holding me, so I try to wriggle free, but he just tightens his hold. "I want to put some clothes on," I hiss.

"Not fucking happening."

"Fine. Here's the truth, Bay. This might have been a game for you but it wasn't for me. You told me you weren't interested and that was fine. I didn't pout or pine, I just carried on with my life and this is what happened. I moved to a place I like, with a person I love. I got a job, I got my own money, I got a fresh start. Just because you realized you made a mistake doesn't mean that I did. But now I think maybe my mistake is you being here and what we just did."

His eyes narrow and his jaw tenses. "Nothing about what just happened between us was a fucking mistake.

You want to stay here, fine, we'll fucking stay in fucking Vermont."

Kicking my legs, I try to get free again, but he just tightens his grip on the arm that's around me until he's holding me so tight I can barely breathe and then he slaps my ass. Hard.

"Aww, you motherfucker," I shriek.

He does it again, spanking my ass so hard the sound of his palm hitting my flesh seems to reverberate around the room. "Don't ever fucking say us being together is a mistake again. If you do, I swear to god, I'll take you over my knee and redden your ass until it's hot to the touch and you won't be able to sit comfortably for a month."

"You can't spank me, I'm not a fucking child."

"Oh, I'm more that aware you are all fucking woman. *My* woman, and I don't care how pissed at me you are, we are never a fucking mistake." He spanks me again, right over the spot he hit me the first time. "You get me?" he demands.

When I don't speak, he spanks me a fourth time. "You. Get. Me?"

"Yes, asshole. I. Get. You."

His lips find mine, kissing me punishingly hard. I wish I could say I hate it, but I don't. The brutal rawness of his touch reignites the heat in my core and I have to fight the urge to grind my sore pussy against him. I'm angry, but so is he and it shows in the way we attack each other's mouths, saying without words that this isn't over, that we haven't even started to forgive, or forget.

When the kiss ends, he rests his forehead against mine,

both of us panting and breathless. "I should have come the moment I realized you were here, I'm so fucking sorry. I'll make it up to you though, Mis. I'll make you so fucking happy."

He moves before I can formulate a response, pulling back the comforter and climbing into bed, still carrying me.

"I need to change the sheets, the blood."

"I'll do it in the morning," he rasps, lying down and cradling me to him. After a second, he lifts me onto his chest and slowly slides me down onto his hard dick.

"Bay," I gasp.

"I just want to be inside you."

His dick fills me completely and my muscles protest, still sore and swollen. After a second, when he doesn't move, I unclench and slowly start to relax. Running his fingers up and down my spine, he soothes until I melt into him, turning my face so I'm fully resting against his chest. It feels odd to be lying on him like this, but not exactly bad, just different. His skin is warm, and I don't hate the way it feels to be wrapped in his arms.

Tonight has been the strangest night of my entire life and lying here now, naked, de-virginized with a man who's told me he wants to marry me twice and with scarily honest sincerity, my mind is spinning as I try to process everything.

If my will was stronger and maybe if I wasn't so desperate to be close to him, I'd ask Bay to leave, or at least sleep on the couch or in Cody's room. But I don't want him to go. I like the way it feels to belong to him, even if it's too quick and too much and I should still be furious at the way he seems to think just because he's here, it means he can take over my life.

His dick is inside of me. Two hours ago, I'd never had an orgasm I hadn't given myself; I had a hymen and I'd never even seen a man naked in the flesh, especially not a man who looks like Bay. But here I am, ravaged and changed and falling asleep with a dick inside of me. I'm pretty sure most men would be seriously offended if a woman went to sleep while they were balls deep, but Bay isn't moving, he isn't attempting to turn this into anything more than this.

"Is it a serious faux-pas if I fall asleep?" I say with a yawn.

"No babe, go to sleep."

"Your dick is in me."

"It's staying in you, just sleep."

"I'm not going back to Montana," I tell him, needing to get the words out. "But I don't hate you. I don't forgive you and I'm angry with you, but I don't think I could ever hate you."

"We can talk about it tomorrow," Bay says softly, still running his hand up and down my spine comfortingly.

"Okay," I nod against his chest, allowing my eyes to fall closed.

***

I'm not sure how long I sleep, but I'm woken by the sensation of fingers moving between my thighs.

"Roll onto your stomach, Imp, I tried to let you sleep, but I need to fill you up again."

"Bay," I croak.

Strong hands lift me, positioning me on my stomach before lifting my ass up until my chest is on the mattress, but my knees are bent beneath me and my ass is in the air.

"My dick's still hard for you, babe. I'll be gentle, I promise. You just lie there and take it like a good girl."

Probing fingers push into me and I wince, but I can already feel wetness building between my legs as he slowly pumps in and out of me. A blunt head replaces his fingers as he slides his dick into me in one firm thrust, and I moan in pain.

"Such a good girl. Your cunt's all puffy and swollen and you still took my whole dick until your hole is stretched wide around me." Slowly moving, he slides almost all the way out, until only the broad head is filling my entrance, then he forcefully pushes back in and a dull thud of pleasure bursts to life in my stomach. Back and forth, he fills me, then withdraws, his fingers pulling my ass cheeks apart so he can watch the way he's fucking me.

"Jesus," he rasps. "Get your fingers on your clit, make yourself come."

Lost to the sensation, I push my hand beneath my stomach and start to rub at my clit while he fucks me. My orgasm comes almost too quickly, barreling through me and exploding like a fireworks display on the Fourth of July. I shudder and shake through my release and Bay starts to fuck me harder and faster, his hips slamming into my ass with each punishing thrust, until he comes, exploding inside of me, heating me from the inside out. His fingers grip me tightly as he holds himself deep for a few long moments, then he slowly relaxes and pulls his dick out.

My sex feels raw and abused and I wince, clenching my butt as my muscles burn and protest the rough treatment. I start to straighten my legs, but Bay grips my thigh, stopping me.

"No, don't move, I want to look at the mess I've made of your sweet cunt for a minute," Bay coos softly. "Go back to sleep if you want, I'll take care of you in a sec."

I don't sleep, how could I with my ass in the air, the feeling of his cum oozing out of me? But I do close my eyes, hiding myself from the embarrassing position I'm in and the way it feels to have his eyes on me.

"I wish you could see how fucking perfect you look," he whispers, running his fingers over my folds before pushing them inside of me, just like he did earlier after we'd had sex. When he's done, I feel the bed dip and a moment later a warm cloth wipes over me. The mattress moves again and Bay pulls me to his side, my back to his chest.

"Lift your leg," he coaxes, lifting my thigh and guiding me to rest my leg on top of his. A moment later I hiss, my eyes snapping open as his dick slides into my abused vagina again.

"No, no," I protest, attempting to get myself off his dick, but using his size against me, he keeps me pinned in place, one hand holding my leg, the other wrapped around my waist.

"I'm sorry you're sore, babe, if you want, we can take a bath and you can sleep while we soak, but I need to be inside of you. I went three months without you, I need this connection."

"It hurts," I wince.

"I know, but it's only because I couldn't hold back and I was too rough. I promise I won't move, not a fucking inch, but I need this."

"This isn't about you," I protest.

"I'm a selfish asshole, Missy, and even though you don't want it, even though it hurts, you're staying right here, your pussy full of my dick. I should be groveling and begging you, but you gave yourself to me tonight. I was deadly serious when I said you belong to me now and if you want to get any sleep tonight, this is the only way it's happening, with your cunt coated in my cum and stretched wide on my cock."

"You're a prick," I seethe.

"I know. Now go to sleep and in the morning, I'll take the best fucking care of you anyone ever has. I'll dote on you, look after you like the queen you are. I'll give you anything you ever ask for; I'll be your willing fucking slave. But at the moment, it comes to this." He cups my pussy, sliding a single finger into me alongside his dick. "This cunt is mine and I'll make you need me so much you'll beg me to do whatever the hell I want. I tried to stay away, I tried not to give in to this fucked-up animalistic need for you. But that's over now. You're mine and I'm yours, I still have no idea what that'll look like in the light of day, but now, in the dark of night, it looks like you accepting that my dick will be in you whenever and wherever and there's nothing you can do except learn to love it."

"Get your dick out of me and get the fuck out of my room," I cry, trying to free myself from his hold and failing miserably. He's so much bigger than me and with me impaled on his massive dick, and physically connected, it makes it impossible to get away.

Grabbing both of my hands in one of his, he shackles my

wrists together in his tight grip. "Calm down," he growls, pulling his finger from inside me and rubbing at my clit.

"No, stop touching me."

"No. You're going to come for me and then you're going to calm the fuck down," he threatens, circling, rubbing and pinching my clit.

I try to ignore the sensations, keeping myself taut, trying to tense away from the way he's pushed the hood of my clit all the way back from the small bundle of nerves and is forcing me to feel the way he knows exactly what to do to make me implode. When my body is forced to surrender, the release is all pain and anger and resentment and I hate it.

"Again," he orders, rubbing my clit until I come with a scream, my tense muscles dissolving against the onslaught of sensation. "Do you need another?" he threatens.

"No, you fucking asshole," I pant.

"Fine, then go to sleep, before I decide your asshole needs to be the hole keeping my dick warm and not your cunt."

"I hate you," I snarl.

"I hate me too," he sighs, relaxing his hold on me until I can breathe, but not loose enough for me to move away. "Sleep, babe. We can work this all out in the morning."

Arguing with Bay, two rounds of sex and more orgasms than I can count, all hit my body at once and a wave of exhaustion washes over me, dragging me down until my limbs feel too heavy to move. I'm not sure if I fall asleep or pass out, but after a while my vision darkens and everything goes black.

Chapter Thirteen

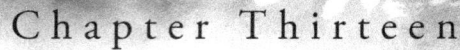
Bay

Until this moment I've never truly understood self-loathing. I get it now, because the way I've behaved tonight is more than reprehensible, it's fucking disgraceful. But the problem is, even though I know I'm being a douchebag of the highest order, I can't stop myself.

Stripping her naked, making her come and then sliding my dick into her virgin body was the most perfect experience of my entire fucking life. Nothing has ever felt as right, as complete as I felt when my cock was all the way in her and we connected in the most primal way. She's mine now, I feel it down to my very soul. She belongs to me, a part of me, a part of my soul, my heart and I'm hers just the same.

I tried to be gentle, but there's just no way to make your first time not hurt. I've got a big dick, it's not setting any records, but it's nine inches and girthy enough that I knew she was going to be sore. If I was a better man I'd leave her alone for a few days, but the moment I placed her down next to me on the bed, I knew I couldn't have her that close and not connected to me in a more intense way.

Laying her on top of me and filling her with my dick wasn't a conscious choice, but the moment her tight, swollen cunt smothered my length, I knew it was exactly what I needed. I wanted to fuck her again, but just being inside of her was enough to douse the urge to take her again. When she fell asleep on top of me, the fire that's been burning in my chest since I lost her settled enough that I could take my first full breath in months.

I wasn't expecting her to let me touch her tonight. I assumed I'd have to beg, grovel or do something crazy like kidnap her before she'd understand how much she truly was mine, but her body submitted to me so beautifully I thought she really understood how things were going to be.

Then she told me her life was here in fucking Vermont. But if keeping her means having an extended vacation from real life until I convince her to come home, so be it, I'm a persuasive man.

I try to let her sleep, but my dick refuses to go soft and after a while I know I just can't resist feeling her come on my length again. Even knowing she's sore, I work her pussy with my fingers until she wakes up, then I roll her to her belly and fuck her from behind, forcing my way into her swollen core and bathing it in my cum.

The moment she let me touch her tonight, I became the caveman monster I knew I'd become if I allowed myself to have her. This possessive, selfish need to possess her is bigger than my desire to coddle and care for her. Like I promised, in the light of day I'll be the sweetest, kindest slave she's ever seen. I'll do whatever she needs, give her the entire fucking world wrapped up in a bow if that's what she wants. But when it comes to sex, to this crazy, powerful, feral thing that seethes between us, I'm not sure I can control the beast she provokes in me.

I thought I sought out strong, independent women, because that's what I liked, but after one night with Missy, it's glaringly obvious that I only liked that because the woman wasn't her.

I don't want Missy to be strong or independent, I want her to be mine. I want to keep her chained to my bed, permanently dripping with my cum, like a pretty little slave.

What the fuck is wrong with me?

Already the thought of letting her get dressed and leave the bedroom in a few hours is making me want to barricade the door and invest in a private island where I can take her and never have to share her with the world ever again.

Objectively, I know the way my mind is working is beyond fucked up, and hopefully once we're home and married and my baby has taken root in her belly I'll calm down, but for right now I need my dick deep inside of her so I know she's still here and I'm not going to lose her again.

The reasonable, rational part of my brain that's still in there somewhere knows that this insane, over-the-top jealous possessiveness I'm feeling is just a serious reaction to knowing she's *my* woman and a serious overreaction to thinking she was gone and lost forever. But even though it's wrong, this feels so fucking right too.

I don't want to share her with this new life she's created for herself, and the fucked-up voice in my head is taunting me by reminding me that if I'd manned up enough to claim her the day I met her, I probably wouldn't have had to. If I'd claimed her when she was homeless, penniless and without any prospects I could have become the axis her world pivoted around. Now I'm going to have to forcefully claim a spot in her life, and knowing that only makes me feel more crazy and possessive.

Missy twitches in her sleep, trying to twist away, but her cunt is swaddling my dick and making it impossible for her to move away. My balls hurt because I've been hard for hours now, but honestly, I can't see my dick getting the message that we can't fuck her again for at least the next twenty-four hours.

Maybe I can convince her to go to a hotel with me, that way I could steal all of her clothes and keep her naked with constant, unfiltered access to her perfect fucking body. And she is perfect. She's gained weight since she left Rockhead Point and the hint of malnourishment, overly sharp cheekbones and shoulders are gone. Now she looks healthy, her skin glowing with vitality, her red hair shiny and as beautiful as I remember it.

I didn't get a chance to really appreciate her tonight. A part of me was worried she'd change her mind, so I got her naked and orgasming as fast as possible. Once she came the first time, I knew I had her, but at the back of my mind I wanted to make her mine and counting every one of her freckles with my tongue wasn't on the agenda. Tonight was about possession and making sure she understands how owned she is, that she belongs to me, just like I belong solely to her.

My dick pulses with the need to move, to drive deep into her and plant my seed in her womb. As good as it feels just to lie with her like this, I know that part of the reason I'm enjoying it is knowing that my dick is keeping all of the cum I poured into her tonight inside of her. I don't know her story yet, but the bits I do know show me that once she's pregnant with my baby, she won't leave. It's underhanded and manipulative as fuck, but breeding her will kill two birds with one stone. It'll tie her to me forever and fulfill this Neanderthal need I have to see her growing with my kid. I can already imagine how she'll look, her stomach swelling, her tits full of the milk she'll feed our baby.

All the reason's I gave myself why I couldn't keep her have gone out the window. I no longer care that I'm stealing her future, I don't care if I'm too old and I've been honest enough with myself to admit that I would love Missy to be as needy, clingy and dependent as possible. I'm all in. No, fuck that, I'm beyond all in. I'm at the point where getting her, breeding her and keeping her are my only priorities.

I've learned a few tricks from watching my brothers travel their own tangled paths to happily ever after. Huck messed with Cora's birth control and then fucked her until she got pregnant while she thought they were protected. Beau refused Bonnie an ounce of space, inserting himself into every aspect of her life until she stopped fighting and gave herself over to him. Granger took control of Alice and tricked her into marrying him less than a week after he met her. Penn stalked Lulu relentlessly, claiming her and her daughter the moment he set eyes on them and Teddy, well apparently my laid-back, youngest brother is a bit of a control freak and he took Juni and refused to let go until she submitted to him.

I'll do whatever it takes to make Missy mine in every way possible, and that might be starting with me mastering her body, but now my moral compass has flown out the window, I'm not above using every trick in the book to get her to come home and marry me.

It takes all my fucking willpower not to give in to the desire to roll her over and wake her up by fucking her sore, abused pussy to orgasm. But I won't. The sun is well and truly up, and even though my dick's rock hard again, now's the time to treat my Imp like a princess, not like a whore.

So instead of pushing my hand between her thighs and stroking her clit, I pepper kisses along her neck, caressing her nipples as she slowly starts to wake up. A soft smile spreads across her lips as she arches her back and pushes her breasts into my touch, her tight pink nipples pebbling in the cool air.

"Good morning, little Imp," I whisper against her cheek.

For a second her entire body goes rigid, tension trembling through her in palpable waves. "What's the matter?" I ask.

"Bay," she exhales as her muscles relax.

"Who the fuck else would it be?" I growl, instantly annoyed that there might have been someone else who could be naked in her bed.

"No one," she says quickly, twisting to move away from me and then grimacing. "How are you still hard? And why is your dick still in me?"

"I'm hard because I'm with you and my dick's been in you all night."

"You really are trying to ruin my pussy, aren't you?" she asks quietly.

"No, Imp, I'm not trying to ruin your pussy," I chuckle. "My dick fucking loved being in you all night though, I slept like a fucking baby knowing I was connected to you the whole time."

"That's weird. Is that something you usually do with your partners?"

"No," I snap quickly. "Never. In the past, I had fuck buddies, casual, nothing more. I've only ever done this with you, because I never cared about being close to anyone else the way I do with you."

"I need to pee, so…" she trails off, not wanting to tell me to get the fuck out of her.

Grunting a displeased sound, I pull back, sliding my dick out of her, not missing her grimace and wince of pain. Rolling to the edge of the bed, she cautiously stands and I watch as she searches the room for something. When she doesn't find it, she sighs, bends and grabs my shirt from the floor, pulling it over her head and covering herself from me before she slowly walks to the bathroom.

I wait until she's pulled the bathroom door closed before I let my smile free. Laughing at how tenderly she's walking will definitely not win me any points, so instead I pull on my jeans, not bothering to button them as I head out of her bedroom and into the living space.

Cody arches a brow at me from where he's sitting at the

dining table, papers spread out in front of him and a cup of coffee still steaming in his hand. "I take it she forgave you for being a dick?"

"We're working things out."

"Oh, I heard you working things out about three a.m.," he scowls.

A chuckle slips from my lips as I open the kitchen cupboards until I find the mugs and then pour two coffees from the pot. "How does she take her coffee?"

"Cream and sugar," Cody tells me.

I doctor her coffee how she likes it, then start to head back to the bedroom, pausing and turning back to Cody. "Is she supposed to be working today?"

"Yes, but as it's after two already, I assumed she was taking a personal day." He smirks. "Are we going home?"

Sighing, I shake my head. "She says her life is here and she's not moving."

Pursing his lips, Cody nods. "What are you going to do? Pretty sure the TSA will arrest you if you try to pull a caveman and carry her onto the plane over your shoulder."

"I'm going to beg Penn to cover for me at the garage until I convince her to come home with me."

"Jesus, I'm going to have to pay for soundproofing on this rental, aren't I?" Cody grimaces.

"Or noise-canceling headphones," I shrug. "I need to go take care of my girl."

When I walk back into the bedroom, Missy's sitting on the edge of the bed staring at the floor. Crouching down, I kneel at her feet and hand her the mug of coffee, sliding my free hand under her hair and onto her neck, stroking lightly.

"What's the matter?"

Bobbing her tongue out to lick her lips, her eyes lift to mine and I see a thousand emotions staring back at me. "This is a lot, Bay."

"It'll all be fine," I assure her, leaning down to kiss her, enjoying the way her lips immediately part, giving me access to her tongue and mouth. "How sore are you?"

Her cheeks flush a beautiful shade of pink and she clamps her legs together. "Very."

Smiling, I push my hands between her knees and slowly part her legs.

"Bay, no."

"I'm not going to fuck you. I just want to see," I coax, putting pressure on her knees until she huffs and stops fighting me, letting me spread her thighs wide until her cunt is on display.

"You're being weird, almost as weird as wanting to sleep with your dick in me. There's a name for that, by the way, I Googled it to see if it's a thing."

"Oh yeah?" I say, carefully parting her folds so I can stare down at how red and swollen her cunt is. She looks like she's been fucked raw all night and my dick twitches excitedly at the thought and the view.

"It's called swaddling, which is a really messed up name, because I thought that had something to do with babies," she babbles

"Huh, I didn't know that. I like seeing your pussy like this."

"What, destroyed? Because it hurts. I'm still pissed at you, by the way, all that shit you said to me in the night, that was messed up."

"Your pussy isn't destroyed, it's perfect, exactly how I want it to be. Puffy and freshly fucked. If you came home, we could be naked all the time, whenever you felt even the slightest bit horny I could have you full of my fat cock a moment later. We could fuck on every surface; do all the dirty things you've only ever dreamed about," I purr, leaning down so my face is only inches from her wet heat, blowing a stream of cool air across her heated flesh.

"I am home," she argues on a gasp, her fingers tangling in my hair. "And I'm off-limits until my vagina recovers, at least a week."

A full-blown belly laugh bursts out of me and I dip my head, pressing a kiss against her cunt and running my tongue softly around the edges of her entrance.

"Bay," she moans, pulling my hair tightly, then pushing my head down, silently asking me to stop, then begging me to keep going.

Reaching up, I push my palm against her stomach and apply some pressure, encouraging her to lie back as I slide my tongue into her cunt.

"Ow, ow, ow, ow," she whines, releasing her grip on my hair and literally slapping the heel of her hand against my forehead, shocking me enough that I pull back and glare up at her.

"What the fuck?" I exclaim.

"It hurts, asshole."

Feeling like a fucker, I curl my hand around her neck again. "I'm sorry, Imp. Did you take any painkillers yet?"

Shaking her head, she leans into my touch slightly and

I kiss her, pushing my tongue that still tastes like her, into her mouth, forcing her to taste herself on me. I reluctantly pull back and stand up. "I'll fill the tub and get you some Tylenol, babe."

She doesn't speak as I push up to my feet. Going into the bathroom I set the tub to fill, then search through her cabinets until I find a bottle of Tylenol. Tipping a couple into my hand, I grab a bottle of water from the refrigerator in the kitchen and then go back to her. Kneeling between her legs again, I hand her the pills, opening the bottle of water and then handing it to her too.

As I watch, she swallows the tablets, then looks at me, her eyes full of a thousand questions.

"Let's get you into the tub, soak that ruined cunt of yours," I chuckle.

"You're not going to try and put your dick in me again, are you?" Her voice is wary and I have to swallow back a laugh.

"No, babe, not right now."

"A week, I'm off-limits for a week. My clit has a pulse and my vagina feels broken."

"Never going to happen. You'll be begging to ride my cock in less than a day."

"I've managed to go almost twenty-one years without sex, I can manage another week," she scoffs sardonically.

"Want to bet?" I ask, taunting her a little as I scoop her up from the bed and carry her into the bathroom.

"It depends what the stakes are."

"Hmm," I say, pretending to think about it. "If you win, then I don't get to fuck you for a week."

"And if you win?" she asks.

"If I win, we get the next flight home."

"No," she answers, not even thinking before she adamantly refuses.

The tub is only half full, but I grab the hem of my shirt and peel it off her, leaving her naked and bare for my view. Pushing down my own jeans, I kick them out of the way and then scoop her off the ground, lifting her up and urging her to wrap her legs around my waist.

Like this, I'd only need to lower her a few inches and she'd be impaled on my cock again, but as much as I'd love to fill her with my cum, right now, taking her would most definitely be detrimental to my cause. Instead, I step into the tub, sitting us down as the water continues to fill around us.

"You want to lie on top of me, or sit in my lap?"

"I want to take a soak on my own," she says, pursing her lips.

"That wasn't one of the options."

"Has anyone ever told you you're bossy?" she asks as she pulls her legs from my waist and spins until her ass is in my lap, her legs tangled with mine.

"No," I answer honestly.

She scoffs and I wish I'd made her lie on my chest, because I can't see her face when her back is to me like this. "Why don't I believe you?"

"I'm not usually bossy, you bring it out in me."

I wait for her to barb something back at me, but instead she falls silent, the sound of the water rushing from the faucet deafening against our quiet.

"What changed, Bay? Three months ago, you were so

adamant that I was everything you didn't want. I know you said you chased after me at the bus station, but why? Why bother, when you openly told me I was a curse?" she asks, the honesty in her tone cutting me to the core. She's not asking, hoping for half-truths and compliments, she just doesn't understand and she needs me to explain.

"I'm forty-two, Missy. I'm not a kid who doesn't know what he wants out of life. I have a degree, a successful business, a great apartment, and an amazing family. I *wasn't* looking for a woman. I definitely wasn't looking for you."

Sucking in a sharp inhale of breath, the muscles in her shoulders tighten.

"I didn't realize I was set in my ways until I watched my brothers meet their women and fall in love. Each of them changed, evolved to make them a better fit for their person, and honestly it was fucking terrifying to see. It felt like in the blink of an eye we went from seven bachelors, living life like we were still teenagers, playing video games and comparing stories about hookups. To my brothers being partners and husbands and fathers. My sane, easygoing brothers went from normal, to losing their ever-loving minds, and I decided that I didn't want that. I didn't want some mythical woman to appear and steal away my life. I didn't want to be that mindless caveman, beating his chest, then throwing his woman over his shoulder and hauling her back to his cave.

"But then I walked into work that day and there you were. You were so young and so beautifully tragic. You were everything that scared the fuck out of me. You had that stuff with your uncle, you were sleeping in Alice's RV, you got fired from your job and you had all this drama happening with your life—"

"I never asked you to become my guardian, Bay." Her tone is snippy, but I don't acknowledge it.

"I know. But I saw you and everything I was terrified of becoming all surged up to the surface and I freaked the fuck out. All I could think was that if I allowed myself to act on what I was feeling, I'd steal your life from you. I wanted to take control, to take over and protect you, but I also didn't want that. I didn't want to be so consumed by you and I didn't know what the fuck to do."

"You never considered just talking to me about it?" she asks quietly.

"I thought I knew better. I thought I was doing what was best for both of us. Then I drove you to the bus station and you got out and I just froze. I had all these intentions. I had an envelope full of cash that I planned to give you so you'd have something to help you through the first couple of weeks. I had a full speech I'd prepared, telling you how I wanted you to be happy and strong and free. But when it came down to it, I choked. I couldn't fucking speak; I couldn't fucking move and I just watched you go." Pausing, I swallow down the gush of emotion that's making my throat feel thick. "I knew straight away that I was a fucking moron. I was out of the truck and chasing you within a few minutes, but... well, you know what happened after that. I was too late and then Cody found you."

I wait for her to say something, but her silence stretches until I'm filled with dread at how she's going to respond.

"That explains why you behaved the way you did, but

not what's different now."

"I realized I couldn't stand another day without you," I say simply. It's the truth, I tried, but my life is worth shit if she's not in it.

"Oh."

That single word is full of shock and disbelief.

"What do you like about me, Bay? We don't know each other. We spent a few hours together and then I left and now you're here and obviously sexually we work. But on a nonphysical level, we're strangers."

"We're not strangers, Imp, we're two sides of the same coin, different, but intrinsically connected, because alone we don't make sense, but together we're a perfect fit. I want to get to know you. I want to know everything about you, every thought, every dream, every nightmare. I want to recognize your moods just from a twitch of your lips, know how to make you feel better when you're sad. I want to bask in you when you're happy. I want to know you on every fucking level, right down to your soul that's interconnected with mine. Because although I've fucked this up, you belong to me, and I might have been stupid enough to let you walk away once, but I'll never let you go again."

Her sharp gasp of shock makes my dick twitch and my heart beat faster. That tiny sound could be joy, anger or pain but I don't know yet, because she's right, we are strangers. "From now on, we're in soul mate boot camp. We'll spend our daylight hours learning about each other. You're in charge of giving me a chance to get to know you."

"I have to work," she says, a defiant tone edging her words.

"That's okay, I'll come with you. I have nothing to do here, other than be with you. My world starts and ends with you. Sounds like fucking bliss. Then once the day shifts to night, I'm in control. Your body is mine and I'll teach you all the ways I can make you pant and scream and cry and come. You belong to me, and during the night, I'll claim you in any way I want until you truly understand how it feels to be owned."

This time instead of a shocked gasp, it's a barely audible moan that falls from her lips and I wish I could see the expression on her face. See if what I just said scares or excites her. My dick is like an iron rod, and I know she can feel it against her ass, but she doesn't rub against it like I want her to, she just sits still, too still, considering what I just suggested.

"So, I'd be in charge in the day and you at night?"

"Yes."

"What if in the day I want you to go away and let me work?"

"No. Wherever you are, that's where I am."

"I have a job."

"And I won't stop you doing it, but wherever you are, I am." I'm being unreasonable and we both know it, but I'm not sure I could let her out of my sight even if I wanted to. Maybe when she carries my name, my ring and my baby, I'll feel less concerned about her disappearing, but I doubt it. Granger and Alice spend all of their time together, or they did until they had Fox. Now Alice stays home with our other sisters and all the babies, we practically have our own day care center, considering how many kids my brothers have produced in the last couple of years. But I know both Granger and Alice hate being separated. Cody has already drawn up plans to build a workshop for him up at the house and Granger is looking for retail space in town so he can move from the space he currently has. They want to be together twenty-four seven, it works for them and there's no reason it can't work for me and Missy as well.

"What if this isn't what *I* want?" she asks, a little caustically.

"Tough."

"Excuse me?"

"You heard me. There isn't another option, babe, this is what's happening and if you try to fight me on this, I'm more than happy to take you somewhere you can't escape from until you realize that us, together, is your only option. If you really wanted to get away from me, you shouldn't have run with my brother. You put a trail of bread crumbs right to your door and I'm the big bad fucking wolf. This, us, is happening, so get on board."

"You're an asshole," she hisses, twisting around to glare at me.

"When it comes to you, yeah, I am. But I'm an asshole who will do whatever the fuck it takes to make you happy. I'll beg, I'll scrape and grovel at your feet. I'll spend the rest of our lives earning your forgiveness. The only thing I won't do. That I can't do, is let you go or give you up."

Her entire body is stiff, but she doesn't move, just sits in my lap, both of us ignoring my hard dick as she processes what I just told her.

"I'd have stayed, you know," she whispers, her voice

breaking the strained silence.

"What?"

"That day we met. If you'd have asked me to, I'd have stayed, or I would have right up until the point that I heard you tell your entire family that you didn't want me."

I cringe. "You heard?"

"Oh yeah, I heard you and Cody arguing after I went to bed. I heard what you said. You told him you didn't want someone you'd have to take care of. That you wanted a woman who didn't need you, who could look after themselves and just exist by your side."

Wincing, I sigh. "I'm sorry."

"What are you sorry for?" she asks, glancing over her shoulder at me. "You were being honest, that's not something you need to apologize for and you were right. That day we met, I did need someone to take care of me. I was lost and scared and alone, and back then if you'd have asked me to stay, I'd have said yes because I just wanted someone to take care of me. Things are different now. I don't need you. I have a job, an apartment, I take care of myself."

"I—" I start, but she ignores me and keeps talking.

"I don't need you, Bay."

I flinch, feeling like she just punched me.

"But I think that's good. I'd like us to have a chance to get to know each other and see if we can live up to the hype. You've built me up in your head into this exotic, mythical creature, but I'm not. I'm just a normal girl, taking charge of her life. When you rejected me, I branded you an asshole, a hot asshole, but an asshole all the same. So how 'bout this? We'll spend some time getting to know one another, but with the aim of actually seeing the real person. If at the end of a couple of weeks we still like the other person, we'll see how this goes. If not, you go home, back to your life, and I get on with my fresh start."

For a second, I consider arguing, but what would be the point? I might not be taking the exact route I planned to get her to agree to this, but who cares how I get there if the end result is the same? Missy and I will be spending twenty-four hours a day together, seven days a week. Soul mate boot camp, and as far as I'm concerned, there's only one possible outcome. Happily ever fucking after.

Chapter Fourteen

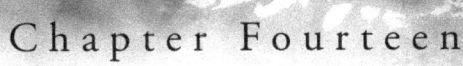

I shouldn't be agreeing to this. My body is aching and sore, my heart is hurting and I feel overwhelmed by all this need he's throwing at me. He rejected me before waltzing back into my world, barging his way into my life, consuming my body… and now he wants my mind, my thoughts and feelings too.

It's too much, and yet I just don't seem to be able to say no. Maybe it's because I've craved this. I've craved the insane, obsessive, possessive want, that Bonnie, Cora and the others described. I'm more than aware of my own desperate need to be wanted and Bay is offering me that, and I'm not strong enough, or emotionally mature enough to say no. Even though a part of me feels like this is all hurtling toward heartbreak and disaster.

The water is starting to cool, but if I get out, I'll have to look at him, I'll have to face him and then maybe he'll see that everything I just told him is utter bullshit. I don't need him, that part was true, but only on the most basic level. I have a job now. I can pay my bills. It'd be harder if I lived alone and it definitely wouldn't be in as nice a place as I live now, but I'd survive. But I do need him, so much more than I'm ready to admit.

I need someone to lean on, someone to share the burdens and hardships, but also the joy and happiness with. I need someone to laugh with, to laugh at, and someone who will laugh at me in turn. I need someone to curl up next to at night, someone to just be with in the quiet moments. I need him, and I think I've known that almost since the first second I met him, but that's not what he wants.

I heard him, I heard him be open and honest and brutal. He might think that's changed because I'm his one, or whatever, but fate can't change everything and if we're going to be together, we'll both have to adapt to be who the other actually needs.

Bay needs an adult woman with her shit together, and that's what I want to be too. I want to want Bay to be in my life, but not need him to be. He put me in charge of our days. He's asking me to show him how capable I am, to give us a chance to get to know each other in my world, not his, and I appreciate that. He said his mistake when we met was thinking he knew what was best for me, and him passing the reins to me is him showing me he can sit back and allow me to make decisions, and set a precedent about how we handle things going forward. He's showing me he can change, and I'm showing him I can do the same.

Bay wants to be in control of the nights. If last night taught me anything, it's that real-life sex is nothing like porn. I thought I had the gist of how things worked, but Bay took everything I was expecting and blew it up. Today I'm sore and aching, but I can still feel the shadow of the orgasms he gave me with every twinge of pain in my sex. He gave me more pleasure under his controlling hands than I ever thought was possible, and I'm happy to cede total control sexually to him, if he makes me feel as good as he did last night. I'm sure once I get the hang of things I'll be comfortable to take over, but for now, I'll happily call him sensei, or anything else he asks me to.

"Water's getting cold, babe, pass me your shampoo and I'll wash your hair," Bay says, pressing a soft kiss to my shoulder.

"Oh, I can do it."

"I know. I want to," he insists, bending me forward as he leans past me and grabs the bottles of shampoo and conditioner from the side of the tub.

Guiding me to slide down until my hair is in the water, he proceeds to wash and condition my hair, massaging my scalp with his fingers until I'm a boneless heap. Once he's done, he sets the tub to drain and turns the shower on instead, grabbing a cloth and rubbing soap into every inch of my skin. The care he takes with me makes my throat feel thick and I have to blink back tears. I've never been taken care of like this. Even as a child, as soon as I was capable of taking a shower and getting reasonably clean without soaking the bathroom, Nana left me to my own devices.

He washes himself quickly, then wraps me in a towel

and lifts me out of the tub, cradling me to his chest as he tips my chin up and kisses me slowly. "Thank you," he whispers against my lips.

"What for?"

"For this. For giving me a chance to make things right."

I nod, but don't say anything else. He kisses me again, before finally releasing me, wrapping the towel around me and taking my hand to lead me back into the bedroom.

"Did you have a bag?" I ask, glancing around and trying to remember if he had an overnight bag with him.

"It's out in the rental. I'll borrow something from Cody."

I nod. "What time is it?"

"Late, after two."

"What?" I shriek. "How can it be that late? I have to work."

"Calm down, Imp, Cody put you down for a personal day."

"I've only worked for him for three months, I haven't accrued any personal days," I cry, rushing over to my dresser, grabbing panties and a bra and wrestling them on. "Why didn't he wake me?"

"Probably because he heard us fucking all night," Bay snickers.

"This isn't funny, Bay; this is my job."

Striding over to me, Bay curls his arms around my waist, stopping me from the frantic way I'm trying to fasten my bra and untwist the straps. "Babe, I know it's not funny. But you work for my brother, he's not going to have a problem with you taking a personal day the day after we got together. I'd love for us to go get some breakfast together, but if you have stuff to do that can't wait until tomorrow, then you work and I'll cook."

Blinking up at him, I swallow down my surprise. I don't know why I thought he'd be an asshole about this, but I kind of thought he would be. "Oh, that would be great. Only our office doesn't have a kitchen, or at least not one you can make anything but coffee and microwave food in."

"Cody's working at the dining table, so unless you specifically need to go into the office, I can cook here."

I nod. "Okay."

Leaning down, he gently kisses me again, his tongue parting my lips and sliding into my mouth. He's leading this, but unlike last night, he's not forcing me to submit to him. The kiss is nice, but honestly, I kind of prefer him not giving me a choice, like he's too desperate to ask for permission. "Get dressed, babe, I'll go raid Cody's closet."

Releasing me, he turns and leaves, closing the door behind him with a quiet click. Exhaling, I stare at the closed door for a moment. It's been less than thirty minutes since I agreed to give us a chance to get to know each other, and I already feel overwhelmed by how different he is than I expected. Last night he was so forceful, so consuming, and this thoughtful, amenable side of him is a surprise. It's not an unpleasant one, but it's a surprise nevertheless.

Shaking myself free of my revelry, I grab a pair of jeans from my closet and pull them on, then find a plain white T-shirt and put that on. If I need to go into the office, I have a cute green blazer I can add over the top. Brushing out my wet hair, I pull it into a high ponytail and secure it with a band. I'll have to wash it again before I can wear it loose, but at least for now it'll be out of my face. Not bothering with makeup, I throw open my door and head out into the living room to face my best friend and boss's reaction to everything that's happened since I got home yesterday and found Bay sitting in my living room.

"Morning, Mis," Cody says with a smirk the moment I take a step into the living space.

"Morning."

"I'm actually impressed you can walk this morning, judging by how loud you were screaming last night when I got home, and again in the middle of the night. I figured you'd be bowlegged and limping," he says, chuckling.

"I hate you, Cody Barnett," I hiss, narrowing my eyes at him as I walk—admittedly a little carefully—over to the dining table where he has his laptop and several papers surrounding him.

"No, you don't, you love me, Missy McCormick."

"Did you get the tender papers back from the board?" I ask, bypassing a chair to grab my laptop from my purse by the door.

We start to talk about work as the front door opens and Bay—dressed in Cody's sweatpants and shirt, both of which are a little tight—walks back into the apartment carrying a leather duffel. Bay's eyes find me and he smiles, closing the door and coming straight to me. Tilting my chin back, he presses a scorching kiss to my lips before he heads back into my room.

"So, you guys made up?" Cody asks, his lips twitching.

"We're going to spend some time getting to know each other," I tell him, clearing my throat as I click into my email and immediately start reading the most recent.

"Considering the noises coming from your room last night, I'd guess you're already pretty well acquainted," he scoffs.

Rolling my eyes, I ignore him as he quietly snickers to himself. After a couple of minutes, my bedroom door reopens again and Bay emerges dressed in jeans that cling to his thick thighs and a shirt that's stretched around his biceps in the most delicious way. His hair is still damp, the sides short with a little length on top that's rumpled and messy. He hasn't bothered to shave, so his cheeks are coated in stubble and my breath hitches in my chest as he pads barefoot into the living room.

"Cody, you eaten, bro?"

"You cooking? I could eat."

"Thought I'd make waffles if you have a waffle iron. Missy, babe, you eat waffles?"

I nod. "Waffles would be great."

Heading into the kitchen, he starts to open the cabinets, pulling things out and getting to work mixing batter and heating the waffle iron on the cooktop. I try to concentrate on work, but I can't seem to tear my eyes away from him and the way his shirt bunches as he reaches for things from the top shelf, or how his butt looks in his jeans as he bends to get eggs from the refrigerator.

I think I'm being pretty stealthy, until he turns and winks at me. My cheeks blush red and hot, and I force myself back to my laptop and responding to emails as he softly chuckles.

"How are things going out here anyway?" Bay asks Cody. "Conquered the Vermont construction scene yet?"

"Working on it," Cody says, flipping Bay the bird without even looking up from his screen.

Bay chuckles and the sound of hissing batter as it hits the waffle iron fills the air, along with the deliciously familiar scent. "Seriously though, how are things going?"

Cody stops typing and turns to look at his brother. "Things are going good. Mis and I have recruited a great crew and we've picked up a few jobs already, but I'm mainly trying to get the contract for some regeneration work that the city has funding for."

"Do you know any of the other companies that are vying for the contract?"

"A couple are my direct competition. They were all surprised to see my name on the tender list, they're not used to me beating their asses for work outside of Montana, so we're going in supercompetitive on a few smaller jobs, hoping to land the whale."

"That's great, man, I'm proud of you. Both of you," Bay says, catching my eye and blowing me a kiss.

I feel my cheeks heat and turn my attention to my inbox again, studiously reading the same email I've read twice already. A few moments later a plate with a steaming, perfectly cooked waffle lands beside my laptop on the table.

"Eat," Bay says, running his knuckle over my cheek, before heading back into the kitchen and returning with bowls of berries, sliced banana and chopped nuts, and a bottle of maple syrup.

"Nice," Cody hums appreciatively, closing the lid on his laptop and pushing it to the side.

The chair beside me pulls out and Bay slides into it,

grabbing the leg of my chair and dragging it closer to his, then laying his hand on my thigh as he drowns his waffles and bananas in syrup. "You need anything else, babe?" he whispers against my ear, his fingers curving around the back of my neck and making goose bumps prickle along my skin.

"No thank you, this is great," I say, sounding breathy and all sorts of wanton.

"Jesus, I forgot what it's like to live in a lovefest. Keep it PG, kids," Cody laughs, pointing his fork at us, and waving it from side to side.

"Fuck you, dude, you've had my girl for three months, you're lucky you're even getting our company at all today and I'm not keeping her in bed."

"I kind of want my woman to show up just so I'm not the odd fucking man out. I don't even remember the last time I got my dick wet."

"Cody," I gasp. "I don't want to know about your dick."

"You sure? There's still time for you to choose the better-looking brother." Cody purses his lips together and pouts, fluttering his eyelashes dramatically.

I barely see him move, but Bay stands, leans across the table and cuffs Cody around the head so quickly it's like someone put him in fast-forward.

"Mine," Bay growls, lifting me out of my chair and sitting back down in his seat with me in his lap, his arm banded around my waist so tightly I can barely breathe.

"Whoa, calm down, Hulk, I was only kidding. I know she's yours," Cody says, his hands raised in surrender.

"Good, don't fucking forget it." Bay's grip tightens a little more, and I push my fingers between my stomach and his arm. "Sorry, babe," he says when he notices me trying to free myself from his iron grip and immediately loosens his hold a little.

"Can I go finish my waffle now?"

Instead of answering, he just pulls my plate across the table until it's in front of me, then presses a kiss to my shoulder as he glares at his brother on the other side of the table.

"So, when do you guys go home?" Cody asks.

"What do you mean?" I swallow down my bite of food and furrow my brow.

"When are you going back to Rockhead Point?"

"I'm not going back to Montana."

Cody looks at me, then toward Bay. "I don't understand."

"We live here, Cody. I know eventually you'll have to go home, but when that happens, I'll just find a new apartment."

"But..." Cody trails off, looking to Bay as if he expects him to explain.

Clearing his throat, Bay tenses beneath me. "I'm staying here."

Cody's mouth falls open. "I—"

Bay interrupts him before he can speak. "Wherever she is, that's where I'm going to be."

"But—" Cody starts.

"But nothing. I fucked this up. I let her leave, so if this is where she wants to be, that's where we'll be."

Cody looks shell-shocked and a little sad... that's odd, why would he be sad?

"You don't have to stay," I whisper, turning to look at

Bay, his beautiful face so close to mine.

"Yes, I do. Where else would I go when my heart is here with you?"

I melt, literally melt and before I even realize I'm doing it, I press my lips against his, taking the lead and kissing him for the very first time. He lets me control the kiss for a few seconds, then his fingers tangle in my ponytail and he pulls, tilting my head exactly where he wants it, as he deepens the kiss, pushing his tongue between my lips and claiming my mouth in a way that makes my panties dampen, despite the ache in my core.

After we've all finished eating, Bay places me back on my own chair and cleans up, loading the dishwasher and washing down the countertops. When he's done, he grabs his cell phone and sits back down in the chair beside me.

For a while I lose myself in work, answering emails, phoning suppliers and sending out introduction emails to the list of contacts Cody hopes to befriend in the state. The whole time, Bay sits beside me, occasionally touching my leg, or arm, feeding me bottles of water and coffee and generally being lovely. We've barely spoken two words to each other since we stopped eating, but his presence is nice.

Once I've completed all of my tasks, I sit back in my chair and exhale slowly. "Right, what's next?" I ask Cody.

"Have you responded to that email from Lester Harris about the zoning?"

"Yep."

"Can you email an intro to The Holdsome Group?"

"Already done."

"Myra asked about social security details for Costas,

the new carpenter—"

"I sent it over to her yesterday."

Chuckling softly, Cody lifts his attention from his laptop and smiles at me. "Then you're done, Mis. Why don't you let my brother take you out? You can show him around town."

"Oh," I say, trying to think of an excuse, and then trying to think of a reason why I need to think of an excuse.

"Perfect," Bay claps, standing up and then lifting me up from my chair. "Grab some shoes, babe."

I move because he told me to, and can't think of a single reason why not. Sliding my feet into some ballet flats, I grab my blazer and purse and then turn to find Bay holding out his hand for me to take.

This should be easy, right? Just slide my hand into his. It certainly isn't the most intimate thing we've done, not even close. But something about taking his hand makes this real. I must pause for too long, because Bay reaches out, entwining our fingers without offering me another choice. Perhaps I should be bothered by that, but I'm not. In fact, I kind of love that he took the choice away from me.

His hand is huge and mine looks tiny in comparison, but he's gentle as he leads me from my apartment and out into the hall.

"Where do you want to go?" he asks as we step into the elevator.

"It's pretty downtown if you want to explore a little."

"Sure." He holds the building door open for me, then releases my hand and immediately drapes an arm across my shoulders, pulling me into his side as we walk across the parking lot and toward the hustle and bustle of town.

"Is there anything specific you want to see?" I ask, unsure where to go or how to behave now it's just the two of us.

"You're in charge, babe, remember?"

Oh shoot, that's what we agreed, isn't it? I'm in charge of giving us a chance to get to know each other better. Right now, I just wish he'd take over and bulldoze me the way he did my body last night. How is it possible that giving my virginity to a virtual stranger felt less awkward than walking and chatting does?

"Church Street Marketplace has lots of nice shops and restaurants, we could head that way," I suggest, plucking the first thing that comes to mind.

"Sounds good." Bay says placidly.

After a few minutes of weird, stilted silence, I stop walking. Bay stops, and looks down at me curiously. "What's up?"

"This is weird," I announce loudly, cringing at the whiny quality of my voice.

Bay chuckles. "This is all you, babe, being with you doesn't feel weird to me. Unless you call having a hard-on that's lasted about twenty hours weird." Reaching down, he adjusts his pants and I can't help but let my gaze fall to his cock. "My eyes are up here, Imp, I'm not a piece of meat."

His voice is so faux outraged that I burst out laughing. "Why is this hard?"

"What, my dick?"

"What? No," I splutter, but now Bay's the one to laugh, smirking playfully at me.

"Babe, you're overthinking this. We're just taking a walk, no pressure. We don't have to figure it all out today. This is only day one of soul mate boot camp, we have plenty of time,"

I feel all the air exhale out of me in a huff of relieved breath. How does he have the ability to affect me like this, to calm me with just a few words?

"Come here," he prompts.

Inhaling, I turn and close the distance between us, until our toes are practically touching and my chin is tipped back so I can look up at him.

"We've got this." His head dips down and his lips find mine. He doesn't kiss me like I wish he would, like I belong to him. Instead, this kiss is all comfort. He's reassuring me, promising me with just the press of his lips. He's telling me I'm his, but reminding me that this is my rodeo right now. When he pulls back, I drag in a deep breath, then let it out slowly. "Let's go and mooch."

"What the hell is mooching?" he laughs.

"It's something my nana used to say, it just means wandering around with no real purpose."

"Mooch. I love it. Let's go mooch."

We spend the rest of the afternoon wandering around the marketplace. Bay buys some clothes as he only brought a small overnight bag with him. He drags me into a bakery and buys a dozen freshly made cider donuts, which we eat with takeaway coffees as we watch a terrible street performer attempt to levitate. After we're bored of the bustle, we walk down to the lake, following the path that skirts the shoreline. Then, when the sun goes down, we find a restaurant and eat overlooking the water at an outside table, beneath the warmth of a patio heater.

"So, what do you think of Burlington?"

"It's pretty, I love being this close to the water," Bay says, perusing his menu.

"I know, there's something very soothing about it, isn't there?" Taking a sip of my soda, I turn and stare out at the still, inky-black water.

"Tell me about your parents? I know they passed while you were a baby, but did your grandmother tell you about them?"

Sighing, I place my glass back down on the table. "I don't really know much, to be honest. Nana was my mom's mom, but she wasn't the type of person who spent time reminiscing. She took care of me because it was the right thing to do, but I never got the feeling they were particularly close before my mom died."

"What about your dad?"

"Nana said she didn't know him. They were meeting for the first or maybe second time the day he died. Cody found some stuff out about him though."

"He did?" Bay asks, his tone a little accusatory.

"Yeah, turns out he had a wife that I'm betting my mom didn't know about," I laugh self-deprecatingly. "But like I said, Nana wasn't one for living in the past."

"Do you look like your mom?"

I shrug. "I'm not really sure. When Nana died, Ernie went through her stuff and donated most of it. I don't remember there being photos. The house I grew up in was a furnished rental, and there weren't pictures out, or on the walls. To be honest, the only stuff we took when we moved in with Ernie was our clothes. Nana had a crucifix, although I'm not really sure why, she never went to church. Wow, that's weird, right? I never really thought about it until now."

"I guess some people just aren't sentimental," Bay says, but I can tell he's trying to make me feel better.

"Your family is close though, I bet you've got hundreds of photos."

Sighing, he nods. "Mama was a nightmare; we have albums and albums of all the embarrassing shit we did over the years."

I smile, thinking of a beautiful woman forcing Bay and all his brothers to dress up and pose for pictures. A wistfulness settles over me and I know that my smile has turned brittle, but I'm not sure how to stop it. I'll bet Bay had an idyllic childhood. He had parents that loved him and six brothers who were so important to him that even now, decades later, they all still choose to live together because they want to be a part of each other's lives in a way I don't think I'll ever fully understand.

"Come here, babe," he croons, scooping me off my seat and into his lap. Curling one of his arms around my waist, he settles me with my back to his chest, his chin resting on my shoulder as he holds his cell phone out in front of us and takes a picture. "We'll make memories and we'll cherish them so our kids can see exactly who their parents are and know how much we love each other."

I don't tell him I don't love him, or that he doesn't love me. It's far too early for declarations, but I don't care. I don't tell him I'm not sure I want children, or that I'm far too young to even think about it. Instead, I turn and bury my face against his neck, incapable of telling him how much his words hit home to me, how much I want that, to leave a legacy of memories so when I'm gone, I don't disappear, never to be spoken about, or remembered.

"It's okay, Imp, I've got you," he coos, running a soothing hand down my hair and gripping the back of my neck in a reassuring hold, one that keeps me in place and comforts me at the same time.

I'm not sure how long we sit together, me on his lap, him holding me like he can't bear to let me go. To the other people in the restaurant, we must look insane, but neither of us cares. Bay put me in charge of us getting to know each other, but just by being here, by listening and understanding, he's broken down almost all of my walls in one afternoon. I don't know him any better on a personal level, but my soul recognizes his, my heart beats in time with his and my brain realizes that I don't want to fight this anymore. I'm not sure I ever really wanted to.

"You ready to go?" he whispers against my cheek.

"Yeah," I agree, reluctantly prying myself from his chest and moving back to my own chair.

Bay pays the check quickly, then curls his arm tightly around me as we walk back to my apartment. It's empty when we get inside, but there's a note on the coffee table from Cody, telling us he's going to find someone to entertain him for the night because Amazon can't deliver any noise-canceling headphones until tomorrow.

Chuckling, Bay crumples the note into a ball, turns the lock on the front door and then spins to face me, his eyes wild with a feral gleam. "Sun's gone down, babe."

"Bay."

"I'm in charge, Imp, now come here."

Swallowing, I don't move, taking a moment to see how I feel about his demanding order... and it is an order.

"Missy." The stern hiss as he says my name has my feet moving without permission, but I wouldn't try to stop this even if my brain was in charge right now.

Apparently, I enjoy being ordered about, because my nipples have pebbled beneath my shirt and there's a hot pulsing between my legs that has me all kinds of excited to see what he's going to do or say next.

"Beautiful," Bay murmurs, hooking his finger under my chin and tilting my head up so I'm forced to look at him. "I don't deserve a gift like you, but I'm going to enjoy unwrapping you anyway. Then I'm going to set you on the dining table and I'm going to eat you like the starving man that I am."

I shudder, a visible tremor rushing across my skin, leaving pleasure in its wake.

"So needy," Bay chuckles softly, sliding my blazer off my shoulders and letting it fall down my arms to the floor. Peeling my shirt up, he discards it, then unfastens my bra and frees my breasts.

"I can't wait to see these fill with milk, watch your belly swell with my kid," he whispers, leaning down and pulling my nipple into his mouth. He bites down on the tip until I suck in a breath and push up onto my tiptoes, unsure if I should arch into or pull away from his delicious touch.

His fingers work the buttons on my jeans, unfastening

them and pushing the fabric over my hips. Releasing my nipple with a pop, he crouches down and pulls my shoes off, then drags my jeans down my legs.

"Look at me," he orders, and I look down and find him on the floor at my feet, his huge fingers curled into the waistband of my panties. As soon as he knows I'm watching, he slowly drags the fabric off, revealing my pussy to him, one inch at a time.

His eyes still on me, he leans forward and presses his nose to my mound, inhaling deeply. "You smell like sin, little Imp. You smell like you're mine."

A whimper falls from my lips and he smiles. "I don't think I want you to wear panties anymore. I want to be able to smell you, smell when your little pussy creams, all eager and desperate for me."

Holding me steady, he pulls my panties off my feet, lifting them to his nose and inhaling deeply, before tucking them into the back pocket of his jeans.

"Spread your legs for me, I want to see my pussy."

His pussy. God, that shouldn't be sexy, but it is, and I can't help doing exactly what he wants, parting my legs and revealing my wet core to him.

"Look at all this cream, little Imp. Is this all for me? Is your little cunt ready for me again?"

I swallow back a stifled moan, embarrassed that he can see how wet I am.

"Answer me, Missy, is all this cream for me?"

I nod, unable to physically say the words.

"Good girl. Do you want me to taste you, or do you want my fingers?"

I am not experienced enough to talk dirty. Yesterday, I was a virgin and, now, he expects me to be a seductress. No, not happening.

"Tell me. Last night when I touched you and licked you, which did you like better?"

"I can't," I whisper, closing my eyes in embarrassment.

"Don't be embarrassed, babe, I want you to be able to tell me what you want. You won't always get it, but I'll always want to know."

"I..." I try.

"Did you like it when I licked you? When I pushed my tongue into your cunt?"

I nod.

"Use your words."

"Yes," I force out.

"Good girl."

The praise heats me from the inside out and I roll my neck, pushing my breasts out and arching my back.

"What about when I pushed my fingers inside you and fucked you with them? Did you like that?"

"Yes," I pant, the word more of a mewl.

"Perfect. Now tell me if you want my fingers or my tongue?" he asks, barely an inch from my sex.

"Fingers," I cry, spreading my legs a little wider, silently begging him to touch me.

"You're such a good girl," he coos, standing up and lifting me onto the dining table. Pushing me so I'm lying back, resting on my elbows, he lifts my knees and urges me to prop my heels onto the table, exposing me to him.

"Bay?" I say, suddenly feeling vulnerable.

"Beautiful." He smiles right before he slides his finger into me all the way to the knuckle.

My sex clamps down on him and I feel a twinge of pain. I'm still sore, but not enough to make me want to stop him. In fact, the hint of pain only increases the hot, itchy pleasure that follows as he starts to pump his finger in and out.

"Look at this pretty cunt sucking my finger in deep," he coos, adding a second finger, but keeping his thrusts slow and deep. "Does it hurt, babe? Your hole's still a little puffy and swollen from when I took you last night. Tell me if it's too much and I'll fuck you with my tongue instead."

"No," I gasp. "No, no, no, don't stop," I beg.

His soft laugh ricochets through me, and I moan just as he adds a third finger, stretching me wide as his thrusts become rougher and faster. "Jesus, Imp," he groans. "I want you to come around my fingers, then my dick needs to be in you."

His thumb finds my clit and I barely last a second as he rubs and thrusts until I come. Lifting my butt off the wooden table, I grind my hips and push myself deeper onto his fingers as I ride out the wave of my orgasm.

"Fuck, your pussy got so tight, I can feel your muscles pulsing around my fingers." Pulling out of me, he rips his shirt over his head, shucking his jeans and boxers as he grabs my thighs and shoves his rock-hard, thick cock into me in one movement.

I scream as he impales me, his dick forced all the way to the base without even a hint of remorse, until I'm completely impaled, panting and gasping through the shock and pain and delight.

"Shhh, good girl, such a good girl. You look so fucking sexy, your cunt gaped wide on my cock. Shhh," he coos, his eyes fixed on where we're connected.

"It hurts," I hiss.

"I won't move, it'll be okay in a minute, your body just needs to remember that you're made for me, that I'm the perfect fit for this tight cunt."

Finding my clit with his thumb again, he stays buried deep inside of me, not moving while he rubs soft circles over my sensitive clit. After a second, I feel myself relax and the pain fades.

"That's it, babe." His voice is gravelly, forced from his lips as slowly, so incredibly slowly, he starts to move. Grinding in shallow thrusts, he pulls back a fraction then inches back into me, his thumb rubbing at my clit the whole time. There's a dull soreness, but as he fills me each time, there's a spark of something that feels odd. Not bad, but not the type of feeling I normally associate with pleasure. When he's made me come before with his fingers or tongue, the pleasure starts off nice, swelling into bliss, but this is different; more.

The way he's rubbing at my clit is familiar, but the faster and deeper he fucks me, the more the strange twinging sensation grows each time he bottoms out inside of me. His palms hold my legs wide and we're both watching the way his dick is sliding in and out of me, my body accepting his, made for him, just like he told me it was.

"Good girl, you're such a good girl, taking my dick so fucking well. Your cunt is so fucking tight, but it knows who it belongs to, opening for me to fill you up with my cum."

"Oh god, we need a condom, we forgot," I gasp, my eyes snapping open when I hadn't even realized I'd let them fall closed.

"I didn't forget," Bay snarls, gripping my thighs tightly, thrusting harder as he angles his thumb to slide over my clit with every slide of his cock.

"Bay, I'm not on the pill."

"Good, you wouldn't be taking it anyway. I already told you I'm going to put my baby in your belly, breed you until you swell and grow with my kid." Each word is punctuated with a hard thrust, making sparks burst to life deep inside my core, igniting and sizzling, building and building, threatening to implode.

"Bay," I cry, the sound strangled and desperate.

"My woman, my little breeder. Come for me, little Imp, come for me, I want to hear you scream."

I honestly don't know what he does next, but it feels like he's everywhere. His mouth on my nipple, his fingers on my clit, his dick in my pussy. Sparks flash and burn, lighting up every nerve ending until I'm just light and flame and joy. The room fades around us and suddenly it's just me and him, joined in the most old-fashioned way. He's a man and I'm a woman, and it's like neither of us has any purpose but to make the other feel like this, to freeze time and bask in this age-old act that people have been doing for millennia. Something I've only done a handful of times, but I want to do again and again, before this time is even over.

When I come back down to earth, Bay is surrounding me, his hands on my face, his chest pressed to mine. "Shh babe, it's okay, come back to me, that's it."

Blinking up at him, he suddenly snaps into focus. His lips are spread into a soft smile and there's a faint sheen of sweat over his skin. "There you are. You okay, babe?"

I nod, or at least I think I do, it's what I intend to do, but I feel so boneless I'm not sure my head complies.

Leaning down, his lips find mine and he kisses me, his tongue forcing its way into my mouth and taking control, owning me in a way I didn't know kisses could own you. We kiss for so long my lips feel swollen by the time he pulls away. We both watch as he slides his cock out of me, leaving me feeling empty and exposed from the way he's staring down at me.

"Fuck, babe," he growls, running his fingers through my folds and then holding me open. "Your hole is all pink, the skin puffy and full of my cum."

I blush. How is it possible for me to feel even an ounce of embarrassment with him after everything he's done to me in the last two days? I try to snap my knees closed, but his soft chuckle and his grip on my knees stop me.

"Do you want to see what you look like?" he asks with hooded eyes and a smoky, sexy tone, that kind of makes me want to agree, just to see if it affects me as much as it's obviously affecting him.

Bending down, he disappears, then pops back up with his cell in his hands. Before I can protest, his camera is between my legs and he's taking pictures of me—of my vagina, with his fingers holding my folds wide.

"Bay," I shriek.

"Look," he says, turning the cell to me and showing me a close-up picture of my pussy and the white liquid barely being contained inside of me. It feels weird to say it's kind of sexy. It shouldn't be... right? I should be squirming, and not in the way I am. I should be uncomfortable with seeing myself like that, but instead I feel hot and maybe... excited?

His lips twitch as he watches me stare at the picture, but he doesn't say anything. Instead, he lowers the cell phone and turns his attention back between my thighs. The fingers that have been holding me open start to move, pushing inside of me, then pulling out, stroking through my sex, before pushing back into me again.

"What are you doing?" I ask. It doesn't feel like when he used his fingers before, he's not trying to make me come.

"I'm pushing my cum back into you. I want to make sure that it all stays right where I want it."

I need to address the whole condom thing. We've had sex multiple times and as far as I'm aware, he's never used a condom. I know how stupid this is. I took health class and I'm more than aware of the risks we've taken, and not just of me getting pregnant but of getting STDs. The twice I've mentioned it during sex he's said no and I was too orgasmed up to argue, but now that we're both of fairly sound mind, we need to talk about it.

"Are you clean, Bay?"

"Of course I'm fucking clean," he snarls, pushing his fingers deep inside of me before he stops moving, just leaving me full of him.

"I am too," I say, although I was a virgin yesterday, so I guess that was to be expected.

"I know, babe." The tension in his shoulders relaxes a little.

"Tomorrow, I need to go and get a Plan B and then we need to start being careful. We might both be clean and not at risk of giving the other a disease, but it's a real possibility that I could get pregnant."

"No."

"I don't understand," I tell him, my brow furrowing in confusion.

"What's to understand? The answer's no. No, you're not getting a morning-after pill and no, I'm not going to use condoms and no, before you suggest it, you're not going on birth control."

My mouth falls open and I stare at him in shock and horror. Suddenly aware that I'm naked, on the dining table, my legs spread wide and his fingers inside of me, I lurch away from him, causing his fingers to fall free, and then roll off the table, grabbing his shirt from the floor and pulling it over my head. It probably isn't my most graceful moment, but within a minute, I'm upright and partially covered.

"You don't get to just say no."

"Sure I do," he says menacingly. "You belong to me, Missy, that includes your cunt that's soaked in my cum and your womb that is hopefully already growing my baby. I warned you that finding our women makes us Barnetts fucking crazy, and I wasn't kidding. I'm forty-two, Imp, and it turns out I want to watch you swell with my kid, almost as much as I want to keep my dick permanently inside of you. So no, we won't be being careful, no, you won't be taking anything that stops me from breeding you, and yes, I do just get to say no, because you gave yourself to me. You gave me you and I'm never going to give you back."

My hands curl into fists and I genuinely have to stop myself from punching his arrogant face. "Tomorrow I'm getting the morning-after pill and you won't be touching me unless you wear a condom."

His laugh is low and rough and full of dark, twisted promise. "I'll tell you what, little Imp, you pack your shit and let me take you home, I'll wear a condom every time I fuck you right up until I put a ring on your finger and give you my last name."

"This is my home. I'm not going back to Montana, and if you refuse to protect me, you don't get to touch me."

"We'll see," he mocks. "But now you won't get my dick until you beg me to fuck you and fill you up with my cum. I won't give you my dick until you beg for me to put a baby in your belly."

I scoff. "Never going to happen."

"We'll see, it can be a little competition. I'll play with your cunt with my fingers and tongue, but you won't get my dick unless you're begging for it."

"You're so fucking full of yourself," I snap, crossing my arms over my chest as I glare at him.

"No, babe, but you're going to be full of me again before the end of the night."

Rolling my eyes, I turn my back on him, bending over to grab my clothes that are all over the floor. "I'm going for a shower."

"Nope. I'm still in charge and right now, we're going to sit and watch a movie together," Bay says, capturing me with an arm around my waist.

"I don't really want to watch a movie with you."

He laughs. Laughs. "You're good for my ego, little Imp. If you don't want to watch a movie, we can pick a series to binge. Either way, we're going to sit together on the couch and relax before bed."

Ignoring him, I try to push his arm away, ready to stomp into the bathroom and wash the cum from inside of me, but the moment I try to take a step forward I'm swung into the air and deposited over his shoulder, my head hanging down his back, inches from his firm and very naked ass. "Put me down, you fucking caveman."

"I don't like hearing you curse, Missy, so unless you want to go over my knee, I suggest you stop fighting and mind your mouth."

"You're an asshole," I cry.

His hand whacks against my ass and I shriek.

"That's the one and only warning you're getting. Next time you call me an asshole or I hear you curse at me or about me, I'm going to redden your ass and then I'm going to fuck it."

"Your dick isn't going anywhere near my ass."

"Why? I can't get you pregnant if I fuck you bare in that tight hole," he laughs, depositing me onto the couch, pulling his shirt up and over my head while he climbs on behind me, holding me between his legs in a tight grip.

"You are not putting anything in my ass! And we can't sit naked on this couch, it's communal. Your brother has to sit here."

He laughs again, long and low and rough, and I tense, refusing to allow the sound to affect me, even though it is. It really, really is.

"Babe, I had my fingers in your ass last night, and you fucking loved it, so don't act like a prude now, when yesterday you were a dirty, dirty little girl."

As he speaks, the heat of his breath warms my ear and I shudder, closing my eyes tight and refusing to squirm, even though I can feel myself starting to heat up with desire in response to his closeness and dirty words.

He waits a long, agonizing moment and then chuckles softly. "What shall we watch?"

To torture him, I pick the girliest, angstiest teenage drama I could think of and force him to watch *Dawson's Creek*. His moans and grunts of annoyance do make me feel slightly better, right up until the point when he starts to touch me.

It begins with his thumb on the arm around my waist, rubbing soft circles against my stomach. When I feel my muscles relaxing and let my weight fall back more fully against his chest, his other fingers start to tease the underside of my breast. Neither touch is overtly sexual, but then he starts to plant soft kisses behind my ear, sighing sexily as he licks my skin and nips at my earlobe.

Until yesterday, I'd barely gotten past second base and now he's igniting my body and sending my sex drive haywire with tiny, fleeting touches. I want more, but I can't ask for it, because then I'm giving in. He doesn't want easily led, he wants strong and capable and that means me not giving in to him the moment he puts his hands on me— no matter how much I want to.

Forcing myself to watch the show, I try to pay attention to Joey, Pacey and the whine-fest that is Dawson, but I couldn't tell you what's happening because try as I might, I can't ignore the way his thumb is now toying with my nipple.

Somehow, he's touching me in a seriously sexual way, but he's not doing it in a sexy way. He's touching me because he can, because I'm naked and sitting between his legs. This isn't foreplay—or at least not in the way we've done foreplay before. This isn't the prelude to immediate sex; he's playing with me with the sole purpose of driving me crazy and it's working.

Warm lips land on the pulse point in my neck and I inhale sharply. Kiss. Nip. Lick, he teases my skin, throwing in a hint of pain the moment I start to relax into his touch. His thumb and forefinger are plucking at my nipple and his other hand is rubbing gentle circles on my inner thigh. It feels like he has ten hands, because he's everywhere and it's as amazing as it is awful because I want this to become more than teasing.

I'm stronger than this. Begging isn't an option. I need to block him out, act as if he isn't affecting me. But he is. He so is. My pussy is melting, literally drooling. My nipples are sharp peaks, taut and eager to be sucked and my neck is so hypersensitive I can feel myself relaxing and tensing every time he lavishes me with his attention.

My barely un-virginized self should have realized that I stood no chance against an experienced seducer like Bay. But I refuse to give in, so I keep my hands to myself and my eyes fixed firmly on the TV screen.

Chapter Fifteen

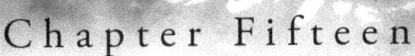

Swallowing down my amusement, I press another kiss against her neck. As soon as my lips lift from her skin, she braces herself, her fingers clenching tightly into fists waiting for the next touch. I kiss her again, soft and sweet and the moment she relaxes, I pull back. She tenses and I touch, she relaxes and I stop. I pinch her nipple, kiss her throat, slide my fingers up her thigh high enough to tease the edge of her pussy. Touch, retreat, touch, retreat.

In comparison to the way I held her open and fucked her on the dining table a couple of hours ago, I'm barely touching her. But it'd be easier for her to try to deny me when I'm dominating her body in such an overwhelming way, rather than taunting with barely there caresses.

Her eyes are firmly fixed on the TV and the stupid teen

drama she's forcing us to watch, but I'm pretty sure I could change the channel and she'd have no clue, because all of her attention is on me.

Today has been pretty close to fucking perfect. I woke up with her in my arms, watched her get all worked up, then calmed her back down again. We ate, then she worked for a little, while I caught up on a novel I've been meaning to read for months. After that, we explored a little, ate food and then we fucked like bunnies on the table, giving me something better to imagine whenever I see her sitting at it all cozy with my brother.

The only down point of the entire day was when she started talking about getting the morning-after pill and going on birth control. Neither of those things will be happening and I won't be wearing a condom either. Call me an asshole, I don't fucking care. I need a way to keep her tied to me, and it's either a cage or a fucking baby. Both options make my dick hard, but a baby in her belly is a hell of a lot easier to explain to the cops than the fucking collar and chains my mind envisages whenever I think about her running from me.

The level of crazy that's been flowing out of me since I first laid eyes on her is fucking terrifying. I know I'm sentencing her to a narrow life with just me, our kids and the small town I *will* be taking her home to, but I want her too much to feel any remorse. She's mine and since I accepted that, that's an inevitability rather than a choice, my moral compass has been spinning in circles, rather than toward what's right or wrong.

We both laid down gauntlets tonight, but what she's

forgotten is that I've got twenty more years' experience playing these kinds of games than she has; and I'm playing for something a lot more valuable than bragging rights. She only wants to win, to prove that she can, but the stakes are much higher for me.

Sliding my finger through the folds of her cunt, I pass over her clit. I'm not applying any pressure or rubbing, the tip of my finger just grazes the tiny bundle as I stroke up and down, collecting her wetness and spreading it over her sex.

"Hmmm," she whines, and I know it's an involuntary sound because her shoulders are tense, like she's trying to fight how she's feeling.

Smiling to myself, I lean down and press a kiss to her neck, feeling her pulse flutter excitedly beneath the skin. She's warm, flushed, and she smells like cinnamon and sex, it's a heady, potent combination that's home and debauchery all rolled into one.

I've fucked a lot of women, but I've never felt this compulsion to consume someone like I do Missy. She's beautiful, but there are a lot of beautiful women in the world, what makes her different is that she's mine. She was made with the sole purpose of belonging to me, and I was made with the sole purpose of worshiping her. I'm going to make her so fucking happy. I'm taking away so many of her choices, but now she's picked me, I'm going to give her the world, I'm going to give her everything she could ever need. I still barely know anything about her, but from what I can gather, she's been mostly alone her entire life. From the way she talks about the grandmother that raised her, she was an obligation rather than a love. I'll never make her feel that way. I've made so many mistakes since I saw her, but I'm going to make things right. I'm going to devote myself to this perfect creature's happiness, pleasure and satisfaction. She's going to be well loved and well appreciated for the rest of her life and it will be my honor to be hers.

I'm going to make it so she doesn't remember a time when she wasn't mine, and all she has to do is give in and give herself over to my care.

Dipping my tongue out, I lick a thin line along her neck, scraping it with my teeth and watching the way she reacts. Alternating between nips and kisses and caresses, I learn what she likes, all while teasing her. Letting her relax only to amp her up again, pushing her and pulling her exactly where I want her to be.

Her fingers are curled into tight fists and I watch as her hands tremble with tension as I graze her clit for the hundredth time, never giving her enough friction to be more than a fleeting delight that fades as quickly as it appears. I can see that I'm driving her crazy, but so far, she's managed to stay silent, taking everything without begging for more.

Moving away from her clit, I stroke through her folds and then circle her entrance, feeling how wet she is. Her breath hitches and I swear she tilts her hips, trying to push me to slide my finger into her, but I don't. Instead, I slide my finger down, grazing over her ass, before moving up again, stroking up and down, taunting her clit, her sex and her ass but never more than a glancing touch before moving again.

With my other hand I pinch at her nipple, gently then harder, then a barely there caress. My dick is like an iron spike, but this is war for her submission. Advance and retreat, building up, then allowing her time to relax, before starting all over again.

Abandoning her breast, I spread my fingers wide and slide them up her breastbone, wrapping them around her throat, collaring her, without exerting any pressure. The moment my palm settles into place, her breathing hitches and a gush of arousal coats my fingers between her legs. My imp likes the feel of me possessing her, my hand around her throat, the threat of my ability to take away her air, tingeing her pleasure with a hint of fear.

I know what breath play is. I also know it's not something that I enjoy, a one-night stand asked me to choke her and my dick deflated faster than a balloon after it's been popped. So, I have no interest in controlling Missy's breath. I do, however, like the way it feels to touch her like this. Handling her this way feels possessive and dominant and it calls to my baser urges that have been in overdrive since Missy appeared in my life.

The wetness beneath her thighs is like a siren call to me and I can't help pushing the tip of my finger into her hot channel. Even after taking my dick tonight, she's still tight and her muscles grip my finger as I slowly slide all the way back out again, swallowing my own groan of frustration as soon as I'm no longer inside of her.

Right now, I'm sure she thinks she's the one being tortured, but I'm driving myself as crazy as I am her. All I can think about is flipping her to her stomach, pinning her to the couch, spreading her legs and rutting into her like a fucking animal. Visions of holding her down, forcing her to take my dick over and over until my cum is seeping out of her is so fucking intense my balls actually start to tighten, preparing to come without any stimulation at all.

I'm not sure how long I play with her. One finger becomes two, becomes three as I stretch out her pussy, playing with her G-spot until she's panting, her hips moving on their own. Then I pull back, withdrawing my fingers and instead paint her nipples with her arousal that's coated my hand, her thighs and the couch beneath us. I'm definitely going to have to pay to have it cleaned, although a fucked-up part of my brain says I should let my brother sit on the fabric, knowing that *my* woman's juices are all over it.

My teeth find the patch of skin behind her ear that makes her shudder and I nip at it, sucking the skin into my mouth and marking her, branding her as owned. My hand around her throat starts to lower and for the first time, she moves, covering my palm with her fingers. "Please," she rasps.

"You like my hand around your neck, collaring you?" I ask.

She nods.

"Tell me."

"I like it," she whimpers.

"What about this," I whisper, pinching her nipple and feeling the way her breath hitches. "Do you like it when I pinch your pretty pink nipple?"

"Uh, huh."

"Say it."

"I like it.

"What about when I do this," I taunt, abandoning her breast to push my hand between her legs, filling her with three fingers and curling to rub at her G-spot.

"Oh god," she gasps, arching her back and pushing herself farther onto my hand.

"You like it when I stretch your cunt with my fingers?"

"God yes," she moans.

"Say it," I demand.

"I like it."

Triumph heats my blood, but this is only round one. Immediately stopping, I drop my hand from her neck, pull my fingers from her cunt and lift my mouth from her skin. The sound that comes from my needy, desperate woman is all animal and I smile, glad that she can't see my expression.

"Bay," she growls.

"What do you need, Imp?"

"Don't stop," she whines.

"Ask for it."

"Please don't stop."

"What do you need, babe? Do you want my hand at your throat, my fingers filling your cunt, my mouth on your neck?"

"Yes, yes, please," she begs.

"Then ask, tell me what you need."

She's silent for a second, her body twitching, desperate.

"All you have to do is ask."

"Put your hand on my throat," she demands.

I chuckle. Yeah, that's not going to happen, she can demand whatever she wants once she's given herself to me completely. From that moment I'll be her motherfucking slave, but now when she's holding back, she doesn't get to play that way.

"Ask nicely," I snarl.

"Bay, please put your hand on my throat."

Doing as she asks, I collar her, spreading my palm wide so my hand cups from beneath her chin all the way down to her chest. "Good girl, see what happens when you ask so prettily. What else do you need?"

"Please put your mouth on my neck."

I feel her swallow beneath my hold and then she rests her head back against my chest, tilting to the side and giving me better access to the spot I've been toying with behind her ear.

"Such a good girl," I coo against her skin, and she shudders at my words. My imp likes it when I praise her.

"Put your fingers inside of me, make me come, please."

"Where do you want my fingers, Imp?" I ask, wanting her to call it her cunt, needing to see how the dirty word sounds on her angelic, innocent lips.

"In my cunt," she whispers.

"You're such a good girl, now ask me nicely."

"Bay, please put your fingers in my cunt."

"Anything for you," I tell her as I fill her completely in one movement, feeling her arousal coat me.

"I need to come, please make me come," she rasps. Her hips roll and she tries to grind against me, but I keep her still, her head back against my chest, my palm around her throat. Without another word I start to move, pumping my fingers in and out of her, finding her G-spot and hitting it each time I fill her. Soft groans and moans slip from her parted lips and she starts to writhe, her internal muscles clamping down on me, letting me know that she's close to falling apart. The moment I feel her muscles start to tremble, I pull my fingers free, leaving her empty.

"Bay," she cries, trying to sit up, but unable to with my hand around her neck.

"What's the matter, babe?"

"Why did you stop? I was about to come."

"I know."

"I need to come, please, please," she begs, grabbing my hand and pushing it back between her thighs. I do as she wants, filling her again, thrusting my fingers in and out of her until she's on the verge of falling apart and then I stop. Ignoring her protests, I start to work her clit, rubbing and squeezing until her hips are bucking and she's trembling, then I stop again. Her whines of anger and protest fill the thick atmosphere, but I ignore her desperate, needy cries for a long moment, then shove three fingers back into her. She's so wet my thick digits easily slide into her and after two pumps, she's on the verge of coming. I stop.

"Bay, please, please, please," she begs after I've pushed her to the edge another three times. Her clit is swollen, the hood hidden as the little mound of nerves stands proudly, begging to be touched again. "Please." She sounds desperate and I love it. I've never been invested enough to edge anyone before, but seeing her this needy has cum leaking from the end of my dick and I'm more than ready to be inside of her.

"What do you need, Missy?" I ask, trying to keep my amusement out of my tone.

"I need to come. Make me come, please, please."

"Ask for my cock, babe."

"Fingers," she demands.

"The only way you get to come is on my dick. So, ask."

"No."

Filling her with my fingers, I fuck her until she's on the edge again and when I pull out, I think she might actually be crying.

"Ask for my cock, ask, that's all you have to do. Be a good girl and say, Bay, fill me with your hard dick."

"Bay," she starts.

"Yeah, Imp?" I toy with her nipple and she moans so loudly I wouldn't be surprised if the neighbors can hear.

"Bay."

"Good girls only get what they want if they ask nicely." I'm taunting her and we both know it. Once she comes, she's probably going to be pissed at me. But it'll be worth it.

"I need your dick," she says so quickly I can barely understand her.

"Go lean over the arm of the couch and then ask me again. Nicely."

Dropping my hand from her throat, I wait, my heart beating wildly in my chest until she eventually starts to move. She has no idea how fucking sexy she looks, crazy eyed and frantic. But if I had my cell in hand, I'd take a picture so I could jerk off to it later.

Curling up onto her knees, she shuffles along the couch until her head is level with the arm, then she leans forward so her chest is resting on the top and her fingers are curled around the edges.

"Good girl," I praise, running a hand up her spine and resting it between her shoulder blades. "Now do you have something to ask me?"

"Bay, please put your cock in me."

My dick is more than happy to oblige, and I guide myself to her entrance and slam my dick home until my hips meet her ass and her cunt is gripping my dick so hard, I almost come.

"I'm not wearing a condom; I'm never going to fucking use them. Ask me to fuck you and fill you with my cum," I demand, grinding my hips in a circle, holding her in place but not fucking her like she desperately needs.

"Fuck me, give me your cum," she growls.

Leaning over her, I wrap my palm around her throat and start to fuck her. Pulling out, I slam forward, filling her completely, fucking her so hard she barely has time to breathe before she implodes, orgasming so intensely I think there's a possibility she might snap my cock in two with how tightly she's gripping me.

Not giving her time to come down from her first high, I fuck her with deep, fast strokes, forcing her straight into a second orgasm, then a third as she screams and cries, begging me for more. Harder, faster, to stop and never stop all in the same breath.

When my balls tighten and I feel the telltale signs of my impending release, I tip her head back and turn her so I can claim her lips with mine. Then I kiss her like I own her as I fill her cunt with my cum.

My knees are shaking as I try not to collapse on top of her, allowing her to feel a fraction of my weight as the last of my release empties deep inside of her. We're both slick with sweat and I'm fairly sure she's going to have marks on her hip from where I've held on while I've fucked her.

She's whimpering, panting and gasping, but she still protests when I slide my fingers from around her throat. I have a moment of panic that I might have lost control and gripped her too hard there, but when I gently turn her face, there're no marks, and nothing to hint that I might have hurt her. I fucking love that me collaring her like that is a turn-on for both her and me. I definitely plan to do it again, maybe next time I'll have her riding my dick, bouncing up and down while my hand is holding her there.

"You okay, babe?" I ask, reluctantly withdrawing my dick as I push my hands beneath her and lift her up from where she's collapsed over the couch. Turning her over, I lay her back down on my chest and she sighs happily, resting her cheek over my heart.

"Missy?"

"Hmmm?"

"You alive?"

"Uh-huh," she replies sleepily.

"You tired?"

I feel the slight movement of her head up and down and chuckle.

"Let's go to bed."

She nods again, and I scoop her into my arms and carry her into the bedroom. Her eyes are closed as she tries to roll onto her side, but I part her legs and push all of the cum that's leaking from her cunt back up inside of her. It's possessive and possibly creepy, but I want all of my release in her pussy. Once I'm happy I've gotten as much as I can back into her, I use my fingers as a plug while she falls asleep, she's so exhausted she doesn't even lift her head to see what I'm doing.

After a minute, I press a kiss to her thigh, pull my fingers out of her and then head back into the living room to clean up after all the fucking we've done. Grabbing some cleaner from the cabinet, I wipe down the table and floor, then collect our discarded clothes and drop them into the hamper in Missy's bathroom. Still naked, my dick semihard and swinging, I put my hands on my hips and stare down at the couch. There are a few damp spots on the fabric of the cushions and for a second, I think about Googling how to clean it, but then I don't. It's childish to need to remind my brother that Missy is mine. There certainly doesn't seem to be anything other than friendship between them. But he took her, he started a new life with her on the other side of the country and the pathetic caveman in me needs to remind him that she. Is. Mine.

So instead of cleaning, or opening the windows to air the smell of sex, I smile like the asshole I am, open the door to his bedroom so the scent permeates into his space and then leave, heading back to my woman.

Lifting the sheets, I climb into bed beside her. Parting her legs, I slide my cock back into her wet pussy. My dick thinks it might be getting round three and starts to harden, but I ignore it, pulling Missy so she's lying on my chest, then I close my eyes and fall asleep.

Chapter Sixteen

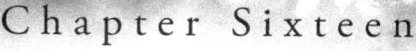

I wake up to the sound of the front door closing. It's not loud, but apparently the fear of someone coming home late at night is so ingrained in me that it's not something I can get over in a few months. I've spent years worrying that each night would be the night Ernie decided raping me was more important than my inheritance, and even though I'm safe now, my heart is still pounding in my chest as I listen to Cody move around.

It's dark in the bedroom and I'm lying on Bay's chest, his arms banded around me, his dick still inside of me, although he's soft and I don't feel stretched or full. Having his softness inside of me is odd. It's not unpleasant, in fact it's kind of nice, in a strange way.

The *thud thud* of his heart beneath my cheek is strong and reassuringly present. Obviously if it wasn't present, he'd be dead, but I'm not sure I've ever been close enough to anyone for long enough to feel their heartbeat like this before.

Nana wasn't tactile and Ernie, thankfully, was never someone who expected hugs or cuddles. My friends and I were excited huggers, like when something good happened, but it'd be weird to spend enough time close enough to listen to their heartbeat for an extended period of time.

I like being surrounded by him. His big body is beneath mine, his arms are wrapped around me, holding me tight and his dick is in me, because he wants to keep us physically connected, even in sleep. Since he got here yesterday, Bay has been apologetic, dominant, sexy, forceful, sweet, attentive, domineering, an asshole, argumentative and at moments, quite frankly insane. There are people with personality disorders who have fewer mood swings than he's exhibited in the last thirty-six hours, but—and I hate to admit it—I like it.

I like that he wants me with an intensity that frightens me. I like that he's bossy in bed and sweet out of it. I like the way he tells me he wants forever with me. I even like the way he seems determined to get me pregnant, even if I'm not sure I'm mature enough or competent enough to be a parent.

Somehow, his need for me settles something inside of me that I didn't realize was ragged and raw. He needs me. He wants me. He's determined to have me and I crave that.

Yesterday, I was overwhelmed by his lust, today, I was soothed by his sweetness and tonight, I was fucked raw by his brutal intensity and stubborn determination.

He's too much and the perfect amount all at once. Pass me the bottle, because apparently, I'm drinking the Kool-Aid. I'm a little pissed that he's refusing to listen to me, or take my feelings into consideration, but the picture he's painting of this perfect world where we live happily ever after is too tempting for me to resist. I'm not sure how this is going to work out between us, but I want it to. I want this life he's offering me; I just need to figure out how to be the person he needs me to be to get it.

It's pretty obvious that Bay enjoys control in the sexual side of our relationship and I am apparently *really, really* good with that. The more dominant he gets, the more I want it and I definitely won't be fighting him to be the one in charge of our physical stuff. But in the day-to-day side of us as a couple, I'm confident I can learn to be the independent, assertive female he craves.

If I'd stayed in Montana, I'm not sure he would have chased me down. He saw the truth of who I was back then, weak, broken down and kowtowed. But I'm confident there was respect in his eyes when I refused to pack up my life here and head back to Montana with him. The way he looks at me now is different, and I know that's because I'm not acting like a frightened mouse.

The sounds of muttering and cursing filters through the walls and I wonder if Cody is okay. Carefully wiggling out of Bay's hold, his dick slides free of me with a wet pop and I cringe a little at the sound, tensing and waiting for Bay to grab me again. When he doesn't, his muscles still relaxed in sleep, I shuffle to the edge of the bed and then slowly sit up. Grabbing my robe from the closet, I pull it on and pad barefoot out of my bedroom and into the living space.

The smell of sex hits me as soon as I open the door and I cringe. It's so disrespectful of Bay and I to get physical in a shared space and I immediately feel guilty. Cody has turned on a table lamp, and the TV is playing quietly as I make my way over to the couch and sit down next to my best friend.

"Hey," I whisper.

"Hey," he says, turning his head to look at me and taking in my robe. "I'm surprised you're awake, I thought my brother would have fucked you into a coma. Do I need to clean the kitchen before I make breakfast in the morning? Or is it just the couch he screwed you on?"

"I'm sorry," I say, bowing my head as shame and guilt fill me.

"I know you're his, I was waiting for him to show up here, but I…" he trails off.

"You're my best friend, you saved me, Cody."

"I know, Mis, you're my best friend too and I don't…" he trails off again.

"Are you?" I swallow thickly. "Are you jealous?"

"Yes, but not because he gets to fuck you. You're my sister, I don't want you that way. But I'm jealous that he gets to keep you and that means I lose you," he confesses on a rush.

"You won't lose me. You're too important to me. Bay is…" I inhale, trying to figure out how to explain what Bay is to me. "Bay is the part of me I didn't know was missing, but I lived without that part and I won't fall apart without him. Maybe before I met you, I might have, but if he rejected me again now, if he packed his bags and went home, I'd be okay because I'd still have you."

"Missy, he isn't going anywhere."

I shrug. "Maybe, maybe not. He seems to have lost his mind a little, but I'm not talking about Bay, I'm talking about you, about us. We're family, Cody, just because Bay came here for me, that doesn't change who you are to me, or who I am to you. You're my best friend and my brother. I love you and regardless of what happens with Bay, I'll always need you."

"Family," Cody says on a sigh, then nods. "Are you okay? Is he treating you okay?"

"I'm good," I say, flashing him a smirk.

"Given the fact that it smells like a whorehouse on a hot day in here, I'd say you're more than good, but I didn't mean the sex. I mean is he treating *you* okay? You said he's lost his mind, what do you mean?"

"He keeps talking about marriage and babies. A part of me wants to believe it's all true, but no matter how good the sex is, we're still virtual strangers."

"It's true," Cody says, sitting up straighter and twisting around until he's facing me. "He means it, he wants you, Mis, you're his and he wants the whole nine yards, wedding, babies, happily ever after. I've watched my brothers fall one by one like dominos and Bay might have been the only idiot stupid enough to fight it, but now he's here, he's *here*. He's all in, there's no chance in hell he'll walk away now. You're his and he's yours one hundred percent."

"I'm not sure I can be what he needs," I confess on a whisper.

"He just needs you to be you, that's all. You're perfect,

Missy."

Shaking my head, I lift my knees up, wrapping my arms around my legs to make sure I'm not flashing Cody. "He wants someone strong and independent, I'm learning how to be that, but I think I'm always going to be a little broken."

Clicking his tongue, Cody scowls. "Don't call yourself broken, you're not. But even if you were, Bay would want you just the same, because you guys are the perfect match for each other. Does he know you're worried about this?"

"No," I gasp. "And you won't tell him."

"You need to tell him."

I roll my eyes and Cody narrows his. "I'm serious, Mis, you need to talk to him, give him a chance to reassure you that you're exactly what he wants and needs."

Flapping my hand through the air, I wave away his concern. "Don't worry about me and Bay. Are you okay?"

"I'll be fine," he says quietly.

"Are you excited to find your girl?" I ask. "You've never really talked about it."

His sigh seems to say a thousand things. "A part of me just wants it to happen. I want what my brothers have, I want someone to love. But another part of me is abso-fucking-lutely terrified. What if I find her and I lose my shit and turn into a meathead caveman and scare her away? I can feel this want for her already and I don't even know who she is, if it's this bad now when she's just an enigma, a faceless figure out there somewhere, imagine how crazy I'll feel once I actually find her. I don't want to fuck it up."

"You won't fuck it up. I just hope whoever it is, she's worthy of you."

Draping his arm around my shoulders Cody pulls me into his side, pressing a kiss to my temple. "Love you, Mis."

"Love you too, Cody."

"Babe, you okay?" Bay's growly voice asks from behind us.

Turning to look at him over my shoulder, I grimace a little when I take in his body language. His huge arms are crossed across his bare chest, his feet are planted shoulder width apart and his lips are pressed into a hard line. He's only wearing a pair of tight boxer briefs, but he still somehow looks impressively intimidating.

"I heard Cody come home, I was just checking he was okay."

"You should go back to bed," Cody urges, squeezing my shoulder lightly before lifting his arm from around me.

"We can talk some more…" I start.

"I'm good, Mis, I'm going to head to bed in a minute anyway. Go, I'll see you in the morning."

"Okay, night."

"Night, guys," Cody says, nodding a little stiffly to Bay, then smiling at me as I climb off the couch and pad back toward my aggravated man.

The moment I'm within arm's reach, Bay curls his fingers around me, pulling me into his side and leading me back into my bedroom.

"I don't like waking up alone and finding you snuggled up on the couch with my brother instead of filled with my cock in our bed," Bay growls angrily.

"He's my friend."

"He's my brother. I still won't have you fucking

cuddling with him. I'm your man, not him, don't let me find you crawling out of our bed and into his arms again, Missy."

"You don't get to tell me what to do. You're making it sound like I was in his lap and I wasn't, I was beside him on the couch. You're being an asshole."

"Do you need a reminder of exactly which Barnett you belong to, little Imp? Because when I fall asleep with your cunt wrapped around my dick, that's where I expect to find you when I wake up."

"You sound like a psycho," I scoff.

"I feel like a psycho, so get fucking used to it. You're mine, not his, and if I have to keep you handcuffed to me until both of you get the memo, I'm more than happy to do it. Now get on the bed," he snarls, his eyes wide and crazy.

"No."

"Get on the fucking bed, Missy."

"No, Bay, you don't get to—" Before I can even finish my sentence, Bay is on me, spinning me around and forcing me to bend at the waist. Holding on to my arms, he pulls them behind me, coupling them together at the base of my spine, while he flips my robe up over my naked ass and pushes his cock into me in one harsh thrust.

"Fuck," I cry, shocked by the invasion of his dick and the speed he managed to get me from upright to bent over and impaled on him.

"Tell me you don't want me," he snarls angrily.

"I don't want you," I pant, lifting my head and trying to flip my hair from my face.

"This wet, hot cunt that's the perfect shape for my fat cock proves that's a lie. Tell me your cunt doesn't belong to me."

"It doesn't," I groan, trying to push my ass back onto him, but unable to move with the way he's holding me immobile.

"This cunt is so wet and creamy it's dripping onto my balls, so that's another lie. Tell me you don't want me, tell me to stop."

"I..." I pause, unable to say anything more, because I do want him. The way he's handling me, his jealousy, it shouldn't turn me on but it does and right now, I don't want him to ask permission, I want him to hold me down and take what he wants. "Please," I whimper.

"Please what, Missy? Please stop?"

"No," I try to shake my head, but with my hair covering my face and hanging almost to the floor, I'm not sure he can see.

"Tell me what you want," he taunts.

"You," I gasp.

"Me?" He laughs, but the sound isn't joyful, it's bitter and harsh. "If you wanted me, you wouldn't be snuggling with my fucking brother, you'd be in our bed."

"Please, Bay."

"Who does this wet pussy belong to, Missy?"

"You," I cry, so desperate and needy I can feel tears filling my eyes.

"Damn fucking right it does," he hisses, pulling his hips back, then snapping them forward, slamming his dick back into me with so much force if he wasn't holding my wrists securely, I'd have flown across the room.

"You. Belong. To. Me," he says through gritted teeth,

fucking me at a brutal pace, each word punctuated with a hard thrust that pushes me forward only for him to reel me back in, filling me over and over. "I know I fucked up, but I can't stand to see you with my brother. You're mine, not his. He doesn't get to have you."

As Bay hurtles me toward a release that I know will shatter me to pieces, he bares his soul. "I can't lose you. I can't survive without you. I need you. I need you to pick me even if I don't deserve you. I'm sorry. I should never have let you go. I'm so fucking sorry." Everything he's saying is exactly what I needed to hear, but didn't want to ask him.

I had no idea that sex could be so cathartic, that such a visceral, physical act, brutal in its intensity could absolve me of my fears and refresh my soul in a way I've never experienced before.

By the time my orgasm hits, I feel renewed. When the pleasure splinters, my knees buckle and Bay releases his hold on my arms, catching me around the waist and holding me upright as he slams into me. Following me over the edge, his hot cum explodes inside of me, scorching me, as his angry confession and sincere apology soothe my ragged heart.

"Are you okay? Fuck, was I too rough?" Bay's frantic voice is followed by him lifting me up and turning me to face him. Movement follows and then we're on the bed, his hands framing my face, pushing my hair from out of my eyes.

"Missy, Missy. Fuck."

Blinking my eyes open I look up at him, surprised to find his damp skin pale, his lips downturned.

"Hi," I say stupidly, my voice weak as aftershocks of release skitter through my nerve endings, making my muscles weak and languid.

"Are you okay?"

I nod, but instead of just my head moving, my whole upper body rocks back and forth.

"I shouldn't. I was too rough. I… I'm…. Fuck, I'm sorry."

"Wow," I say, letting my lips tip up at the sides.

"Wow?" Bay questions.

"Wow," I say again.

"So not too rough?"

I shake my head from side to side.

His lips slowly curve into a smile and some of the color returns to his cheeks. "Fuck, Missy, you are absolutely perfect for me."

"Sleep," I slur.

"Okay babe, sleep."

"Talk in the morning."

This time when he nods, his expression is more solemn. "Yeah, in the morning."

***

Opening my eyes the next morning, I'm not surprised to find Bay is plastered around me, his softening cock still semihard inside of me. My skin feels clammy and disgusting and I've no doubt my thighs are sticky with dried-on cum. I need a shower. But after last night, Bay and I need to talk, really talk. Except, as much as I know we need to, I don't want to have a stark conversation and ruin this thing that's developing between us by being too honest.

"Bay," I say, freeing my hand and cupping his cheek. His cheek twitches, but his eyes don't open and I take the moment to trace his face with my gaze. I thought he was beautiful from the moment I first saw him, but up close, while he's still, I can really take him in. His skin is tan and there's a smattering of almost imperceptible freckles across his nose and cheeks. His nose is austere, but there's a small bump on the bridge that could maybe be from a break once upon a time. His cheekbones are sharp and his jaw is square and chiseled. There are a few fine lines at the corners of his eyes, but it's his lips that keep demanding my attention. Full and parted slightly in sleep, his mouth is enticing, a neat stubble coating his chin and above his upper lip.

He's so gorgeous I want to take a picture so I can remember this moment when he was so peaceful. Awake, Bay has a desperate energy that seems to exude from him. I don't know if that's the way he always is, or if in the short amount of time I've spent with him it's just been drama and stress. I'd like to see how he looks when he's settled, happy and relaxed. The only time he seems totally calm is after sex, but last night he was anything but chilled.

"Bay," I call again, leaning forward and pressing my lips against his in a soft kiss.

The moment my mouth touches his, he jolts awake and kisses me back. "Morning, Imp," he whispers roughly against my lips

"Hi."

"I like waking up like this, I think you should kiss me awake every morning," he smiles, making the lines by his eyes crinkle and curve.

"You do, huh?"

"Yep, I think a new rule should be that neither of us gets out of bed without kissing the other awake."

"What if I have to get up to pee in the night? Or if you have to get up to pee, you are older than me, middle age does that to a guy, right?" I smirk.

Flipping me to my back, Bay pins me down, his fingers digging into my sides and tickling me. "I'm not old, little Imp, you're just young, practically a baby."

Laughing, I try to squirm away from his fingers, but instead as I jerk, my hip hits his rock-hard dick, that had slid out of me when he rolled us over.

"My dick wants you," he purrs against my cheek.

"Your dick is on a ban, I'm sore," I groan, feeling my internal muscles wince with pain as my core clenches.

Bay's amused expression instantly sobers and I hate that I made all the playfulness leave. "Did I hurt you last night?"

"No, at least not in a way that I didn't like. But you were angry."

"I was," he agrees. "I..." Inhaling slowly, he sits, then pulls me up, lifting me and placing me in his lap, my legs straddling his thighs, his hard dick pressed against my stomach.

"I shouldn't have behaved like that last night; I shouldn't have handled you like that."

"I don't have a problem with you handling me, Bay. I liked you taking over and holding me in place. What I do have an issue with, is you losing your shit and acting like a jealous idiot. I'm not your toy, I'm a person and I have a relationship with your brother. I like you; I want to give this thing between us a try, but if you expect me to pick between you and Cody, right now I'd pick him."

Bay jolts back like I've slapped him. "You'd pick my brother?"

Scoffing, I shake my head. "Not like that. I have no interest in Cody in any way except as my best friend and brother. We're close, Bay, that's not going to change just because you and I are having sex. He was here for me when I needed someone, he saved me and I won't give him up, even if that means losing the chance of something between me and you."

"So, you'll always pick him over me?" Bay's expression is murderous, but I'm not prepared to back down. He's behaving like a child who doesn't know how to share.

"I'm not picking him over you. I'm telling you, if you force me to choose because you're too immature and jealous to deal with me having a close relationship with your brother, then right now I'd pick him."

Bay's lips part and he stares at me like I've just betrayed him.

"You rejected me, Bay. You drove me to the bus station and let me walk away, knowing there was every chance we'd never see each other again. I know you came after me, but I didn't know that until two days ago. As far as I was concerned, for the last three months you were just a guy who decided I wasn't who you wanted and didn't care what I was doing or who I was doing it with."

"You're mine," he growls like a barbarian.

"I am," I nod. "I'm yours, I want you, Bay, I want to see if we can make something of the connection we feel for each other, but I finally found someone who cares about me with zero ulterior motives. Cody doesn't want anything from me, he doesn't see me as young, broke or needy, he just felt like we were destined to be in each other's lives and we both made that happen. I have never had someone be there for me with no hidden agenda, sense of obligation, or..." I pause, then say. "Or weird mystical, fated connection. I won't give him up and if you ask me to, then you're not the person I hoped you'd be and definitely not the man for me."

On the outside, I'm trying to sound confident and strong, but on the inside, I'm a mess. If he walks away, or asks me to choose, I honestly don't know what I'll do. I want him, despite all the crazy he's feeling right now, despite the fact that he's walking all over me and I'm letting him. He's too strong and too determined, and I know being with him will be a constant push and pull, but I want him. If the connection he feels for me is anywhere near as intense as the one I feel for him, then I can understand why he's acting so insane. I want him and I want this, whatever it is, but I can't let him walk all over me, no matter how much I'm tempted to just lie down and let him take over entirely.

"I can't just sit there and watch my woman cozy up to another man. I just can't."

Ice fills my veins and I lift myself up from his lap, feeling like my bones are going to crumble to pieces without his touch. "Then you need to leave."

"What?"

"I want you to leave."

"I'm not going anywhere."

Jumping off the bed, I take a step back, holding my

hands up to ward him off as he reaches for me. "Go, Bay, this is over. You want me to pick two days of great sex with you, over the most important friendship I've ever had just because you're too jealous to deal with it? No, I won't do it. I heard what you said that day at your house, I heard you say you didn't want someone like me, that you needed a strong and independent woman, well this is what happens when you get everything you ever asked for. This is me being strong and independent and right now, you need to show me some respect and leave when I've asked you to."

I'm sure that my monologue would have been more impactful if I wasn't naked while I said it, but it's taken every ounce of strength I have just to force the words out of my mouth. Everything about asking him to leave feels wrong, but I refuse to be a doormat and give in to his caveman, possessive bullshit. I haven't done anything wrong and he knows that. Cody is his brother, and both he and I have assured Bay that our relationship is one-hundred-percent platonic. We consider each other brother and sister, siblings, and I won't abandon my best friend for a guy who only wants me because it's driving him insane not to have me.

Slowly rising from the bed, Bay stares at me like I've betrayed him, but I keep my gaze level and calm. As I watch, he snags his pants from the floor and pulls them on, then yanks his shirt over his head. "You keep telling me what I said I wanted, but that was me lying to myself, feeding myself bullshit to hide from how fucking terrified I was of losing myself to you. Before you, yeah, I sought out women who had their own shit sorted, so the only thing they needed from me was my dick. Then I found you."

A shudder causes goose bumps to pebble across my skin and I grab my robe, wrapping it around myself.

"You changed everything, Missy, but you scared the shit out of me. You're so fucking young and sweet and when I looked at you, I saw all this need from you and I didn't know how to give you what you deserved and get what I needed too. I knew that if I took even an inch from you, I'd steal the rest and then I'd take away all your choices, all your wants and hopes and I'd force you to live the life I want and need for you. So I drove you to that fucking bus station and I watched you go, like the fucking asshole idiot that I am. I knew it was wrong, but then you were gone and when I came out of my pity-induced haze, you were here with my brother."

"Cody and I—"

"I know, but I didn't know that then. For the last three months, every time I've closed my eyes, I've seen visions of you and him. I've tortured myself imagining the way you'd sound when he touched you, how it'd feel to see you two together. By the time I got on that plane to come here, I didn't care, I was determined to take you. You belong to me, not him, after all. But then you were never his, or at least not in the way I was imagining and when you let me kiss you, touch you, when you gave yourself to me it was heaven on fucking earth."

"Bay."

"I don't need you to be strong. I don't need you to be independent. Fuck, I don't want you to be anything like those women I wasted time with until I found you. I want you to need me for everything, I want you to come to me when you're happy, when you're sad or hurt, or horny. I want to know your every thought, fear or desire. I want it all from you. But more than anything, I need you to pick me. To want me, to choose me."

He's barely an inch from me now, not touching me but close enough I can feel the heat of his breath as he speaks.

"And I need you not to ask me to choose," I whisper.

We're both silent as his shoulders slump, and we stay that way as he turns, grabs his cell and walks out the door.

Chapter Seventeen

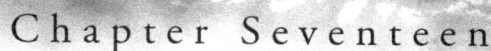
Bay

"Fuck," I hiss as I shove my feet into my sneakers, grab my keys and walk out of the door, ignoring my brother's incredulous glances from where he's sitting at the dining table.

"Fuck," I snarl again, storming down the stairs and into the lobby, where a family scatters, a mother pulling her kids into her, like I'm about to attack.

Uncaring, I throw open the door and rush onto the sidewalk, my jaw clenched so hard it feels like my teeth could break. How the fuck did this happen? How did we go from waking up with soft kisses, her naked body pressed against mine, her pussy still wrapped around my dick, to me being alone out on the sidewalk trying to figure out what the fuck to do?

More than anything, I just want to go home. I want to turn to my family, to Beau's wisdom and unapologetic attitude. He'd tell me what to do, he'd set me straight and let me know if I'm being an asshole, or if she's being unreasonable.

A part of me knows it's a bit of both. It's unfair of me to expect her to abandon her friendship with Cody just because we're together. But the caveman inside of me still sees him as a threat, even though, rationally, I know he isn't one. The only people who are going to stop Missy and me from working out are me and Missy, and right now, we both seem to be doing a pretty fucking good job of it.

Last night when I'd woken up alone, I'd been worried. I'd assumed she was in the bathroom, or maybe getting a drink or something, so when I'd opened the bedroom door and found her curled up on the couch with Cody's arm around her, I'd seen red. It'd taken all my self-control not to rip her away from him and reacquaint his face with my fist. Instead, I'd taken my frustrations out on Missy. We'd argued and then I'd bent her over and fucked her hard enough to brand my possession of her inside and out. I'd behaved like little more than an animal, a true alpha, reminding his mate who she belonged to.

After we'd finished and my mind had cleared, I'd been terrified that I'd hurt her, that she'd see me as a monster. But instead, she'd loved my display of dominant ownership and we'd tumbled into bed happy, with a promise to talk things out this morning. I just never realized that talk would end up with me leaving.

Is that what I'm doing? Leaving? Vermont is two hours

ahead of Montana, but I know Beau will already be at work, and up on the mountain, cell reception is almost nonexistent away from the offices.

I should turn around and go back inside. I should sit her down and talk through this, but I'm angry. How can she say she'd pick Cody over me? How is it even a choice? There is no one and nothing in the world that I want more than her, apparently, she doesn't feel the same.

She told me I shouldn't have asked her to pick, and fuck, maybe she's right, but I thought she'd pick me.

"I heard what you said that day at your house, I heard you say you didn't want someone like me, that you needed a strong and independent woman, well this is what happens when you get everything you ever asked for."

Her voice echoes through my mind and I wince. I did this. I ruined all this by spouting all that shit about her not being what I wanted. The fucked-up thing is that now I have her, I can't think of anything more torturous than her being strong and independent without me. I need her to need me, just like Cody said I would.

Fuck.

Sliding into my rental car, I start the engine and pull out of the lot. I don't know where I'm going. Where do you go when you're leaving your heart behind? And that's the truth, Missy is my heart. I barely know her and most of the time I've spent with her, has been either arguing or fucking, but my soul knows her soul, my heart knows her heart and I can't walk away again, even if it'd be the best thing for both of us.

Driving around the corner, I spot a Best Western hotel,

the blue-and-yellow logo calling me like a beacon from the highway. Parking, I go inside and book a room, ignoring the fluttering eyelashes the receptionist bats in my direction and then flop down onto the white bedspread, exhaling wearily.

My cell is buzzing in my pocket, but I can't find the energy to pull it out and see who's trying to get hold of me. I'm pissed at Missy and Cody and fate, or whatever the fuck it is that made Missy mine and then made me fuck it up before I even had a chance to make it work. I don't know how to make it better. She would rather lose me than my brother. That knowledge is like a kick in the gut and I don't know what to do with it.

My cell buzzes again and I force myself to reach for it and bring it to my ear.

"Hello."

"Bay, what the fuck is going on?" Cody demands.

"It's over."

"What's over? You and Missy?"

"Yep. She picked you."

"Picked me? What the hell are you talking about?" Cody demands angrily.

"I needed her to pick me and she didn't, she chose you." My voice is flat and lifeless, and maybe that's better than the fury that was flowing through my veins earlier.

"Bay, Missy and I are friends, she's my fucking sister, because she's your fucking woman. She's just like Bonnie, Cora, Alice, Lulu and Juni, she's my sister."

"I know, but you don't snuggle on the couch with any of them. You haven't spent months living with any of them. You're her savior and I'm the guy she'd give up rather than lose you." Wow, I sound bitter, but I am.

"You're being an asshole," my brother warns. "We're best friends, why the fuck would she have to give me up? Is that what you told her? That to be with you, she had to stop being friends with me, you fucking dick."

"I want her to want me."

"Having you doesn't mean she doesn't get to have anything else," Cody yells, then ends the call.

Pulling my cell away from my ear, I stare at the home screen, feeling like a dick. He's right, they're both right and I'm a fucking asshole. Clicking into my contacts, I pull up Cora's number and hit call.

"Hello," she answers distractedly after the second ring.

"Hey Cora."

"Bay? Hi, are you okay? Did you manage to get everything sorted with Missy? I'm assuming that's where you are? You could have told us, you know we want to do whatever we can to be there for you guys."

"I need to ask you a question."

"Okay," she says warily.

"Have you ever cuddled on the couch with any of us except Huck?"

"Err, that's a weird question. I'm going to assume Missy and Cody are touchy and you're losing your caveman mind over it. But yeah, it's not something I do often, but when I was pregnant and feeling shitty, all of you hugged me and comforted me if Huck wasn't there."

"Right, but that was a hug to make you feel better, she got out of our bed and went to cuddle with him on the couch."

"How were they sitting?"

"They were beside each other and he had his arm around her shoulders and her head was rested on him."

"Sounds a lot like the way you've hugged me in the past. Let me ask you a question."

"Okay."

"Do you want to fuck me, Bay?"

A spluttering, shocked sound bursts from me. "What, no, fuck, of course not."

"So why would you think Cody wants to fuck Missy, or that she's interested in him that way?"

My voice dies in my throat. She's right, of course she's right, it's the reason I called her and not any of my other siblings. "Fuck."

"How bad is it?"

Exhaling slowly, I cover my eyes with my hand. "I basically told her I couldn't watch her cozy up with my brother and that she needed to pick, me or him."

"Bay, why the fuck would you do that?"

"Because I'm an asshole."

"God, what is wrong with you? Are you trying to push her away? I figured when you left that you were going to do your Barnett voodoo and bring both Missy and Cody home, but apparently not."

"She's not going to forgive me, is she?"

"Honestly, Bay, at this point, I'm not sure. You rejected her, abandoned her, then when you chase after her finally, you give her an ultimatum and basically accuse her of betraying you with your brother. I'd have kicked you in the balls, punched you in the face and then possibly pushed you into the lake. Where's all the Barnett charm? Even when you're being OTT jealous and possessive, you guys still have an endearing charm."

"I don't know. It's like when I'm around her I lose my mind. I thought we were sorting things out. I apologized and we were good, then I said something about us going home and she basically told me to have a good trip. She says she's a different person than who she was in Montana, that she has a new life out here in Vermont and that she isn't coming home with me."

"Did you give her orgasms? When Huck gives me lots of orgasms he can convince me to do whatever he wants," Cora says on a chuckle.

"Lots of orgasms, so many fucking orgasms, that side of things is good, really good. But she seems happy here, they both do. They live together and work together, she and Cody have this rhythm that I'm not a part of and I'm jealous. She says he's her best friend and the most important person in her life. I don't know how to compete with that."

"Why do you need to compete?" Cora asks rationally.

"Because she's mine. I've spent the last three months in fucking hell without her but she's been fine, starting over with my fucking brother," I growl.

"So, this is all jealousy?" Cora says bluntly.

"Yes," I snap. "I'm so fucking jealous. He has this closeness with her and I fucking hate it. She's mine, she belongs to me and Cody can't fucking have her."

Cora's sigh is loud and I grimace waiting for her brutal honesty, but instead when she speaks, her voice is soft and a little sad. "I don't know what to say, honey. I get why you're jealous and upset. You've spent the last few months knowing you made a mistake and hating yourself for it. You've driven yourself crazy thinking the worst of Cody and Missy and now that you've pulled your head out of your ass and finally gone after her, she isn't falling at your feet like you expected her to. But what you have to realize is that just because you've been pining after her and feeling like your life was over without her, doesn't mean she was. I can't tell you what she's been thinking, but I can explain a little about how it was for me when Huck and I got together."

"Okay," I say.

"From the moment Huck carried my drunk ass home after girls' night, he was relentless, he was always there and he just never gave me an opportunity to pull away. He sent me texts and turned up at my house, he overwhelmed me and knocked me completely off-kilter, but then never gave me a chance to balance myself again. From the first moment, I felt like I was snowballing downhill, but even as scary as his hundred-mile-an-hour approach to our relationship was, he was always there, always reminding me that I was his and that he was mine. He did some fucked-up things, but even though I was angry and I doubt I'll ever fully forgive him, he refused to back down. The girls all agree that the reason we never fought the Barnett bulldozer romance approach is because we were never given enough time to actually sit back and think about anything. Missy's had three months to think about your claim on her and how you didn't want her. She's had time to plan and plot and stew in her anger and hurt without you there to soothe the raw edges you've created. Did you really think just showing up in Vermont would be enough to make things good between you?"

The stupid thing is, I think I did think that just being here was enough. I figured that showing up, telling her she was mine and then fucking my possession into her after I apologized for being a dick, would allow me to hit reset on our relationship and start fresh, but obviously it's not. "I..." I start, then trail off, because really, what the fuck can I even say?

"Cody is the person who's been there for her every day. He's the one who's been holding things together, he's been the constant in her new life, the person to support her in something that was probably pretty scary. Put yourself in her shoes, Bay, when she left Montana, she had nothing but the clothes on her back and a few hundred dollars. No family, no friends, nothing but a need to leave and start fresh. If that were you, and someone came into your life who was there for you in your most vulnerable moments, who not only supported your dreams, but helped you achieve them, would you give that person up? Would you choose a virtual stranger who was nothing more than apologies and orgasms, or the person who uplifts you and helps you? You should be her Cody, but you fucked up and you're not. You don't have the right to ask her to choose and I'm sorry, Bay, but I think she made the right choice. In this moment, you're not uplifting her, you're holding her down."

"Fuck," I hiss, shame and guilt barreling through me and threatening to drown me beneath the onslaught of emotion.

"We all want you to come home, *all* of you, but I think you need to prove to Missy that you deserve her and accept that because you fucked up, she forged a bond with Cody that isn't going away. If you were really thinking about her needs more than your own, you wouldn't want it to. If you were truly worthy of her, you'd want to give her as much family who loves and supports her as you can, and she has that in your brother. Don't allow your childish jealousy to make you act like any more of an asshole than you have already."

Thoroughly chastised, I exhale a shaky breath. "What do I do?"

"Honestly, I don't know. In normal circumstances, I'd tell you to do what Barnett men always do, but I think you've missed your chance for the caveman routine to work. So maybe apologize and then give her some space."

"I'm not sure I can do that," I confess.

Her shrug is so loud I can hear it through the phone line. "Sometimes, it's not about you. Stop being a selfish asshole and start putting her needs and wants above your own."

The line goes silent and I pull my cell away from my ear and see she's ended the call. I deserve that, because she's right, everything she's said is right. I've made this all about me, and what I want and need, and that needs to change.

Going into my contacts, I start to scroll to Missy's name before realizing I don't have her number. A thought rattles through my mind, back in Montana she didn't have a cell phone. Beau tried to give her his number and she didn't take it because she didn't have a cell.

Has she got one now? Surely Cody would have gotten one for her, for safety reasons as much as anything else. Because Cody isn't an asshole and of course he'd look after her, because that's what he's been doing since he met her.

He's been taking care of her, because I wouldn't.

Fuck.

Exhaling sadly, I pull up my brother's number and hit call.

"What do you want, douchebag?" Cody snarls.

"I'm sorry."

"Yes, you are, but I'm really not the one you need to apologize to first."

"I don't have her cell number."

Cody's bark of laughter is full of disgusted mirth. "Fuck me, you don't deserve her."

"I know."

When the line goes silent, I know Cody's ended the call and I can't even be pissed at him. Sitting up, I shove my cell into my pocket and push up to my feet, then leave the hotel room, driving my car back toward the two people I've hurt.

There's someone coming out of the door when I reach their building and I grab the door, smiling charmingly at the woman who exits before stepping into the building and calling the elevator. By the time I'm standing outside their apartment door, my palms are sweating and I feel a little pool of dread building in my stomach.

Lifting my fist, I knock at the door and wait, then wait some more. Knocking a second time, I hear some noise behind the thick wooden barrier, then a moment later the door opens a couple of inches and my brother's angry face appears in the gap.

"What?" Cody snaps.

"Can I come in?"

"Nope. Missy doesn't want to see you and honestly, I'm

not that interested in talking to you right now either."

Sighing, I place my hand against the door and try to push it open, but my brother is as big as me and more than capable of stopping me from forcing my way inside. "I need to fix this."

"You're right, you do, but that isn't happening right this second. If you hadn't basically told the girl I consider not only my best friend, but also my sister that she needed to cut me out of her life, I might have been willing to help you, but right now I'm picking a side and it isn't fucking yours. So go get a hotel room, or fly your ass the fuck back home. Right now, you're not welcome here."

Before I can even part my lips to apologize, he slams the door closed in my face, leaving me alone, out in the corridor, feeling like the world's biggest jackass. For a second I consider knocking again and again, forcing them both to come out here and deal with me, but that would be me looking after my own needs instead of Missy's again. So instead, I head back downstairs and drive back to the hotel.

I stay in my room, mindlessly watching TV and ordering room service, while I try to decide how the hell I fix this. Thinking about Cody taking care of my woman still rankles, but if not me, then who better to look after her than my brother? As much as I need to fix things with Missy, I need to make things right with Cody too.

Clicking into his contact, I decide against calling him and instead open up the text app.

ME

> I'm sorry. I'm an asshole and honestly the only excuse I have is a pretty shitty one. I'm jealous as fuck.

> **ME**
>
> You've had her for three months, you know her, you get her and you have a bond that I'm terrified I won't ever be able to live up to. I've done nothing but make one mistake after the next since the moment I laid eyes on her, and when I saw the two of you on the couch it pushed me over the edge. With me she's wary and I hate it. Physically we connect, but on every other level we're strangers. She loves you, you're her best friend and it was wrong of me to ever ask her to pick between us. I might be older than you, but when it comes to Missy, I feel like a kid who is trying to attract his first crush. I fucked up with her the day we met, and now I don't know what to do to bridge this gap between what I want from her and what she's willing to give me. But that's on me and I should never have blamed you or your relationship with her for the fact that I feel like I've missed my chance. I'm so fucking sorry, bro. I love you and I'm grateful she has you in her life. You were there for her when I wasn't and I'm glad she has you. Can we talk?

It's practically a fucking essay, and it's not even a drop in the ocean of all the things I need to say to him, but it's a start. Hitting send I stare at my screen, waiting to see if the ticks appear to say he's read it. After ten minutes, they're still missing and I let my head fall back against the wall and drop my cell to the comforter.

A part of me wants to go over to their apartment and demand entrance, but like Cora said, I've fucked up so badly the usual Barnett bulldozer approach probably won't be well received.

My cell beeps and I fumble with it, almost dropping it over the side of the bed in my rush to open my text.

CODY

> You're right, you are an asshole!!!! I'm so fucking pissed at you, but I'll get over it. Missy is hurt and honestly, that girl has had enough pain in her life without you making things worse just because you're a jealous idiot. Why would you say that to her? Why the fuck would you even suggest that she has to pick between the two of us? I get that you're jealous, but that's a YOU problem and by giving her that ultimatum you made it a HER problem. I knew you'd come for her sooner or later. I guessed a lot sooner, but I do honestly believe that you thought staying away was the best thing for Missy. But YOU are the reason that you've missed the last three months with her. YOU are the reason she was alone and about to get on a bus to the other side of the country. I thought when you turned up that you'd work the Barnett charm and we'd all get to go home, and it was working. Then you pull this shit and right now you're not even back to zero, I'd say you're sitting at negative fifty with her. I love you, but I love her too and I won't allow you to hurt her any more, she's been through enough, fuck, she's still dealing with it. It genuinely hurts me to say this, but Bay, you need to go home. Give her some space and yourself some time to get over your petty jealousy. Once you get yourself figured out, then come back, but I'm not going to lie, it's not going to be easy to win her over.

With each word I read I get angrier and angrier but also guiltier, because even though I hate it, every word he says is true. I have royally fucked up, but even if he's right, he must be out of his mind if he thinks I'm going home without her.

I stew for the next couple of hours, trying to decide what the fuck I do next. For a hot minute I seriously considered the Huck school of romance, but I don't know Vermont at all. And unlike back home where everyone knows we're nuts for our women, but would never actually hurt them, if I throw Missy over my shoulder and kidnap her here, I'm pretty sure someone would call the cops.

Getting back into the apartment is the first step to fixing things, but if I tell Cody I'm coming back to force her to listen to my apology, I'm pretty sure he'll refuse to open the door. Instead, I get into my rental, drive to their building and then press every door buzzer except Missy and Cody's and wait for someone to unlock the lobby door. It clicks a moment later and I wrench it open and quickly make my way to their floor. When I'm outside the door, I send my brother a text.

> **ME**
> Can you let me in for a minute please, I need to grab my stuff before I leave.

Hitting send, I let all the fear and sadness show on my face, forcing my eyes downcast, my shoulders slumped as I wait for the door to open. The moment it does, I snap my arm out and throw the door wide, barging past my shocked brother and straight over to Missy who is curled up on the couch beneath a blanket, her eyes red like she's been crying.

Scooping her up and into my arms, I rush into her room, closing and locking the door behind us before Missy has a chance to react.

"Bay, what are you doing?" she asks as I slowly lower her to her feet and cup her face in my hands. Her lip quivers and I fight the urge to lean down and bite it. I hate the desolate look in her eyes, I hate that I can see the tears threatening to fall and I really, really fucking hate that I'm the reason she feels this way.

"Bay," Cody hammers on the bedroom door.

"Fuck off, Cody, she's fine," I yell, not glancing away from Missy.

"I'm fine, Cody," she says wearily, blinking her attention back to me.

"I know I'm an asshole. I'm jealous, insanely possessive, over the top and a control freak. I will hate every fucking man who looks at you, and you being closer to Cody than me will probably always make me a little crazy. But if you let me, I will love you unconditionally, irrationally, endlessly, psychotically for the rest of my days. I will worship the ground you walk on; I'll be your fucking person. The one you can rely on, the one who's always there for you even if it's just to get you some disgusting pregnancy craving in the middle of the night. I promise to do my absolute best not to make you cry again, unless it's happy tears or while I'm making you come. I'm sorry, little Imp, I'm so fucking sorry, but I can't leave, I can't fucking do it. I hate being this far away from you," I motion to the few feet between us. "If I let you go again, I'll break and I'll never put myself back together, because without you, my pieces don't fit right anymore. I'll make this right, I'll fix this and I swear I'll never fucking utter a word about you needing to pick between me and my brother ever again. But please, please let me love you, let me be yours," I beg, falling to my knees at her feet.

Curling my arms around her waist, I bury my face into her stomach, breathing in her scent and wondering if my baby is growing in her belly right now.

For an indeterminately long time she does nothing, just stands stock-still, her hands motionless at her sides as I hold her tightly. Then after what feels like an eternity, she lifts her hand and runs it through my hair.

"Bay," she whispers.

Chapter Eighteen

"Bay," I whisper, pushing my fingers into his dark hair and pulling slightly. He doesn't lift his head, so I let my knees go weak and sink down to the ground, forcing him to relinquish his tight grip on my waist, until I'm kneeling beside him.

"Bay," I say again.

Lifting his hand, he cups my cheek, his rich dark eyes solemn and filled with moody intensity. "Yeah, babe."

"I hate you a little right now," I confess, confused that his speech has cooled some of the anger that's been barreling through me all day.

"I hate me too," he agrees, running his thumb back and forth over my cheek. "I can't give you up though. I'm too fucking selfish to walk away, even if it's what's best for you. Before it was because I didn't want to tie you to my narrow life, now I can't leave because I refuse to be without you. I've tasted your sweetness, I've had a glimpse at what the rest of our lives could look like and the only way I'll let you go is if I'm dead. And right now I think I'm obsessed enough with you to come back and haunt you, until you follow me into the afterlife so we can be together again."

"You sound like a psycho," I tell him, fighting to keep the amusement from my voice.

"I am a psycho, but I'm your psycho."

"Being around you hurts," I confess.

"Because I fuck you too much?"

"No," I snap, "it hurts because you want everything *you* want in spite of what I want and I'm trying to be strong and—"

Bay cuts me off before I can finish my sentence. "Do you enjoy being strong?"

"What?"

"I asked if you enjoy being strong? Do you like it? What do you think it means to be strong, Missy? Is it doing everything yourself? Is it being an island, shouldering the burden? Is it having to keep it all together? Tell me what you think being strong means."

"I…" I trail off, unsure how to answer.

"I have five sisters. They're all very different women. Cora is one of the most badass girls I've ever met. She's forthright, outspoken, blunt. She keeps Huck on his toes and refuses to take any of his shit. Bonnie is amazing, she's a natural caregiver, she wants to look after everyone, she takes on too much and runs herself ragged trying to be everything to everyone. Alice is sweet, she's quiet and shy, when we first met her, she barely spoke two words, she had all kinds of baggage. Lulu is a force, she was a single mom, she moved across country to make a better life for her and Poppy. The woman is a straight-up genius, a total girl boss, she's going to be a lawyer and she's going to be amazing at it. And lastly there's Juni, she turned Teddy's world around, she refused to let him walk all over her, she made him work to win her. All five of my sisters are total badasses. They are five of the strongest people I've ever met. But they're not alone. They aren't doing everything themselves, because they have my brothers and as couples, they figured out what being strong meant to them as part of a team."

Inhaling sharply, I hate that my breath is shaky as I listen to him.

"Bonnie lets Beau help her find balance, she allowed him to take some of her responsibilities and make them his, and now they're both the caregivers. She might only be twenty-three, but she's mother hen to all of us, and instead of giving everything to care for others, she's strong enough to let Beau take care of her. He takes care of her, so she can take care of us. Cora was the queen of casual when she met Huck, he messed up, probably worse than I have, but her strength is that she decided to stay when she had every reason to walk away. She is the only person I've met who can handle my brother and even though they fight, they love just as hard. Alice says she was broken and that Granger is the thing that holds all her shattered pieces together. I don't know all what they have going on, but her strength is that she willingly gives herself over into Granger's care, trusting that he's strong enough to make the right choices for both of them. Lulu's strength is her trust, being with Penn was scary, allowing her life and Poppy's life to change for a man she barely knew was tough, but she was strong enough to have faith that Penn would be there for them both. And Juni, well, her strength is that she understood her own worth and forced my brother to look past his bullshit and see her, it wasn't smooth sailing but she had the capacity to admit her own failings and then work with Teddy to figure out how happy looked for them both."

Bay's brows furrow together and he leans forward and rests his forehead against mine. "Being strong doesn't just have one definition, strength can be shown in a million different ways. I know what I said about wanting a woman to be strong and independent. Those things were what I looked for in a woman to have a casual fling with. I didn't want someone to ever think things could be more than a physical release, and the easiest way to ensure that was to find women who weren't looking for a husband."

Thinking about all the women Bay's had "flings" with makes me cringe, but he just smooths out my expression with his thumb and carries on speaking.

"The absolute last thing I want from you is for you to be so strong and independent that you don't want or need me. I know the last few months have changed you, and even if I hate how it happened, I'm really fucking proud of who you are and what you've achieved. I know I have no right to ask anything of you, but I'm begging. I'm on my fucking knees, Missy, begging you to stop being strong, just for a little while. Be weak for me, babe, allow yourself to be weak and let me see who you are. Just you, not the person you think I want you to be, not the person whatever you have going on in your life demands you be. For a minute, just be you, the real, raw, ugly and honest you that you hide from everyone else. Let me show you that although I'll take you however you come, I want the you hidden beneath all the layers of defense, all the hurt and anger and fear. I started to fall in love with the scared girl I met sleeping rough in an RV. I'm falling in love with the tough little badass who moved halfway across the country for a fresh start. I'm already in love with the little hellcat who likes to be owned in the bedroom, who's ready to let me lead her to a world of pleasure. So please, babe, please let me love *all* of you."

"I'm scared," I confess weakly, not sure I trust him enough to make myself that vulnerable. He hurt me today. I thought I could let him leave, that I'd survive without him, but I was wrong. I would have lived, but I know I'd never be whole. I'm not sure how he's done it, but in a couple of days he's burrowed under all of my defenses, and when he told me I needed to pick between my relationship with him and my friendship with Cody, my heart broke.

"I'm scared too," he whispers. "It's okay to be scared, as long as you don't let that fear own you. That's what I did when we met. I saw you and I saw this innocent, beautiful, scared little fae creature, all crazy red hair and terrified eyes and I knew that even though you were mine, you were meant for more than I could ever give you."

"But you never asked what I wanted."

"I know," he nods. "I should have, but as much as I want to say it doesn't matter, I'm twenty-two years older than you. I'm old enough to be your dad and when I looked at you, all I saw was me tying you to me and holding you back from this huge adventure your life could be."

Anger wells up inside of me and I push his hand off my face as I shake my head. "You want to see the real me?" I demand. "You want to see the person I am beneath all the fear and defenses that have kept me afloat for almost three years?"

I pause, allowing myself a glance in his direction. "I want to be loved," I yell. "My parents died when I was a baby and I was raised as an obligation. When I was sixteen my uncle came and found us and for two years, he treated me like family. He cared for me, provided for me, he was there when my nana died and then on my eighteenth birthday, he pinned me to my bed, rubbed his dick all over me and said I either had to pay back his hospitality on my back, or by signing over an inheritance I never even knew I had. He never cared about me, he played the role of doting uncle and then he threatened to rape and abuse me if I didn't give him money. When he found out that I had more money coming my way when I turn twenty-one, he used threats of selling me and sharing me to keep me under his thumb. He forced me to take a job, then took all of my wages, he kept me completely reliant on him and he only agreed not to force himself on me or pimp me out to his disgusting friends as long as I promised to sign the rest of my inheritance over to him. The day I decided to sleep in that RV rather than go home, was because he'd gotten drunk and forced his way into my room in the middle of the night. Until I slept at your home, I hadn't slept a full night without waking up terrified of finding him or someone else in my room in almost three years. The person I am deep down inside, is a scared, lonely little girl who wants to be loved. You say you started to fall for me that day we met, but instead you rejected me, so I need to be strong, I need to carry my own burden, because you let me go once and if I give myself fully to you, when you walk away again, I won't survive."

Once I finish my tirade, I slump down, falling to my butt as all the anger melts from me, replaced by sorrow and exhaustion.

"Babe, Missy." Bay picks me up and places me down in his lap, his arms wrapping tightly around me, holding me against his chest. "Fuck," he rasps against my head, his voice shaky. "Fuck."

I'm so tired that I just close my eyes and let him hold me. I shouldn't, I shouldn't be letting him get any closer than I already have, but my confession, telling him everything that's led to this moment has left me raw and exposed, and as much as I'm angry and hurt by his behavior, I've also never felt safer than when I'm in his arms.

It's such a cliché, isn't it, that a man who rejected and hurt me is also the one who makes me feel better, who can comfort me, even when he's the reason I'm in pain. I melt into his embrace, taking his strength when mine has evaporated. Maybe he's right and I don't have to be strong in the way I think I do, but if I let down my guard, what do I do when he leaves again?

"You've been strong for so fucking long, Missy, let me be strong for you for a little while. When you're ready, I'll help you build those walls again if that's what you need.

I'll do whatever you need me to do, I just can't leave you, please don't ask me to."

Exhaling, I try to figure out what to do. I could push him away, ask him to leave and refuse to see him when he comes looking for me, or I can give in and accept what he's offering. Neither of those things is really what I want. Experiencing Bay's all-or-nothing attitude today was awful and giving in to him feels like I'll be letting him win. Allowing him to think he can be an asshole and it'll all be okay as long as he grovels afterward isn't a precedent I want to set.

"I..." my voice shakes and I push out of his lap, sitting down on the floor beside him, our legs still touching. "I don't want you to leave, but I'm not asking you to stay."

"What does that mean?"

"I like you, Bay, I'm falling for you and it's scary because you hurt me and you keep hurting me. I don't want you to give up on me, but I'm not ready to let down my shields and give myself over to you."

"So, what are you saying?"

"I guess I'm saying I think we should date."

"Date?" he says, spitting the word from his lips, like it's left an unpleasant taste in his mouth.

"You wanted me to just fall in line with your plan for us and I've done that for the last couple of days, but when things don't go your way, you turn into an asshole and demand things from me that are selfish and unreasonable. I want to be with you, but I want you to be with me for the right reasons and not just because of some fate-driven urge to own me."

"That's not—" Bay starts, but I lift my hand, silencing

him.

"I know you want me, Bay, I know you think you're falling in love with me, and maybe you are. But we don't know each other and I need to get to know you, just with some boundaries. So, I think we should date."

"I haven't dated anyone since I was in college," Bay grimaces.

"Well, I've never dated anyone, so it'll be a learning experience for both of us," I smile shakily.

"How long?"

My brow furrows at his question. "What do you mean?"

"I mean, how long do you want us to date before you agree to marry me?"

"How long do normal people date before they make such a huge commitment?"

"Nope, that's not happening, this thing between us isn't like what other people have. We know we're meant to be together. We know that it's more than coincidence or lust that brought us together, so we can't put the same time line on our relationship," he argues.

"Fine," I concede. "Six months, we date for six months and then at the end of it we reassess."

His laugh is so dry I swear I could cut it with a knife. "No, a week, we date for a week and then we get married."

"A week is ridiculous."

"Fine, a month, but that's my final offer. We'll date for a month and then I put my ring on your finger and give you my last name."

Honestly, I'm surprised he's agreed at all, so a month is probably better than I could hope for. "Okay, a month."

Holding out my hand I wait for him to take it.

Glancing down, he smirks, the sides of his mouth twitching with amusement, but he grips my palm with his and shakes. Then he leans forward and claims my mouth in a passionate kiss, parting my lips and pushing his tongue into my mouth, exploring and branding it as his.

Something about sealing our agreement with a kiss feels right, and even though I'm still hurt and angry, knowing I'm not losing him settles the fear and worry that's been sitting on my chest since he left this morning. I expect him to pull back, but I don't know why, our physical connection is the thing that's the easiest between us. When we're naked we agree on everything, he likes to take charge and I like him to. It's outside of sex that we seem to be having problems figuring things out.

His hands curl around my back, holding me to him as he devours my mouth. This is more than a kiss of agreement, this is him cementing his claim on my body, even if my mind isn't fully on board. I don't try to fight him. I know that having sex won't solve our problems, but it really does feel amazing and Bay is a giver, especially when he's apologizing. So, I don't argue when he strips my clothes, nor when he spreads my legs and devours me until I'm wrung out from all the orgasms. Only then does he take off his own clothes, lift me onto his lap and slide his dick all the way into me in one slow glide.

We've never had sex with me on top, but his fingertips grip my hips, showing me how to move, and guiding my pace until I'm riding him like a cowgirl. My hands cover his, holding on while he arches his hips, meeting me thrust for thrust. Until this moment, I've never understood the expression "topping from the bottom," but that's exactly what Bay's doing. He's put me on top to allow me the impression that I'm in charge, but it's him calling the shots. I don't care. When it feels this good, why does it even matter? As my orgasm peaks, I throw back my head and scream, my stomach tensing as my nerves burst to life, sparks of pleasure-filled pain arcing across my skin.

His hold on my hips tightens and he lifts me up and drags me back down, fucking me from his position beneath me until he comes with a groan, pulling me down to his chest as his lips seal over mine yet again.

After our breaths have calmed, Bay rolls us to the side, somehow managing to keep his dick inside of me even as we move. I don't bother arguing with him about his obsession with having his dick inside of me after we've finished having sex. He likes it and I don't hate it, so why cause an argument?

If we're going to fight about anything, it should be about the fact he didn't use a condom again, but I'm too relaxed to care right this second. Today has been a hell of a day and even though nothing has really been resolved between us, I feel calm and at peace right in this second. All the problems, issues and insecurities can be tomorrow me's problem. Today's me is enjoying the afterglow with a man I could so easily fall head over heels for.

"Tell me about your uncle," Bay says, his softly spoken voice filling the silent air.

Sighing, I try to decide how to explain it, then I realize I blurted it all out earlier, so I might as well tell him the truth.

"Ernie turned up on mine and Nana's doorstep when I was sixteen. He said he'd been searching for us and then he asked us to move to Montana to stay with him. He said he adored my dad and that as soon as he found out about me, he had to find us and make sure we were taken care of. My nana was old and sick and honestly, when he showed up, we were on the verge of losing our apartment, so we packed up and moved. Nana died six months later and Ernie was amazing. He assured me he'd take care of me, that I had a home with him, family. He was doting and supportive and everything I could have wished for. He didn't have many rules, but he didn't approve of me dating or having a boyfriend. He said I was too young to date, that I needed to concentrate on my education. Until the day I turned eighteen I would have called him my savior. He was my family, and I loved him, I thought he loved me too."

"So, what happened after you turned eighteen?" Bay growls, his face twisted into an angry grimace.

"The night before my birthday, he was sweet as pie, telling me how excited he was for my 'big' birthday. The next morning, I woke up to him lying on top of me." Swallowing, I try to speak past the revulsion in my throat. "His dick was hard and he held me down on my bed and told me I owed him. He said that he'd taken care of me and paid for everything, and now I had to pay him back for all the money he'd spent on me. He knew I didn't have any money, so he told me I could start to pay off my debt by sucking his dick and fucking him, or I could sign over my inheritance to him."

"That fucking asshole."

Sighing, I turn my face and press my cheek into his chest. "He took me to a lawyer's office and had me tell them that I wanted to have the money transferred into Ernie's account. That was when I found out that he's not my uncle at all, he's my second cousin. He knew my paternal grandparents had left money to me, but apparently, he didn't realize that it was left in trust. I only got access to part of it when I turned eighteen. I get more when I'm twenty-one and then again at twenty-five."

"So why didn't you leave after you gave him the money? Why stay?"

"I was eighteen, I was still in high school and without money or family, where could I go? I considered sleeping rough, but when it came down to it, I was in danger no matter where I was. Ernie told me I could stay on the agreement that when I got my inheritance at twenty-one, I signed it over to him again. I only had a few weeks left at school, and once I graduated, he got me a job at Mountain View Pines. I didn't realize until I got my first pay stub that he'd put his bank account details down and my wages were being paid directly into his account. My boss was his friend and she wouldn't let me change where the money was being sent. When I told him I'd earned that money and that it was mine, he gave me a bill for a hundred thousand dollars. He told me that's how much it's cost him to take care of me and that any money I earned would come off the money I owed him."

"Jesus, what about your friends?"

"I never told them what happened and then they went to college and I didn't. I've spent the last almost three years trying to scrape together enough money to leave. He promised to keep his hands to himself, although he always let me know that I could work off my debts on my back and he told me if I tried to leave, he'd take what he was owed by force and when he was finished, he'd give me to his friends. Keeping me broke, alone and scared was his way of controlling me. The day we met, was a couple of days after he got drunk off his ass and broke into my bedroom in the middle of the night. I managed to get away from him, but I knew I had to leave. For the first time, sleeping rough was the safer option and, well, you know the rest. I'd managed to stash some cash in Mr. Prentiss's room. Any time I'd managed to save any money, Ernie always found it and took it. I was hoping to avoid him for a few more weeks, make some more cash doing shifts for other people and being paid under the table, but then I got fired and the rest is history."

"Fuck, Missy, I'm so sorry. What happened to your grandparents? Why didn't they come for you?" Bay asks, cupping my cheek and rubbing soft circles over the skin.

"I don't know much, but Cody had a lawyer look into my family for me. My dad's family all still live in Ireland. I have a half sister. Apparently when my dad met my mom, he was already married. I don't know details, but from what Cody managed to find, his family didn't know he was dead until quite a few years after it happened. They put money into a trust for me just before Ernie turned up on our doorstep and they both died shortly afterward. Cody thinks they didn't know about me until then, which is possible I suppose."

"When do you turn twenty-one? Can that fucking dick get your money without you? Did you sign anything when you accessed your trust at eighteen?"

"My birthday is May 4th and honestly, I don't really know what I signed. That day, my life fell apart and I barely even remember going to the lawyer's office. I don't want the money; he can have it for all I care."

"Babe, that money's yours and even if you want to give every penny away to a charity that knits hats for furless cats, that would be better than that dick getting even a single dime off you again," Bay snarls angrily.

"Hats for furless cats?" I snicker.

"Those little bastards get cold," Bay jokes.

"I just don't want to deal with him. If I never see him again it'll be too soon, and I know if I step foot inside that lawyer's office, he's going to turn up to get his money."

"No, fuck that. When you go to claim what's yours, the money your family wanted you to have, you'll do it with a wall of fucking Barnetts behind you. You never have to be scared of him again. You got away and you fucking owned your fresh start. That asshat is nothing but a road bump in the rearview mirror. I swear I won't ever let him touch or threaten you again, we're fucking lumberjacks and there's plenty of places up on the mountain that a person can go missing and never be seen again."

I can't help it, I smile. "Are you offering to kill my not-uncle for me?"

"Too fucking right I am. If I ever see the motherfucker again, I'll take great pleasure in ripping him limb from limb."

"Another reason why I don't ever need to see him again."

"I'm serious though, babe, that money is yours, and even if you don't want it, he absolutely shouldn't get it either."

Sighing, I spread my fingers out on his chest. "Cody said the same."

"He's a smart man," Bay says, his tone a little dry, but not openly antagonistic.

"You need to go," I say on a yawn.

"What?"

"We're dating, that doesn't include sleepovers, at least not yet."

"Are you serious?" he asks on a bark of laughter.

"Deadly. You hurt me today, Bay, I can't just pretend nothing happened."

His sigh is solemn and loud. "I'm sorry."

"I know you are, but that doesn't mean it's all forgotten. I need some time and some space."

"I don't like space," he growls.

"Space doesn't have to be a bad thing," I say, trying to sound upbeat, even though if I was truly honest with both him and myself, the absolute last thing I want is to put space between us. Today, without him, has been awful. I've spent half the time crying and the other cursing his name to any deity that'd listen. Our relationship is right on the verge of toxic, but even after such a short amount of time together, he's a drug that I just can't seem to quit.

A part of me knows I'm being too forgiving, that allowing him to think I belong to him, in any capacity is a big red flag, but I want to be his so much that I simply can't resist, or maybe I just don't want to.

"Space is always a bad thing. Space allows time for doubt and there's no room for doubt between us."

"Bay," I breathe sadly.

"Can I stay tonight? I don't think I can actually leave you here without losing my mind."

"Okay, but just tonight," I agree.

Not sounding so eager might be a good start to actually making him do as I'm asking, but I don't want him to go, and this way I don't have to stand by my guns and watch him leave.

***

Waking up in his arms is like heaven, his body heat wrapped around me is like being embraced by the perfect temperature comforter, and a blissful sense of safety surrounds me whenever he's near. I like him being here, and that is so scary to someone who has been completely alone for almost three years.

"Penny for them?" Bay asks, his voice rumbly and gruff.

"You scare the hell out of me," I admit on a rush, instantly wishing I could swallow the words back down again.

His whole body tenses behind me. "Why?"

"Because until I met you and your family, I was so completely alone. The only person I had was Ernie, and we both know what he's like. Then all of a sudden there you were, this man who was supposed to be mine and even after you were gone, there was Cody and suddenly I wasn't alone anymore. Now I have you both and it's terrifying because I'm not sure I'd be okay being all alone again."

Rolling me to my back, Bay hovers above me, his body pressed lightly against mine, his weight held up on his knees and elbows. "You'll never be alone again, Missy. I'm never going to let you go and even if I wasn't there, you'll always have Cody and the rest of my family. You have so many people now, babe, you'll be sick to death of them half the time and begging for a moment's peace without a dozen people all wanting to talk to you all the time."

I laugh, but I can feel the emotion clogging my throat. What he's offering is tantalizing. Family. People who care about me. Him. I want it all so much my lungs seem to stop working and for a long moment, I can't do anything but stare up into his earnest, honest eyes.

"They're all yours, Mis, I know I fucked up yesterday by trying to come between you and Cody, but I promise I'll never ever try to take any of them from you, or step between you and them. They're all yours, just waiting to know you and love you."

Tears fill my eyes and I try to blink them away, but they spill over my lids and drip down my cheeks.

"Babe, don't cry, please don't fucking cry."

Strong arms band around me and a moment later, I'm lying on Bay's chest and he's the one on the bed beneath me. One of his arms is banded tightly around me and the other is stroking the back of my head, holding me to him as he coos reassurances into my hair.

When my tears are dry and Bay's promised me a thousand times that he's sorry, that I'm not alone, that I have him and all the people who love him love me too, I lift my face from his chest and press a kiss to his lips. It's not aggressive, or meant to lead to more, it's sweet and chaste and kind of perfect.

"Do you have to work today?"

"Yeah, I'm probably already late. Good thing my boss is a softy who won't fire me for being the worst employee in the world the last few days."

"You guys rent an office space, right?"

"Yeah, it's a few blocks from here, close enough to walk."

Bay nods. "Do you have a spare desk I can use? We've been meaning to set up a digital appointment system for a while, I might as well get to work on it while I'm here."

"Yeah, we can find you some space, do you have a laptop with you?"

"Yeah, it's in my bag. You shower and get ready; I'll speak to Cody and make us all some breakfast."

Nodding, I reluctantly lift myself off his chest and climb out of bed.

"Missy."

"Yeah?"

"We're going out on a date tonight."

"Isn't it customary to ask, not just tell a girl?"

"Maybe, but I'm not asking, little Imp. I'm taking you out tonight and every night until you agree to marry me."

"We can't go on a date every night." I laugh.

"Why not?"

"Because that's crazy."

Pushing himself up to a sitting position, the sheet falls down, revealing his deliciously toned chest, stomach, and the sexy trail of hair that goes all the way down to where his dick is hard and ready to go.

A dart of lust hits me and my stomach and sex clench excitedly.

"What's the matter, little Imp?" Bay asks, sliding his hand down to his cock and gripping it. Pushing the sheet all the way off and giving me the perfect view of his hand, the swollen head of his dick and the glistening bead of precum pooling at the tip.

"I need to get ready."

"Okay," Bay says, slowly sliding his hand up and down his length, his lips parted slightly as he watches me watching him.

"I need to go to work."

He nods.

"Can you stop doing that?" My eyes widen a little as he reaches between his legs and cups his balls with his free hand.

"Why? Do you want to do it instead? Or would you rather I fill you up? Is your cunt all needy and empty?" His voice lowers until each word is a taunt.

"You're not playing fair."

"I'm not playing at all, Mis. If you want my dick, all you have to do is ask. It's yours. Any time, any place. Just ask. So do you need me, Missy?"

Swallowing, I watch his fist squeeze and gradually increase the pace, moving up and down.

"Does this dick belong to you?" Bay asks, dragging my eyes away from him jacking his cock.

"Err."

"Who do I belong to, Missy?" His tone hardens, he's

demanding an answer, and my body and mind react.

"Me, you belong to me."

"Good girl. That's right, I belong to you. So, who does my dick belong to?"

"Me."

"Yes it does. So tell me what you need. Do you need me to fuck you?"

I read the term dick drunk once in a book and until this moment I never really understood what it meant, it seemed so ridiculous that someone could be so desperate for sex they'd lose their minds. In this moment I get it. We had sex last night, I should be good, I shouldn't be so horny my thighs are damp with arousal. But I want him. No, I need him. "Yes."

"Yes, what, Imp?"

"Yes, I need you to fuck me."

Smiling, he releases his dick, lifts his hand and crooks his finger at me, beckoning me to him, and I go, like a moth to a flame. Turning his hand over, he offers it to me palm up and I slide my fingers across his hand, entwining my fingers with his and letting him pull me back to him.

"Fast or slow, Imp? Do you want to feel like you're running the show, or like I'm taking charge?"

A guttural moan slips from my lips, I don't care how we do things, I just need him to touch me, to do something to quell this need inside of me.

"So needy, aren't you? Come and sit on my face, let me take the edge off."

Reeling me in, he lies back on the bed, then guides me to crawl up his body. Once I'm positioned with my knees on either side of his head, he pulls me down and feasts on me until I've orgasmed twice and his face is wet with my arousal. Then he spins me around, pushes me forward so my cheek is to the comforter and my knees are beneath my chest. I'm bent like a pretzel, but he doesn't check that I'm okay, or give me the chance to move, before he's shoving my thighs wide, grabbing my butt and filling me with his dick.

He fucks me like he's on a mission to come and he does, but not until I've exploded all over his dick twice. Then he chases me to the finish line, releasing inside of me on a groan of bliss, his fingers still holding me tight as his hips jerk.

"Jesus, Mis, you feel so fucking good, I'd happily die with my dick buried in your tight cunt." I feel his weight move behind me and then a sharp pain as his teeth sink into the skin of my butt.

"Oww," I shriek.

"Sorry, babe," he chuckles. "I couldn't resist, your ass is just so fucking bitable. I can't wait to fuck it."

"Your dick isn't going anywhere near my butt," I hiss, slowly unfurling myself from my position, face down on the bed.

Lurching over me, Bay's heavy weight topples me forward just as I get my legs out from beneath myself, and he's pinning me to the bed with his chest pressed against my back. "Is that a challenge, little Imp?"

His hard dick prods against my ass, sliding between my cheeks and gliding over my hole.

"You're heavy," I gasp, and he instantly lifts his weight

off me, but his hand pushes between my thighs, his fingers collecting his release that's dripping out of me and pushing it back inside. I know I shouldn't be letting him do it, but as much as I hate to admit it, I find it sexy that he wants all of his cum in me.

Once he's finished slowly fingering me, he lifts off me completely and slaps my ass with his open palm. "Time to get up, babe, you've got work to do."

He laughs when I turn and glare at him, then blows me a kiss, before he bounds off the bed, scoops me into his arms and carries me into the bathroom, depositing me next to the shower as he reaches in and turns on the water. Kissing me sweetly on the lips, he pads naked out of the bathroom, leaving me alone to shower.

By the time I'm clean and wrapped in a towel, Bay is still naked, his dick soft, but still impressively large. "Bathroom's all yours."

"Thanks, babe." Smiling, he passes me as he walks into the bathroom and I blink at the familiar domesticity of it. Is this how it'd be if we lived together? Waking up together, having mind-blowing sex and then taking turns in the bathroom to get ready for work. An image of stepping out of his rooms to have breakfast with all of his family around the huge table at their home flashes into my mind.

Shit, where did that come from? I live in Vermont; this is my home. Isn't it? Being here with Cody is the happiest I can ever remember being, this apartment is home. So why, when I'm thinking about a future with Bay, am I picturing it in Montana, the one state I vowed never to go back to ever again?

Maybe it's because being around Cody and Bay is making me think about family so much. I knew when Cody and I got here, that although I planned to stay, his home is back in Rockhead Point with the rest of the Barnett clan. Not wanting to think about losing him, I just sort of pushed thoughts of him leaving to the back of my mind.

When Bay showed up and talked about forever with me, a part of me thought that having two Barnetts here might be enough to convince them to stay, but I realize how selfish that is.

Bay promised me that his family was mine now. That even if he wasn't here, they were all just waiting to get to know me… to love me. Is that true? The other wives seemed very close, and whenever Cody's spoken about them the last few months, he's called them his sisters, not his sisters-in-law. From what I've garnered, being with one of the guys is an instant invite into the exclusive Barnett club. I've never been a joiner, but this is one club I'm desperate to be a part of.

I'm jolted back into the moment when Bay appears in front of me, a white towel tied around his hips. "What's the matter, little Imp?" he asks softly, cupping my chin in his hand, tipping my head back and forcing me to look up at him.

Sighing, I try to smile, but I can't force my lips to move.

"Don't you dare regret this or forgiving me. I'm an asshole, but I'm your asshole. I'm not fucking perfect, but nothing we do together is a fucking regret," he snarls angrily, his grip on my chin tightening.

"It's not that," I exhale.

"Then what? Talk to me, Mis, let me shoulder some of that burden for you."

God, it's the perfect thing for him to say. I know I should still be mad. I know I should be playing hard to get, making him grovel, but I just want to give in. When I lost my shit and yelled at him last night, it's like the last wall that was holding me back from him shattered and now I have to decide if I want to rebuild it or not. He knows everything, all the nasty little truths that I'd normally hide.

"I…" I start.

"Baby."

"Eventually you're going to want to go home, aren't you?"

Silently cursing, Bay tips his head back, clenches his eyes closed and then exhales. When he opens them again and looks at me, I brace myself for what he's going to say. "You're my home, Missy. Wherever you are is the only place I'll ever want to be. So if you're here in Burlington, that's where I'm going to be too. We can find a nice little house, I could even open up a garage here, or I could help Cody."

"You'd move here, permanently?" I ask, shocked.

His eyes soften and he crouches down, still holding my face in his hand, but at eye level now. "There's nothing I wouldn't do for you, Missy."

I melt. I'm nothing more than a puddle of goo on the floor. He's being truthful. I might not know him that well, but I can see the sincerity in his gaze. He'd do it, he'd move his life, leave his family. For me.

I know what I have to do too.

That night he takes me on a date. I expect dinner or the movies, but instead he packs us a picnic and drives us down to a small beach I didn't even know existed. He lays out a blanket and then unpacks the beautiful food he's prepared for us and we eat it as the sun goes down.

After, we have sweet, torturously slow sex in my bed and I don't make him leave.

The next night, he takes me to the aquarium and we watch the colorful fishes and jellyfish in the see-through tunnels that lead a path beneath the water. We laugh at the penguins as they joyfully waddle and dive, and I don't make him leave that night either.

For the next three weeks, just like he said he would, he takes me on a date every single night. Sometimes he arranges activities where Cody can come too and even though I sometimes catch him glancing at his brother and me together a little enviously, I think he's gotten over his jealousy of our friendship.

We ride bikes, go rock climbing, take cooking lessons, eat at amazing restaurants, see movies in the park and even sail a boat around the lake. He's drowning me in romance, sweet gestures and more orgasms than I even thought it was possible to have. He spends every night in my bed and we play silly get-to-know-you games each night before we fall asleep, his dick still inside of me, just like we both enjoy. Every morning, I wake up enclosed in his safe arms and I've never been happier in my entire life.

Chapter Nineteen

These have easily been the best three weeks of my life.

I've spent my days in the office with Cody and Missy, getting the online booking system for the garage set up and then transferred all of our current appointments to it. Then I set up three tablets, so the guys back home can put all their notes and any parts required straight into the record form for that customer and car. At the end of each day someone can just print out a list of all the parts that are needed and the system even automatically creates an invoice for the customer. It's something Penn and I have been talking about doing for a couple of years, but we've been so busy with cars, that we haven't had the time to actually do it.

I hadn't realized just how burned out I'd been until I've

had these weeks to just unwind and take stock of what's important. Missy is everything. She's sweet and funny and at times goofy. Cody warned me the day I turned up here to claim her, that she wears her strive for independence like a bulletproof vest and back at the start, that was true. But everything changed the day she told me all she wanted was to be loved.

It baffles me that she doesn't feel like she's ever had that, because I fell in love with her the moment I laid eyes on her. The way I feel about her now, makes that initial want feel like nothing more than a drop of water in an ocean. Now I know her, I can see how she's feeling by the way she smiles, the turn of her lips and the way she fidgets when she's unsure or nervous. I know her and she knows me, right down to stupid things, like how she hates panties that go up her butt and grimaces if a pickle even glances in her direction

I'm head over heels in love with her and I hope she feels the same way. I think she does. Neither of us have brought up the subject of me moving to Burlington permanently again, but if this is where she wants to be, then I'll do whatever it takes to make her happy. I had an appointment with a local realtor yesterday and tonight's date is going to be me taking her to see the nicest house I've found so far. It's not far from the apartment she and Cody are sharing and still close enough to the office so that she can walk, although I also plan to teach her to drive the moment she agrees to get behind the wheel. She says she's not insured to drive my rental and won't risk Cody's car in case she gets in an accident.

"Mis, you almost ready? Our reservation is at seven, we need to get going if we don't want to miss it," I call into the bedroom, then pad back over to the couch and sit down next to Cody who is sprawled out in sweats, a bottle of beer in his hand.

"Where you taking her tonight?"

"We're going to that sushi restaurant. She's never had sushi, can you believe it?" I chuckle.

"That's because sushi is disgusting," Cody grimaces.

"If she hates it, we'll grab something from one of the food trucks up on the road by the lake. Then we have an appointment with a realtor," I say quietly.

"What? Why?"

"Shh," I hiss, glancing over my shoulder to check if Missy is still in the bedroom.

"Why are you meeting a realtor?"

"I've been looking for a house for us, I want to show her my favorite."

"You're going to move here?" he asks, appalled.

"Well, I'm sure as fuck not going to leave her here. This is where she wants to be, so yeah, I'm moving here."

"Shit," Cody exhales, his shoulders slumping.

"What?"

Inhaling slowly, he sighs. "I want to go home, Bay. I miss everyone. The babies are growing up and I'm missing it. I really thought you'd convince her to come home with you. I never really thought you'd stay."

"Are you going to go home then?" I ask shakily. I'm not a fucking kid, I've lived away from my family before, but I'd just assumed if we stayed here, that Cody would stay too.

"If she needs me to stay, I'll stay," he nods, but it's clearly hard for him.

"No, bro, I can look after her and we can come visit. Go home, love on the kids and tell them Uncle Bay and Auntie Missy will be coming to visit soon. I'm not sure I ever thanked you for looking after her, but I'm so fucking glad she had you. I was jealous and I acted like a dick, but I never stopped being thankful that she wasn't alone. She's as lucky to have you as I am. I love you, bro."

Reaching for my baby brother, I pull him into a quick hug, pounding his back before releasing him, just as Missy opens the bedroom door and steps out. My heart beats faster as I take her in. She's fucking gorgeous in a cute pair of shorts and top, her feet clad in flat strappy sandals, her hair down in glossy curls, just how I love it.

"You ready, babe?" I ask, jumping up from the couch and striding over to her, palming the back of her neck and pressing a hot, claiming kiss to her lips.

"Yep," she says breathlessly when I pull away from her mouth.

"Have fun," Cody calls, his attention on the TV, but I can see the sadness on his face. I really hope my brother finds his someone soon.

Taking Missy's hand, I lead her out of the apartment and down onto the sidewalk. Instead of walking, I guide her to the car.

"I thought we were going to eat?"

"We are, I just need to stop somewhere first."

"Oh, okay," she nods, letting me fasten her seat belt and

close her door.

The house is just a few minutes' drive, so we get there just as the realtor is pulling into the driveway.

"Come on," I say, stopping at the curb and climbing out to open her door.

Her brow furrows. "What are we doing here?"

She doesn't argue when I unfasten her belt and lift her out of her seat. The rental isn't as high as my truck, but after I explained that I love lifting her in and out, she stopped complaining and instead lets me carry her around, just because it makes me happy.

"What do you think?" I ask, towing her up the driveway and toward the front door.

"I don't understand," Mis says, glancing between me, the house and the woman who has unlocked the door and then stepped to the side.

"I know you love living with Cody, but I thought having some privacy would be good for us." Stepping into her, I lean down and whisper. "Then you can be as loud as you want, without anyone hearing."

"You rented us a house?" she asks slowly.

"No. Renting is a waste of money. If you like it, I'll buy it. Come and look around, see what you think."

Her steps are a little sluggish, but she follows me into the house, wandering in and out of the rooms as I tell her all the things I think we could do to the place to make it feel more like home.

The realtor Hannah politely excuses herself to allow us to chat and Missy waits until she's gone before she speaks. "You want to buy us a house?"

"Yes. It doesn't have to be this house, if you don't like it, we can keep looking or we can even buy a parcel of land and build our own. We know a good contractor," I laugh.

"You want to buy a house here in Burlington?"

My brow furrows as I take in her conflicted expression, her mouth is downturned and she's nibbling at her bottom lip with her teeth, her fingers picking at the skin on her thumb.

"Babe, what's going on? I thought you liked it here in Burlington? I know it hasn't been the full month yet, but what fucking difference will a week make? I love you, Missy. I know you and I love you, and I want to fucking marry you and live together."

"You love me?" she gasps.

Reeling her toward me, I cup her cheeks in my palms. "Of course I fucking love you."

Her silent hitch of breath and the tears that fill her eyes fucking kill me. "I love you too," she whispers, a single tear spilling over and rolling down her cheek.

"Me loving you, and you loving me isn't something to cry about," I tell her, pressing my forehead to hers for a long second, needing a moment to process.

"They're happy tears. I love you, Bay, so much it terrifies me."

Smiling, I close my eyes and let her words wash over me, changing me, making me new and complete and undisputedly hers. "Don't be scared, little Imp, I'm going to take the very best care of you, because I love you more than anything else in the world. I love you so much, you consume every thought I have and I wouldn't change it for anything."

I'm not sure if she kisses me or I kiss her, but somehow our lips touch and it's more than just an action, it's a revelation. Its acceptance and relief and unison and need and fucking love. Blinding, consuming, obsessive, wonderful fucking love.

When her lips are kiss swollen and my dick is so hard I'm pretty sure it could cut through my pants and her clothes given the chance, we finally separate. "So," I pant. "The house."

"I don't like it," Missy says breathily.

"Okay, tell me which parts you do like, if there are any, then I'll know what sort of thing to look for."

"It's in the wrong place."

"Oh," I ask, a little confused. "I thought you'd want to be somewhere close to the water."

"It's not that."

"Okay, so what is it?"

"It's not home."

"I can look into maybe buying the apartment if you're that attached to it."

"No. Bay, it's not home. Because home is Rockhead Point in a big house full of family."

Blinking, I stare down at the woman I love, who looks... nervous. I tamp down the hope that's surging up in me. "What are you saying, Mis?"

"I'm saying I want to go home, Bay. To your home, with Cody and your brothers and sisters and nieces and nephews."

Forcing my whoop of joy down, I narrow my eyes and

watch her carefully. "Is that what *you* want, or what you think I want?

"It's what I want. I love you, Bay, and if it's just you and me for the rest of our lives I'd be happier than I ever imagined I could be. But when I close my eyes and think about our future, it's not here on our own, it's in a house full of family and kids. I want it all, I want the crazy and the loud and the home full of love and memories and happiness."

Rushing her, I lift her off her feet and swing her around, whooping for joy. "We're going home, babe."

Missy laughs, wrapping her legs around me and her arms around my neck as I carry her out of the house, ignoring the shocked looks of the realtor, as I shout of my shoulder. "She doesn't like it." Striding past my car, I cross the street and straight down to the shores of the lake that's only fifty feet away. Then I lower Missy down, and let go of her.

"Bay, what are you doing?" she giggles.

Shoving my hand into my pocket, I pull out my wallet and grab the engagement ring I've been carrying around for weeks now. It's not the ring I picked before I left Montana. The ostentatious diamond wasn't Missy, so I returned it and bought her this one instead. It's a princess-cut emerald, set in a platinum band. The green is deep and rich and the moment I saw it I knew it would look perfect on my imp's hand.

Dropping to my knee at her feet, I hold the ring out to her with one hand and take her fingers with the other. "Missy McCormick, I love you more than anything in the world. You are the center of my universe and the most important thing in my life. I'm too old for you, too selfish to let you go, and I plan to steal all of your options that don't lead you to me. But if you let me, I'll make you so happy, and so loved you'll forget every moment before me. Please, babe, please say you'll marry me."

Tears are flowing down her face, but she's smiling as she nods, dropping to her knees next to me on the ground as she holds her hand out to me so I can slide my ring onto her finger.

Chapter Twenty

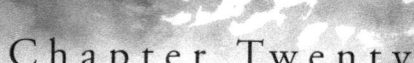

The day Bay asked me to marry him, we ended up skipping dinner and going home instead. As well as sealing our engagement with a kiss, we sealed it with a dozen orgasms. The next morning, Bay told Cody we were all going home and he forgave us for keeping him awake all night.

Now, two weeks later, we're on day three of the epic three-day drive back to Montana and I have never seen either Cody or Bay so excited before. I feel incredibly selfish that I kept them both away from their home for so long, but whenever I bring it up, they both assure me it hasn't killed them to be away from their family for a few months.

"Babe, you hungry?" Bay asks from the driver's seat.

"I could eat," I shrug.

"Thank fuck. I'm starving and this asshat wouldn't stop

while you were sleeping," Cody says, twisting around to face me and winking so I know he's kidding.

"Fuck off," Bay growls. "She's fucking tired, don't be a dick."

"She wouldn't be so tired if you stopped giving her your dick and let her sleep occasionally," Cody barbs back.

Sucking in a shocked gasp, I glare at Cody. "Cody," I hiss.

"Sorry, Mis, but it's true, I'm amazed you're not bowlegged with how much you pair fuck."

Without taking his eyes off the road, Bay reaches over and punches Cody in the arm. They continue to bicker and fight until Bay pulls off the highway and into the parking lot for a diner. A huge neon sign declares that they have the best pancakes in the state. We've been on the road for so long I don't even know what state we're in, but my stomach growls at the thought of pancakes as Bay opens my door and lifts me out. It's a weird habit we've gotten into, I'm guessing it's the caveman he barely bothers to try and tamp down coming out to play. I kind of enjoy being carried, so why question something we both enjoy, just because it's not supernormal?

Once my feet hit the ground, Bay leans down and kisses me. Entwining his fingers with mine, he lifts our joined hands up so he can press a kiss to where the engagement ring he got me is sitting on my finger. The emerald is huge and stunning, I don't remember telling him they were my favorite stone, but I must have for him to have picked the absolutely perfect ring for me.

"Come on, babe, let's go feed you."

Cody is already halfway to the doors when we start to move, but Bay thoughtfully slows his stride to match my much shorter one. He holds the door to the diner open when we step inside and Cody waves to us from a booth in the window.

For a roadside diner, it's surprisingly clean and modern, busy with a mix of families, teenagers and single guys. I'm smiling, right until the smell of bacon hits my nose, then saliva fills my mouth and my stomach revolts. Covering my nose with my free hand, I rip away from Bay and rush for the bathrooms, barely making it into a stall before I throw up.

Once my stomach is empty, I wash my hands, then swill my mouth with water from the tap, dabbing cool liquid onto the back of my neck. The immediate nausea has gone now that I've been sick, but the dull, unpleasant feeling in my stomach remains.

The moment I step into the hall, Bay circles me, his eyes wild with worry. "Mis, are you okay?" Lifting his hand to my forehead, he runs his free palm over my cheek.

"I'm okay. I threw up," I confess miserably. When it comes to being sick, I'm a huge baby, I hate throwing up. My nana had zero tolerance for illness, so as a kid, unless I was comatose or projectile vomiting, I went to school and learned not to moan. Being around Bay is making me soft, because even though I know I'll be fine, all I want now is for him to coddle me.

"Do you think it's something you ate? Could it be traveling in the back of the car? I told you to sit up front."

I shrug pathetically, not even attempting to protest when

Bay scoops me up into his arms and carries me out of the diner, sitting with me in his lap on a picnic bench a little way from the door. His cell phone rings, vibrating beneath my butt, and he lifts me slightly, pulling it from his pocket and bringing it to his ear, cradling me to his chest with the other arm wrapped around me.

"Hey. She got sick; I brought her outside to get some fresh air."

Bay listens for a minute, then looks down at me. "Do you think you can eat anything, babe?"

"Soup and grilled cheese and a bottle of water, please."

Repeating my order into the cell, he ends his call and wraps the other arm around me too. I melt into his chest, happy to be surrounded by his minty, comforting scent. Closing my eyes I relax into him, content to stay here in his arms for the rest of forever.

"Hey Mis, how you feeling?" Cody asks, placing three paper bags onto the picnic bench and handing me a bottle of water.

Inhaling slowly, my stomach growls. "I feel fine now, wow, maybe it was just motion sickness or something? I'm starving though."

Chuckling, Cody looks at Bay, then smirks as he unpacks the food, handing me a take-out container full of tomato soup and two huge pieces of gooey grilled cheese. I eat like I've never seen food before, shoveling spoonfuls of soup into my mouth between huge bites of squishy, crispy grilled cheese.

When I'm finished, I lick my fingers to get the last of the cheese grease off my skin, before wiping my hands with a napkin and dropping my empty containers into the trash. "That was the best grilled cheese I've ever tasted," I announce, patting my full stomach.

"Want me to go ask for the recipe so I can make it for you once we get home?" Bay smirks.

"Actually yes, that would be great," I tell him, ignoring his amusement.

Cody snorts. "Get to it, bro, what the lady wants, the lady gets, you remember what Cora was like."

Bay pales a little, but doesn't say anything as he kisses me quickly, lifts me from his lap and then disappears back into the diner.

"What's that about Cora?"

"Oh nothing," Cody says, waving me away. "Just when she has a taste for something she gets super into it. I once saw her eat an entire pie straight out of the pan with a fork, she nearly stabbed Huck when he tried to take a bite."

"That must have been some good pie. Do you have the recipe for that too? Wow, I could eat pie now you're talking about it."

Cody bursts out laughing, his head thrown back. "I'll go see if they have any. Any preference on type?"

"Peach, oh no, apple, ohhh or custard."

"I'll get you a selection," Cody laughs, pressing a kiss to the top of my head as he leaves.

Bay is coming back outside and they stop and speak for a moment before Cody heads inside and Bay comes back to me, lifting me back into his lap again.

"We've still got about four hours until we get home. You going to be okay, or do you want to find a hotel and head out again in the morning?"

Furrowing my brow, I look at him. "It's lunchtime, why would we check into a hotel now? It's only four hours, we could be home by dinner and I'd much rather sleep in your bed than in a hotel again."

"I just don't want you to get sick again," Bay says, stroking my hair out of my face and tucking it behind my ear.

"I'll be fine, it's probably just how I had lain down in the back seat."

"You can sit up front then and if you feel like you're going to get sick again, you let me know and we can find somewhere for you to rest up for a while."

"Okay," I agree, loving how sweet he's being.

Cody makes his way outside carrying another huge take-out bag, and we all climb back into the car and get on the road. Bay drives again and Cody gets into the back seat, immediately resting his back against the door, closing his eyes and going to sleep.

I dig into the pie, offering Bay bites of each different type before finishing off three slices myself. "Oh my gosh, I've eaten too much," I complain, rubbing my engorged belly and groaning.

"I think you look sexy with a belly," Bay winks.

Rolling my eyes, I shove the trash down by my feet and before I know it, I must fall asleep.

"Babe," Bay calls, his fingers stroking my cheek softly.

"Hum," I groan sleepily.

"We're home, Mis."

"Home?" I question, blinking slowly awake.

"Yeah, babe, home."

Bay's smile is blindingly wide and I smile back, almost as happy to be here as he is. Reaching over me, Bay's huge hand unclips my seat belt and I reach up and wrap my arms around his neck, letting him lift me from my seat and out of the car. He places me on the ground, but doesn't release me, leaning down to press a soft kiss against my lips. "Welcome home, little Imp."

Chapter Twenty-One

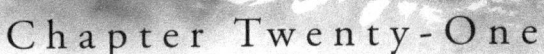

"Welcome home, little Imp," I whisper against her lips a second before I claim them with mine again. The last time we were here together I had my head up my ass, determined not to claim her. Now she's unquestionably mine, my ring on her finger and if I had to guess, my baby in her belly.

When she darted out of the diner and toward the bathroom to puke, I was too worried about her to think about what might have made her sick. Then she ate grilled cheese and tomato soup like she hadn't eaten in a month and I remembered the last time I'd seen a woman throw up, then eat like they were starving. It was Lulu when she was pregnant with the twins.

By the time Cody reminded us how Cora had savagely

protected pie like it was her precious and she was Gollum, I was desperately trying not to drive straight to a drugstore and demand my fiancée pee on a stick.

I've been waiting for the penny to drop for Mis, but I'm pretty sure she hasn't connected the dots yet. It's been nearly six weeks since I went to Vermont and started filling her with my cum as many times a day as she'd let me. I know she's not on any birth control, so there's every chance she's pregnant.

I'm not sure I'm lucky to have knocked up my woman within a month of claiming her. Although Huck did with Cora, so maybe strong swimmers run in the family.

Missy's lips part, granting me entrance into her mouth and I take it, tangling my tongue with hers and kissing her until she's grinding her wet cunt against my thigh and practically begging me to fuck her.

"Babe, as much as my dick wants in you, my family is all inside and they're really fucking excited to see us. I promise the moment we're alone, I'll spread you like a buffet on the dining table and feast on you, but for now we need to go say hi."

"I want you to fuck my face," Missy says breathily.

Groaning, I reach down and palm her ass, squeezing harshly. "Temptress." After one of our dates where I took her to a drive-in movie and finger-fucked her through five orgasms until she was begging me to stop, Missy decided she wanted to try sucking my dick. Turns out, my little imp gets off on me using her mouth, emphasis on "using." She has zero gag reflex and gets so fucking wet when I hold her head and fuck my dick down her throat. My little imp can be a dirty, dirty girl.

"Bay," she whines needily.

"Later, babe, I promise."

Reluctantly nodding, she inhales, then slowly exhales, straightening her shirt and smoothing down her denim shorts.

"You ready?"

She nods.

"You don't need to be nervous; you've spoken to them all every day for weeks, they already love you, now you just have to deal with all that love in person, not over video chat." The moment we got engaged and I told Cody and the rest of my family we were coming home; every Barnett I'm related to has gone crazy over Missy. The girls added her to their wives' WhatsApp chat and her cell is constantly dinging with messages from my sisters. Our nightly video chats have gone from a few minutes, to at least a couple of hours each night and I think my family may be more excited to see Missy than either me or Cody.

Linking my fingers with hers, I lead her toward the door, scooping her into my arms bridal style as I carry her over the threshold and into the house. Her laugh is infectious and I lean down to kiss her briefly, then lower her to her feet and embrace the chaos that is a Barnett family welcome.

Hours later, we've eaten, chatted and basked in the familiar warmth of being home. I would have moved to Burlington permanently if it'd made Missy happy, but I'm so fucking glad she wanted to come back to Montana, because being home is like taking a full breath after weeks of being deprived of oxygen.

The kids stay up late, the drinks flow and I have to slyly swap out Missy's wine cooler for the nonalcoholic ones Cora is drinking now she's pregnant again. There are several bottles of the nonalcoholic stuff in the trash, so I'm guessing more than just Cora and possibly Missy are expecting.

It's late by the time all the babies have been put to bed and a neat row of baby monitors sits on the coffee table. The doors to all the "wings" have been left open so we can hear if any of the kids wake up.

"Now everyone is home, let's all raise a glass to our newest sister, Missy. Welcome to the family, sweetheart," Beau says, lifting his bottle of beer into the air.

Everyone follows suit, welcoming my woman home and she smiles happily, basking in the love and attention she's getting. Seeing her happy is everything I want and I relax as I realize that this is right, that she'll be happy and content here.

"I have news," Teddy announces, smirking at a glowering Juni. "Juniper is pregnant, I'm going to be a dad."

We all cheer and Juni blushes, her cheeks stained pink.

Cora cackles, pointing a finger at Juni. "I warned you not to let a Barnett anywhere near your birth control."

"I was on the shot. But this one deleted the reminder appointment out of my calendar," Juni says, narrowing her eyes on Teddy.

"I swear I didn't," he says, laughing, holding up his hands.

"Aren't you happy about the baby?" Missy asks, silencing everyone, her expression concerned.

"Oh, I'm over the moon," Juni assures her, placing her

hand over her stomach, "but we'd decided we would wait a while, so this one is just a little earlier than I expected."

Missy's concern dissolves and I lift her onto my lap and squeeze her tight.

"We have news too," Cora announces, her belly pronounced. "We're having a girl."

We all cheer, then rib Huck about having a girl and having to fend off horny guys like us.

"Might as well tell them," Penn says, smirking proudly at Lulu.

Lulu rolls her eyes. "I'm pregnant again too. It's early days, I'm about eight weeks."

"Super fucking sperm," Penn yells proudly. "I've got super fucking sperm."

"Don't even think about it," Bonnie yells, jumping up and pointing at Beau. "I'm not having another baby for at least a year."

"Whatever you say, baby girl," Beau nods, grinning.

"I'm serious, Beau," she warns.

"I know you are." Pulling her to him, he sets her in his lap, resting his chin on her shoulder as he smirks.

Caught up in the excitement of there being at least three more Barnetts coming in the next year, I consider announcing that Missy might be pregnant too, but then I swallow down the fucking words. She definitely needs to know before I tell the rest of my family. I only just got back in her good graces, telling anyone else she could be pregnant before she figures it out is definitely going to put me in the doghouse again.

After Missy's fifth yawn, I scoop her up and stand.

"We're going to bed, guys, it's been a long fucking day, but I'm glad to be home."

There's a chorus of "glad you're backs" and "sleep wells" as I smile and then pad over to my door, exhaling happily as I push it open and carry Missy inside.

"Welcome home, baby."

"You already said that," Missy grins, resting her head against my chest.

"Yeah, well I'm excited. I'm so fucking glad we're here. I would have settled anywhere you wanted to go, but I'm going to be honest, I'm over the fucking moon that you picked here."

Carrying her into the bedroom, I pull back the comforter on the bed and place her down on the mattress. My hands move to the button on her shorts and unfastening it, I peel them over her butt and off, dumping them on the floor. As I tug the hem of her shirt, she lifts up a little to help me get it off, and that lands by the shorts too. Her bra goes next, then her panties, until she's naked and laid out on my bed like a gift.

"I need a shower," she whines, her eyes closed.

"You want me to help?"

Her lips dip into a pout and she nods so pathetically, I chuckle. "Okay, little Imp, I'll take care of you." Stripping out of my own clothes, I pick her up again and carry her into the bathroom. Pressing the button on the fancy shower control I had installed on the wall, I smile as the water instantly steams, then cools to the perfect temperature. Stepping into the stall, I turn us so the warm water cascades over her back and she hums contentedly. I only have my normal shampoo and no conditioner, but I wash her hair and then her body, then my own, all while she hangs off me, helping when I need her to, but mainly letting me care for her.

Once we're finished, I set her on the counter and wrap her in a huge fluffy towel, rubbing her skin until she's dry. Quickly drying my own body, I use a towel to squeeze as much water as I can out of her hair and then search for a brush, but I'm a guy and so I don't have anything.

"Babe, I don't have a brush, do you need me to go get our stuff from the car or will it be okay until the morning?"

"Be fine," she says sleepily, her voice slurred. "Too tired."

I wanted to talk to her about the baby tonight, but her eyes are shut and I know she probably won't remember any conversation I try to have with her. Smiling, I pick her up, carry her into the bedroom, turning off the light in the bathroom as I go, then place her on the bed, crawling in after her.

"Sex?" she asks, but I'm not sure if she's asking for it, or telling me she's too tired to want it. Either way, I'm not going to fuck my probably pregnant, exhausted fiancée, no matter how hard my dick is.

Pushing my hand between her thighs, I slide one finger inside of her, pumping it in and out, before adding a second finger and fucking her until her cunt is dripping and stretched enough for me to slide my dick into her. This isn't the first time I've prepped her to swaddle my dick and once she got over how weird it kind of is, she admitted she doesn't hate sleeping with me inside of her.

Lifting her leg, I slide into her and she sighs and smiles in her sleep. "Love you," she murmurs.

"Love you too, Mis." Wrapping my arm around her, I pull her into me and fall asleep with her back pressed against my chest.

***

I wake up just as the pale morning sun is rising into the perfect Montana sky. I can practically smell the crisp mountain air and once again, I thank Missy and God and fate and whoever the fuck else helped get me and my woman back home. Happiness bubbles through me and I smile as Missy twitches in her sleep. The sheet has fallen as we've slept and now her perfect full tits are there, ripe and full and begging to be kissed or fucked. Her lush body and endless curves are still pressed up against me, and my dick rises to the occasion, eager to be inside of her for more than just a warm place to nap.

As my dick hardens and fills her, stretching her around my length and girth, she whines and moans, her nipples pebbling as I push my hand between her thighs and cup her cunt. Spreading my fingers on either side of where my dick has her split open, I groan at her wetness coating me. She's dripping, like she always is when she sleeps with my cock in her, and her arousal helps me as I roll my hips, pulling out an inch, then sliding back in as she sleeps peacefully, completely unaware that I'm fucking her.

Holding her folds open, I watch as my dick slides into her, glistening with wetness when I pull back out again. I'm pretty sure she'll kill me if I suggest setting up my cell to video us fucking, but I'd love to be able to see how her pretty pussy looks spread wide on my fat cock.

I fuck her for a few minutes before she starts to wake up, a soft moan of pleasure coming from her lips as her eyes blink open.

"Bay?"

"Yeah?"

"Oh god," she whines as I start to rub at her clit, increasing my pace now she's aware enough to know what I'm doing. "Were you," she swallows, tilting her chin up as a sigh huffs from her mouth. "Were you fucking me while I was asleep?"

"Couldn't help myself, little Imp," I tell her, lifting her leg and pulling it a little higher over my thigh, spreading her wide and allowing my dick to slide deeper into her cunt.

"Oh fuck," she gasps.

My fingers at her clit move quicker, circling, then pinching, until she's writhing, her hands clenching into fists, searching for something to hold on to. It doesn't take long for her cunt to tighten around my dick and she comes on a cry, slick arousal dripping down my cock as her muscles lock down. Lifting her leg up, I pull her on and off my length, rolling my hips and fucking her hard and fast for a few intense minutes, until my orgasm hits and I pump her full of my cum.

"Oh god," she pants, her chest heaving up and down in time with mine, a fine sheen of sweat coating her cheeks and chest.

My hips keep moving slowly and the wet sound of my dick in her soaked pussy join the ragged rasps of our breathing, in an erotic orchestra that makes my dick jerk excitedly, despite having just come.

"Morning," I chuckle against her cheek.

"Holy shit, you fucked me awake," she laughs, unfurling her fingers and lifting her hand to push her damp hair out of her face.

"Perfect damn way to start the day. How does it feel to be home?"

"So far, so good," she laughs again, then exhales loudly, her muscles melting as she collapses, her weight resting back on me.

"How'd you sleep?" Curling my arm around her waist, I get as close to her as I can while I spoon her.

"So good, your bed is like a cloud."

"Our bed."

"Our bed," she parrots, her cheeks turning pink.

"Did you know it's been almost six weeks since I came to Vermont?"

"It has? Wow, it seems like longer. I can't believe how much has happened in such a short space of time."

I can't see her face properly from this angle, but I can just make out the smile tipping up the corners of her lips. She's happy and although I know I'm not the only reason, I'm pretty sure that us being together, being in love and engaged is definitely part of why she's smiling, naked, filled with my cum and in Montana right now.

Part of me knows I need to prompt her to think about the fact that she hasn't had a period since we got together. But even though she's here in our bed, wearing my ring, this thing between us still feels perilously balanced on a knife's edge. Will telling her I think she might be pregnant tip us off the edge of happily ever after and back into fucked up and fighting?

"I want to marry you," I announce, unsure where the words have come from, but feeling a peace settle on me now I've said them.

"What, right now?" she chuckles like I've said something funny.

"I'm not sure we can do it today unless you want to take a trip to city hall? We could fly to Vegas, though, if you want?"

Wiggling forward enough so she can look over her shoulder, Missy flashes me a confused look. "What are you talking about, we just got home and now you want to fly to Vegas?"

"I want to marry you," I tell her honestly.

"I want to marry you too, Bay, but not today."

"Why not?" I demand a little desperately.

"Let me up," she says, pushing my arm and trying to free herself from my touch.

"Are you going to try and leave?" I demand.

"No," she snaps, "I just think this is a conversation I'd like to be looking at you for."

Reluctantly, I loosen my hold on her and she slides off my dick, twisting around and lying back down on her side facing me. "What's going on, Bay?"

Chapter Twenty-Two

His expressive eyes blink up at me and a tremor of fear rushes through me. He looks worried. It's not an expression I've seen on his perfect face before and I hate it. Bay isn't scared, if anything he's overly confident, sometimes even bordering on cocky. Only now he looks worried.

Is this the moment when he shouts "punked" and a celebrity jumps out at me to let me know this has all been some elaborate prank?

No, that's crazy. Bay loves me and I love him. We're engaged, we just moved halfway across the country to be here with his family who have been nothing but endlessly supportive of us. Nothing about Bay is fake or pretend, he's real even if it makes him sound like a psycho, even when he's telling me I belong to him, like a person can be property.

But I do feel owned. Not in a derogatory, demeaning way though. I belong to him and with that belonging is love and faith and permanence, because Bay isn't a man who would ever willingly walk away from me. He made mistakes right back at the start but he's more than made up for letting me leave all those months ago.

What we share isn't average, it isn't casual or relaxed or normal. It's intense and crazy and overwhelming. Bay is a walking red flag, alpha male through and through. He's mine and he belongs to me, just as much as I do to him.

"Bay?" I say, when he just stares at me with earnest, fear-filled eyes.

"I love you, Mis. Promise me you'll marry me."

"I already told you I'd marry you. I moved all the way back here with you. What's going on?"

Bay curses beneath his breath, then rolls to a sitting position. Lifting me up, he sits me back down in his lap, his arms behind me, holding me tight.

"You got sick yesterday."

"It was motion sickness; I feel fine today," I say, waving away his concern, then placing my hand down on his bicep and squeezing.

"Yeah. I'm not so sure that's all it was," he answers carefully.

My brows squeeze together as I feel confusion spread across my face. "Well, if I ate something bad, I'd be sick more than a couple of times. Plus, we all pretty much ate the same food, so we'd all be sick."

Exhaling, Bay pinches my chin with his fingers. "Imp,

when was your last period?"

I freeze. Ice lances through my veins and I become a statue as his words ricochet through my mind. My period. When was the last time I had my period? A couple of weeks before he came to Burlington maybe?

They've always been pretty regular, so I've never really worried about keeping track, just sort of mindfully aware it came at roughly the same time each month.

"Babe?" Bay calls. "Missy."

"You think I'm pregnant?" I ask slowly.

He nods, a cautious smile playing with the edges of his full, tempting lips.

This is what he wants. He hasn't ever shied away from telling me that he wanted kids. With me. He wants kids with me. Lots of kids. As many as I'll give him. I'm pretty sure those were his exact words. But I'm twenty. Do I even want kids?

Thoughts ping around my head like a silver marble in a pinball machine and then I look at him. This man who loves me, who wants me, who asks nothing of me but to love him and want him back. If I am pregnant, Bay would be the dad, he'd be my baby's daddy.

Bay, my fiancé, my person, my man would also be this tiny person inside of me's person. He'd be their love, their person too. I can see it. I can see him holding a tiny creature, half me, half him. I can see it and maybe I want it. Having his family is great, but starting our own would be even better.

Suddenly I'm not scared. I should be. I should be freaking out and angry and confused and terrified. But I'm not. Maybe this isn't exactly on that ideal map of when things should happen. Pregnant at twenty isn't everyone's dream, it definitely wasn't mine, but that doesn't mean it's not my happily ever after.

"You think I'm pregnant?" I ask again, a bright smile blossoming over my lips even as tears fill my eyes and spill down my cheek.

"Yeah, little Imp, I think you might be."

***

Given the fact that Bay is a Barnett, it's probably not a huge surprise to find out he was right, I'm pregnant. Twenty and a pregnant bride, wow, I'm really ticking off all those clichés. The moment those two lines showed up on the stick covered in my pee, Bay went on a mission to make an honest woman out of me.

So, two weeks ago we got married in the garden of our home. Cody walked me down the aisle and Beau got online ordained and performed the ceremony. Instead of letting me come to him, before I was even halfway down the aisle, Bay marched over to me, scooped me off the ground and carried me the rest of the way to where Beau was presiding, while I laughed, holding on to my crazy man.

Before he made me Missy Barnett, Bay took me to the lawyer's office Lulu worked at and had them draw up a prenup declaring that no matter how much my inheritance is, it's mine and he doesn't want a penny. I never for a moment thought he was interested in the money, but I was touched by his thoughtfulness all the same. When I tried to get them to draw up something to say that I didn't want any of his money either, he scowled at me and his eyes promised retribution the moment we got home.

My punishment for suggesting he protect his assets was him spanking my ass until it was red and sore, then fucking me hard enough that if we didn't have soundproofing, I'm pretty sure the people in the next town over would have heard me. Safe to say, I get it now why Bonnie finds Beau spanking her such a turn-on.

My life is pretty perfect, all except for my twenty-first birthday looming on the horizon like a harbinger of doom. I've lost count of how many times I've told Bay I don't care about the inheritance, that Ernie can have it. But both he and Cody are absolutely determined that my not-uncle doesn't get to take another dime from me.

"Babe, you need to contact the lawyer's office and set up an appointment," Bay reminds me for the hundredth time already this week.

"If you care so much, can't you just go in my place?" I whine from my spot on the couch, the green fluffy blanket I fell in love with and Bay bought for me draped over me.

"Mis, you know I can't. Just take the meeting and sign the paperwork, then you can forget all about the money if that's what you want to do. How are you feeling?"

"Urgh," I grunt. Whoever called it 'morning' sickness was an asshole, because I'm rarely sick when I wake up. Instead, bouts of nausea hit at random points through the day, sneaking up on me and leaving me sprinting for the closest bathroom.

"Oh babe, have you gotten sick today?"

With Penn and Lulu expecting another child and me being pregnant as well, Bay and Penn decided to promote one of their existing mechanics to shop manager and take on more staff so they could both reduce their hours down to part time. They take it in turns alternating days, and today was Bay's first day back at work since we got back from Vermont.

"Five times," I groan, eagerly curling into Bay's chest when he lifts me off the couch and cradles me in his lap.

"Have you stayed in the apartment all day? Why didn't you go into the main house, then the girls could have taken care of you while I wasn't here."

I don't admit that I never considered burdening his family with pandering to me while I'm feeling crappy. Being a Barnett is taking some adjusting to, and relying on a huge group of people isn't something I've ever done in the past.

"I didn't…" I pause, not sure how to say it.

"You didn't think they'd care," he says, reading my mind.

I shrug, then nod.

"Babe, you're not alone anymore, and no one is pretending to care about you. You know my entire family likes you more than me, if you're sick and I'm not here they'll want to look after you. You just need to give them a chance to prove it to you."

Tears fill my eyes and I nod as they spill, dripping down my face. So far, being pregnant is making me an emotional mess and I've lost count of the number of times I've burst into tears over stupid things. I've tried to hide my weepy moments from Bay, but when he found me in the bathroom, stifling my crying jag with a towel, he was not happy. Now

I lose my shit right in front of him and just like usual, he scoops me into his arms and holds me, telling me he loves me and our baby and how everything is okay. Then he gets me pie. Pie makes everything better.

"Tomorrow, we'll make that appointment, your birthday is next week and you need to get in touch with them and let them know Ernie is not acting as your proxy."

I nod against his chest, inhaling his calming scent and using his warmth and strength to comfort me.

"Cody's cooking tonight, he's making pot roast. Do you fancy it, or are you craving something different? We can always eat in here if you're not up for being social."

Lifting my cheek from his chest, I tilt my neck and look up at him. "Bay, you need to stop enabling my cravings, if Cody cooked for us, we should go eat it," I say seriously. Since I starting hankering after certain foods, Bay has been amazing, he even drove all the way down the mountain to the store when I had a sudden craving for thick, creamy New York–style cheesecake and blueberry jelly.

"Mis, you're building our baby, I'll get you whatever the fuck you want. All I did was feed your cunt my cum, you're doing all the hard work, so now it's my job to make sure mama and baby are happy and getting what they need."

If it was possible to swoon while basically lying down, I would. My husband can be an overbearing, jealous, possessive asshole, but he can also be the sweetest, most caring person in the world. "I love you," I say, pressing a kiss against his chest.

"I love you too, little Imp."

Epilogue

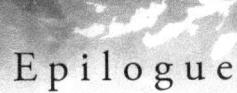

On her twenty-first birthday, I wake my beautiful wife up with my tongue on her clit and my fingers in her greedy cunt. After she's come all over me, I crawl over her limp body and press a kiss to her full, pouty lips. "Happy birthday, wife."

"Thank you," she giggles, her boobs that are even bigger now she's bred and growing our first baby, jiggling with her amusement.

"It's your day, babe, so how do you want my cock? You want to ride me, you want to take charge, you want me to take over? Birthday girl's choice."

"I want you to take charge." Her cheeks go pink and she bites at her bottom lip. "And I want you to spank me."

My lips spread into a wide grin. My little imp is starting

to learn to ask me for what she wants. I don't always give it to her, but if she wants a birthday spanking, I am more than happy to oblige.

"On your belly, babe, chest to the bed, ass in the air. I want your legs spread wide, so I can see all of my cunt, wet and ready for me."

A mischievous grin tips at her lips as I sit back and watch as she positions herself. When she's exactly where I told her to be, she glances back at me, then slides one of her hands between her thighs and rubs at her clit.

Shaking my head, I smirk. Apparently, my Imp is feeling bratty and I know exactly what to do. Pushing my hand between her spread thighs, I cover her fingers, stilling them, but keeping them in place. "Who does this cunt belong to?" I demand.

"You," she giggles.

"So why are you touching my cunt?"

"Because you weren't," she sasses.

Releasing my hold on her hand, she pulls it back and then before she has a chance to do anything else, I spank her pussy. She screams, then I do it again. Grabbing her hips, I guide my dick to her entrance and slam into her, lifting my hand and spanking her full ass hard as I pull back and push into her cunt again, starting a slow, deep grind that has her wiggling her hips, urging me to go faster and harder.

"Bay," she whines.

"Who does this cunt belong to?"

"You," she gasps.

"Who do you belong to?"

"You."

"Who loves you more than anything in the world except that baby that's growing in your belly?"

"You do."

I work her butt with a flurry of spanks, while she gasps and mewls, pushing her butt back into me, begging for more. Swapping hands, I spank her other cheek until her cunt is clamping down on me and I know she's on the verge of orgasming.

"I love you, Missy Barnett," I tell her, holding both of her hips tightly as I start to fuck her fast and hard. When she hits her release she screams, her fingers raking at the sheets as she struggles to keep herself in position. A moment later I follow her over the edge, filling her cunt with my cum, my dick shiny as I watch myself slide in and out of her.

"God, I love you," she rasps, her voice scratchy and hoarse.

"That what you wanted, babe?" I tease.

"Yes," she pants. "Jesus, yes."

I fucking love that as hot and serious as sex is between us, we can still laugh and have fun. I love everything about her and I'm so glad that she's forgiven me for being such an idiot when we first met. I nearly lost her and now I've stopped being an insecure, jealous asshole, I'm so fucking grateful to Cody. He stepped up when I was too fucking scared to, he took care of my girl when I didn't, and I fucking love him for it.

After we're showered and dressed, I pull a gift from behind my back and present it to her. Her eyes light up as she takes the box wrapped in shiny green gift wrap.

"You didn't have to buy me a gift."

Scoffing, I look at her, expecting her to laugh, but she's serious. "Babe, it's your birthday."

"So?"

"So, it's your birthday so that means gifts and cake and celebrating."

"I've never really bothered with the birthday thing," she shrugs.

Gritting my teeth, I close the distance between us and lift her into my lap. "Well, you're a Barnett now and Barnetts do birthdays. So, open your first gift, then we need to go into the main house, because everyone is waiting for us."

"My first gift?" she exclaims, shocked.

"Yeah, babe, this is just your first one."

Smiling, a little bewildered, she rips the paper off the box and opens the lid, then lifts out the huge stack of college prospectuses. Her eyes lift to me and confusion flashes in her gaze.

"I know that college wasn't an option when you graduated high school. But I've seen the expression on your face when you talk about not going, so those are prospectuses from all the schools within a couple of hours of here. If there's somewhere farther away that you want to go to, then that's fine, we can just buy a house near campus and come home when you're on break."

"Bay, I'm pregnant."

"So?"

"So how exactly do you expect me to go to college with a baby to take care of?"

"You're not doing it alone, babe, I'm happy to take care

of the baby while you're at school. Or if you want, most schools do an online degree, then you can do it part time. It's up to you, babe. Or if you don't want to do it at all, then that's fine too. But I want you to have the option to do whatever you want in life. I've been selfish tying you to me with a ring and a baby. I won't ever let you go, but I'm more than happy to stand at your side while you get everything you've ever dreamed of."

Tears fill her eyes and she throws her arms around my neck and kisses me. Her tears coat my cheeks too, but I don't care. I want everything she has to give me, kisses and tears and everything in between. I want it all.

We eat breakfast with the family in the main house and with each gift she receives, Missy cries, then apologizes. Her main present is outside, but I also thought it'd be fun to get her twenty-one gifts, one for each year I didn't know her or get to celebrate her being mine. So in between her opening the gifts from our family, I hand her one from me and our baby.

Some are expensive. A trip to the spa with my sisters, a pair of emerald earrings and a necklace that match her engagement ring. Some are silly gifts, panties that say property of Bay Barnett across the butt. A huge box of red Swedish fish—her favorite—and a year's membership to the pie-of-the-month club, where a different flavored pie comes through the mail each month.

Once we've eaten and Mis has opened all of her gifts, I cover her eyes with my hands and lead her outside to where her final gift is. Lifting my hands, I watch her blink, staring at the black SUV with the massive red bow on the hood.

Turning, she looks at me, then back at the SUV. "You got me a car?"

I nod, smiling. "Do you like it? If you don't, we can trade it in and you can pick something else. It needs to be an SUV because the roads can be slippery in the winter, not that you'll be driving yourself anywhere if the weather's bad."

"You got me a car," she screeches.

"Yeah, babe, I got you a car."

"You can't buy me a car."

"The fuck I can't. You're my wife, I can buy you whatever the fuck I want."

"I can't drive, Bay," she shrieks, the color draining from her cheeks.

"I know, babe, that's why I'm going to teach you. Between here and Hal's place there are plenty of quiet roads for you to learn on."

For probably the hundredth time this morning, she throws herself into my arms and hugs me. I'll never get used to her being so excited over things that she should take for granted, but I'll never turn her away if she wants to hug me like this.

"You never get on a bus again," I whisper into her neck. "I'm never going to let you leave me, but if you ever try, it's going to be in your own car."

When she pulls back she's laughing, even as tears flow down her cheeks.

"No more tears today, babe, you're killing me," I say, wiping the wetness from her cheeks with my thumbs.

Nodding, she smiles widely. "I love my car. I love all

my gifts. But most of all, I love you."

"Love you too. Now we need to get going, else we're going to miss our appointment."

Her smile melts away and a grimace replaces it. "Fine, let's get this over with."

Lifting her chin with my thumb, I press a kiss against her lips, then pull back, take her hand and lead her over to the big SUV we keep for when we want to go out as a group.

"Why are we going in this? I thought we'd go in the truck."

"We can't fit in the truck, babe?"

Her brows furrow. "What? Why?"

"Because there aren't enough seats." As I finish speaking, the front door opens and my brothers start to file out.

Missy's lips part and she stares at me, then at them. "What's going on?"

"I told you, you'd have a wall of fucking Barnetts at your back if you had to face that asshole Ernie again. I think we both agree it's pretty fucking likely he'll turn up thinking he can bully you into giving him money again, so we're all going."

I'm hoping that she'll eventually get used to knowing she's not alone, but for now it's still a shock when she realizes she has people at her back.

"You're all coming?" she asks my brothers.

"Of course we are. We won't let that asshole think he can take anything from our baby sister," Beau tells her, pressing a kiss to her head as he passes us and climbs into the driver's seat.

The lawyer's office is in Bozeman and the closer we get, the more tense Missy gets, until she's like a board in the seat beside me. I want to pull her into my lap, but it's not safe, so instead, I try to surround her as much as I can, curling my arm around her shoulders, while the other is across her thighs. "It's going to be fine, Imp, we won't let him anywhere near you," I assure her.

"I know," she nods.

She's shaking by the time we get to the door of the lawyer's office and just like I suspected, Ernie the little worm comes marching across the lot the moment we step out of the car.

"Finally," he growls. "Where the fuck have you been, you little bitch? You owe me and it's time to pay up. I want my money."

Without speaking, I guide Missy into Cody's side, waiting until he has her positioned behind him, my other brothers boxing her in from all sides. Once she's surrounded with protection, I step forward, grab Ernie's shirt and yank him toward me.

"What the fuck kind of man speaks like that to a woman, let alone his blood?"

"Who are you? This is none of your business, this is between me and my little bitch of a niece."

I scoff dryly. "She's not your niece, she's my wife and I suggest you shut the fuck up."

"Wife?" he shrieks.

"Yes, my wife. And these," I motion behind me. "Are all her new brothers. Now I suggest you take your disgusting, abusive, waste-of-life self back to whatever hole you crawled out of and forget that my wife exists. Because if you speak to her again, if you even glance in her direction, I'll fucking kill you, then I'll bury your body where no one will ever think to look for you."

"You can't threaten me," Ernie says, but his skin has gone a sallow-gray color.

"Is that right? Maybe I should threaten to break into your room at night, pin you to your bed and rape you. Maybe I should describe in detail all the sick, messed-up things I'll do to you if you don't do exactly what I tell you to. Is that something you'd understand more? Because that's what you did to her, isn't it? That's what you told her on the day she turned eighteen and every time she stepped out of line. You threatened her while you held her barely more than a child body down and rubbed your pathetic little cock all over her, isn't it?"

"I..." Ernie starts, sweat rolling down his brow

Lifting my hand, I silence him. "You don't know her. You'll never see her or come near her again. She doesn't exist to you. You get me?" I demand.

"She owes me," he says, puffing up his pudgy chest.

Shoving my hand into my jeans, I pull out a dime and flick it at him, hitting him in the cheek before the coin drops to the floor. "There you go, consider her debt paid, because that's the only money you'll ever get from her and if you even try, I'm sure the police would be interested to hear all about the fraudulent way you extorted money from a teenager."

Before he has a chance to speak, I reach through my brothers for my wife, pulling her into my side and shielding her so she doesn't even have to look at the man who pretended to be her family, then betrayed her in the worst way. My brothers close rank around us again, opening the door for us to walk into the office, while they stay outside, making sure we're not disturbed.

An hour later, Missy's eyes are still like saucers, and she's still gripping my hand so tightly it's started to go numb. When the lawyer called her through, I offered to stay in the waiting room, but she refused to let go of my hand, forcing me to come into her meeting with her.

"A. Million. Dollars," Missy whispers again, still sounding as shocked as the first time the lawyer advised her how much her grandparents had left for her. "Bay."

"Yeah, babe?" I say as I guide her out of the door and back toward the SUV where my brothers are waiting. Beau texted me to tell me that after trying to barge his way into the office a handful of times, Ernie had eventually given up and stormed off. Apparently, he tried to bribe my family with offers of money if they'd let him through. When that didn't work, he told them Missy was a compulsive liar and he'd never done any of the things she'd accused him of. When that hadn't swayed them, he'd given up and left, still ranting about Missy owing him, but at least he'd gone.

"Pinch me," she says.

"I'm not going to pinch you, babe."

"This can't be real."

"It's real, Mis. You have all the legal papers in your hand."

Her grandparents had it set up that she inherited a small amount on her eighteenth, then a million on her twenty-first and an additional million on her twenty-fifth birthday. They might not have known about her, but once they did, they made sure she was set for life.

"What do we do with that kind of money?" she whispers.

"We don't do anything, babe, that money is all yours."

"No, it's ours. Because it's not me and you, it's us. Right?"

Smiling, I pull her into my chest and kiss her. "That's fucking right, babe, it's always going to be us."

Epilogue

Missy

A million dollars. A million dollars. Nope, it doesn't matter how many times I say it, it still doesn't make any sense. I have a million dollars and according to the lawyer we just met with, I'll have another million when I turn twenty-five.

How is it even possible that less than six months ago I had less than three hundred dollars to my name, no family, no home and no clue what I was going to do? Now I have a husband, a baby on the way, more family than I really know what to do with and a million freaking dollars.

A part of me doesn't want it. It seems wrong to take money from people I never even met. But when I said that to the lawyer, Bay reminded me that my grandparents wanted me to have it. They left that money for me because they wanted to take care of me, a stranger they never even got a chance to meet.

I feel shell-shocked. This morning has been so perfect. Bay woke me up in the most decadent way. I've been spoiled with gifts and the support of my new brothers. Seeing Ernie was hard, but Bay eviscerated him. He told Ernie all the things I've dreamed about saying, but have always been too scared to. My brothers protected me and it really started to sink in that I'm not alone anymore.

Today I have everything I'll ever need to run away and never be found. But for the first time, there's nowhere I'd rather be than exactly where I am. I have people. I have family and I'm loved. I'm more than loved, I'm adored. Bay is everything to me and I'm everything to him, and this baby I'm growing will be everything to both of us.

"Missy?" a soft female voice calls. "Missy McCormick?"

Turning toward the voice, my eyes find a woman staring back at me, her hands twisted together, a cautiously hopeful expression across her oddly familiar face. She's tall, much taller than me. She's beautiful, with creamy skin and hair almost as bright as mine, only instead of it being long and curly, her hair is cropped into a short pixie cut. She's wearing a tight, cropped tank top, wide-legged ripped jeans and scuffed doc marten boots. There's a silver hoop in the side of her nose, several earrings in each ear and tattoos covering one of her arms.

"I'm Missy," I confess, stepping out from behind Bay, even though I know he's probably glaring at me.

The woman's expression morphs into a bright smile and her eyes run over me, taking me in like I just did to her.

"I'm sorry, do I know you?" I ask.

"No, you don't," she laughs. "God, I'm sorry, I know I'm staring, it's just you look so much like her it's kind of weird."

Her accent is American, but there's a soft lilt that I can't quite place.

"Who do I look like?" I ask.

"Like our grandmother."

"*Our* grandmother?"

"Yes. I'm Betty McCormick, your sister."

Epilogue

Cody

(Yes, you read that right, Cody)

Oh fuck, it's her.

The End

But not really

Loving the Mountain Man
MONTANA MOUNTAIN MEN #7
Coming Soon

Acknowledgments

Well, that's a wrap on book number twenty! This book just wouldn't end and now I realize it's because Cody's story has been such a part of this one too, so maybe it won't feel done, until I've told his story.

I love this family, I want the Barnetts to be real and so I'm excited to tell Bay's story, but I don't want to, because that means it's almost over and I'm not ready for there to be no more Barnett brothers left to fall in love with.

This book is over 100k and I've kind of run out of words, so I'm going to bullet point my thank-yous.
- Sarah Stanley, I love you, thank you for helping me stop writing in circles.
- Sarah Goodman, thank you for making my words pretty, I hope you like Bay as much as his brothers.
- Hudson Indie Ink, you guys rock!
- Kerry Heavens, I think this cover is my fave.
- All my wonderful readers who love the Barnetts almost as much as I do, I see you, I love you and thank you.

About the Author

Gemma Weir is a half crazed stay at home mom to three kids, one man child and a hell hound. She has lived in the midlands, in the UK her whole life and has wanted to write a book since she was a child.

Gemma has a ridiculously dirty mind and loves her book boyfriends to be big, tattooed alpha males. She's a reader first and foremost and she loves her romance to come with a happy ending and lots of sexy sex.

For updates on future releases find her on:

Facebook
Twitter
Instagram
Amazon.

Other Authors at Hudson Indie Ink

Paranormal Romance/Urban Fantasy
Stephanie Hudson
Xen Randell
C. L. Monaghan
Sorcha Dawn
Harper Phoenix

Sci-fi/Fantasy
Devin Hanson

Crime/Action
Blake Hudson
Jack Walker

Contemporary Romance
Gemma Weir
Nikki Ashton
Anna Bloom
Tatum Rayne

Printed in the USA
CPSIA information can be obtained
at www.ICGtesting.com
LVHW092013030224
770773LV00066B/779